TURNING
POINT

John Kurt

"Has anyone told you lately just how wonderful you are? You are!"

To Christina, my very very good friend! Best wishes always! Love [signature]

Dedications and Acknowledgements:

"Through him all things were made; without him nothing was made that has been made." John 1:3

I want to dedicate this book to my mother Alice Marie Samuelson Kurt who encouraged me to write it in the first place, my daughter Jillian who inspired me, and in memory of my late father who I am sure would be pleased to see this come out in print if he were around today. I thank my entire family in particular my brother Bob, and my brother Jim, both of whom went out their way to help me during a difficult time.

Special thanks to Dan and Reva Dubiak, who without their help I doubt I would see this book in print myself! In addition I want to thank the many friends who helped me in so many ways including opening their own homes to me when I had no where else to go! And, to all my children who I hope will know that I love them.

Chapter 1

For the first time ever, we have confronted in reality the sinister power of uncontrolled nuclear energy.

Mikhail Gorbachev May 26, 1986.

Friday, September 22, 2006

The car came to life, the rumble of tuned exhausts reverberating off the walls of the steel-hulled *Victoria Express,* a vehicle ferry that ran between Vancouver Island, BC, and Port Angeles, Washington. Nick Peters throttled up and eased out on the clutch, joining the procession of cars in front of him. After a brief exchange with the customs official through his window, he pointed the car towards Highway 101. He would deliver the package, an aluminum attaché case, to the federal courthouse in Seattle on Monday. He carried a Letter of Congress authorizing its delivery, but he was bringing it into the country covertly for his own reasons. In his gut, he sensed a setup.

He had selected this route to Seattle, via a privately owned and operated terminal, as the one least likely to be monitored by the authorities. Other points of entry would have held a higher priority for the feds or anyone else looking for him, and it was the "anyone else" whom Nick was mostly concerned about for the moment.

The late September morning was crisp, the skies cloudless blue. Majestic mountain peaks greeted his gaze in all directions—some even with traces of white snow still remaining, and although the sun blazed hotly overhead, the cold, green-hued waters he had just crossed over maintained the ambient temperature at a very pleasant seventy-two degrees. He had hoped to see some whales in the crossing from Vancouver Island, but he was not so lucky today. Instead, there were only some small boats, freighters, and a handful of hopeful anglers scattered about the Strait of Juan de Fuca.

He had grown up in these parts, but he had been away for a long time, nearly thirty years now, and his memory of most everything about the area had waned—or perhaps, everything had actually changed that much! What he remembered though, were mostly things like the high school he had attended in Renton, a suburb of Seattle, and his first schoolyard kiss with a girl named Theresa, and his first job delivering newspapers when he was just twelve years old. But, even those fond memories had become clouded over time, but remained still as fond memories.

The pine trees, the mountainous terrain, and the smell of salt water were all very familiar to Nick, for it was these things that had endeared him to the deep-water fiords along the frigid Siberian coastlines of Russia, too. His adeptness in rough terrain, skills he had acquired as a boy living in the Pacific Northwest, had played a significant role in eluding the *Federalnaya Sluzhba Bezopasnosti*, the Federal Security Service—better known as the KGB, its original acronym, and more recently the FSB. These skills had saved him more times than he cared to remember. He had spent most of his adult life behind the Iron Curtain, risking his freedom, and his life, for a cause that was now nearly forgotten. It was the memories of his upbringing here in America that had kept him loyal to the cause—the cause of keeping America strong. But, it was his Russian heritage—and his understanding of the Russian culture, that made him a great diplomat for both countries.

Now, he was attempting to start over—to leave his former covert life behind him by returning to the place of his youth, the place he fondly thought of as home, to retire. But, leaving it all behind, quitting the business, retiring—was easier said than done! He had made enemies over the years, enemies that had reason to want him dead. According to official records, he had died many years ago, and for the sake of his secret past, which could not be resurrected, it was to his advantage to keep it that way. For that reason, he had created a new identity for himself, one that would be difficult to question and even more difficult to trace. And, although he was unlikely to be discovered, he knew some of his enemies would never stop looking for him. So, he had taken up the identity of a ghost, a spook, a man who was feared by many, admired and respected by many more, and one that only a handful of people had ever met in person—a man few could challenge!

He had taken up the identity of the legendary Mr. Smith, who in the world of espionage was a man so surreptitious in life that in death, he went completely unnoticed.

Since the end of the Cold War—the fall of the Soviet Union, Nick had maintained his primary residence in Zurich, Switzerland, a country renowned for neutrality.

His agency was located not far from the Grossmünster Church there. The three-story building it occupied looked like the others in the neighborhood. It had cost him more than ten million dollars US to excavate the three subterranean levels beneath it, where his real operations took place—the covert ones. At street level were retail shops, shops that rented the storefront space; and on the second floor, World Trade carried out the normal business activities of any international trading company, it moved cargo around the world! His offices, and his management team's offices, were all on the third floor.

The fifty or so administrators, and analysts, that managed the covert operations of World Trade—worked below ground, in a labyrinth of offices and workshops without windows, and without daylight. They were connected to the outside world by cable, and satellite transmission, and telephone. Every effort was made to counter claustrophobia in this subterranean world without sunshine, without fresh air, with only re-circulated air to breath which many employees commented—was too clean! The ceilings were many meters high and domed, much like the openness of old cathedrals—or the historic subways of Moscow. The floors were made of marble, and the hallways were wide and echoed with the footsteps of people going about their business. Artwork adorned the walls, and the lighting was engineered to give the effect of natural sunlight.

Nick's underground complex was a self-sustaining environment, including its own generators at the lowest level. Fresh water came from the city's system, but the condensers for the HVAC system backed up the complex's water system. Nick estimated that, should a catastrophe occur, the subterranean complex could operate for a minimum of thirty days, but food stocks were maintained for double that amount of time.

Access to the subterranean levels was through neighboring buildings so that the entrance could be kept completely secret—hard to do with fifty employees coming and going. A myriad of tunnels led to one central hallway—the main entrance. Nick had the only direct access to the lower levels via a private elevator from his office, which was concealed behind a bookcase, and only a select few even knew of its existence, much less the pass code it required. He maintained a flat within walking distance, and except for a parking garage two blocks distant where a limited number of parking spaces were maintained, there were no accommodations for private transportation. It was a matter of policy not to be noticed.

Nick went private after his departure from the CIA, and he had taken with him a good many intelligence agents from both sides of the fence. World Trade did exactly that but not just in goods—the organization supplied reliable unbiased intelligence to any legitimate country with a bank account large enough to write six, seven, or sometimes even eight-figure checks. Nick ran a very lucrative business that had made him, and his agency many enemies! But, at the same time, many allies too. Foreign governments found his intelligence reliable, sometimes more so than their own, so they tended to turn a blind eye to his activities. Some of his high-placed contacts, against the wishes of their own superiors, even tipped him off if they got wind of a plot to undermine his operations.

The reason Nick had such allies was simple. Unlike national intelligence agencies that held allegiances to one side or the other in any given dispute, World Trade stood firm on one single philosophy: to maintain the balance of power worldwide by providing unbiased intelligence to those needing it the most. This insured that the underdog in any conflict knew that any intelligence coming from World Trade was worth the price, and probably many times over. Nick wasn't always paid in hard currency, however. He sometimes bartered for a ceasefire, the removal of forces, an exchange of prisoners, or an unpublicized agreement to otherwise cease hostilities. As a result, World Trade had become the single most influential diplomatic service on the planet, a fact known to only a few at the very highest levels of governments around the world. Nick's operation remained a secret because it was a safe haven for any top operative from around the world destined for early retirement, the usual consequence of a government deciding that an agent was disposable due to their old age, or budget cuts. World Trade was a brotherhood of burnt-out agents who looked after their own. They knew whom the top agents were who would replace them, and they knew whom the string pullers were higher up within their former organizations, and often, on the other side as well—all good information to know. They all came with their own network of reliable snitches and sources, sources that trusted only them! The money, or any false allegiances to patriotic duty didn't motivate them anymore—not after having been tossed aside, thrown out, and discarded like a spent tissue! The business was simply in their blood, and most found that they couldn't give it up. Importantly, however, no government official wanted to admit to knowing about Nick's operation because they feared the many secrets he and his agents kept to themselves—the secrets, the skeletons they kept in their own closets.

Zurich, for the most part, was a safe place for Nick. He had enough authorities on his payroll to know who was new in town, and he maintained a very low profile at all times, and avoided publicity completely. As far as anyone knew, he was just another businessman who worked out of a small office. His life had been about his work, but he was tiring of it all—tired of the killings, the deceit, and trying to figure out whom was playing whom! He was planning his own exit strategy, but even that proved to be more difficult than he imagined.

Then, out of the blue, comes a former Soviet comrade who needed a favor! He shows up at World Trade to call in an old debt. In the spy business, old debts typically come due with immense interest tacked on—this old debt was no different. When Alexander Mayakovsky made the appointment to see him, it was under the pretext that he had some important information about Nick's daughter Natasha, but that proved to be a diversionary tactic—though in part true! Instead, he had asked for Nick's help in a more delicate matter altogether. Alexander wanted to run off and wed Natasha's mother, Nick's long ago lover, Tatyana. To complicate matters even further, Tatyana was married to Victor Zubkov, a very dangerous man. For this reason, and many others too numerous to list, Nick was reluctant to accommodate Alexander's wishes. But, his own history with Tatyana meant he held little choice in the matter. Had the woman been anybody else, he would have simply declined the request and offered Alexander the door! But, Tatyana was his former lover, his only true love to be heartrendingly exact, and the mother of his only child—and that made him reconsider.

"I just need four days, Nikki," Alexander had pleaded with him. "Give me four days, and Tatyana and I will be safely in New York City and well out of Victor Zubkov's reach."

Seated behind his uncluttered mahogany desk, Nick replied dryly,

"It sounds a bit risky to me, Alexander."

Tapping his fingers on the polished wood desktop apprehensively, completely uncertain where all this was going, and definitely not wanting to make a commitment, he commented, "Zubkov might just have plans to terminate you, my old friend!" and, he added. "Then, I become the mark on your behalf! I owe you, to be certain! But, I don't think I want to take a bullet for you, comrade."

"It's not for me, Nick!" Alexander barked back, slamming his fist down. "I ask for your help only for Tatyana and Natasha! What do you think will happen to her when Zubkov finds out that we have been having an affair? And, what about Natasha? Tatyana would never leave her behind! You know, Nikki, Natasha believes Zubkov is her real father, and Zubkov believes it too! How would you react if another man tried—not only to take your wife away, but your beloved daughter too?"

Nick grimaced, clearly remembering the favor he had asked of Alexander in the first place—so many years ago! "What do you want me to do, Alex?"

"Buy me some time! That's all I ask! Nick, I have a Letter of Congress for you. You may find it useful."

"Letter of Congress?" Nick replied warily.

"It gives you the authorization to deliver the attaché case without interference from the authorities, and it protects you from prosecution before the fact. You know," he shrugged indifferently, "just in case you happen to break a few laws in the process of delivering it? Zubkov has had this congressman in his back pocket for years now, and this congressman has been instrumental in writing legislation that will allow this deal to fly through Congress, and enable him to avoid any antitrust lawsuits. The deal is between Stalintsia Steel, a Russian steel manufacturer, and Providence Steel, an American company that is losing market share. The merger is worth many of millions to Zubkov personally, and quite a bit to the congressman as well. As you know Nick, Stalintsia Steel is the largest steel producer in Eastern Europe, and its labor force works for a third the pay that American steel workers do. Also, the raw materials to manufacture the steel, are also half the price in Russia compared to that in America, meaning that Russian-made steel can be imported to America and sold for far less than it could be manufactured there in the USA."

Alexander, still eyeing Nick warily, paused to catch his breath. "Providence Steel," he went on, "has been in negotiations with the various labor unions for more than two years now, and the company has been unable to get any concessions from them. Other US suppliers are currently importing steel from China, and that is killing their business. Consequently, Providence Steel has been losing market share for a long time. If Providence Steel merges with Stalintsia Steel, the combined company can utilize its vast steel distribution network throughout America, and abroad, to become a dominant player again in the steel market. In the meantime, American Steel goes bankrupt, which is where what antitrust lawsuit is all about. The US government has a legitimate concern about closing down one of the few remaining domestic steel manufacturing plants in the US, and with it, the loss of union jobs and the potential, some would say inevitable, collapse of the Steel Workers Union altogether. So, the fly in the ointment is the labor union, and the reason a Letter of Congress might come in handy at some point."

"It sounds dangerous, Alex. I am guessing that this Letter of Congress won't protect me from a union hit man? Or perhaps a bullet to the head either! Will it, Alexander? Why me?"

Alexander nodded ever so slightly, agreeing with Nick's assessment of the situation. He stood and began pacing about the room. Now it was show time! He knew Nick, and he knew he was a wary man. He would have to be—anyone in this business would have to be! So, he chose his words carefully. "Because you owe me, Nick! Because you slip into the

States all the time anyway, and because you can travel freely throughout Russia, and that is where we need to make the exchange." He paused and looked directly into Nick's eyes before he continued. "And because you are still in love with her—Tatyana, aren't you Nick?"

Nick remained silent, refusing to answer.

"I can't lie to you. It will be dangerous Nikki," he added, his face turning cold. "Zubkov wants this deal to happen, and the American labor union doesn't! The union will try to stop me from delivering this package, or in this case, try to stop you from delivering it. I would recommend that you use your renowned skills to make the delivery covertly."

"What am I delivering, Alex?"

"Documents that prove ownership of Stalintsia Steel by a European conglomerate and not the Russian Federation, which is what the argument the attorneys for American Steel are using. They are using this argument to establish that Stalintsia Steel represents a national security threat to America, as a way to block the merger. In truth, once steel manufacturing was a nationalized industry in Russian, but the documents you will be delivering will prove that it is otherwise now. That not only was the company privatized, but it was also sold to this European conglomerate that has no governmental ties whatsoever!"

Nick had nodded, now understanding the importance of delivering such documents—and the risks involved. "So, you are asking me to possibly die on your behalf? Seems a pretty steep repayment fee, considering what I asked you to do so long ago, which turns out to be finding the love of your life!"

Alexander approached his old friend and stood before him. "You are too clever and too lucky to die, comrade. You are the only man with sufficient motivation to pull this off—the well being of the only two women you love! You have the motivation to pull this off—not to mention your skills, and your contacts. I predict that, as always, you will indeed pull it off."

Nick stared coldly at his old friend for a few silent seconds before replying. "Tell me your plan first Alex, then I will tell you if I will do it."

Alexander nodded enthusiastically as he raised the attaché case to eye level and showed it to Nick. "Here is an identical attaché case to the one I will have with me in Moscow, Nick," he began. "I won't have the merger documents until the very morning of our departure. We will switch attaché cases at Sheremetyevo Airport in Moscow. You'll be flying into Vancouver in my place. All the required travel documents are in the attaché case I am leaving with you now. We will make the switch under Zubkov's nose, but he won't suspect a thing! His people will be watching me, but they won't be able to get to the gate. So once past security, we make the exchange. You will take my place on the flight, while I go in the opposite direction. It's a sixteen-hour flight, more than enough time for me to slip away. As long as you get off that plane in Vancouver on Friday morning as Alexander Mayakovsky, Zubkov won't have a clue that anything has changed until the following Monday morning, when you deliver the documents on my behalf, and by then it will be too late for him to stop me."

"And what's this about a Letter of Congress?"

"Like I said before Nikki, it is Plan B—just in case! There are people who don't want this merger to take place — the union is but one faction in this little game. If someone tries to stop you, the letter authorizes you to use force if need be to protect yourself and the package, and it exonerates you from any prosecution before the fact. I can't imagine anything going wrong. Anybody trying to intercept the documents will be looking for me, not you, and besides, no one stateside even knows what you look like."

"Have you ever heard of FedEx, Alexander?" Nick replied sarcastically.

Alexander grinned at his old friend. "I have convinced Victor, and it was a good story too, that I will be needed to offer testimony on his behalf in the antitrust hearing! He bought into the idea, and he even coached me on what to say if they did call me to the stand! It is a perfect excuse for me to slip away with Tatyana!"

Nick thought about it—he wanted to believe what Alexander was telling him was the truth. It seemed simple enough, buying his old friend some time to escape the watchful eyes of his nefarious employer—Mr. Victor Zubkov, and of course to run off with the very beautiful Tatyana. He wondered if Alexander ever told Tatyana that it was he that had tasked Alexander to watch over her all these years? He doubted it. Alexander probably fell in love with her straight away, just as he had so many years before! Alexander was a double agent for the CIA, and had been feeding the CIA information about Zubkov and his political and business ambitions for many years now. Zubkov knew he worked for the CIA, but believed he had an agent in his pocket! What no one knew was that Alexander was there, because Nick had put him there in the first place. It was a very dangerous role for him to play all this time, and Alexander was correct in his assumptions—Nick did indeed owe him for looking after Tatyana and Natasha. Reluctantly, Nick agreed to help Alexander, not only to settle an old debt, but more as an act of penance for his own past, especially for his failure to follow his heart so many years ago, and marry her!

He had watched Alexander Mayakovsky close the door behind him, and only then did he pick up the attaché case and examine its contents: a fake visa, a passport, and a round trip ticket to Vancouver, British Columbia. He wondered briefly the reason Alexander had booked a flight into Vancouver instead of Seattle? But, he rationalized that Canadian customs agents were less stringent than those in the US—ever since the World Trade Center attacks anyway. He picked up his phone and dialed his operations manager.

"Ulyana. Something has just come up that I will need to attend to. Have Jules reschedule all my appointments—push them all out. I want you to fill in for me for anything that can't be pushed out."

"But Nikki," she pleaded. "According to the intelligence reports coming in, something big is going down in Siberia. You need to be here."

Nick sighed. "Ulyana, you are the operations manager here—just handle it!" He hung up on her, feeling badly for being short with her, but he had needed to think—think about why he was doing this favor? He had no answer because there was no answer! The only answer there was, was that he was doing it for a woman he never stopped loving! Besides, if he were ever to retire as he had been planning for some time now, he would need her to run things without his input, and she was more than capable! She was just used to the boss taking on all the tough tasks—though in reality, she was the boss!

Having made it up the ramp at the ferry landing, Nick removed a radio scanner from a backpack resting on the seat next to him, and turned it on. Immediately, the device started scanning emergency radio frequencies. It had a special chip inside it programmed to pick up on key words—courtesy of the CIA! The device squawked once.

"Damn," the voice said. "Roadblock on Highway 101." The chip had picked up on the word *roadblock*, and as a result, the device replayed the entire sentence that was stored in memory from just seconds before. The voice belonged to an angry truck driver who was being pulled over by the cops. Nick pushed a button on the scanner that allowed him to hear the whole conversation. He then pulled over to the side of the road to listen.

"Damned State Mounties! They have a roadblock up here near mile marker 280 heading east. Looks like they are stopping everyone going that way, searching for something or someone!"

"Come back, this is the Pathfinder," a phantom voice replied on his CB radio. "I have a heavy load going west. See any scales?"

"Negatory, the cops are looking for something eastbound only. No scales, just looking. Looks like us east-bounders are in for a wait."

Nick punched another button to return the device to auto; he did not care to listen to chatter between two truck drivers. He removed a laptop from his backpack and plugged a GPS unit into it, and a few seconds later, his position was displayed on the plasma screen along with a detailed map of the area. He keyed in the mile marker, and the computer zeroed in on it. The roadblock was only thirty miles away, and unfortunately, on the only direct path to where he was going. To his left was the coastline of the Strait of Juan de Fuca, and to his right were the Olympic Mountains, where only logging roads led—to the forests of the Olympic Peninsula, but they went nowhere!

He wondered to himself, "Is the roadblock meant for me?"

He punched in a command to find an alternative route. The curser blinked at him while it searched. The scanner picked up on another transmission just as something caught his eye in the rearview mirror.

The red and blue flashing lights of a highway patrol car appeared in the distance behind him, coming up on him fast. Nick took a deep breath, and reminded himself it might be nothing.

With tires smoking and wheels locked up, the patrol car skidded over to the shoulder of the road right behind him. Nick caught the words "gray mustang" emanating from the scanner just before he shut it off. He pulled out a map while the laptop continued to work out a solution for him. Apparently, it was more than *nothing*!

Calmly he shut the lid, wrapped up the cord from the GPS, and put it back into the backpack. He made sure that the four-point seatbelt held it all secured as he glanced in the rearview mirror. The officer was still on the radio with dispatch, but then Nick saw him put the radio mike back in its cradle, and get out of his patrol car.

"Afternoon," the officer said nervously when he reached his window.

Nick fumbled with a road map that he had just pulled from his glove box—playing the part, and looked up in surprise. "Afternoon officer," he replied casually and smiled.

"Any trouble here?" the officer asked.

Nick shook his head and frowned at the map. "No officer, I just pulled over to take a look at the map. I seem to be turned around. Why do you ask?"

The officer looked anxious. "License and registration please," he replied.

Nick looked puzzled. "What for, officer? Parking on the shoulder of the road?"

The officer stood there staring at him through dark sunglasses that hid his eyes—hid his thoughts and emotions! He had an aluminum clipboard in his left hand, and Nick assumed it must be his habit to take it with him—to write tickets on. But, it was apparent that the cop had no intention of writing a citation this moment. His right hand went to his hip, and it came to rest on his service revolver. Nick also noticed that his hands were trembling. There was adrenaline obviously pumping through this officer's bloodstream, from fear or anxiety Nick could not guess! It pretty much confirmed that the roadblock up ahead was indeed meant for him.

Nick reached for his hip pocket, and the officer nervously unsnapped the leather strap that restrained his gun. Nick froze and smiled. "I am just getting out my wallet, officer. Okay?"

The officer dropped his clipboard to the ground and shouted, as he took a three-point stance—a stance he was trained to take when he meant business!

"Get out of the car now!"

The gun was pointed directly at Nick's head, and the end of the barrel was twitching about a bit too much for comfort.

Nick raised his hands. "If you would be so kind, officer. Please open the door for me. Under the circumstances—your gun and all, I want to keep my hands where you can see them."

The officer fell for this ruse, and he hesitantly moved forward. Reaching for the door handle, and all the while keeping his gun aimed directly at Nick's head, he reached for the door. When Nick heard the catch on the door release, he lunged into it with his left shoulder. The door sprang open wide. It clipped the trooper's left knee, throwing him off balance, and causing him to drop to the ground. His weapon went off like a cannon, the bullet passing by Nick's left ear and piercing the roof of the Mustang.

Nick rolled out of the car and made his move. There was a crunch of cartilage being crushed as he jabbed the heel of his hand into the officer's nose. The patrolman went limp, immediately losing consciousness.

Before Nick could consider what to do next, there were more sirens in the distance! It was apparent that backup was already on the way—probably called in when the officer pulled over and was on the radio to dispatch. Nick took the officer by the armpits, and dragged him to the ditch behind his car. "Sorry buddy," he muttered, and then he retrieved the officer's weapon from the roadside. He unloaded it and threw the rounds into the woods, and wiped his prints off the weapon, and then placed it by the downed officer's side. The weapon was probably worth a week's salary to him.

Nick peered down the road in the direction of the sirens. There were now three state patrol cars racing toward him with sirens wailing and lights ablaze. He ran back to the Mustang and started the engine. The squad cars were coming at him incredibly fast! Their images growing quickly in his side view mirror as he started the car. He slammed the shifter into first gear while popping the clutch. The Mustang fishtailed, spewing gravel everywhere, until the tires took purchase on the asphalt. The Mustang laid down twin black patches of rubber as it rocketed forward. White smoke from burning rubber filled the air behind it as it sped away. The supercharger was just beginning to breathe when Nick slammed the gearbox into second. The speedometer flew past sixty in a heartbeat.

"Jesus," he muttered out loud. "This isn't what I planned for!" His voice was lost in the screaming of the engine.

There was no place for him to go but forward. He slammed the gearbox into third at six thousand RPM and pushed the gas pedal to the floor again. The supercharger began working hard now—pumping horsepower to the wheels! The speedometer indicated he was moving at well over one hundred MPH when he pushed the gear selector into fourth gear. He looked in the rearview mirror again! Two of the patrol cars had stopped gaining on him—the third had presumably stopped to assist the downed officer. The Mustang topped out at one hundred and sixty-five miles an hour and things began getting crazy for Nick!

Highway 101 was in most places only a two-lane highway possessing only a modestly paved shoulder on either side. Nick blew past the first set of vehicles easily enough by swerving into the left lane. But oncoming traffic soon forced him back into his own lane. He was going too fast to slow down for the vehicles in his own lane—he needed to do something! He downshifted, and braked hard, shooting the gap between an enormous RV and an SUV, and sliding onto what little of the right shoulder there was. The right wheels of the Mustang hit the soft dirt and squirmed, but Nick had anticipated this! The car got loose and drifted, but Nick compensated. He looked ahead for another lane. He powered past the next group of vehicles on the right shoulder, stones and debris flying everywhere behind him. Other drivers started laying on their horns in anger! He shot back into his own lane, and was once again faced with more traffic. This time he shot across the left lane and into the opposing traffic, and took that shoulder! Fortunately, no one was there. He had lost sight of his pursuers, but knew it was a temporary condition.

Up ahead—was a fork in the road! It looked promising, considering that Highway 101 was choked with traffic. He was still on the left shoulder, and still traveling at well over one hundred miles per hour when his time ran out! Highway 101 curved off to the left, and the side road he was approaching rapidly broke off straight. The immediate problem—was getting to that side road! Another challenge cropped up! A semi heading straight for him! It seemed the shoulder was ending too, blocked by boulders. It became immediately apparent that it was time to move once again!

The truck driver was flashing his lights—sounding his horn, doing whatever he could to clear the lane in front of him! Nick downshifted, pushed the gas pedal to the floor, and aimed for another small gap between a logging truck and a pickup truck ahead of it!

The semi approaching him now veered off to the right side of the road to prevent a head-on collision. The trailer began to jackknife! White smoke billowed from the trailer tires, as they howled in protest. The driver no longer bothered with his horns. He was now doing his best to counter-steer. The whole rig started to slide sideways, and the drivers of vehicles traveling in the opposite direction were slamming on their brakes, as well—and taking their own shoulder, as the truck-and-trailer rig skidded into their space.

Several cars entangled when drivers lost complete control. Vehicle debris flew everywhere! Air dams and chunks of plastic bumpers skidded onto the roadway! Headlights and taillight lenses exploded like fireworks! The sounds of locked up tires, and the *whump* of metal folding on impact, filled the air!

Nick shot the gap between the two vehicles ahead, and then steered for the side road. Turning his wheel slightly, he realized that his escape route was not what he had thought it was! From his previous vantage point, the country road kept going straight, while the main highway curved off to the left. But, it was an optical illusion!

What he didn't realize—not until this very moment, was that running adjacent to the main highway was a railroad track! The track bed was twenty feet lower than the road he was on, and was impossible to see it from the highway! The side road, which was his aim—his last hope, dipped to a railroad crossing that ran adjacent to highway 101. To his horror, there was now a train stacked high with logs—directly in his path!

He was already committed, though, and instinctively—perhaps foolishly, he floored the gas pedal again, and prayed for deliverance!

The engine redlined! The Mustang leapt forward in response! It became a projectile at one hundred forty miles per hour. The pavement dropped away from under the wheels and the car arced through the air like an artillery shell.

"Oh, my God!" Nick muttered, as he braced for the imminent crash and he cursed Alexander!

He nearly cleared the train, but not quite. The wheels of the Mustang slammed onto the top layer of logs with enough force that it ripped apart the chain binders holding them together! It then skipped off them like a flat stone on water and crashed back onto the roadway eighty feet further away. The impact of the vehicle slamming to the ground jarred Nick's head severely! It felt as if he had been hit with a sledgehammer! Airbags exploded all around him! He should not have survived this crash, so he knew it was God's will he did! Nick blacked out for a moment, and when he regained consciousness, he was slowing down rapidly in a field of soybeans—or, something that looked like soybeans. He instinctively planted his foot firmly on the brakes, churning up clouds of dust. The Mustang spun 360 degrees several times, before it finally came to a complete stop—pointed in the wrong direction! Nick crossed himself, and breathed deeply, as dust settled around him. His heart was pounding in his chest—fiercely!

His laptop beeped at him. He looked over at it, surprised to see it still intact in the seat next to him. He took a few more deep breaths while the Mustang idled roughly—like a spent stallion after a hard run on a hot day. He removed the laptop from the backpack. The computer had plotted his alternative course. This turn-off, along with multiple logging roads that weren't on any printed map, were his way out—courtesy of CIA satellite mapping. This road would take him up into the mountains and eventually, almost, to where he needed to go.

Nick looked back toward Highway 101 and could see the train was still lumbering along; a load of logs had spilled onto the siding—the result of a two thousand pound vehicle hitting it with immense force! It effectively blocked the road. He could see vehicles stopped all along the shoulder of Highway 101, creating another roadblock. The trucker who had driven the semi that Nick barely missed, was now pulled off onto the shoulder, and was standing next to his big rig, smoking a cigarette!

Getting out of the car, his own legs wobbly—he verified that he could still walk. He ripped the air bag from the center steering column, and tossed it to the ground. Climbing back into the vehicle, he strapped himself in. He dropped the Mustang into first gear, and spun it around in the soft dirt to point it in the right direction.

The highway behind him would be shut down for several hours—while the authorities sorted out the mess! His own escape route was pretty much secured. The tangle of logs that had broken loose from the train made sure of that! Looking at the map again, he plotted his course. Deciding where he needed to be before dark, he mentally swore that Alexander was going to see his face again, only this time, he better have answers—some really good ones!

He knew that the highway patrol would tighten the noose on him again, and he wondered what he had with him that was so damned important for them to get so aggressive about apprehending him and it—whatever it was!

"Documents, my ass," he muttered out loud. Alexander had a lot of explaining to do! But, it would have to wait. Right now his immediate concern was to elude those who would stop him, and it appeared that there were many!

"Paybacks are hell," he muttered out loud to no one.

He was now being reminded of another anomaly of the Pacific Northwest. The weather changes rapidly! Storm clouds were rolling in over the mountains, and thunder could be heard in the distance. It reminded him of being back in Siberia.

"Great!" Nick thought to himself knowing full well his Mustang could easily get mired down in mud. He looked toward the highway once more, where the truck driver was giving him the finger. Nick thought about giving it back to him, but instead he dropped the clutch and pulled the beat-up Mustang back onto the country road. He was amazed that it still ran. He floored it. In a few seconds, he was gone from sight and heading up into the mountains.

Plan-B was now in effect!

Chapter 2

FBI agent Bill Blakely was at the roadblock at mile marker 280 when the report came in that the Mustang had been spotted thirty miles west of him, just outside of Port Angeles. Within minutes, a flurry of frantic communications came in: officer down, Mustang fleeing the scene at high speeds, Mustang escaped, and a dozen other reports of mayhem.

"Damn it!" Blakely cursed. "This is getting out of hand. Get me a chopper," he commanded to one of his men.

Blakely, a career FBI man, had been with the force for nearly twelve years. In his late thirties now, he still maintained a youthful look that led many to believe he was just a rookie straight out of training. It had always been a problem for him, especially when dealing with elder subordinates who deemed themselves much wiser and more deserving than he. His brown hair was cropped short, and being of medium height and slender build to begin with, it added to the illusion that he was too young to have experience, much less authority.

It was not the case! After having spent ten years in the field, he was considered a senior field agent by the FBI—and was, by any definition of the term! That too worked against him, because he should have been promoted out of the field years ago!

Blakely had a tendency to bend the rules—not listen very well to orders! The result was he had been passed over for promotion several times already—much to the chagrin of his wife, Anne Marie, who expected upward mobility, including pay raises! Because there were no promotions, there were no big pay raises!

Blakely's wife was another worrisome concern for him, but right now things with his work seemed to be spiraling out of control, and he didn't have time to dwell upon his bad marriage. It seemed in his profession—

everyone had a bad marriage!

He had worked all types of cases before, from kidnappings to hostage negotiations, but this was a new one to him. He was briefed just the day before when handed a thick file to study. There was nothing in the FBI manual that quite covered anything like this.

His orders were to the point: "Stop Nick Peters and detain him by the order of the President of the United States of America!" It was subsequently made clear that lethal force was not an option—someone, somewhere, had plans for Nick Peters. The file he was given was remarkably uninformative, considering its size.

First of all, his name was not Nick Peters. He was born Nicholas Dimeitry Petrovisky. His parents were Russian immigrants who were given political asylum in the US shortly before WWII ended. During the war, his father had done something—what that was, there wasn't a clue in the file. Whatever it was he did to earn a free and speedy passage to the United States, along with complimentary American citizenship for himself and his family was a mystery! The file did not elaborate, except to say the Soviet Union had proclaimed him an enemy of the State for his actions, which forced a name change for the family. The KGB had standing orders from Stalin himself to kill all of them. The US government decided upon the last name of Peters, the English equivalent to Petrovisky. Nick was raised as Nick Peters, and his friends knew him as Nikki. He was fluent in Russian, something that would later result in his recruitment into the CIA.

Blakely had spent the previous afternoon reading and rereading the file, hoping to come up with a clue as to where Peters point of entry into the country might be; he had no luck. The authorities knew he had flown into Vancouver early that morning, but from there he had managed to slip away using a false ID. They had assumed, incorrectly, that he would be traveling as Alexander Mayakovsky. But, Nick Peters had gotten clever, and instead he booked another seat under another name. How he got his visa punched in Moscow was unclear. But, he probably knew the customs agent there! After all, that was what he did for a living—wasn't it?

Peters entire adult life had been classified—according to the file. At the age of nineteen, during the height of the Vietnam War, he was ordered by the draft board to report for enlistment into the army. It was discovered that he spoke fluent Russian during the induction process. The CIA immediately snapped him up in the hopes of using him behind the Iron Curtain—which they did. They put him into an academy for covert ops, from which he graduated with honors, and he later took a master's degree in foreign languages.

After spending two years in France, and two years in Germany studying the native languages as Michael Dobson—an assumed name, Peters then ended up spending several years on the Grand Prix circuit as a driver for Ferrari. The CIA utilized his freedom of travel throughout Europe to their best advantage, making him once again a courier. Speaking five different languages fluently, and considered to be quite dashing—and a ladies man, he became one of the most talked about eligible young bachelors in Eastern Europe. But Michael Dobson had become too well known, and too dashing for that matter!

In the file was an article published by a popular magazine about a spectacular car crash during a time trials run in East Germany. The dashing American Michael Dobson was declared dead upon arrival at the hospital. There were plenty of photos taken by both the news media, and the CIA. He appeared to be dead, but of course, he wasn't! The CIA needed to remove him from public view! And, everything had been staged for just that affect!

After six months in Switzerland, and a great deal of cosmetic surgery, he was slipped into East Germany, and later, behind the Iron Curtain. He had a new face and a new identity by that time. The dossier had little more in it than that. Officially, Nick Peters, *aka* Michael Dobson, was dead! Killed in a racecar accident! There were no more photos of him after the accident. No one knew what Nicholas Dimeitry Petrovisky looked like today, not even the CIA, or so it seemed. Somehow, all of his records, as had those of so many other top operatives for both sides, disappeared in the aftermath of the fall of the Soviet Union. He never officially returned to America.

"So, who the hell is this guy? And, what's so damned important about him?" Captain Jorgenson of the Washington State Highway Patrol demanded, coming from out of nowhere! Blakely was taken by surprise by the loud outburst. Turning around to face an outraged Jorgenson, who had stormed up from behind him, he considered his answer carefully. "I presume you are referring to the driver of the Mustang?"

Jorgenson nodded. "Damned right I am!"

"His name is Nick Peters. He's a fifty-five year old Caucasian male with no previous convictions. He's a courier, a very clever courier."

Captain Jorgenson stared back at him quizzically, and then spat on the ground. "What the hell are we are chasing here, Mr. FBI man? Is he a summons server, a FedEx man, or a pizza delivery boy? What precisely do you mean when you say that he is a courier? And tell me, what's so damned special about him?"

Captain Jorgenson, approaching fifty years old himself, was a big man, well over six foot tall and with a linebacker's frame. Blakely thought he probably was of Norwegian descent, and noted that he appeared to work out regularly. He was also clearly a man who liked to be in control, a man not to cross.

It was obvious that his men knew it too, for they acted with absolute deference around him, and Blakely took an instant dislike to him. He too felt intimidated, just by being in his presence, and under his wrath.

Blakely paused once again—he needed time to consider his answer. Field agents weren't supposed to give out too much information to outside agencies. But, it was probably better that he let the captain know that he wasn't up against a murderer, or a pedophile, or some other equally distasteful character, which might make it a bit too palatable for him, or his men, to justify gunplay or brutality, which Jorgenson, seemed to be capable of either, or both. They needed Peters alive, and intact! At least his orders said so, and his superiors ordered him to work with the man whether he liked him, or not.

"A courier," he continued. "A delivery boy—in this case Peters, is hired to deliver packages! Except that this courier, carries a Letter of Congress from the United States of America! It puts him somewhat above the law, your law anyway."

"The hell with what you say — no one is above the law!" Jorgenson spat back. "If he knows we are looking for him, why doesn't he just give himself up if he thinks he is immune to prosecution?"

"The Letter of Congress he carries means, as far as he is concerned anyway, that he doesn't have to be bothered sufficiently to give himself up. As far as such a man is concerned, he hasn't broken any laws yet. Again, why turn yourself in if the laws in question don't pertain?"

"The hell you say! I have a man down, and this courier resisted arrest—and he was the one that put my officer down! He's broken every traffic law there is, endangered the lives of civilians, and is now fleeing and eluding the law! You mean to tell me that I have half my force sitting at roadblocks jacking off, and the other half out on patrol looking for this guy? And, he's done nothing wrong?"

"That is correct, Captain."

Jorgenson stared back at him with an expression of hatred, and of utter confusion.

Blakely continued. "Peters is carrying a Letter of Congress, and he has only one goal in mind, to make his delivery on Monday morning. He doesn't know what's inside the package, and he probably doesn't care what it is. He is under no obligation to surrender anything. Therefore, his best line of defense is to elude the law. And even if we do manage to catch him, his Letter of Congress protects him from prosecution before the fact!"

"And just what in the hell, is a Letter of Congress?"

"A Letter of Congress authorizes him to use whatever means necessary to deliver his package. It exonerates him from most criminal acts in doing so. The only thing that overrides a letter of Congress is an order from the President of the United States himself, and I have just that! But, I have to serve him first."

"Well, what the hell is this all about anyway?" Jorgenson demanded. "What if someone other than the authorities attempts to take the package, or what if my boys were to stop him for a simple traffic violation, try to search him?"

"You are wondering if he will resort to violence, or if he will perhaps use a weapon?"

"Well, hell yes I am! He has already resorted to violence. He assaulted one of my officers and put him in the hospital, and what the hell is that pile up he caused, if not an act of violence?"

"If someone other than the authorities tries to separate him from his package, or try to prevent him from delivering it, he is authorized to use lethal force, if necessary, to protect himself and/or his goods."

"You are joking, right?"

"Sorry Captain, but I am not. He is protected under a federal law much like a bounty hunter is protected. The law was passed back in 1868 when the country was half lawless, and the Spanish American War was imminent. Back then; the Congress needed a way to deliver documents from point to point reliably. At the time, the postal service was unreliable and often got looted by renegades. So, they hired men like Peters, to ride the coaches and the trains, to make sure that the documents meant for delivery arrived as expected. They would be given a Letter of Congress authorizing them to do whatever was deemed necessary to make their deliveries without fear from prosecution later. The original laws were never taken off the books. Though a Letter of Congress is rarely used anymore, the law is still valid. I wasn't even aware of this law until just yesterday myself! Now you know what I know about this situation." He handed Jorgensen a photocopy he had made on the topic.

Jorgenson read the photocopy of the referenced law, and grimaced. A blood vessel on his left temple began to throb. "And, what if one of my boys were to have a run in with this Peters again?"

"Have you talked with your officer yet?" Blakely replied.

"No, not yet," he grumbled.

"Odds are that your officer overreacted and pulled a gun on him. Under those circumstances, Peters had no choice but to disarm him. He is a well trained operative, and according to what I have been led to believe about him, he is very well disciplined, and unlikely to use lethal force—unless he needs to! I doubt he even has a weapon on him because he just came in through customs and wouldn't have chanced it. His first line of defense will be to elude."

Blakely now stared hard at Jorgenson, that to make a point with his eyes.

"We requested that you stop and detain him, not put him on the run. The tip about the Mustang was anonymous, and either someone is setting this guy up or someone is trying to warn him off, knowing that we would put up roadblocks."

"What the hell is this guy delivering that is so important?" Jorgensen asked, and then he spat tobacco juice to the side of the road.

"That I don't know," Blakely replied honestly. "One thing I do know, is that this guy is very clever, and that he was a former spook for the CIA. He spent most of his life behind the iron curtain under extremely hazardous circumstances, and I wouldn't want to set him off."

"Why don't we just put a bullet into him? Sounds lots easier than trying to apprehend him."

"A presidential order—for one," Blakely replied. He then shrugged his shoulders indifferently. "I don't know, Jorgenson. My orders are to detain him and not to harm him. My best guess is that the president—or someone, has something he wants this guy to do! Something that only he can do, and something someone needs him for. Otherwise, I agree with you, why not just take him out with a bullet?"

Jorgenson mulled over what Blakely had just told him, feeling for the first time as if he and a federal agent that he had something in common with! If only the desire to plug somebody, instead of chasing him down!

"And what about all the mayhem he has created, the damages and injuries to private citizens?" Jorgenson replied heatedly.

"Until he kills someone, or until he injures someone—seriously, with malice, he can't be prosecuted anyway."

Jorgenson turned purple with rage! He slammed his fist down hard on the roof of the car, crushing it as easily as if it were a beer can! Blakely began to wonder just how stable Jorgenson was? He wondered if he was going to lose it right here, right now, and go seriously ballistic on him? The weight of his own weapon on his hip, suddenly felt reassuring to him! And, considering the size of the man—it would take a forty-five to bring him down!

"Listen Captain," Blakely continued as calmly as he could, not wanting to push him—infuriate him, any further. "I am sorry your officer got hurt, and I apologize for not briefing you entirely earlier today. Now that I have briefed you, here are my orders," and he handed him the papers. "And, I hope that you like driving a taxicab if you decide to ignore them! Because, if you do, it will be one of the few jobs left that you will ever be able to get if you breach these orders!"

Jorgenson spat once again onto the road, and nodded, after reading Blakely's orders.

"There is more to this than meets the eye," said Blakely.

"Go on," Jorgenson muttered.

"The congressman or woman who issued this letter, has now opened themselves up for public scrutiny! Everything was kosher so long as this guy—Nick Peters, could deliver the goods on time and intact without any fuss. But, if he gets caught, and if he exercises this Letter of Congress, it exposes the whole gig—whatever the hell it is! If Peters gets caught, it would be a big problem for someone, somewhere, and no telling what that might lead to!

Jorgenson did not like what he was hearing. He spat out his spent wad of tobacco, and loaded up another one, puckering out his right cheek as he stuffed the wad in. Blakely was sickened just watching him. He was about to continue when Jorgenson held his hand up, and turned away from him. He apparently needed a moment to consider his options—this new situation, and to cool down a little.

Blakely got the message. He left the man leaning over his newly dented patrol car and went over to his own car to retrieve a pack of smokes. He lit one, then stood by his government-issued sedan and took a deep drag on it. He had been trying to quit smoking for a year now—but without much success. The Nicorette gum he had been trying was turning his stomach inside out! He told himself that he would have just this one smoke, and get back on his routine in the morning.

Peters had already managed to elude the highway patrol on the ground, and he had created such mayhem in his wake that it would take hours to catch up to him now. Blakely was hoping that, by using the chopper, he might spot the banged-up Mustang quickly! But now the weather was turning—what was the likelihood he could find him, when a chopper would have zero visibility? Thick dark storm clouds were blowing in over the mountains from the south, and soon, it would be dusk—further adding to his problems, and he knew the chopper would be of little value.

Jorgenson waved him back over just as he finished his smoke, and he crushed it out on the tarmac. Jorgenson had been on his radio for the past ten minutes, probably checking out his story.

"Good luck," Blakely thought to himself. No hick-town law library was going to have any reference to law concerning Letters of Congress, which was written back in the eighteen hundreds and long forgotten about! Jorgenson would be told by his superiors to just drop the matter and to do as he was told. There would be a big federal grant coming the department's way soon—so, just make a big wish list! Christmas time has come early for the Washington State Highway Patrol, and Blakely knew that someone, somewhere, already had the money spent!

Jorgenson looked to be a bit more humble when Blakely came back. "What now?" the Captain asked him, his tone less abrasive than earlier.

"Well, it seems that you and your boys are out of the chase, at least for now. You pushed Peters a bit too hard today, and now he has fled. Whether he meant to or not, he shut down Highway 101 behind him, and he blocked any pursuit down the side roads. He is now heading up into those mountains, where I believe he will abandon his car eventually and go on by foot."

Jorgenson looked skeptical, and so Blakely elaborated.

"Look Captain, Peters is not a normal thug, not the type of criminal that you know, anyway. He is a former CIA operative with thirty years of field experience in places like Russia—Siberia, Russia! Where the stakes are very much more serious for him if he is caught there, than if he is caught here."

"Remember, he carries a letter—a license, to do just exactly what he is doing now. So far, he has not exceeded his license! The federal government will pick up all the property damages incurred. Your job was to spot him and to detain him. My job was to serve him with a subpoena, and to get him to surrender his parcel. He is not a stupid man! His vehicle was made, yet he got away anyway. He will either switch vehicles now or go on by foot. He is a skilled woodsman according to his file, and so proceeding on foot out there is going to be an option for him." He nodded toward the mountains again.

"He has a backup plan, believe me," Blakely stated with confidence.

"And, how will he get to Seattle—can he swim the Narrows? He either takes a ferry at Port Townsend, Bremerton, or Port Orchard, or he has to drive the Tacoma Narrows Bridge," Jorgensen said dryly. "Either way, he can't walk there."

"True, but once he gets to the mainland, he can take a bus to the court house if he wants to, and I doubt that anyone will recognize him—because, that is what he does best: not get noticed! My guess is that he will steal another ride at the first opportunity."

"And how did he know where our roadblocks would be?"

"Maybe he didn't. Your officer put him on the run, remember? Now that he has been made, he'll have to ditch the car."

"So who the hell screwed up in Port Angeles and let this guy through customs?"

"No one, Captain. He had a perfect cover. He was just another businessman coming back from Canada. How was customs to know?"

"Still, why didn't they nab him?"

"Because we don't know what he looks like," Blakely exclaimed! "The man has been abroad for twenty years. He's a freaking ghost, a spook! We don't know how he gets into the country when he is here, or what name he goes by when he is here. Officially, he died in a racing accident in Europe over twenty years ago. His own former agency, the CIA, doesn't even have recent photos of him. The guy can speak five or six different languages fluently, and he could have a passport from anywhere, and pose as anybody! He got through customs minutes before we could get a description out on the car! As soon as we did, one of the customs people reported having just seen it leaving the terminal, and that was when your people got the call. Before anyone could do anything about it, all hell broke loose! Your man in the hospital is the only person right now who could ID this guy, and I am surprised that this Peters didn't take him out just to protect his own identity."

"If you didn't know what he looks like, how did you expect to ID him?" Jorgenson asked.

"He was captured once by the KGB, and they tortured him. He was thrown into a gulag where they branded him with a number burnt onto his forearm. The markings are fairly discrete—and not garish, like most tattoos are. They would go unnoticed by most—unless one was looking for it! And, what markings there are, are in Cyrillic anyway, and most people wouldn't know what they meant! Over the years, the scars have faded, and are now barely discernable. But, according to the file, if one looks closely enough, one can still see the raised scars of the Cyrillic numbers seventeen and eighteen burnt into his flesh! Those numbers are representative of the year that Czar Nicholas II abdicated the throne to Russia, 1917, and the year it was decided to kill his entire family before he could change his mind, 1918! The KGB had Peters marked for death! But, once again he eluded them too! His records went missing after the Cold War ended, and only that tidbit about him survived. It's the only way we know of to get a positive ID on him, and the only way I'll know I have the right guy."

It was getting cold, and daylight was fading rapidly to dusk.

Captain Jorgenson spat his wad out and said, "Let's get in the car."

"Sir, the chopper will be here in forty minutes—it's being prepped now!" said one of Blakely's men who had just rushed up from behind him.

Blakely sighed. "Right! Find someone to return my car. With the rain coming in, I doubt we will see anything after dark, but it's worth a shot."

The two men got into the patrol car and Jorgenson turned on the overhead light. "I guess you are right," Jorgenson said. "I'll send a man over to the hospital to see if my officer can ID this guy."

A Washington State patrolman approached the car and shouted loudly enough to penetrate the closed windows.

"Captain! What do we do? Shift's ending soon!"

Jorgenson looked at Blakely, who sighed audibly.

"He's up in the mountains somewhere, no telling where! He will abandon the Mustang and switch vehicles at some point, or he'll go on by foot and acquire another ride later. He has two more days to get to his destination. I probably should have just waited for him to show up in Seattle, but that's water under the bridge! Now, I want to find that car! It may give us a clue as to where he will hole up next, or where he might show up next! Have your men patrol all the back roads and all the logging roads. I doubt that he would just abandon his ride by the side of the road— it will be hidden somewhere. Have your men look everywhere: behind a shed, down a private drive, in the local junkyard, if need be. Remember, the overtime is on Uncle Sam."

Jorgenson rolled down his window and answered his officer. "Pull all the roadblocks officer, but I want a car on this road here, off to the side,

24/7. I want every officer out there, driving around looking for this guy! No speeding tickets tonight, no drunk drivers, and no goofing off! Work twelve hours, go home and go to bed, sleep eight, and then be prepared to work another twelve. Got it?"

The officer nodded, grabbed his walkie-talkie, and passed the word on to the rest of the men. Jorgenson knew this was good timing for the young officer. The young officer's wife was pregnant again, and they could use the overtime pay.

"Now what?" Jorgenson asked.

"You need to find out what your officer, the one who got hurt, knows. I am going to make a sweep from the air, but it is doubtful! Where is your officer now?"

"Olympic Medical Center in Port Angeles," Jorgenson replied.

"I'll meet you there after I make my sweep. And, also, there is a fair chance that your man got a good enough look at this guy, for a drawing of some sort. So, in the meantime, I'll have an artist sent over to see if he can make a composite drawing of our so-called Nick Peters."

Chapter 3

Resorting to plan-B meant that his cover was blown, just as it had been—back in St. Petersburg, back in 1975, when he was courting the beautiful young Tatyana! The KGB had tortured him for three days after they captured him, and he spent nearly a year in a Siberian gulag before finally escaping. It was in that year, that Tatyana had given birth to Natasha—Nick's own daughter, and by then, her current husband, Victor Zubkov, was already courting her.

Peters knew that he would have to ditch the car somewhere soon or wind up in jail once again—something he feared more than death itself! He checked his map again; locating the place he would abandon the Mustang—the place where he could acquire a new ride. Now, he just needed to stay out of sight until he got some answers about what to do next. As he drove up into the mountains, the road became narrower and narrower, and at the same time, the world around him became darker and darker as dusk blanketed the valleys. He turned on his head-lamps. The rain had begun an hour ago, and now it intensified, making matters even worse. The Mustang was a hell of a car, but it was not a four-wheel-drive truck and it lost traction several times on the slippery muck called a road! It wasn't long before he found himself tailing a logging truck that took up the entire lane, making it impossible to pass. The tires of the big rig spewed mud the entire way and the Mustang's wipers were making a mess of it on the windshield. Finally, the truck turned off onto a gravel road.

The rain started coming down in a torrent now, and Nick turned the wipers to high, hoping the rain would wash the windshield clear. But, the wiper blade smeared even more, and then the visibility really went straight to hell. The windshield was now more dirty than clean. As he struggled to see where he was going in the darkness, through a smudged windshield, he caught a glimpse of a vehicle pulled off to the side of the road directly ahead. As he came upon it, he moved over to pass. The driver door to the Jeep Cherokee flung open wide at just the wrong time! He swerved to the left to avoid it! But, he caught the door nevertheless! It snapped off the hinges cleanly, like a dried chicken wishbone does when one makes a wish with it. He locked up the brakes and skidded to a stop. He threw open his own door to get out! When he did, he immediately fell to the ground himself. The dirt road had turned to mud—no, to snot! Picking himself up, he rushed over to the Cherokee as quickly as he could. The sloppy muck made more of a mess of him! He only hoped it was only a door that he took off—and not someone's arm, or worse!

"Oh my God, are you okay?" he yelled above the downpour.

Inside the Jeep was a woman. Her head was pressed against the steering wheel and she was sobbing. Nick stood there, not knowing what to do for her. The pouring rain rinsed much of the muck from his face and his clothes as she continued to sob, her shoulders heaving with emotions. Finally she looked up, turned her head toward him, and she exploded into a tirade.

"You bastard! What—are you some drunk?" she screamed at him. "You nearly killed me!"

Nick replied excitedly, "No, no—give me a chance to explain! My windshield got smeared with mud—your car was in the dark without any lights on, and everything just happened so fast. Are you okay?"

"No, I am not okay, you idiot!" she screamed back. "This piece of crap just quit on me! The battery must have failed or something, which is why the lights weren't on! I barely made it off to the side of the road and then you—you come along! When I finally do open my door to get out, you tear the damned thing right out of my hand! If I had already stepped out, I would be a dead woman right now! It isn't like we are in New York City here, with so much traffic that I need to be wary of idiots like you! What are the odds? That, when I go to open my door to check out why the car stalled out, that another car is right there? There ready to take it off the hinges? On this bleak road in the middle of nowhere?"

Nick stammered trying to collect his thoughts. He wanted to apologize to her, but he had no idea how to begin.

As he got soaked even further, he apologetically replied, "I am very sorry, ma'am—miss! It was just a coincidence—you being here and all! It was a coincidence that no one could predict! The thing is, you still haven't answered my question—are you all right? I will pay for any damages to your car, and I accept full responsibility for everything."

She looked at him directly for the first time, and now she was visibly trying—with all her might, to calm down!

Nick noticed the beauty of her strikingly beautiful large brown eyes.

Standing there thoroughly soaked in the rain, actually, as soaked as a man could get, and with mud splotches still on his face, he stared back at her with complete blamelessness. She noticed that he was a handsome man, and a very fit looking one at that—judging from how his wet shirt pasted itself to his lean torso. He had a lithe and athletic build to him, and he appeared to be in his late forties or early fifties. It was also apparent to her that he was not from around here.

"Where are you from?" she asked defiantly.

"Ah, Portland. Portland Oregon," he replied.

"So, what in the hell are you doing up here on the Olympic Peninsula?"

Nick stood there dripping wet! He wondered if he should answer her questions or not? He wondered if he should just get back into his car and drive off? He knew he could not tell her the truth! That he was eluding the law! But, he needed a plausible story for why he was in the mountains in the first place! Why he was driving a beat-up Mustang in the pouring rain on a road that went nowhere!

With his palms facing upward, he gestured expressively toward the heavens, as if pleading to God for guidance of some sort! He stammered, and went on. "There was a traffic jam on Highway 101 because of some sort of accident," Nick told her truthfully, and continued. "And, I waited there for hours, before deciding to try a back road to get around it," he lied. "But, then I got myself turned around. I ended up getting behind a logging truck that I couldn't pass, because the lane was too narrow. Then my windshield got covered with dirt and mud from the logging truck! When it started raining even harder, I turned on my wipers to full, but then the windshield smeared even worse! The next thing I know, the logging truck turns off the road, and you are right there! Still, halfway in the middle of the road, and with no lights on! Then I take your door off! So, are you hurt or not? Do you want me to look at your car? Maybe I can fix it?"

He felt awkward—like an awkward teenager would! Like a teenager would when talking to a very pretty girl! There he was blurting out everything he knew like his mouth was on autopilot.

Her expression softened, as did her tone.

"So what about my door, mister? I can't drive this piece of junk without a door, can I?"

Nick stammered, "Is a thousand enough?"

Caught off guard by his response, she replied, "This wreck isn't worth six hundred, much less a thousand. You got a deal mister! However, I don't take credit cards, checks, or promissory notes either, if you get my drift?"

Nick nodded, now utterly soaked by the downpour. He reached for his wallet, counted out ten soggy one hundred dollar bills, and handed them to her.

She looked at him, and then she looked at the notes suspiciously—before counting the money carefully. "Okay, we're square, except for one thing."

"And what's that?" he shouted loud enough to be heard over the downpour.

"I need a ride, and I want to go with you. Take me someplace far away from here."

Nick looked at her incredulously as water dripped from his hair and his nose. She stared back at him with defiance.

"Look mister," she said. "Are you going to leave a young woman stranded out here, in the woods, in the middle of the night? This piece of crap car can't take me anyplace. It doesn't even have a door now, thanks to you! I need a ride."

"I'll take you home, okay?" He stated, thinking she couldn't live far away.

She stepped out of the car and screamed into his face,

"I don't have a home buster! That was what I was leaving when you came along and tore my door off! All I have in the world is in the back of this old clunker—a backpack and a suitcase, and that's it! Is it asking too much of you to take me, and my two damned bags, the hell away from here?"

Nick hesitated. She was a very pretty woman—probably in her early thirties, he guessed. Her straight black hair and her skin color indicated that she was of Latino heritage, or possibly even a combination of African American and Latino. She wore no make-up, but she didn't need to either—she was remarkably beautiful! She was about five-seven, and if she weighed over a hundred and thirty pounds, he would be surprised. She was wearing a white blouse and blue jeans. Her blouse had saturated quickly in the rain, and it became apparent that she wore no bra under it. Her bronze breasts were clearly visible under her rain soaked garment, and her nipples pointed defiantly at him in an alluring way, and it became difficult for him not to stare.

Stammering as a result, he said, "Of course I wouldn't leave you here stranded. But ma'am—miss, I have to tell you something first."

"Well, what is it?" she yelled over the rain.

"I didn't quite tell you the whole truth a minute ago. I just wanted to be on my way, and to know that you were okay, so I skipped a few details."

"So, get on with it!" she yelled again. "Every man lies to me—I expect it! What didn't you tell me?"

"That the law wants me," he answered, also shouting to be heard over the downpour. "The part about the highway being blocked is true, but I took the back roads in the first place to avoid the law. In fact, I was the cause of the traffic mishaps that closed down the highway in the first place!"

"Yeah, well I can believe that from the way you drive. Look what you just did to my car!" She pointed at the water dripping into the driver's seat. "So are you going to give me a ride or what?"

Nick was getting worried that someone else might happen along at any moment, and he replied, "Where are your bags?"

He loaded her stuff into the trunk, and then moved his own gear from the passenger seat to the trunk too, and slammed it shut. As he got into the driver's side, he once again couldn't help but notice, in the light from the overhead dome light, just how attractive she was. He pushed the thought aside and dropped the Mustang into first gear. They didn't say anything for a few minutes as the car spun its way up the road.

"So why are the cops looking for you?" she asked finally.

Nick looked at her in the darkness and replied,

"Does it matter?"

She pulled a cigarette from her purse and lit it.

"Mind if I smoke?" she said before answering him, exhaling in his direction.

Nick didn't reply. If she was trying to show she could be defiant, she wasn't gaining any ground with him. He really didn't care if she smoked or not.

Finally, she answered his question.

"No, it really doesn't matter to me why the cops are after you. Just take me somewhere far away from here, and don't get any funny ideas either. I know how to take care of myself."

They drove on in silence for perhaps an hour, until they finally reached the plan-B destination, at the end of an old logging road.

"This is it, miss. This is as far as you go with me," he said as he pulled the Mustang to the side of the narrow lane and shut the engine down.

He looked over at her when she did not reply. He realized that she had fallen asleep in the warmth of the car, her cloths now nearly dry. He assumed her adrenalin rush must have worn off a few miles back, leaving her drained! For now—she was sound asleep, her head resting on the window, and she snored softly. It was apparent that she had not heard a word he said.

He got out trying not to awaken her. "It would be better this way," he thought to himself!

Apparently the lack of movement from the car awakened her! Or, perhaps the fact that Nick had slammed the door a bit too loudly! She looked around in surprise, and found herself in an empty car. Nick was in back rummaging around in the trunk, packing what he needed into his backpack.

"Where the hell are you going?" she asked him after getting out of the car and slamming the door angrily!

It had stopped raining, and here in the woods it was completely silent save for the chirping of crickets or frogs. There was no sound of traffic, sounds of vehicles or cop sirens! There was no light from a town, or a house, or any other source in any direction. The trees surrounded them everywhere! They were high up in the mountains standing under a canopy of pine boughs. And, the only light there was, emanated from a small bulb from the opened car trunk.

"I need to go on from here by foot. Take the car and go wherever you want."

"Listen mister," she replied. "I *ain't* taking your tainted car anywhere! The first town I get to, I'll be pulled over! No doubt the car has already been ID'd by the cops, and there will be an APB out on it! Nice try, but I am not that stupid! You haven't been driving around in these mountains for your health. You know a way out of here, and you're supposed to take me somewhere, remember? This is about as close to nowhere as I have ever been. You hear me?" she shouted at him. "This *is* nowhere! I know you are going somewhere, and you look like the type of man that knows what he is doing—so, I am going with you. Do you understand me, mister?"

Nick looked at her and shook his head otherwise.

"Pretty woman," he said. "You don't even know my name, and I don't know yours either. We met by coincidence, not by design—and I owe you nothing! I paid for your damned car door! And I am leaving you with a car that has a clean title in the glove box. Even if you only sold it for scrap, it is worth a few thousand dollars. The cops want me, not you! And, they won't give a damn about the car, or how you got it. Get on with your life and leave me alone!"

She watched him hike his backpack onto his shoulders and slip away into the woods. She was so angry with him she couldn't speak! She stomped one foot on the ground with all her might, as if a show of defiance would impress the utter darkness! She grabbed a jacket, and a few other items from her suitcase — took her purse, as well as her own backpack, and headed off after the exasperating man! She was not a woman brought up to be afraid of the woods, the dark, or hardship, though *mountain lions* and *bears* were another matter altogether! But, she wasn't about to be intimidated by any man! All her life, she had had been proving herself to someone, and if it meant trailing this guy—this guy that fate had obviously thrust upon her, she was determined to do so. He was right about one thing: she didn't even know his name. But, she sure as hell was not going to get dumped on the side of the road by this stranger, and things were not going to end on his terms—her mind was made up, and that was final!

She had failed to get the last word in, and that simply would not do!

Stepping into the woods in the same place he had, she looked around for a path that he might have followed. She found the trail right away, and began double-timing it in the same direction he did. It didn't take her long before she had caught up with him. He had heard her coming up from behind, and was reluctantly, waiting for her by a shallow stream. It was so pitch black she nearly ran into him, and was startled! She could not see him in the nearly complete darkness until he spoke.

"So why do you follow me?" he asked her, as the stream bubbled noisily nearby.

Catching her breath, she replied, "I told you mister, you are going somewhere and I am going with you."

"I left you a car, and I left a thousand dollars more than what I already gave you in your purse. What more do you want from me?"

"You left me another grand?" She giggled. "I never checked my purse. I have it though, so let's see.

"I'll be damned," she said, struggling to see the denomination of the bills in the dark. "You did leave me a thousand dollars more. What? You want it back? I'll give you a thousand dollars to get me away from here!"

The two of them stood there by the noisy stream in silence, hearing nothing but the sound of water bubbling over smooth rocks. There, barely able to see each other, neither one knew what to say to the other. They moved closer to one another—until there was but a few inches between them.

"I don't even know your name," he said quietly.

"Roberta Sanchez, and I won't be dumped by the likes of you! Just let me go with you until I can find a bus or train station, and then I'll be out of your hair."

"I want you to go back to the car and find your own way to town. Just follow the road back the way we came, it will eventually take you to a better road, which will eventually take you to the highway. I can't help you."

"And why do you want to get rid of me so quickly? I might be able to help you."

"Because, Roberta Sanchez, I still have a job to do, and no, you can't help me."

"The cops are looking for a man traveling alone, not a man and a woman traveling together," she replied curtly. He started to move down the trail again without replying, and she followed him.

"So what's your name?" she asked.

Realizing she wasn't going to go away, he plodded on ahead of her in the darkness. She was right, and the thought annoyed him. The cops were looking for his car and a lone man. Finally, he replied over his shoulder,

"Nicholas Dimeitry Petrovisky".

"Hmm, sounds foreign," she replied.

"It's Russian," he muttered, and they walked for another mile in silence until they came up upon a gravel driveway. He immediately knew where he was and turned right. A short distance away was a cabin and a tin shack. "What is this place?" she asked.

"Where we get another ride," he answered.

He went to the shack and threw open the small door. Inside was an old beat up Kawasaki 250 motocross bike. He rolled it out, checked the tank for gas, and kick started it to life to make sure that it still worked. He then shut it down and pleaded with her.

"Roberta," he said. "You should stay here where you will be safe. The key for the cabin is on a nail in the outhouse out back, to the right as you sit on the pot. There is a phone inside the cabin, and you can call 911 and have the police come and get you. Just give me a twenty minutes head start. That's all I ask! If you get on this bike with me, there is no turning back for you, and I can't guarantee your safety."

Roberta rolled her eyes and folded her arms. "What is your problem with giving a woman a ride?" she asked irritably. "Yeah, I can call the cops to come and get me, but then what? They take me back to the station, call my family, hold me for questioning about you—and for who knows how long? When everything is said and done, my ex-boyfriend finds me again, and starts beating on me—again! I want to get the hell away from here, and I want to get away clean. Do you get it now, mister?"

"I am a bad man, Roberta. You don't want any part of me."

She rolled her eyes once more, and then grabbed the front of his shirt and pulled him to within inches of her face.

"Screw you, Nicholas Dimeitry Petrovisky! You aren't losing me this easily! My gut tells me that you aren't a bad man, and it tells me that you won't hurt me either! So, let's just get the hell out of here!"

She surprised him with her fierce determination! But, he did nothing, but stare back at her—not wanting to say yes or no! She made up his mind for him and pushed him away, raised her leg, and mounted the bike behind him. Wrapping her arms around his waist she told him,

"Go for it, mister! I'm holding on."

Nick kick started the engine back to life, and revved it up. He dropped it into gear, and they sped away into the night, spewing gravel behind them. Nick wasn't sure why he was allowing her to talk—no, rather bully him into this! But he was pretty sure that it was mostly because she was pretty! Something, he knew was a flaw in his character, one that had gotten him into trouble in the past, and more than once! He was angry with himself for succumbing to her charms—if one could call her bravado and constant attitude, her charms! He thought he had time enough to get her somewhere safe—or, was that his balls talking? He reminded himself that she certainly would pose problems for him—no matter what, if he kept her around for very long.

"So, what man doesn't do fool things for a pretty woman?" he rationalized and sped away.

He wound the throttle back to the stops, pushing the tired old bike to its limits. He changed gears, first up shifting to accelerate and then downshifting to brake. She clung to him tightly and screamed with delight as he powered the bike down the narrow gravel road at dangerously high speeds, often pushing it into turns and drifting across the lane, and barely able to see the next bend in front of him! The headlight was marginal for the speeds that he demanded from the machine, which made the ride even more perilous, but Roberta clung to him without protest. "Perhaps he would frighten her enough—she would demand to be let off?" he allowed himself to believe for a moment. But, then she would squeal with delight again—negating his supposition.

The faster he went the more it seemed to thrill her! When he leaned, she leaned. When he stood for a jump, she stood, almost as if she were part of him. It had been a long time since he had such a young woman holding onto him, let alone challenging him without any fear for herself. It was as if Roberta feared nothing, and he wondered how this could be.

The question soon left his mind, however, for he was having some fun himself! He was even starting to like this woman's spunk, but something wasn't right about her—he instinctively knew. She was too pretty, too adept, and too young for such a coincidence, running into her out here in the dark—in the middle of nowhere as he had. He buried the thought, for the time being anyway, and rolled the throttle back again, pouring on the remaining power left in the tired old bike. Together they flew through the night as one, on a machine built really only for one.

Within a few minutes, almost to his disappointment, they came upon a blacktopped, County Road 2480. He turned right, knowing immediately where he was, and drove several more miles until he picked up the highway. He headed south on 101 again, towards Olympia. This would be a somewhat roundabout way to get to Seattle, but the cops would be looking for him to make the crossing to Seattle at one of the more common ferry terminals well north of here. He needed to find a safe place for the night, and he needed something to eat and a reasonable night's rest. Tonight would be plan-B, and tomorrow he would resume as originally planned.

He wasn't too worried that the cops would know anything about the motorcycle because it didn't belong to him. He knew of the cabin only from his boyhood, and it was just a guess that it was still used during deer and elk season or even that the bike would still be there and drivable. The cabin belonged to a friend of his father, and he had spent many a weekend there with his dad back in his youth. He had assumed that Reggie, the man's son and once a hunting buddy of his, still owned it and would continue the hunting tradition with his own son. Obviously, he had, and Nick was grateful for this little bit of luck.

After twenty miles, Nick pulled off of the highway and onto a narrow gravel road. A few minutes later, a house appeared to his left near the end of the lane. He turned onto the familiar paved driveway and drove the bike around to the side of the garage. Under a carport next to the garage, he killed the engine. Roberta instinctively got off while he searched for the kickstand with his heel. Propping the bike on it, he dismounted too.

"Where are we?" she said, rubbing her sore backside.

"My place, kind of."

"Kind of?" she muttered.

"C'mon," he said. "This way."

He started down a brick path that led to the back of the house. Roberta was getting her bearings as she followed him. The house was large, and looked like newer construction. It had two floors, and as she walked behind him, lights came on, illuminating their way. The backyard was manicured like a putting green, and fifty feet away, it dropped off precipitously. She could hear the waves crashing on the rocks below and assumed from the smell of salt water that the Sound was not far off in the dark.

Flowers and manicured bushes were laid out nicely in ornate gardens as only professional gardeners could accomplish. Her heart started pounding as she now wondered what she was getting herself into. This guy said he was wanted—wanted by the law, and yet he seemed to have fancy digs hidden away here in the trees. He walked up to a large double French door, punched in a code on the keypad to the right of it, and pulled the door open. She followed him into a large living room having creamy white carpeting and appointed with fine cherry hardwood furniture, and sofas made of luxurious dark green leather. The room was nicely peppered with well-appointed furnishings all around. There were oil paintings, all framed eloquently, and she wondered if they were genuine oils or prints. The room had a European flavor to it, open and expansive, with high ceilings decorated in the style of the early eighteen hundreds with ornate carved wood moldings. She also wondered if the furniture were a genuinely antique or well-made replica instead.

Nick removed his backpack and dropped it to the floor by the door. He moved into the kitchen off to her right, and the lights came on automatically again, touch less.

"Roberta," he said. "It's late. Are you hungry?"

She looked around his place and wondered what this was all about, the whole being-chased-by-the-law thing! This was not the kind of place a fugitive owned or even holed up in. She knew the only reason he had allowed her to come with him was because she was pretty.

Nick came back into the room and noted her worried expression.

"What's the matter? I'm not going to hurt you, Roberta. Like I said, do you want something to eat or not?"

"What's wrong?" she answered emphatically. "This is not the place of a man on the lamb! Who the hell are you, Nicholas, and what are you about? Are we breaking into someone's house, here?"

Nick scoffed. "What is your problem? I asked you to go on by yourself hours ago, and when you refuse and I bring you here, then you act like I am a threat to you."

She stared at him so intently, he continued quickly,

"Come over here, Roberta," he said, a bit miffed himself, and his tone reflected it. He went off to her left and opened another door. Once again lights came on without touching a switch. She followed him down a long hallway to a garage. Inside it were three shiny and clean vehicles, a gray Ford Bronco, a black Cadillac CTS-V, and a red Ferrari. From a pegboard with hooks on it, he plucked off a set of car keys. "Here," he said. "Take the Cadillac, and get out of here! It is an untainted car, and no one will be looking for it."

She was now even more confused. "Why in the hell would you give me a sixty thousand dollar car when you have a cheap-ass Bronco right there parked next to it? This is the supercharged V-model, isn't it? Everything you said about yourself so far has been a lie."

"I haven't told you anything about myself, Roberta. I was hoping you would go on your way long before now, but you haven't. And now that you are here, I can understand that you might have changed your mind about being here in the first place and now you want to leave. If that is what you want, then go! Here are the keys. You can lock them in the car when you get to where you are going. I'll find it later using the North Star tracking system. Myself, I am hungry and tired. As soon as I grab something to eat, I am getting some sleep."

He placed the keys in her hand.

"I have no designs on you, Roberta. I still have a job to do, and you still have nowhere to go. Besides a ride, my home is all I can offer you. I don't have the time right now to take you into the city or to buy you a bus ticket someplace, and I don't have the inclination to explain my life, or anything else to you! So, either take my car or make yourself comfortable here! When I am finished with what I need to do, I will take you to the city myself. Either way, it is your choice!" He punched a button on the wall and the garage door opened.

The message was clear: it was her choice to leave or not. She looked at the set of keys in her hand and considered it for a moment. Then she put the keys back on the hook on the wall and said,

"I'm hungry too," and she hit the button on the wall reversing the garage door.

"Answer me one question though," she demanded.

"What's that?"

"You said *'Kind of'* when you said this was your place."

"It was willed to me, and I stay here when I am in the States. I thought I might want to retire here, but I have since changed my mind. The place is not me, and I am considering putting it on the market."

"I thought you said you were from Portland?"

"You asked me where I was from, and I had just come from Portland a few weeks ago. I didn't say I lived there — you just assumed that to be the case, but technically it wasn't a lie either."

She turned for the kitchen, and this time she led the way. She sat down at the kitchen table. "It's your kitchen, Nicholas. What do you have for a hungry woman? Mind if I smoke?"

Nick rummaged through the cupboards until he found her an ashtray, which he placed before her. "I have cold cuts. How about a smoked turkey sandwich?"

"What, no caviar? No Champaign?"

He laughed. "You are poking fun at me. I suppose you wonder why I don't have an accent if I am Russian." She nodded.

"I don't have an accent because I was raised here in America, but yes, I am of Russian decent. My parents were first-generation immigrants, and I spent many years in Russia as an adult, in the service of the American government. Sometimes I switch my words around because I often think in Russian, and that gives me away."

"You said your parents *were* immigrants."

Nick caught her drift. "My parents have both passed on."

"I am sorry," she said.

Nick smiled at her. "Believe me, my parents led very happy lives together, good long lives together, and I am grateful that neither suffered in the end nor were alone for too long."

"So this was their house?"

"Not hardly," Nick replied, and he proceeded to put out two plates. "My parents were poor immigrants. The man who owned this house was a very wealthy man. In a way, he was my mentor; and as he had no family himself, he left it to me when he died."

"That was very generous of him," Roberta said suspiciously. "But when most rich people die, especially those who have no family, they donate everything to a cause with the hope a street, or a park will be named after them."

"I was his cause, Roberta! And, he wasn't the type of man who needed recognition—enough with the questions! Here, eat!"

He had made her a sandwich of smoked turkey with Dijon mustard, sliced tomatoes, and lettuce. He found a bag of chips, placed a pickle spear on her plate, and handed it to her. "I have wine, beer, and soft drinks, or you can join me in a glass of iced tea."

"I thought Russians drank lots of vodka," she quipped.

He laughed once again. "Yes, of course you are correct, but what would an American woman know about the Russian culture? The American government can't seem to get it right, and they spend millions of dollars each year trying to undermine a culture they can't seem to comprehend much less understand."

She remained silent for a moment, and then said, "Well, I was always told that communism is bad and that Russia is a communist country."

Nick smiled. "Yes, there are many misconceptions about communism. In fact, as a political belief, communism is benign. However, the Soviet Union only professed to be communist. The USSR was really no more than a dictatorship disguised as something else entirely. Do you know what the direct translation for the word Soviet is?"

She shook her head.

"Soviet means to '*consult*.' The Soviet Union was meant to be much like the United States is, with independent sovereignties that governed themselves — as our States do here in America! Instead, all property in the Soviet Union, and all industry were nationalized, and the so-called Politburo replaced the royal families and took over. The result was a dictatorship that was even worse than when the country was ruled by the Romanov's!

"The *stated* goal of the communist regime was to eliminate the distinctions between the haves and have-nots! But, it never worked out that way. When anyone achieves power, greed and ambition takes over! And, even if the members of the Politburo believed idealistically in the beginning, and worked for that goal, in the end the haves and have-nots merely got shuffled a bit. The flaw in communism has always been that people are not equal! And, they never will be! Communism cannot address the inherent differences in all people. It cannot reward the talented, the gifted, or the resourceful, which is the reason it has failed nearly everywhere." He paused as if to catch his breath.

"Would you care for some iced tea?"

Roberta nodded, and Nick poured two glasses of iced tea and joined her at the table.

She pondered on what he had said for a moment, and then shrugged. "I don't understand much about politics. So, why don't you have a woman?"

Nick nearly choked on his sandwich and covered his mouth as he cleared his throat. He replied after he swallowed,

"How do you know that I don't have a woman?" He held up his left hand to her, and pointed to the wedding ring."

Roberta rolled her eyes and said, "That's *BS*. Where are all the photos? Where are all the knickknacks?"

"Knickknacks?"

"Yeah, the stuff that most women like to put around a house to make it a home, the stuff that they pick up at garage sales and in antique stores. This place is like a government building. There are no adornments of the sort anywhere, just designer furniture. If you had a woman in your life, there would be little things everywhere to remind you that she was a part of your life. That is what women do."

"So, you don't like my home?" he said trying to change the subject

"Let's say it has unrealized potential."

Nick shrugged his shoulders and smiled.

"You are right, of course. There is no woman in my life." He finished his iced tea and went on. "I have lived out of hotel rooms, mostly in Europe, most of my adult life. There were woman, of course, but I was not allowed to stay in any one place for very long because of my job. In what few romantic relationships I was lucky enough to blunder into—there wasn't enough time for any to blossom!"

"Bullshit!" Roberta stated with conviction. "Relationships don't blossom. They explode! You just haven't met the right girl yet."

Nick plucked a potato chip from the bag and thought about what Roberta said.

"Perhaps you are right once again," he said after a few moments. "There were certainly moments, though." He finished eating, and then picked up the plates to load into the dishwasher.

"Have you ever wanted a woman in your life?" she taunted him as she grabbed another handful of chips.

Like a light switch, though, Nick turned off.

"It is late, Roberta." He smiled. "Let me show you to your room—to where a nice hot shower awaits you!" He finished cleaning the table. "There are some things—errands that I must do tomorrow, so do not be concerned if I am gone when you awaken. You may have free run of the place. I have shut down the alarm system, but be careful not to lock yourself out! I will be back well before dark."

"Nick," Roberta replied, smiling. She was now a bit confused. "You told me a lot about yourself, and it would seem that you have a vested interest in keeping most everything secret. Why did you tell me these things?"

Nick smiled back. "Because, Roberta, you are a very pretty woman, and I am a foolish old man—one who doesn't know when to shut his trap! Does it surprise you, that in the company of a pretty woman my resolve wavers—falters?"

Roberta thought about it. "Yes, maybe it does, but I don't believe your resolve has been weakened! You are too confident a man to be foolish. My instincts about you tell me that you only reveal what you want to reveal, and that you are not worried what I might do or say. What if I picked up the phone right now and tried calling the police?"

Nick shrugged and acted indifferent. "If you do, you do. I already gave you the opportunity to do something besides traipse along with me back at the cabin, and you declined, so what has changed? I presume your question is rhetorical? What would be in it for you if you did — what would you gain? Will you tell the police that some guy came along and put two thousand dollars in your purse, gave you a lift, and is now holding you hostage after feeding you a sandwich and offering you a hot shower?"

"I could tell them what you told me, that you are on the run," she replied.

"And I could say that I picked you up in Olympia, paid you two thousand dollars to come home with me—with the expectation of a little intimate adult entertainment for two, and that you became delusional from the drugs you must have taken before I solicited your services in the first place! And, just exactly where will you tell the police they can locate the car that will verify your story? The Mustang is the only thing the police have on me. They don't even know what I look like."

"Touché," Roberta replied, and she laughed. "See, my instincts about you are correct. You know what you are doing and where you are going, but don't worry. I won't call the police."

Nick shrugged. "I wasn't worried, Roberta. I have no intention to harm you, and it seems that you have your own reasons for tagging along, your reasons why to remain hidden for now. We are in the same boat momentarily, and quite frankly, the boat is not that bad, so I have no worries."

"You are not worried that in your absence I might leave and take whatever I can with me?"

"Now you have a point." Nick laughed. "I will handcuff you to the bedpost before I leave in the morning!"

"You wouldn't dare!" she exclaimed, laughing but uneasily, for in truth, she did not know this person beyond what little he had told her, and what her own instincts told her about him.

"Once again, you are right, Roberta. It would not be necessary to restrict you in any way. I would find you if you took anything I didn't want to live without," Nick replied calmly. His tone was not threatening, but his eyes told her it was true. "But there is nothing much here I would want to hang on that tightly to anyway."

"It's too early in our relationship for handcuffs," Roberta answered with a smile, now trying to lighten the mood. "Don't you think?"

Nick knew that she was baiting him, and perhaps even challenging him at the same time.

"If I needed handcuffs to keep you here, you wouldn't be here! It's getting late, and I need my rest. We can talk tomorrow about the handcuffs, but I agree." He now laughed too. "It's a bit too early in our relationship to determine a good use for handcuffs."

He then led her upstairs and showed her to her room.

"My room is on the first floor. I think that you will be comfortable up here, and there are locks on the door if you feel that you need them."

He showed her around briefly, opening the door to the attached bathroom. "You can take a shower or bath in here," he said. "All the towels in the closet over there are fresh," he pointed. "But if you need more, there is another closet down the hallway filled with fresh linen."

He turned and walked out, leaving her standing there alone! Before closing the door behind him, he said, "Good night."

Roberta looked around. If this was the guestroom, she wondered what the master suite was like. She pulled back the comforter on queen-sized bed and felt the sheets, which to her delight were white satin. The pillows were down-filled and plump and also covered in satin. More paintings adorned the walls in this room, and as she looked closely at them and felt the texture, she decided that these were all originals.

Once again the furniture was made of fine cherry wood and was of a French design, as if it came from long ago even though it appeared to be new. The delicate crystal lamps scattered about the room looked fragile. She definitely didn't see anything that looked like it was bought in a Wal-Mart. It all seemed to be very expensive, in fact, from warm dark teal carpeting underfoot to the very high ceilings with crown moldings—it all exuded money! Double hung French doors opened onto a balcony, and she shivered a bit as she stepped outside. The night air had gotten even chillier. In the gardens below her, all the lights had turned off, probably automatically, just as they had come on earlier, she assumed. She could see the city lights far off in the distance, over the waters of the Puget Sound, and from this vantage, she could hear the gentle clang of a buoy and the soft moan of a foghorn somewhere off in the distance.

With all the lovely night sounds and smells of the Puget Sound in the air, her spirits lifted.

Within a few minutes, she became too chilly to be out, and she went back inside to her comfortably warm room, locking the French doors behind her. Now she was excited, and she scrambled to the bathroom for a look. There was a Jacuzzi tub and a freestanding shower, both big enough for two, awaiting her use. The shower door was made of frosted glass and there were twin showerheads inside—how romantic! The Jacuzzi was made of shiny high-gloss white porcelain with ornate chrome fixtures. She opened a mirrored vanity—and there found soaps, nail clippers, and Band-Aids. She noted there were no medicines of any kind at all, not even aspirin! She looked under the vanity and found shampoos and conditioners, oils, and lotions with French labels on them. Opening a drawer, she found toothpastes of all types, and an assortment of packaged toothbrushes. She giggled to herself with delight, and then she turned on the faucet to the Jacuzzi tub.

Then, suddenly, she realized that she still needed to get her stuff from downstairs.

While the tub filled, she ran to the bedroom door and flung it open. She nearly tripped over the silver tray that set just outside it in the hallway. Her backpack and purse were nearby. On the tray was a bucket of ice, and in it, a bottle of French Champaign was chilling. A slender-stemmed champagne glass was next to the ice, and there was a silver bowl with a silver lid chilling in crushed ice next to that! Lastly was a plate of crackers, and a card.

She reached down and carefully plucked the card up: "Champagne and black caviar for your sampling. Sleep well. Nick."

"Wow!" she exclaimed to herself. She carried the tray into the bathroom and placed it on the vanity, then searched for the bubbles. Finding something that appeared to be bath soap, she poured it into the tub. The fragrance of lilacs immediately wafted up with the steam, filling the room with the fragrance of flowers while foamy layers of suds filled the tub. She ran quickly for the hall to get the rest of her things while the tub filled.

She turned the spigot off, poured herself a glass of champagne and tasted it. It was wonderfully bubbly and cold, and she felt that she was in heaven after just one sip.

"A good bath, plenty of women's soaps, and a glass of bubbly. How could it get better?" she wondered to herself.

She peeked into the silver bowl curiously. She had never tasted caviar before, and it looked horrible. The robust black fish eggs appeared to be slimy. She raised it to her nose to smell it. If it smelled like fish, she would not sample it. To her surprise, it smelled more like olive oil. She touched it, and it was a bit rubbery, but she knew that it must be very expensive if it was good caviar, and she suspected that this might be the best.

"Oh my God, what have I gotten myself into?" she said out loud, and then she giggled.

Using the tiny silver spoon, she smeared a thin layer of the black substance onto the cracker. She raised it to her mouth and hesitated: should she be doing this, she wondered? She looked around, and finding herself completely alone, she shrugged. She looked at the cracker in her hand and said out loud to no one,

"Oh well, what the hell. Best ride I ever had!" She bit into it. At first she tasted nothing but the cracker. But then she tasted the caviar, which was reminiscent slightly of the sea—salty like, but was a bit sweet at the same time. The black sturgeon eggs had a peculiar flavor that left her uncertain if she should have more or not? She had never tasted anything like it before, and she wasn't sure if she liked it or not! She washed it down with the champagne and said out loud, "Ughh!"

She poured another glass of champagne, stripped naked, then sat on the edge of the tub, draping one leg over the side to test the water with her toes.

"Ouch! Too hot," she squealed. She let some cold water pour from the spigot and tried it again, swirling the water around with her foot until it felt just right. There was an aftertaste left in her mouth from the caviar, but it wasn't unpleasant at all. She thought to herself that it almost tasted like a man did, salty and sweet. She giggled again—becoming sillier with each sip of champagne. She finished her second glass of champagne and decided to try another cracker. This time she smeared the cracker with the caviar until it dripped off the sides, then put the whole thing in her mouth, and chewed it slowly. It tasted completely different this time, rich and creamy, so rich that it made her belch.

"Oh my," she excused herself, and she giggled again.

The champagne was going to her head, and the caviar was having a strangely amorous effect on her. She decided that she felt very, very good. She took another sip of champagne and slid into the tub.

"Oh, my God, this is wonderful," she said out loud. She took the thick cotton washcloth, enveloped a bar of soap in it, and then started working on her feet and legs. She then worked all the way up to her face. She scrubbed herself clean, and then she lay back in the huge tub to enjoy the warm water. She noticed a big silver button, and she pushed it with her toe. The whirlpool started, and jets of warm water began massaging her body. Her eyes rolled back with pleasure, and she couldn't believe how relaxed she was becoming. Then a jet of warm water found just that special spot—and gave her a start! She wriggled around trying to find it again, and when she did, waves of pleasure embraced her.

"Jeeze, who needs a man when you can have this? And without any of the hassles!"

She allowed herself to be stimulated by the jets of warm water until she was on the brink of orgasm. She tried to pull back at the last second, but she went over the edge, and wave after wave of pleasure surged throughout her body. Her head tipped back in ecstasy, and the room began to swirl around her. She giggled again out loud, wondering what had come over her! Quickly, before she began to rise to the top again, she touched the big silver button with her toe and turned off the jets of water. She laughed out loud and said, "Wow!" Her hands looked like prunes, all wrinkly.

"Enough is enough. Time to get out." She sighed. When she stepped out of the tub, she was so relaxed, or perhaps because she was so overtaken by the champagne or the orgasm—she wasn't sure which, that she nearly fell over! She giggled again and grabbed for a towel to dry herself off before she became chilled.

Then, before wrapping herself with another towel to keep warm, she took a moment to admire herself in the mirror. She poured herself the very last of the champagne, and took a tiny sip. She wondered how she could have finished off an entire bottle by herself?

She giggled again when she realized that the bottle was only a half-liter. "Damn, I love that tub," she muttered. "My oh my, girl. What have you found here, and what have you gotten yourself into now?"

She opened her towel once more critiquing herself in the mirror. At thirty-two years old, her breasts hadn't yet begun to sag, but that was because she had always been small on top, she knew! Then she wondered, "What about the rest?"

Her tummy was still round, soft, and flat, but as she turned to look at her behind, she frowned. "My ass is too big," she acknowledged bitterly! She quickly wrapped herself up again, not wanting to think about it.

She sipped on the last glass of champagne as she smeared her body with fragrant body creams. Wanting a cigarette now, she found her purse, which had a nearly empty pack of smokes in it, took one out and lit it. She looked around for an ashtray, but there wasn't one anywhere! She stepped outside onto the balcony before an ash could fall to the carpet.

The air outside was once again chilly. But, her body had soaked up so much heat energy from her bath that the cool night air felt refreshing. She stood there in the darkness for a few moments longer, puffing on her cigarette and wondering once again what she had just gotten herself into. It was all very quiet, except for the night sounds emanating from around her everywhere.

"This man had not wanted to answer my questions about another woman. He must still be in love with her," she thought to herself reflectively. The cigarette burnt her fingers, and she tossed it over the balcony instinctively, hoping to remember to pick it up from the manicured lawn in the morning.

Going quickly back inside and closing the door behind her, she washed her hands and brushed her teeth. Then she turned off the lights, dropped her towel to the carpet by the side of the bed, and slid her slender body between the satin sheets, sighing with a sense of pure bliss. She pulled the comforter over her and wriggled a bit, relishing the feel of satin against her soft warm flesh, and nearly immediately fell asleep. But, just before she did, she thought,

"I wonder what his life is like?"

Chapter 4

Nick Peters awoke at dawn, painfully aware that he needed another four hours of sleep. He thought about the woman upstairs, and about his own dilemma, a dilemma brought on by misinformation and subterfuge. He had until Monday morning to deliver the attaché case, and it was now Saturday. Although Plan-A had plenty of time built into it for contingencies, what had happened yesterday had taken up much of that time, and what time he had left needed to be carefully utilized. The Mustang was disposable—collateral damage! But, the woman was not, which would certainly make his tactics tougher to pull off now. What concerned him the most was that someone had obviously tipped off the cops, possibly even the FBI!

The million-dollar question was pretty easy to identify:

Was he being set up, or was he being warned off? A roadblock is a pretty obvious, and reasonably safe way to warn him off! But, who would send such a message? Could it be that this mysterious attaché case wasn't meant to be delivered in the first place? Could it be that instead, it was meant to be intercepted all along? If so, who could have the juice to put such a plan into action? He couldn't know! Not unless he looked at what was in the attaché case!

He stepped into the shower. The hot water soothed his tired muscles and brought him back alive. As he stepped out, and dried off, he knew what he would have to do.

Never before had he ever looked at the contents of what he carried as a courier! But, then again this wasn't his usual gig either! He knew too little about the game, having only taken Alexander's word for the particulars. He opened the attaché case, removed everything from it, and laid it all carefully out on his desk top for examination. He searched for a false bottom or secret compartment, but he found none! After nearly an hour of intense scrutiny, he had found nothing at all! Which was puzzling enough in itself! There were no encrypted messages, no microdots, nothing of any apparent significance other than the legal documents related to the Stalintsia Steel merger, all of which seemed legitimate. The entire contents of the attaché case were of no more consequence than Alexander had indicated it was! But, there was one thing—a small pocket drive, sometimes called a flash drive, tucked away neatly into a pocket intended for business cards. He removed it from the pocket and plugged it into the USB port of his laptop. He tried to read what was on it, but it appeared to be encrypted. All that came up were garbled symbols with smiley faces.

"This will take an expert to decipher," he thought to himself.

He made a call to Russia on his international cell phone. It would be noontime there by now. The number rang several times before a very familiar voice answered.

"*Dah, sto eta gavareet* (Yes, who is speaking?")), the man grumbled into the device. It was the voice of his old friend, Boris Sakharov.

"Boris, this is Nick. I need your help."

"*Dah, dah, kaninshna minya pa druzia* (Yes, yes of course, my friend.) How can I help you?"

"I need your computer skills, of course! I have something for you to decipher for me, and it is on my computer."

"So, what is the big deal? Send it to me, and I will do as you wish. How are you doing, my old friend?"

"Boris, I need you to look at this now! It is encrypted—I think."

Boris sensed the urgency in his friend's tone. "My friend Nikki, my darling Lyudmila has planned a big day for us and Pavel. Pavel is playing in the soccer finals. I do not have the time now. How important is it?" he asked.

"I am sorry to ask this favor of you Boris, but it is very important! Why else would I call you? It is not New Years—or your birthday, is it?" Nick laughed. "How are Lyudmila and Pavel?"

Boris also chuckled. "My Lyudmila is as beautiful as ever, and my son turns sixteen in three days. Are you in trouble, Nikki?"

"Perhaps, Boris."

The connection went silent for a moment.

"If that is the case, then tell me what I must do."

"I need you to connect to my computer remotely. In the USB port is a pocket drive, and I need to know what's on it."

"Okay, my friend. I will do it now, but first you must talk to Lyudmila and tell her how much you miss her. Otherwise, I will be in big trouble for ruining her plans. Is your computer online?"

"It will be by the time you get to yours."

"Then here is Lyudmila. Speak to her while I go to my computer and take a look at your silly problem."

Boris handed the telephone to his wife, and Nick said 'hello' to her while he got online. In the meantime Boris headed to his study. Boris smiled as he climbed the stairs of their Sochi Villa seeing the look on Lyudmila's face when she picked up the phone. He heard her gleefully saluting Nikki. He knew she had always liked him, probably even more than what he knew! One day, maybe she would tell him the whole story—the story about her and Nick. Nevertheless, her joy brought him happiness, and Nick was a trusted comrade.

Lyudmila was a delightful, and very pretty woman. And when Nick had first met her—back when he was a much younger man, he was convinced he knew the reason why Russian men gave up their lives so readily to protect their country! It wasn't the homeland that they fought so fiercely to defend, but instead it was their beautiful Russian brides they fought so fiercely for!

Hard Russian life kept Russian women fit, trim, and very sexy looking for far longer than was considered normal in Western countries. Russia lacked fast food and frozen dinners—things that are so common in America! Instead, for Russians, their daily staples consisted of steamed vegetables, rice, and small portions of meat had to suffice. Soda pop of any kind was a luxury. Tea was more common than coffee, and coffee was served in small cups, not mugs. Free refills on anything, much less second helpings, was not part of Eastern European culture. Typical public transportation meant walking to a bus, trolley, or train; few people owned cars in Russia. Those who did owned only one! And typically, only the man of the household used it—and even then, only sparingly, for the occasional outings in the country, where public transit was limited. Very few women in Russia even held a driver's license! They walked most everywhere, and when necessary, they resorted to public transit. Whereas, western women stayed fit, only if they have the time, and money for it! That usually meant a fitness center membership. Staying fit was just a way of life for most Russian woman!

Russian women tended to make good wives. Sadly, the same could not be said for Russian men as husbands. Russian men tended to drink too much and to take on mistresses! But, after years of military conflicts, and premature deaths as a result of prevalent alcoholism, good men were in short supply in Russia. Lyudmila had found herself a good man in Boris, however, who was neither an alcoholic nor a womanizer.

She was so happy to hear Nick's voice that they conversed in Russian for ten minutes. She spoke mostly about her son Pavel and about Boris. As was typical of a Russian woman—she said very little about herself, as if her life was inconsequential.

Nick was watching his computer screen as he talked to her. Boris had found his computer and was now in control of it. The screens changed at Boris's keystrokes, and within seconds, he had located the pocket drive. Nick asked Lyudmila for her help.

"Of course, Nikki. Are you in danger?"

"Lyudmila, I am in much danger. There are things that I do not know, a lack of knowledge that is putting my life at risk, and I need Boris to help me solve a puzzle. Will you both help me?"

Lyudmila did not hesitate. "You were here for us when we needed you, Nikki, and now we will be here for you."

"*Spiceeba* (thank you) Lyudmila. I am so sorry to ruin your day."

Lyudmila replied, "You are like an uncle to Pavel, and he will understand. I am so proud that you have even asked us to help you!"

"Lyudmila, may I speak to him? Pavel, I mean."

"Yes, of course. But Nikki, do not worry. Boris is a very clever man, and he has friends too, and he will help you, believe me!"

"Lyudmila, you are wonderful!"

"Have you found yourself a woman yet, Nikki? You know I have many pretty women friends here who are looking for good husbands."

Nick laughed. "If only they were you, my Lyudmila."

She scoffed at him. "Here is Pavel, and he wants to speak to you too."

Nick spoke with Pavel for another ten minutes. If he ever had a son, he hoped he would be much like Lyudmila's boy. Pavel was quiet and shy, but he had much common sense. Like all boys do, he hated to study! But he hit the books anyway at the instruction of his mother, and as a result he did well in school. He loved his parents and his country, and he took pride in his athletics, and he excelled in them all!

Finally he said, "When are you coming back, Uncle Nick?"

"Soon Pavel, soon. I want to see you play soccer."

"I will score a goal just for you, Uncle Nick!"

His words of confidence caught Nick by surprise, and they moved him almost to tears. "You do that Pavel, and in the meantime, you watch over your mama and papa for me."

"You got it Uncle Nick," he said proudly in English, showing that he had been keeping up with his English studies.

Nick looked down at his computer. A window had popped up on the flat screen. In Russian, it read, "Give me eight hours."

Nick keyed in, "Thanks!"

"Pavel," Nick finished. "You have a good game today, and I'll see you all soon, okay?"

"Hey, Uncle Nick," Pavel replied. "Are we still on for that vacation in Australia, all of us?"

"Is your passport in order?"

"*Dah, kaninshna* (yes, of course)!"

"And what about your grades, Pavel?"

There was a moment of silence on the other end. "I am working on it," he replied.

"Well, do that Pavel. Yes, we are still on as long as there are warm sandy beaches there."

"I've got to go Uncle Nick," he said elatedly, and he hung up.

Nick then made another telephone call to Switzerland this time.

"Her name is Roberta Sanchez: American, about five foot six or seven, very slender and very pretty, and either Hispanic, African American, or both. She is in her early thirties, I think."

"What is it you want me to do, Nikki?" Ulyana replied dryly—actually miffed that her boss found himself another woman. A woman, no doubt, that would be nothing but trouble for her, and another distraction for him.

"I want a background check done on her. Run the fingerprints I lifted off her glass from last night—I am sending them now."

"How soon do you need it, Nikki? Are you in trouble?" She sounded concerned.

"The sooner the better, Ulyana."

He was about to hang up when she added, "Nick, I don't know what you are doing over there, but something big is going on in Siberia."

"What do you mean by '*big*,' Ulyana?"

"Big enough to put the Kamchatka Peninsula on alert, and big enough that an American carrier is in the Bering Straits, and big enough that the Russian Politburo cancelled sessions indefinitely. Something is going down, Nikki!"

"So, what do you know, Ulyana?"

"Nothing yet, but the signs are ominous. You should get back here. I have agents out sniffing, and the UN is getting nervous. Both Russia and the United States are squelching rumors, and yet both are also moving assets."

"But you have nothing solid yet? Is that right, Ulyana?"

"Affirmative sir," she replied.

"Then keep sniffing Ulyana; and Ulyana, run those prints!"

Chapter 5

The car was where Nick had left it, the keys still on the floorboards where he had dropped them for Roberta the night before, assuming that she would take the car, but obviously she didn't.

When Blakely and Jorgenson arrived, the sun had just risen.

Blakely looked at the nearly empty suitcase in the trunk, at the remaining woman's clothing and shoes. The tags on the clothes told them she wore a size 5 or 6.

He thought to himself, "Now why would a woman leave behind her clothes? Was she that afraid to stay behind, or was she forced to leave?" Taking a woman along didn't fit the profile of Nick Peters, who was known to be a loner and too much of a professional to get sidetracked by a woman.

"I want prints taken from everything, so nobody touch anything until my people arrive. And everybody, please!" Blakely shouted, "Quit walking around the crime scene! We may need the footprints!"

"Relax," Jorgenson replied. "There is no way out of here except for that path over there, which leads to a hunter's cabin a few miles away, and my men have already been there. There is evidence to suggest that your man and woman have escaped on a motorcycle, whereabouts still unknown."

"And how do you know that?"

"There are footprints of a man and a woman on the trail and fresh tire tracks on the dirt road where the path leads," he replied. "My men and I are not quite as stupid as you might think. We are looking into who owns the cabin to see where that information might lead us, if anywhere."

Blakely replied, "Good, but my people still need to come to their own conclusions. Fair enough?"

Jorgenson nodded, knowing full well that Blakely was within his jurisdictional rights. He put the word out for his men to tape the place off and to quit moving around the scene.

Blakely pulled out another cigarette, having failed miserably once again at quitting the damned things. As he suspected, Nick Peters had abandoned the car and gone on by foot. He assumed Peters must have known about the cabin. After all, he was raised in these parts. But where did the woman fit in?

Jorgenson came up with the answer.

"Blakely," Jorgenson called out, and he motioned for him to come over. He was still on the radio at his car. "We have an abandoned Jeep with a door torn off a couple mountain ridges over, and we think it might be the reason this Mustang has damage on the right front fender. The paint seems to be a match."

"Any ID on the woman yet, since I assume that he picked her up there?"

"No. The jeep was reported stolen two days ago. We're fingerprinting it now, but there is something else."

"What's that?" Blakely asked.

"It looks like a setup."

"What do you mean?"

"There is nothing wrong with the vehicle! It was parked with a near full tank of gas on the side of the road—just far enough over so that anyone trying to go around it had to hit the driver door if it were flung open at just the right moment. The vehicle also had a fully charged battery, meaning the lights were off and no flashers were on. There were cigarette butts in the mud on the driver side, suggesting that someone had been waiting there some time, and the butts had lipstick on them, leading me to believe that it was a woman in the car. The key lock on the steering column had been busted out, apparently how the car was stolen, but when our mechanic gets there—the Jeep started right up! He tells us that—after inspecting it, he can't find anything mechanically wrong with the damned thing! Whoever this woman is, she was just waiting there for this Nick Peters to arrive! There were no footprints in the mud to indicate that she had even gotten out of the car to lift the hood—like most people would! She just sat there in the dark—and with no lights on, with no hazards on either, and with the hood down. She was waiting—waiting for her mark! Now, I know that you think that we are all stupid hick cops around here, but to me? It looks like a setup! No one around these parts would behave that way!"

Bill Blakely threw his cigarette to the ground, crushed it out, and lit another. "Good work, Jorgenson. Bring both vehicles in after we are done with forensics. Do we have a timeframe?"

"Yeah, that too," Jorgenson replied. "A drunk ran over the torn off door on his way home, and it took out his oil pan. He had to call Dully, the local towing service, to haul his car in and give him a ride home. The call was made at 10:45 last night. A resident who lives just up the road swears that the Jeep wasn't there at 9:00 when he and his wife came home from dinner, and they would have passed right by there on their way home. That places the incident between 9:00 and about 10:15. It would have been plenty dark by then too! Dark enough that it would have been crazy not to have running lights on!"

While Blakely and Jorgenson talked about the evidence, Nick was getting into his Bronco. He backed it out of the garage and pushed the button to the electric garage door, closing it behind him. He then turned around in the driveway and headed toward Olympia. Daylight was just breaking over the Cascade Mountains.

"Too many things were going wrong," he thought to himself as he dialed a number on his cell phone.

Nick Peters had joined the CIA as an alternative to being drafted into the Army back when the Vietnam War was still raging in the late sixties. Becoming an agent was a coincidence, actually. After he graduated from high school, he enrolled in a community college and applied for a deferment, like most kids did back then. He was able to ride out his deferment for a year, but then his grades were not good enough to maintain his deferment status any longer, a *turning point* in his life for sure! He received his notice from the US Army in April of 1968.

His mother was devastated by the news, and his father just smacked him on the head and cursed at him for letting his grades slip. Both of his parents were first generation immigrants to America, and they had led very hard lives to give him a good start in life. His father had been a colonel in the Russian Army during WWII, and by aiding the Americans against the Japanese in the Kuril Islands on the North Pacific front. Somehow, he had earned himself a free ticket to bring his family to America. His father's memories of the war were all the more reason he did not want his son to be drafted. He had kept whatever it was he had done a secret from Nick, and in fact, he had never talked about it his whole life—not even a word!

Regardless of what his father had done for the U.S. military though, his father's free ticket to America was anything but first class. After trying many low paying jobs while he learned English, washing dishes or cleaning public restrooms, his father finally managed to land a job as a dock supervisor with the Lockheed Corporation in Renton, Washington. It would later become known as the Boeing Corporation. The job was well beneath his father's abilities, but he never complained about it, because he only got the job through an American war buddy whom he had met in the North Pacific Theater. He was grateful for having the inside track on it in the first place! Besides, to go back to Russia meant his certain execution, and his family too! And, although all the jobs he had in America were well below a man of his caliber, such menial labors were preferable to a bullet in the head back in Russia.

Nick was raised the typical son of a blue-collar worker in Seattle, and he did his best, like all teenagers do, trying to just fit in. So one day he found himself standing in line at the draft bureau, being shuffled from one line to another and filling out tons of questionnaires and forms, when some old salt addressed him.

"Says here son, that you speak and read *Rooshkie*. That right?"

Nick nodded.

"Wait right here! There's a guy over there looking for guys like you."

That was another turning point in his life. At nineteen years old he managed to flunk out of college, get drafted, and then get recruited by the CIA to do covert ops behind the Iron Curtain instead of going to Nam, and all because he got lazy and let his grades slip! It was only because he spoke both Russian and English fluently that he was even considered for a covert ops position. The Cold War was at its apex at the time, and since Russians all look much like mainstream America does, the trick for the CIA was to find young men and woman to use as operatives who could speak Russian fluently and free of any accent which might sound foreign. It was a difficult task for the CIA—not many people fit the bill! Nick was Russian as well as fluent in the language, which made him that much more interesting to them.

The man he met that day at the recruiting office called himself Smith, and he was the most unlikely looking agent imaginable! He was overweight, balding, and soft-spoken, and he had a grandfather's demeanor to him unlike that of a field agent's! Like all good spooks, however, he was not who he appeared to be. He was very quick witted despite his mannerisms that made him look befuddled most of the time, and when he became angry, his eyes seemed to crystallize and turn gray, and his whole personality changed! His words would become much more succinct, his voice icy cold. Somewhere in his past, Smith had seen battle, which the deftness of his movements made clear when he forgot that he was supposed to be an old and harmless befuddled man. Nick was to become his protégé, though at the time he didn't know it. Their common destiny began the moment that Smith stepped up to him in the draft line and they conversed in Russian.

After twenty minutes of demanding questions, all in Russian! And in a small office that contained only a table and two chairs, Smith was visibly impressed, and very pleased with his new find. The young man before him had listened to all of his questions in Russian, and understood every word as if he had lived in Moscow his whole life. The young lad had answered all his questions without hesitation and with flawless Russian! Politically, the young boy—Nick, was completely ignorant of any current events happening in Eastern Europe, or within the Soviet Union for that matter! But, he knew everything about the Russian culture, from the royal families down to the great artists and composers!

Smith threw a large book in front of him. "Tell me about this book," he said in Russian.

Nick picked the book up, and without opening it, he said, "This is an epic historical novel by Leo Tolstoy, originally published as Voyna i mir in 1865-69. It is about Napoleon's invasion of Russia and about his defeat. Haven't you read it?"

The book had been published in Russia and bore no English symbols. "And did you read it in English or in Russian?" Smith had asked excitedly.

Nick had looked at Smith with a miffed expression. They had not spoken a word of English since they had entered the room. He wondered if this guy—this pudgy Mr. Smith thought him an idiot? He looked at the large mirror on one wall, which he now assumed was a one-way mirror. It made him uncomfortable, and in English he said defiantly, "I'm thirsty, may I have a Coke?"

"Answer the question, or you take your chances with the Army in Southeast Asia," Smith said coldly in Russian.

"*Dah, dah, pa Rooshkie, kaninshna!* (Yes, yes, of course in Russian!)"

"So, you can read Russian as well as you speak Russian?"

"Why wouldn't I? Both my parents are Russian! My father was a colonel in the Russian army, and my parents come from royal blood. We are not stupid immigrants who fell off a potato truck!" he replied defiantly, his voice rising. "My father risked his life, and my entire family's lives, to aid the American's during WWII. He was branded by Stalin, and the USSR—as an enemy of the State for his actions! But, he and mother love their motherland—the place of their birth, regardless!" Nick had paused to catch his breath and to calm himself. "Besides, my mother," he continued in a defiant tone, "would never permit me to read a great work of Tolstoy's translated into English—there is no complete translation of this work anyway." He then stood with anger, pushing his chair away. It toppled over and clattered on the tile. "My mother and father have not forgotten where they come from, and they taught me the Russian ways. I was the one who first learned the English language, and I am still the only one in my family who subscribes in the least to the American ways."

Then the door opened and a young woman brought in a plastic tray with a bottle of Coke on it. She placed it on the table before him and left as quickly as she had appeared. Smith went to the wall where the chair lay toppled on its side, picked it up, and placed it once again before the table.

"Sit," he said calmly, and Nick did.

Smith pointed to the Coke. "As you requested. Enjoy, please." He was now speaking in English. Smith then sat down across from Nick. "Sorry

Nicholas, but I had to push you. I had to find out if you are what we are looking for. It is only a coincidence that I am here today. Normally, I am abroad, in Russia to be exact, but by coincidence I was visiting an old friend who works here, and I put out the word to bring anybody who speaks Russian to me. I am absolutely amazed by your facility with the Russian language, believe me."

Nick sensed that Smith was telling him the truth. He could never figure out why he trusted the man so quickly, a man who had such brutally different sides to him, but he did. In time, his instincts became justified.

Chapter 6

Roberta awoke at nine o'clock to the sound of a vacuum sweeper. She squirmed under the satin sheets, loving the feel of them as she wriggled a little more—hoping to put off the inevitable! But her curiosity got the better of her. Sunshine was pouring into her room, and she had to take a look outside to finally see where she was. Still naked, she reached for the towel that she had dropped to the floor the night before and wrapped it around her torso.

Opening the French doors and stepping out onto the balcony, she gasped. A panoramic view of the Cascade Mountains and Mount Rainier was before her! And, the Puget Sound, speckled with boats, was far below. At ground level were the gardens that she only caught a glimpse of the night before—unbelievably colorful and pristine, surrounded by an impeccably manicured yard!

She looked first to her right, then to her left, leaning far over the balcony. All she could see were pine trees. The mystery man had no neighbors, it appeared. The vacuum sweeper seemed to be getting louder now.

"Was Nick vacuuming?" she wondered to herself. She was about to put on her clothes when there was a knock at her door. Still wrapped in a towel, she went to the door to take a look. A shapely woman with blond hair and blue eyes appeared there, smiling.

"Yes?" Roberta said, barely opening the door.

"Miss Sanchez, Mr. Smith called my store early this morning and explained that your baggage was on its way to Japan without you, and that you needed a complete new wardrobe with accessories. May I come in?"

"Mr. Smith?" Roberta asked.

The woman looked confused. "Yes, of course. Mr. Smith! This is his house, isn't it? You are Roberta Sanchez, right? He said that you would be on the second floor, and he said that the maid would let us in. He said that you needed everything to wear, and that you were a size four or six.

May we come in?"

"We? Who are we?"

"My staff, of course," she replied. The young woman then pushed the door open and walked in with confidence. "Mr. Smith said that you would be suffering from jet lag, but that it would be important that we get you outfitted before noon. We have only a few hours to do that, and believe me, he is paying a premium for it, if you will excuse my candor."

Roberta stepped aside as a procession ensued. Three young women walked in carrying parcels, which they laid out on the bed after first making it. "Let's start with your lingerie. "My name is Gloria," the shapely blonde said, holding out her hand.

Bewildered, Roberta shook her hand.

Another woman came in with a tray, apparently the maid. On it was black coffee in a carafe, sugar, and cream, and cinnamon raisin toast. She set it on a French side table and said,

"Miss Sanchez, Mr. Smith said to prepare breakfast for you. Is there anything that I can make for you?"

Confused even more now, Roberta shook her head.

"Oh, one more thing, Miss Sanchez," said the maid. "Mr. Smith asked me to go to the gas station down the road and to get you this." She handed her a pack of Parliament Light Menthols and an ashtray.

Roberta looked at her with disbelief but took the items anyway.

"How in the hell did he know what brand I smoke?" she wondered to herself. But before she could dwell upon the thought, Gloria laid out an assortment of fine lacey women's undergarments before her and urged her to start trying things on. One side of her brain was excited by the prospect of a new wardrobe, but the other side was sending off alarm bells.

"What is this man going to want from me in return for all of this?" she thought to herself. The feminine side of her brain won out when Gloria held up a lacey bra and said, "You are an 'A' cup, right?"

Roberta giggled, then frowned.

"Sadly, yes," she admitted. "He told you that?"

"Oh, nonsense!" Gloria said. "You have a model's build. He told me you looked like a runway model! Most models are 'A' cups so I assumed as much! The right bra can do wonders, and you know what?"

Roberta shook her head.

"Some men actually hate big boobs! I dated a man once who was like that, and we broke up mostly because my boobs didn't suit him. He told me that all he could think about when making love to me is what my boobs might look like when I was forty." The blond laughed. "I was eighteen at the time. Screw him!"

She laughed again. "It turns out that he married a friend of mine who thought she would never find a man because she was an 'A' cup. So, it became a proven fact that—that at least for this man, he really does like a woman with tiny tits! They have three kids now, and he adores her. Go figure! All men hope to have big penises, and all women hope to have big boobs! But, as I am sure you already know my dear, it is all a matter of what turns you on, and how you use what you have. This will drive the man in your life crazy, guaranteed! Go ahead now and try it on!"

Gloria handed Roberta a pair of matching white panties. "Go try them on and let me see how it looks on you," she encouraged her again.

Confused and excited at the same time, Roberta went to the bathroom and tried on the underclothes.

Blakely flipped opened his cell phone and barked out orders. "Have the chopper pick me up at Eagle Point! How long?" He listened to the reply and closed his cell phone. "Jorgenson," he said. "How is your man doing, the one Peters put down on the side of the road?"

Jorgenson replied, "He's got a broken nose is all. He was released from the hospital last night after they determined he did not have any head trauma, and he is working with the artist to come up with a composite drawing of this guy. But to be truthful, he doesn't remember too much about him, other than he is suave and very quick! He says this Peters guy put him out before he could get a good look at him. My man was too busy watching his hands to pay much attention to his face." There was a moment of silence between Blakely and Jorgenson, and then they shook hands.

Blakely apologized. "Your guys have done a good job here Jorgenson, and I am sorry that I gave you the impression that I think you and your men are all country bumpkins. The job puts me in contact with lots of locals, and to be honest, more often than not, they are hicks! But, your guys have come up with some really good leads. Tell them thanks, but this investigation is not over yet and so you might keep them on their toes too. Peters is on this Peninsula somewhere, and we still need to find him. You have my number—keep me posted." A few minutes later, the chopper arrived. "I'll send someone for my car," he shouted over the noise of the helicopter, and he tossed Jorgenson the keys.

Jorgenson nodded, catching the keys in one hand and waving him off with the other. "First damned Fed I ever liked," he thought to himself!

Chapter 7

CIA director Harold Toman was about to tee-off on the first hole when his pager vibrated. Quickly, he looked at the number and then resumed his stance at the tee. He took a normal swing at the ball, and it tinged nicely as the little white ball flew off in a nice straight loft, and landed about two hundred and fifty yards down the fairway, slightly to the right, but about where he wanted it go. He was pleased, and his partner congratulated him and clapped him on the shoulder.

"Nice drive, Toman! Now let's see if I can do as well."

His partner was Deputy Director Struthers, and they were playing against Congressman Wilshire from Washington State, and one of his favorite lobbyists, Malcolm Stanovich! Malcolm lobbied for whoever paid him the most money at the time and Wilshire was just one of the many Congressmen that Malcolm had in his stable—back pocket! Stanovich was an amicable man, and he had deep pockets to boot. In fact, he was picking up the tab for everything today, and he would be the last to tee off— just so he could decide how he wanted to play this round. He was very well connected in Washington DC and he could arrange nearly anything for anybody, including the perks that most politicians had come to expect. Whether the request was for a woman, a man, or a discrete orgy, it didn't matter to Malcolm. In fact, he had no conscience at all when it came to granting favors, or when asking for favors back in return. He was known to cover gambling debts, arrange college grants for the children of favorite congressmen, and he had a portfolio of friends who owed him favors in return. And then there were the dossiers—including the videos and photos, he kept on them all! It made him one of the most persuasive and successful lobbyists in the history of that dark craft.

Toman got into his cart to return the call on his cell phone while the rest of the foursome took their turn on the tee. He listened intently to the voice on the other end, and finally said, "Do it!" Despite it being the weekend, immediately wheels were set into motion and phone calls were being made back at headquarters.

"Any problems, buddy?" Struthers asked as he got into the cart.

"No, the usual," he replied—actually a bit miffed that his Saturday was being interrupted.

"Well, let's not have anything from the office affecting your game right now. This Stanovich is a scratch player, and I have fifty bucks on this game."

"In the bank, pal. Stanovich needs a favor from me." Toman chuckled and winked. "I'll bet ten bucks that Stanovich blows the next putt." They both laughed, enjoying the beautiful autumn morning.

By the time the foursome had reached the ninth hole, a man in Chicago had already packed his sniper rifle into its case and was preparing to depart from O'Hare airport for SeaTac International. He would be in Seattle by early nightfall, and his instructions were very clear: he was to terminate the courier before he could deliver his package on Monday morning, and before he made it to the Federal building in Seattle.

Nick was on his way to Olympia for an early morning meeting. He had a bad feeling about this one. Things didn't generally go bad in the courier business, unless lives were at stake—in this case his! It wouldn't hurt to have some backup, so he was enlisting Ron Kowalski. They had worked together in covert ops before, and Kowalski was a reliable gun-for-hire. Nick had come to trust him as a friend as well, and to respect his abilities, and he had requested that they meet down by the docks where the tourist boats gathered. Nick arrived on time, parked the Ford Bronco in an alley where it wouldn't be noticed, and went on foot from there to meet Kowalski.

Ron was already waiting on the pier. He held a Starbucks paper cup in his hand and was feeding the gulls some breadcrumbs. His blond hair was being tousled by the wind, and when he turned to greet Nick, he clapped him on the back as he smiled broadly. "Hey, Nikki. Have you had any breakfast yet?"

Nick shook his head. "No."

"Then let's go grab a bite to eat and you can bring me up to speed." They then headed for a small café down by the water.

As Nick and Kowalski finished their meeting, Roberta was still at Nick's house and didn't know what to think.

"Who the hell is Smith?" she thought to herself.

It was a question that would have to wait until Nick got back. Gloria and her crew had just left, leaving behind a week's worth of very, lacy lingerie, three pairs of designer jeans, two separate outfits, one casual, one dressy, a half dozen blouses, and six pairs of shoes—three were heels, three were flats. They had also left her makeup and hygiene products, as well as various accessories to go along with the clothing—a nightgown, a robe, slippers and two brand new suitcases—all of which took her hours to decide upon as if she were paying for it herself.

Gloria had told her that Mr. Smith was not placing a dollar limit on her but had only indicated that they were to be sure that she had enough clothing to fill two suitcases. When Roberta heard this, she smiled. Nick was obviously making sure that she left his house with as much, or more than, she had left behind at the abandoned car. So, she had chosen her selections very carefully, making certain that her choices could cover a wide range of activities, but—at he same time, without taking advantage of his generosity.

She couldn't fathom what was on this man's mind! So far, he hadn't made a pass at her. He seemed to be intent on finishing something! Yet, he took the time to attend to her needs as well. He had left her caviar and champagne the night before! And before she could even dress this morning, he had a staff of people attending to her wants and needs. The two thousand dollars he had handed her the night before was still neatly tucked away in her purse.

"So," she thought to herself. "The man must be wealthy enough to drop this kind of money without even batting an eye," and she wondered once again if a payback was to be expected—a payback that meant going horizontal with him!

She had discovered the maid's name was Maria, and Maria had insisted that she eat something more than just toast. As such, she had prepared a breakfast for her consisting of scrambled eggs, bacon, and fresh orange juice. As Roberta sat to eat, she asked her offhandedly,

"Maria, how long have you worked for Mr. Smith?"

Maria smiled. "I have come to his home to clean, shop, and cook for him for nearly five years now. He pays me very well, even though he is rarely here, and he always leaves me special gifts for each holiday."

"Really?" Roberta exclaimed.

"Oh yes. Mr. Smith is a very generous man. He is not here very much because I think he travels for business, but when he is here, he will take the time to talk with me. He always asks me about my family, and every time I tell him about something special, like my son Jose graduating from high school, he does something special for me. I told him that Jose was graduating from school with honors, and that he was accepted into the University of Washington with a scholarship, but it was not a full scholarship, and that we did not know where to come up with all the money for the remainder. Then one day I come to clean his house and there is a big white envelope on the table where you are eating now. It was addressed to me, and when I opened it, I found a letter from the University of Washington saying that Jose had qualified for an additional scholarship to cover his entire tuition, his books, and his room and board. In addition, there was a note in Mr. Smith's handwriting."

Roberta sat at the table eating her breakfast.

"What did it say, Maria?" she asked excitedly.

Maria smiled broadly and sat at the table across from her, leaning toward her in confidence. "It said that Mr. Smith had discussed the matter of Jose with a very good friend—a friend who knew the dean at the University of Washington, and that there were some additional grants that Jose qualified for based on his academics. The letter went on to say that there was a part-time job for Jose at the university bookstore, so he could make some extra pocket money! Mr. Smith's note said to tell Jose to keep up the good work and he would be there for his graduation." Maria beamed as she told the story.

"And did Jose graduate?"

"Oh yes," Maria said proudly. "And with honors, last year."

"And did Mr. Smith attend his graduation?"

"Yes, of course he did! He took us all there in his boat, my entire family! He took us all the way to the University of Washington, and there we docked at the University's private dock! We walked to the ceremonies like dignitaries, and watched the entire ceremony in seats reserved only for rich people! And, then he took us all out to a fine restaurant, again by boat! Everyone got very drunk on tequila except for of course Mr. Smith, because he was the Captain! Later he brought us all back here, and put us up for the night—so that no one had to drive home! It was something Jose will remember forever!"

"So Maria, you must be very loyal to Mr. Smith."

"Yes, of course! My entire family would do anything for him. He speaks to us in our own language, and we know that he cares for us."

"But you told me he is gone most of the time. Why should he care about you?"

"This I do not know." She shook her head vigorously. "He is a very different man from any other man I know. He is very quiet when he is here, and always very pleasant to me. He used to leave his instructions for me with my agency, using the Internet. He paid for all services electronically. My former employer has never even met Mr. Smith! He instructed her that I am the only person to have access to his house. The agency couldn't send anybody else into this house unless I approved first! Finally, a year ago, Mr. Smith dismissed the agency, and hired me fulltime. Now, I work only for him! He pays me what the agency did, but he also pays for full medical for my entire family. He has given me a 401K, and he leaves me bonuses in cash every holiday. I only work here three days a week, but he pays me for six. He told me that I am part of his family now, that his home is my home, and to treat it accordingly. I think Mr. Smith has no family of his own, and I think he adopted mine."

Roberta finished her meal.

"Maria," she asked almost in a whisper.

"Do many people come here?"

Maria smiled, and reached across the table to touch her hand.

"Miss Roberta, you are the first person that Mr. Smith has ever had here as a guest. It is about time that he has had a lovely woman stay over. I have always teased Mr. Smith that he should find a nice woman and bring some life into this place."

"And what did he say, Maria?"

"He would just kiss me on the cheek, give me a big hug, and remind me that I am married."

"Wow!" Roberta sighed.

"Miss Roberta," Maria queried. "Can I ask you something?"

Roberta nodded.

"I don't know who you are or how you got here, but Mr. Smith is a very nice man. Do you think he is interested in you?"

"Maria, I am scared to death that he is doing all these things, like the clothes—because, he expects something from me in return."

Maria removed her hand from Roberta's after patting it gently, and replied, "Oh my dear, Mr. Smith is a very wealthy man, I think. In all the years that I have worked for him, no young lady has ever been his guest here in this house. Yet if he wanted a woman to be here, there are many women who would do anything to be with him—for his money alone! He is not that type of man. If you find him attractive, then go for it girl, because he needs a woman in his life."

"Maria," Roberta replied. "I am twenty years younger than he is, and I am mixed race, in case you haven't noticed."

Maria smiled. "Mr. Smith has good tastes in young women, then doesn't he?" She laughed. "I guess you don't know him that well yet. He doesn't care about skin color—he cares about what's in here," she said putting her hand over her heart. "He sees the good in people and he understands the bad. I don't know what he has been through in his life, but I do know that he is a reliable man and that he has a big heart. I have seen him work out in the gym downstairs, and it is frightening to watch him! I am sure that he could kill a man with his bare hands if he wanted to—for he is very strong! So yes, he is twenty years older than you are, but his heart is as strong as a young man's heart, and much bigger than maybe any man's."

"Why are you telling me this, Maria?"

"Because Mr. Smith has never called me at five o'clock in the morning before to tell me he was worried about a young lady sleeping upstairs in his house, and he has never asked me to come to this house on a Saturday morning. Then he asked me to pick up cigarettes on my way into work for you, and he doesn't even smoke himself. I think that he might be attracted to you, my dear," she said enthusiastically. "And it is about time that I changed some sheets around here that needed to be changed!"

Roberta blushed, not knowing what to say, but Maria continued.

"It's up to you, dear. You could do a lot worse than Mr. Smith. Look around you, girl. You ask me questions about him because you are worried that he might want something from you, but look around you! What woman wouldn't want to live like this? But never mind—it is none of my business!" She sighed and got up from the table.

Roberta said, "No wait! Please finish what you where about to say."

Maria looked at her over her shoulder. "I have to go now, and I have already said too much. I would trust Mr. Smith with my own daughter, so don't worry about his intentions. Worry about your own, but give him a chance. You both deserve it; I can tell by our little conversation." She then put on her jacket and left, adding, "I'll be back to clean up. Just leave your dish in the sink."

Roberta rinsed her plate and went back upstairs to brush her teeth. Now that everyone was gone, and the house was completely empty, she needed to find what she came for. She opened the door to her room and looked down the hallway in both directions. "Why not start up here?" she thought. Directly ahead of her were the stairs that went down to the great room, and to each side was a balcony that overlooked the rooms below. In each direction were corridors, so she picked one, deciding to go to her left.

At the end of the hallway was a den or office. It must have been directly over the three-car garage below because it was just as big. It had built-in bookcases filled with books on two walls, and the remaining walls were paneled in dark wood with very ornate trim. The room would have been very dark if it had not been for the cream-colored carpeting, soft white paint on the cathedral ceilings, and the large French designer windows opposite each other that profusely lit up the space.

A huge wooden desk was in front of one set of glass-paneled windows that overlooked the front of the house and the driveway below. On the end of the room was an oversized fireplace with split logs ready to add to a fire to. Directly across from the desk was another set of double French doors that went out onto the same balcony that her room let out onto, facing the gardens below, and Puget Sound beyond.

She made her way to the desk, and sat in the high-backed leather chair. The chair was on a plastic mat that allowed for freedom of movement over the thick carpet under it, and it tilted and moved freely when she sat in it. She spun around gleefully like a little child would. On the desk was a flat screen PC monitor, a wireless keyboard, and a mouse. There was an ornate brass mug filled with pens, pencils, and letter openers within easy reach. There was a brass-reading lamp with a pull chain dangling under a dark green crystal shade. Other than that, the desk was completely clear of clutter.

She touched the mouse, and the flat screen monitor came to life. It requested a password. She thought to herself,

"What the hell?" and typed in Smith. The monitor told her that the password was incorrect. She tried various combinations of Nicholas Dimeitry Petrovisky and Smith, but she finally gave up! She tried the drawers. The top left drawer opened easily enough, and in it was nothing but office supplies: legal pads, paper clips, a stapler and staples. Below this drawer was a large door, and within it she found the PC and printer. She opened the top right drawer and found a gun, a Glock! It must have been a new model because she hadn't seen one quite like it before. She picked up the weapon for a closer look, and found it to be very well-balanced, and very lightweight—even for a Glock! She removed the loaded clip, and pulled the chamber open. Once again she was impressed with its smooth action. She returned the weapon to where it belonged. The rest of the drawers were locked. She wondered, "So where is the attaché case?" She went to the bookshelves. The first volume she pulled from the shelf was written in Cyrillic, a language she recognized, but could not read. She put it back and pulled several more books at random—most of them written in languages other than English.

She then left the den to continue her search. She found that there were three bedrooms on the second floor, but the attaché case was nowhere to be found! So, she concluded it must be downstairs. So far, she had found nothing of interest to tell her anything about who Nicholas Dimeitry Petrovisky was—or was it Mr. Smith? But, she reminded herself that she was there to find the attaché case.

She went to the master bedroom on the first floor. This room was spacious and luxurious, with a king-sized bed and the usual furnishings, but there was also a French looking desk—a desk that caught her attention. This room had double doors that led outside onto a brick patio, and also dormer windows that faced the front of the house. It had a bathroom like the room in which she stayed, but this bathroom looked much more like a man's would, a bit messy! His razor was laid carelessly out on the vanity, as was a tube of toothpaste and a toothbrush. There was a hairbrush and shaving cream left out as well, adding to the bachelor look. She looked around further, wanting to know more about him—despite her real objective! She opened the medicine cabinet. Once again she found no prescriptions, only the usual stuff like aspirin and bandages.

She went over to his bed next and pulled back the comforter. His sheets were made of cotton instead of satin. There were no stains on the sheets that she could see, but she knew that meant nothing! Maria would have already remade his bed this morning. What was she doing checking his bed for semen stains for? She wondered if he had a lover, even though Maria emphatically stated he didn't. Why did she care? Carefully, she remade the bed and went to his dresser. Opening each drawer, she once again found nothing unusual, just underwear folded neatly in the top drawers. The lower drawers were all empty. She went to a large walk-in closet and opened the door to find a modest amount of clothing hanging on the racks. He had half a dozen suits, most of which had Italian labels on them and all of high quality. He had a dozen dress shirts and a rack filled with silk ties. He had polo shirts, and plaid cotton flannel shirts, a few durable sweatshirts, and an assortment of dress slacks and casual slacks, including jeans all hung neatly. The shoe rack had only two pairs of fine leather shoes on it, and the rest were casual footwear. He had an assortment of hiking clothes, but for a rich guy, the huge closet was mostly empty space, and a disappointment for her—there was nothing old in it! She wondered what this closet filled with so little had to say about Mr. Smith or was it Petrovisky?

She went to the French desk, and like the desk upstairs, it was bare! This one—even without a computer screen on it! The only thing on it was a desk pad, and nothing was written on it either. She pulled back the delicate French-made chair and sat down. She was becoming frustrated! There was only one drawer to the desk to look at, and she pulled it open. Once again, there was an assortment of office supplies in it, but there seemed to be nothing else of importance. Reaching to the very rear of the drawer, she felt something solid, and pulled it forward into sight. It was a small photo album! With excitement she pulled it out, hoping to learn more about him—and at the same time wondering why she should care? She momentarily put aside what she was there for.

Chapter 8

Blakely was in the helicopter heading back to the federal building in Olympia when his cell phone rang again. He knew before answering it that it was his wife, Anne Marie.

"So, where the hell are you now?" she asked. "Are we going to that party together tonight or not?"

Anne Marie, despite her petite size, was anything but demure. By nature she was a very demanding woman! She was driven by appearance, power, and money. She liked to dress up, and she like to spend money—both of which were difficult for Blakely to facilitate. He supposed it was because she grew up poor, and money and power validated her as a *real* person. If it weren't for their two young kids, he would have cut her loose a long time ago—but, not because he didn't love her, but instead because her aspirations were poisoning their relationship! He questioned himself continually about her devotion to him—or rather, her lack thereof.

Their love life had deteriorated to the point of making appointments with one another, and cashing in coupons for sexual favors. The coupons she handed out were in return for getting something that she wanted—but did not necessarily need. Rather than arguing with him about getting it, a promised sexual favor was her way to diffuse any objections before the fact. At first it amused him, but as time went on he figured out that she was just manipulating him to suit her own whims. She knew that her good looks got to him, but he felt that she couldn't care less about him as a man—sex was only a tool to get what she wanted from him. Her good looks and her sexy body were all part of a toolkit. And, she was proficient at using it to get her way! Nevertheless, he was still in love with her, or at least he thought he was.

"Actually, I am on my way home right now," he replied.

"Good, because I was really looking forward to meeting with the

Trundles tonight. Harry is running for Congress next year, and Margaret, his wife, is just the most fascinating woman! Besides, I have this new dress that I am dying to show off. You will like it, Bill. It's very low cut but very fashionable. It will be great that we can go together, because actually, I didn't want to go this party alone wearing such an outfit. Someone might get the wrong impression, if you know what I mean. I am so excited!" she squealed.

"I can tell, Anne. I'll be there soon. I can hardly wait to see your newest outfit," he replied, almost too dryly.

"And Bill," she said. "You will refrain from drinking tonight, right? You know how argumentative you get after two drinks."

"Yes, dear. Ginger ale for me all night long."

"Good. I am really excited about going to this party! Everyone will be there! How are you doing with the smoking, dear?"

"Oh, just fine. I hardly even crave one anymore. I just wish the people around me would get on the ball. I hate it now when my clothes smell like cigarettes."

"Well dear, you have to remember that some people still smoke. Harry Trundle is the type of man that is on our side, and if it was up to him, cigarettes would be illegal."

"I can hardly wait to vote, Anne. See you in a couple of hours."

She said goodbye just as he lit another cigarette.

The pilot said, "It's against the rules to smoke up here."

Blakely looked at him with irritation, and the pilot laughed. "Hey buddy, I don't care. Go ahead and burn it. The frigging do-gooders write the rules, not me."

Roberta stared at the brown leather cover of the picture book in her lap. There was no writing on it, but there were floral designs imprinted into the leather outside, a bit too feminine to be a man's book. The cover was very worn, and it looked very old. In fact, it looked as if it had traveled a million miles. She opened it. The first photo was of a small boy of about six years old. The photo was in black and white, and the boy was standing in front of a church holding a young woman's hand. His mother's, Roberta guessed. The child was dressed in church clothes, but his hair was resisting staying in place. The photo was taken somewhere in the US, because in the background there were 1950's vintage cars parked at the curb, and one in particular, she recognized as a '55 Chevy pickup like the one her father used to drive when she was little.

She flipped the page, and there she saw a photo of a handsome young soldier standing at a ship dock. Behind him was a black submarine. He was wearing a uniform that did not look at all to be American, and he was smiling with delight while standing at attention. In the background were snow-covered mountains, and in the foreground there were mounds of freshly shoveled snow. This picture was also a black and white photo, and the overcast skies overhead were gray. It looked to be very cold wherever the photo was taken. She wondered if this man was Nick's father. He had said his parents were first generation immigrants.

There were several photos of family outings, various combinations of the three of them together, the mother and boy, the father and boy, the mother and father, and all three of them together.

About the time the young man became a teenager, the photos changed to color. A dozen photos later, he had become a man, and he wore a graduation gown. The photo was taken on some university campus, and he held a scroll, presumably his diploma.

Then there were photos of the young man with racecars, and in one he was holding a very large victory bottle of champagne and smiling broadly. These photos did not appear to be taken in America. The architecture of the buildings in the background was completely different. European looking, Roberta thought.

As she neared the end of the book, she found a picture of a very lovely young woman, a slender brunette with long flowing hair. She stood in front of a palace ornately trimmed in gold. Roberta had seen this palace before, but she couldn't remember where at first, and then she remembered where it was. It was the Winter Palace in St. Petersburg Russia; she had seen it in the movie Dr. Zhivago or was it Anastasia? But, she couldn't remember which one for sure—as if it mattered anyway!

Other photos were of the woman and what might have been a handsome young Nicholas. He looked in his mid-thirties and she in her early to mid-twenties. They made a handsome couple, and they were obviously in love with each other. There were six photos of them as a couple, and then the next photo was that of a little girl, perhaps six years old, walking with her mother to what appeared to be a school, and the mother was the very same young woman as in the previous photos, only a bit older. The photo was grainy, as if taken from far away and blown up, but unmistakably, the woman in the photo was the same woman as in the previous photos. It might have been the little girl's first day in school, or so Roberta allowed herself to imagine. The little girl carried a satchel—one large enough to have held her school supplies, and they were both dressed in autumn jackets and hats.

"So, he has a daughter too," she thought to herself.

The last photo was of a very young woman—a teenager, with long flowing dark hair and beautiful bright green eyes. She was looking away at something behind the camera, and the photo looked as if it had been taken when she was totally unaware of being photographed. The photo must have been the little girl grown up; the resemblance to her mother was remarkable. She was standing in a street market, and in one hand she held a grapefruit and in the other a cotton satchel used for holding groceries—a loaf of bread protruded from it. That was the final photograph.

Roberta sighed deeply, knowing that there must be some amazing stories behind those photographs. She then put the album back where she found it and sat there in silence, thinking about the sequence of photographs—the sequence of his life! She had just pried into a man's past, and instead of learning something more about him; the photos raised even more unanswered questions. Nick had changed dramatically—in appearance anyway, from the early photos to the later ones! She opened the album again and flipped to the racing photos, then compared them to the ones taken with the young woman. It was as if his face had changed completely! His nose was utterly different, as was his cheekbone and jaw line. The later Nick had a rougher appearance to him, but she noticed that the eyes were the same.

Now she wished that she had never snooped around in the first place. How could she tell him that she had found his photo album? She knew she could keep her intrusion secret, of course, but at the same time she wanted to confront him about the photos. Strangely, she also felt like she needed to hear the stories behind the photos too. She had just met this man, so why was she compelled to know more about him? The question hung in her mind like a bad painting that reminded of her someone she knew she should forget. Besides, she reminded herself, there hadn't been any romantic overtures between them, and in fact she had only met him less than a day before. She hadn't slept with him yet, so she didn't need to know anything about him, did she? Yet, she was intrigued by his indifference toward her, and also by his acceptance of her, and she was beginning to find him to be a fascinating man. Besides, the attaché case wasn't here—she had looked everywhere—and so he must have taken it with him. She chastised herself for all this silly pondering about a man she barely knew, instead of doing her job! Becoming hungry she made her way hastily to the kitchen.

Roberta was finishing a bowl of soup when she heard the garage door open. He walked in and smiled when he saw that she was still there.

"I see you are still here, and the Cadillac is too."

"I found your photo album in your room. Sorry, but I had to look around," she blurted out sheepishly.

He smiled tensely, and said cautiously, "I told you last night that you had free run of the place, but of course I wasn't expecting you to open my drawers, though there is nothing for me to be concerned that you might find."

"So, this is not your place, is it? And by the way, who is Smith?"

Nick got a beer from the refrigerator and sat down at the kitchen table across from her. "This is my place—I own it!" He took a swallow of beer and waited for her next question.

"So, who is Smith?"

"I am Smith," he replied.

She became upset and raised her voice. "You told me last night that your name is Nicholas Dimeitry Petrovisky, and now you are saying that you are Smith!"

Nick looked at her and smiled once again, saying, "Now would you care for a glass of wine, a bottle of beer, or something else to calm you down? How did you like your caviar and champagne last night?"

Roberta was fuming at his calm replies to her questions, but she didn't know why it bothered her so! "I liked the damned champagne and the caviar just fine. So please answer the *damned* question!"

"After you answer my question first: beer, wine, or what?"

"I'll take a cold beer, okay?"

"Good. Let me get one for you. Why are you so angry with me anyway?" He brought her a bottle of Heineken and opened it for her. "I should be the one who is angry with you for looking through my private belongings, and yet it bothers you that I'm not. I do not care what you discovered in my absence," he said as he lowered himself back into the chair across from her.

"You tore the door off my car last night, and you tell me that you are running from the law! Then you bring me here to a place that is apparently owned by a Mr. Smith and calmly sit there and offer me a beer. Yet, you say that you aren't hiding anything? Is any of that normal?"

"Look Roberta," Nick had to smile, though he tried not to. "We just met last night, and quite by accident, as you know. I am not sure what I am obligated to tell you about myself or what I am not obligated to tell you, but I have tried to accommodate your needs. I am sure that I wouldn't have deviated from my initial plans if you were not such a pretty, and persuasive, woman. Nevertheless, I do not owe you any more explanations, and I hasten to remind you that you are here of your own free will. But to ease your fears: yes, I am evading the law, but what you don't know is that I have a license to do so. I am a courier tasked to deliver something for a congressman of the United States. Technically, I have not broken any laws yet, according to my license. I carry several identities, and one of them is Smith. I carry different identities because it is my job not to be known, and technically, Nicholas Dimeitry Petrovisky does not exist, and yet I promise you, that is in fact, my birth name. As confusing as all this may be to you, it is all the truth."

She stared at him in disbelief, and then took a large swallow of beer.

"How can any of this be true? And what do you mean about a license—a license to break the law?" Then she belched from the beer that she had just swallowed too quickly.

"Sorry," she said, covering her mouth.

"Go get the picture album, and I will explain a bit more."

She pushed away from the table with irritation, almost as a wife would do when she caught her husband in a lie—and she had the proof to back it up! She went to his room, and retrieved the photo album from his desk. She returned and handed it to him defiantly.

"Sit," he said. "Sit here, next to me, so that we both can look at the photos together."

She moved from her previous chair and sat down next to him as he had requested, and he opened the book.

"Look at the photos and ask me anything," he said.

"Who are these people?" She pointed to the young boy and his mother.

"That is me when I was four or five, and I am with my mother at church," he replied.

"The boy doesn't look at all like you, but where were you?"

"Attending church."

"Where?"

"The church was in Renton, where I grew up. It is a small suburb of Seattle. My father worked at the Renton Boeing plant there until he retired."

"So why doesn't this photo look at all like you?"

"Probably because I was only four at the time. I hadn't yet started to shave, and of course the body was probably much trimmer back then."

She laughed in spite of herself! "No, here. Look at this photo of when you graduated," she said flipping the pages forward." She showed him the photo of himself wearing a cap and gown. "See," she said. "Here you can see the resemblance to the boy in front of the church, but now you look completely different."

"When I was a young man, I raced the Grand Prix tour in Europe for the Ferrari Company. I crashed my car one day in a practice run and got broken up pretty badly. I was also a CIA agent at the time, working under cover for the Agency. The Agency capitalized on the crash, and for all intents and purposes, they killed me off to get me out of the public's eye. They then sent me to Switzerland to recover, and while I was there, they reconstructed my face, changing my features in the process. Six months later, they slipped me behind the Iron Curtain and I worked covert ops in Russia for the CIA for nearly two decades."

"What did you do?"

"Different things, but mostly I moved people and documents across the borders when it was required."

She raised the Heineken to her mouth and looked at him with disbelief, and then she swallowed another large gulp of beer. "Did you ever kill anyone?"

"I did what I had to do for my country."

"You carried a gun and you shot people?"

"I rarely carried a gun," Nick replied. "It was too dangerous to have a weapon in Russia, but there were times when the circumstances required it."

"What about the gun upstairs in your desk drawer?"

"What about it? It is registered," he replied innocently. "Many Americans have weapons."

"Registered to a Mr. Smith, I would guess?"

"Yes, of course," Nick replied. He then stood up from the table, went to the pantry adjacent to the kitchen to where Roberta had found a can of soup, and beckoned for her to come and look. He pulled on something, and the entire wall moved outward, exposing a hidden room behind it. "These are all weapons that are not licensed, which is why they are hidden."

Her jaw dropped as she looked past him. The hidden room was about six feet deep and the same width as the pantry. It was cedar lined, and from top to bottom, it was stocked with different military arms, pistols to automatic rifles, and things she had only seen in the movies. He pulled an automatic rifle from a rack and handed it to her, a fully automatic Kalashnikov AK47 with a sixty round clip.

"Is it loaded?"

"Of course. What good is a weapon if it is not loaded?"

She shook her head, not wanting to touch it.

He put the rifle back in the rack and pushed on something again, and the pantry wall slid back into place. He put his hand on her shoulder and guided her gently back into the kitchen where they both sat down again at the kitchen table. She was visibly shaken by what she had just seen.

Her hands trembled when she reached for her beer, and her voice faltered.

"So, who are you? What are you?"

"I am retired CIA. I spent most of my adult life in Russia serving my country, the United States of America in case you are still wondering—that's *who* I am. That closet is not filled with street weapons. The rifle that I just showed you is a collector's item given to me by Mikhail Timofeevich Kalashnikov himself. It is the last AK47 of that series produced in Russia, and he gave it to me out of gratitude for helping a close friend of his out of a bind. The stock is autographed in his own hand. Most of the other weapons in that closet are weapons that the CIA issued to me for various assignments, or weapons acquired by Mr. Smith."

"I thought that you are Mr. Smith?"

"I am, and in a minute more, you will understand things better, but you have to hush. May I continue?"

She nodded.

"Over the years," he continued, "these mementos accumulated in an old warehouse that Mr. Smith and I rented jointly in Moscow, and when Smith finally retired about ten years ago, he had them all shipped here. Actually, this was meant to be his retirement house, not mine, but he died of cancer before he got to enjoy it, and as I told you last night, he willed the place to me. These items are evidence to prove that I am who I say I am because, technically, the CIA killed me off a long time ago. The death certificate the CIA filed for Nick Peter's—my American name, for the race car accident, completely erased my previous identity.

I was born in Russia and named Nicholas Dimeitry Petrovisky by my parents, as I told you already. But when I came to America as a young boy, the US government declared that I was to be called Nick Peters. All my papers were in that name, and at the age of twenty-eight, according to public records, Nick Peters died in a racecar accident. I no longer officially existed in America! And, in Russia, because Stalin proclaimed my parents enemies of the state—all my birth records were destroyed there too! When the CIA used me in Russia, they gave me back my given name. However, again technically, there is no American known as Nicholas Dimeitry Petrovisky. Nicholas would in fact exist only in Russia, but all his records were purged after Stalin died. Nick Peters, who went by the CIA name of Michael Dobson, the aspiring racecar driver, is also officially dead. So, when I decided to come back to America, who was I to be?"

"It is starting to make sense now. Go on."

I have a dozen passports, a dozen different identities, all with different names, and all are perfectly legal but also illegitimate at the same time. I have no past, and I do not exist on any document of record either here in America or in Russia. That is how I can slip across borders so easily without detection—I simply don't exist!"

"Wow," she said. "How is it then that you can own property and pay your bills?"

Nick smiled at her, lifted his bottle, and said, "That is where Mr. Smith comes in. Mr. Smith recruited me into the CIA when I was a very young man because I spoke fluent Russian, and he was looking for new operatives at the time to put into Russia. In a way, he was my mentor and my guardian, and we worked together until he died a few years back. Toward the end of my tenure with the CIA, I had become very well connected there in Russia. When the Cold War was over and the Russian Mafia was, for all intents and purposes, running the country, I came under suspicion by my own agency. Priorities had changed in the CIA," he continued. "From thwarting the Communist's expansion in the world to controlling major arms movements from the Russian military into the black market.

"Huge sums of untraceable money were involved, and at one point, the CIA became convinced that I was involved in the arms movements because I was friends with so many higher-ups in government, most of whom were involved in arms deals out of necessity. I was guilty only through association, even though I was paid by the CIA over the years to develop those associations."

"But the CIA must have had their reasons to suspect you?" Roberta said cautiously.

"Yes, of course," Nick replied. "I withheld and distorted information to protect my Russian sources, my Russian friends! After all, I lived there most of my adult life, and I saw what was happening as Communism crumbled into the dust of Russian history. The pensions for the people who ran Russia were gone, and of course, they had no investments unless they were sneaking money out of the country. The military, including the soldiers, were not getting fed let alone paid. Soldiers became beggars on the streets of Moscow; it was humiliating to witness!"

"Smith," he continued, "knew of my predicament, and he agreed with my decision to protect our sources. He knew too that, if certain people in the Russian government and the Politburo did not remain in power, the Russian Mafia would replace them completely. We both agreed to turn a blind eye to many activities that would allow them the financial resources to stay in power, but we both also knew that my days were numbered with the CIA."

"Smith was the one who came up with a solution and a plan. In the early days of the Soviet Union's demise, the tanks, ground to air missiles, and aircraft were being sold off to foreign governments, mostly in the Middle East and Africa. These weapons posed no national threat to the US government, but there were millions to be made in brokering deals. The Russians were willing to let these items go for twenty-cents on the dollar, which allowed for plenty of profit to be made while still being able to offer a bargain to a foreign government that had no other access to such high technology weaponry. Smith brokered a two hundred million-dollar deal for a few tanks and a half dozen Soviet fighter planes, all of which were obsolete of course, with an African country wanting to be better able to protect itself from its predatory neighbors. His cut in the deal was over twenty million, but he needed my contacts, as well as me, to make it happen."

Nick got two more beers because he noticed that hers was empty and then he continued.

"I was already under scrutiny by the CIA even though I had done nothing wrong up to that point, but since I couldn't prove that I wasn't involved in arms dealings, Smith convinced me to be a partner in crime with him, and I agreed. When he came to me with his plan, he said, 'Look, Nikki. It is time for you to get out of this business for good. How many years have you given up for your country, and for what? You protected your sources so that you can give another ten years of service to your country, but again I ask you, for what? The Soviet Union is caput, no longer a threat to the United States of America militarily, or even to Eastern Europe for that matter! It is time for you to disappear, Nikki, time to start a new life.'

"I asked him what exactly he was talking about, and he said, 'I am talking about a whole new start in life, before you are too old like me to enjoy it. I am talking about when I die—there will be no one in the Agency who will know what you have sacrificed for your government. Soon, after I am gone, they will bring you down. They will put you in prison as your reward for giving up everything. The writing is on the wall.' Are you still with me Roberta?"

"Yes, I think I am," she said. "But why are you telling me all this?"

"I don't know," he replied. "You wanted to know about Smith and how I became him, and this is how it all happened. It makes no difference if you know or not. Any information I have just offered you is either unknown by anyone else altogether or classified. Bottom line: nothing can be verified, except for what is in that closet over there." He pointed with his beer.

"Go on, then. Tell me about Smith's plan."

"Smith knew that he was dying, and like me, he had no family. We had worked very closely together for more than twenty years, and in a way, I became his son and the only family he had left. Smith was a very clever man, a strategist at heart. Before he ever approached me with his plan, he had all the details already worked out. After he died, I was to assume his identity, and if we could pull off this one deal together, the money was all mine to keep. Because Smith had been diagnosed with terminal cancer by that point in time, he knew he would never see the inside of prison cell, and yet, I was about to be put away *possibly* for life, for something I didn't do! So—he convinced me to go for it."

"What happened to Mr. Smith?" Roberta asked, still trying to comprehend everything. "And this deal, selling weapons to some foreign government, wasn't that illegal?"

Nick smiled. "Mr. Smith took care of all that. It was illegal for an American to sell arms to a foreign country, but it was not illegal for a Russian national. Smith, it turned out, was a Russian national. His American name was as made up as my own was. He set me up with an Internet identity that could not be traced, and he set up numerous bank accounts that could not be touched by anyone to fund me. He set me up with a whole new life."

"Wow," she said to herself numerous times as he continued his story. "So, Mr. Smith leaves you with a fortune and a new identity, and then he dies?"

"Something like that," Nick muttered. "He died quietly in Moscow, and I had him buried in the town of *Volsky* next to his parents, the town where he was born."

"Oh, that is so sad. I am so sorry," she said softly.

"It is what he wanted," Nick said. "And he died happy, knowing that his well-thought-out and well-executed plan succeeded."

"But, if you are rich, why are you on the run now, or is everything related?"

"Part of the Internet identity created for me by Mr. Smith was devised around utilizing my network of contacts, and why not? I had two decades invested in building them," Nick explained. "Mr. Smith saw an opportunity above and beyond doing arms deals after the Berlin wall fell. What was to happen to all the agents on both sides of the Cold War after Perestroika and Glasnost? Could the governments on both sides of the Cold War be trusted to bring in their field operatives and retire them with dignity?"

"Excuse me Nick, 'glass' what?" Roberta asked.

"Ah yes, excuse me. Let me explain. Perestroika and Glasnost mean reform and openness respectively. President Mikhail Gorbachev introduced both terms to the West, and indeed both terms as programs for reform, in the late eighties as Communism crumbled. It was in a last ditch effort to prevent all the republics of the Soviet Union from pulling out. It backfired, of course, and the Soviet Union crumbled anyway. As I was saying, Mr. Smith saw this as an opportunity to bring in the Cold War warriors, so to speak, and to give them all new identities, like he had done for me, a way for them all to make a living too. So, he created a secret organization with his newfound twenty million dollars, and he opened an office in Switzerland that is staffed with former members of the CIA and the KGB. Ironic, isn't it?" Nick laughed. "Imagine, all of us arch enemies now working together toward a common goal?"

"And what would that goal be, Nick? Toppling governments, supporting terrorist activities, or selling nuclear weapons?"

Nick smiled. "Quite the contrary. We intervene in all those activities you just named, and we sell the information back to the appropriate agency. Believe it or not, the Smith Foundation is a top secret, privatized organization manned by the best agents from all over the world, and it works far more effectively than any government agency could ever hope to. You see, Smith recognized very early on in his career that all covert operations are driven by the same goals: to protect a country from an unfair advantage by its enemies—one that could lead to a first strike. There is no way that Russia could ever hope to invade America with conventional armies, and there is no way for America to invade Russia with conventional armies—not since the advent of nuclear weapons anyway. However, a nuclear arsenal in both countries meant that complete obliteration was never out of the question either. The purpose of the Cold War was for both sides to keep tabs on each other, because both sides were determined to develop a weapon that would give them first strike superiority. With few exceptions, Russia was always a few steps behind the Americans in that quest; but America was driven more by protectionism than by imperialism, and in the end, the Soviets had to concede because the Russian economy couldn't support the quest anymore. Once they said *uncle*, Russia was no longer an adversary for America, and I suspect that one-day the country will be an ally with America in fighting global terrorism.

"The Smith Foundation helps all sides," he continued. "We monitor the movement of arms around the world, and we monitor and infiltrate terrorist cells. We watch for large movements of money, and we are unbiased in our objectives, which makes us the only unbiased covert agency anywhere in the world. The Russians buy our services just like the Americans do, the Israelis, and the Iranians. However, payment or no payment, we help any government when we come across credible information that we believe they should know about, especially information that has to do with one country acquiring weaponry that could cause the balance of power to tip one way or the other in a region."

"So, how do you decide which plot to thwart?"

"We are a consultant to the United Nations, and the United Nations makes that decision. Publicly, the Smith Foundation is known as *World Trade*, an import and export company doing business all over the planet. In reality, we trade intelligence for funding, but the world thinks we operate on behalf of shipping companies."

"I was under the impression that the United Nations was a joke, that it has no power, and no authority to act," Roberta replied.

Nick laughed and raised his bottle for a toast. "You are absolutely correct." He touched his beer bottle to hers. "But, all major powers belong to the United Nations! So, how better to remain unbiased than by acting under the auspices of the UN? Such an alignment keeps the major powers in check and ensures that we don't lose our funding. No one can bury us because they all want to know what we know."

"So, are you on a mission now?"

"Yes." Nick smiled. "But it is not a mission that has anything to do with the Smith Foundation or World Trade, and it was supposed to have little if any consequence. It is a personal job. I owed someone a favor, but now it seems that job has turned sour on me. I should be done with it in a few days, nevertheless."

"Why did you have someone bring me a wardrobe? It must have cost you a fortune."

"Because," Nick said, "last night we met quite by accident, and I told you that I would accept full responsibility for that accident—I meant it! Coincidence brought us together, but I don't like owing anyone. You were forced to leave your things behind because of my actions, so I felt obligated to replace those things. Was it presumptuous on my part to send you on your way with a fresh wardrobe?"

Roberta giggled. "No, to be honest, it was great fun to have everyone bringing me outfits to choose from. I was just worried about what your expectations might be in return for your generosity."

Nick nodded. "Well, we are even now! But, as a matter of fact I do have a favor to ask of you."

"Oh really? Surprise, surprise! So, there are strings attached after-all! What is this favor?" Roberta answered apprehensively.

"There is a very formal dinner tonight at the Governor's Mansion and a reception afterwards. I'd like you to accompany me, as part of my cover, of course."

Roberta stared back at him intently, trying to discern if he were joking or not, but she simply could not tell and so decided to ask. "You are joking, aren't you? The law is hunting you, or so you have indicated, but you want to go the Governor's place for dinner? Besides, I don't have any formal wear!" she exclaimed.

"Formal wear is on its way," he replied with a boyish smile. "Gloria has been putting an outfit together all day. She needed to see you first, so I had her come over this morning with your wardrobe so she could size you up. She works for my organization."

"You bastard!" She laughed and tossed the remnants of her beer at him. "So much for not wanting to owe someone something!"

Nick jumped backward but got covered in a beer shower anyway, and he laughed. "C'mon, it's a formal occasion, for God's sake. You'll have fun!"

"Do I get to dance a waltz or something like that? Every young girl dreams of having that one special dance in a ballroom filled with beautiful and prominent people in a Cinderella setting!"

"Center stage, if it pleases you, Roberta," Nick replied, smiling boyishly again at her while toweling up the spilt beer.

"I need some air," she said smiling. "Can we go for a walk?"

"Of course. Let me show you around the place while there is still some daylight."

The sun was starting to set when they stepped outside, and it was getting chilly again as the sun slipped slowly behind the Olympic Mountain Range. Nick brought her a jacket and slipped one on himself.

"Thank you," she said, putting on the tanned leather jacket, which was many sizes too large for her. "Your gardens are beautiful!"

"Smith considered himself part of the royal family, and this was the way he would have liked to have lived. I haven't done much with the grounds other than maintain it all as he had it laid out. There is a path that will take us to an overlook. Would you like to go there and watch the sunset?"

"Yes, of course," she replied, even as she was wondering if she should.

The path was all up hill, and it followed the cliff's edge. As soon as they left the manicured lawns, they entered the magnificence of the Pacific Northwest woods. Huge pine and cedar trees lined both sides of the path as they trekked upwards. The path wound around huge boulders, narrowed, and then expanded again. Once in the woods, they heard an owl off in the distance and the chirp of chipmunks protesting their presence. The ground was covered with moss and fallen boughs, and the path in the forest was soft underfoot. The air was damp and musky and filled with the scent of pine and cedar. Roberta let Nick take the lead, and before long, they reached a clearing in which a tree of huge proportions had fallen.

Nick climbed up onto the huge tree trunk that overlooked the Sound below and took a seat. He motioned for her to join him, and offered her his hand to help her up to his perch.

"Wow," she said as she sat next to him.

"Yeah," he said. "Wow is a good way to describe it."

Before them was a panoramic view of the Puget Sound, and the sun setting behind them showered the Cascade Mountains in front of them in a fiery red/orange caste.

"Follow me," Nick said as he got up again.

"Where to?"

"You'll see," he said, as he took her by the hand and led her further out onto the tree trunk. She followed his lead until the ground fell away into the darkness below them. Frightened, she clung to his arm tightly.

"Just a few more steps," he said, and then he sat down again.

They sat there atop a huge tree trunk that had fallen in a storm many years ago. It extended out over the cliff's edge and seemed to float in space over the channel far below. Their feet dangled in the air, and the Puget Sound below them sparkled from the reflections off the mountains. The waves below held a crimson and blue hue but appeared to be capped with fire from the orange reflection cast from the granite-capped peaks to the west as they reflected the sunset. Only a few glorious minutes later, dusk enveloped the entire area as the sun dipped completely behind the Olympic Mountains, and then suddenly the world around them was very dark and the forest seemed to quiet even further. They could see the mainland from where they sat, and it was lit up like a Christmas tree, but over here on the Peninsula, only a few lights twinkled in the night.

"Oh my God Nick, this is really great, but it is also freaking scary as hell," she said, holding him even closer.

"I like it here, and the sunrise is even more dramatic!" he said. "When I was a young boy, my parents and I spent a lot of time camping in the Pacific Northwest. Those were my favorite days, and the reason why I felt so strongly about America. This place reminds me about my youth with my folks, and about why I did everything I did."

"Do you have any regrets?" Roberta asked him softly, holding more firmly to his arm and pulling herself closer to him. She looked down fearfully, knowing full well that she was hanging over a cliff.

"Of course Roberta," he said. Sensing her fear sitting there, he put his arm around her and held her firmly. She responded by holding him even closer and putting her head on his shoulder, not daring to look down again.

"I have many regrets," he went on. "And many sorrows, like we all do."

"Do you still love her?" she asked timidly.

There was a long silence between them then, the only sounds were those of the night, as a few birds called back and forth. "Do you?" she asked him again.

"Yes, and I love my daughter more than anything."

"Is that why you don't have another woman?"

Nick was silent again for a moment, and then he replied almost in a whisper,

"*Dah, dah, kaninshna.*"

Roberta raised her head from his shoulder and said, "You answered me in Russian, Nick, which I don't understand at all—please translate."

"I am sorry," he replied. "English, Russian, they are all the same to me. Sometimes I think in English, and sometimes I think in Russian. I said yes, yes of course. I will never stop being in love with Tatyana."

Roberta found his answer to be honorable and honest, albeit a little disappointing too.

"Nikki, why don't you go after her now that you can?"

He squeezed her tightly and sighed. "Because she has a good life with another man, and she has had a good life with him for many years now. I cannot in good conscience ruin it for her, if indeed I still mean anything to her at all and I doubt it."

"How do you know, Nikki, that she does not feel the same way about you?"

"You have called me Nikki twice now. What does that mean?"

"It means," she said as she put her arms around him and pulled him closer. "That I am starting to like you."

She found his mouth in the darkness, and she touched her lips to his. At first he hesitated, but then he pulled her closer, and his tongue hesitantly found hers. Her lips were soft—supple, and her tongue did a magic dance of shyness at first, and then danced more boldly as their passions began to rise. The spell was broken by the screech of an owl finding its prey nearby.

"Wow, what was that?" Roberta exclaimed.

Nick smiled at her in the darkness and ran his hand through her hair.

"It is a warning to get back before we can't see well enough to find the path" He paused and smiled again.

"Besides, we have a party to go to tonight."

Chapter 9

The Boeing 747 touched down at SeaTac airport right on time. Morgan retrieved his bags and flagged down a taxi. "SeaTac Hilton," he told the driver. By the time he checked into his room, it was already lunchtime. He went down to the restaurant and ordered something to eat, refraining from hitting on the waitress. There would be time for that later, he reminded himself. Something wasn't right about this hit, and so he put in a call to an old friend.

At the same time, Kowalski rounded up his men and briefed them. He had two marksmen and four well-trained ex-seals on the team. They loaded their equipment into a black Ford van and headed off for their destination. Ron had known Nikki for a long time, and he knew that something bad was potentially going down tonight, and so he had geared up accordingly. He watched his men load up flash charges, smoke grenades, and assault rifles. He was reassured by the men's optimism—that they were up for it! This was, after all, what they did best as trained soldiers, and they were all eager to get on with it.

Back in Washington DC, the bloodletting began shortly after the housecleaning was done—meaning the erasure of all files or other tangible evidence which might show a connection between the three soon to be dead men, and the courier bringing the attaché case into the country. It was necessary to protect the conspiracy.

Congressman Wilshire was the first to die. Shortly after leaving the golf course, a city dump truck blew through a red light and slammed broadside into the side of his Lincoln Town Car, crushing him in the process.

As Malcolm Stanovich made his way to his Fourth Avenue apartment he looked forward to taking a nap and doing nothing for the rest of the afternoon! A very lovely young brunette got into the same elevator with him and gave him a smile. His body was found there shortly thereafter, his throat slashed.

No one remembered seeing the pretty brunette after that.

CIA director Harold Toman was found later that night at his desk in the CIA building, a fatal gunshot wound to his head, and a suicide letter on the writing pad his head rested on.

The letter said, simply, "Sorry, dear."

In a city the size of Washington DC, these three deaths were unremarkable in spite of who the men were. It was just another day in a big city where murder was as common as suicide, and where traffic accidents happened just like anywhere else. CIA Deputy Director Struthers' fate was a bit more complicated, however, in that he was marked as the patsy who would take the blame for these deaths and much else, and his life was spared for that purpose. Evidence was planted to indicate that he authorized the killing of the courier to cover his tracks regarding his involvement with the Stalintsia Steel merger and his involvement with Congressman Wilshire and Malcolm Stanovich.

What these four men did not know was that more than a multimillion dollar merger was at stake, and that a much more complex conspiracy was now underway.

Department heads would receive immediate orders to transfer out, and others would be offered lucrative positions within the private sector, too lucrative to turn down if they were sane. Anybody who resisted or made noise, so much as a squeak of protest, would be dealt with in a very uncivilized way. Harold Toman had no idea when he gave the go ahead to eliminate the courier that he was signing his own death warrant too!

FBI agent Blakely had gotten home just in time to be swept off to a soccer game that afternoon with the kids. Jackie, his twelve year-old daughter, was on the soccer field, while his nine year-old son, Aaron, played some handheld video game on the bleachers next to him. Jackie moved the ball down field expertly and passed it off to one of the other girls who kicked it into the net. The parents of the home team cheered! Blakely was grinning ear-to-ear and Aaron barely looked up! Anne Marie had decided it was more important for her to get her hair and nails done than it was to attend the soccer game with them, so Bill had gladly taken the kids himself.

After the game was over Aaron had caught him at the car smoking a cigarette while waiting for Jackie to pack up her gear.

"I thought you quit smoking, Dad?" he muttered, never taking his eyes off his handheld game.

Bill handed him a five. "It's just between us, okay?"

"Cool," Aaron said, again not looking up from his game, but pocketing the money quickly. He knew his silence was going to be very well rewarded. By the time they got home, the kids were starved, and Blakely ordered a pizza for them. He then hurried upstairs to get ready for the big event.

Nick and Roberta had just returned to the house when the doorbell rang, and Nick went to answer it. A young man was at the door holding a garment bag. Nick went for his wallet, but the young man objected. "Gloria told me to tell you that everything has been handled."

Nick smiled and took the garment bag. Roberta had followed him to the door, so he handed it to her.

"Your clothes for tonight my dear! Take them upstairs and try them on—I am sure that you will look fantastic in them! Gloria does a fabulous job."

Roberta looked doubtful. "How long do I have to get ready?"

Nick went to her and kissed her gently.

"Is one hour enough?" he said, noting the time was approaching 8:00 p.m.

"We could have made love, and I still would have had enough time to get ready," she teased him.

"Really?" Nick laughed. "I didn't realize that an offer was on the table. Besides, one hour is barely enough time with a woman like you!"

Roberta stuck her tongue out at him and said,

"Yeah, yeah, yeah. All talk!" She grabbed the garment bag and turned to go to her room. Nick could barely take his eyes off of her lovely behind. He wondered if he had just missed a golden opportunity to mount and ride this lovely woman? Probably, he told himself, but then again, he wondered if he could have lasted even an hour with her. He doubted it, knowing that the years were working against him.

"How long has it been, Nick?" he wondered to himself.

Roberta made her way to the room, laid out everything on the bed, and held up the dress against her body to look at it in the mirror.

"Be back in one hour, and then see what you just passed up Mr. Petrovisky, or is it Smith tonight?" she queried sarcastically through the open door as he passed by.

"For tonight, Miss Roberta, it is Mr. Smith," he said.

"Fine," she said, closing the door behind her.

He continued down the hallway to his office, wondering if in fact he had offended her or if she was only teasing him. He shut the office door behind him and went to the computer, punched in the password, and it came to life. On the screen was a message from Boris.

"My friend," it read. "You are in deep *shit*!"

Kowalski and his men did not have far to go that evening, as the Governor's Mansion was not far from downtown Olympia to begin with. Kowalski had wished, though, that Nick had given him more time to check out the lay of the land during the daytime. The approaching darkness would make it more difficult to find good positions, but they would work with the Intel they had. The men checked out their gear and put on their night-vision goggles. Wearing total black, and wearing something new to the CIA that Nick had gotten his hands on, outerwear that shielded infrared signatures, they departed into the semi-darkness like phantoms.

The two shooters headed for their positions, one in front and one toward the back of the mansion. Each had a spotter with him equipped with night-vision goggles. The other two were experts in explosives, and they would advance on the perimeters, planting flash charges and smoke grenades to use as diversions if needed. Ron Kowalski stayed back near the van to wait for Nick's arrival. He observed everything through binoculars while he listened to the reports from his men in the field over his headphones. The fun, if it could be called that, would not start until close to midnight, which would be enough time to figure out all the security and surveillance positions held by the governor's guards. Kowalski's men settled in, anticipating a long wait! In the meanwhile Kowalski took notes on positions and how the guards moved about.

People began to arrive at eight o'clock from three different directions, but most came to the front entrance by car or by limo. Others came to the rear entrance by yacht, and a few even came by helicopter and entered at the side entrance nearest the helipads. Kowalski's men were positioned to cover all three approaches, and they were instructed to observe everything.

Kowalski's two explosive experts returned to the van after placing their devices. They began monitoring the feed coming back from the night-vision goggles worn by the two spotters accompanying the shooters. One monitored the video while the other monitored the audio, and both looked for infrared heat signatures that would indicate someone was approaching the now darkened hillside. The black Ford van was pulled well off into the trees, where it would be difficult to be spotted from the road. Kowalski looked for the thumbs up before heading to a vantage point from which he could oversee the operation. He took a rifle with him as well as his monitoring equipment.

Nick Peters noted the time, a quarter to eight, and then re-read the message on his computer screen:

"My friend, you are in deep shit."

Attached to the email was a zip file. Nick double-clicked on the icon to reveal half a dozen files there. He had spent the past forty minutes reading what he could, but he knew there was much more to absorb, and so he dialed Boris's cell number to get a synopsis of the situation. The phone rang and rang and finally it went to voice mail—not a good sign under the circumstances! Nick hung up without leaving a message. Something told him that his friend was in big trouble too. He fired off a hasty email to his

Agency. He clicked send and waited for the verification, which came back a few seconds later. With that done, he felt irritated with himself.

"What the hell have I gotten myself into? But, more importantly what have I gotten my friend Boris mixed up in?" he wondered.

Roberta called out from the hallway, and Nick looked up from what he was doing.

"Ready or not, here I come!" she exclaimed, opening the door wide. She stood there hesitantly, in the hallway—completely done up, and looking absolutely stunning!

"What do you think, Mr. Smith? Do I look good enough to attend a ball at the Governor's Mansion?"

Nick's jaw dropped slightly, not in surprise, but in awe at how lovely she looked! Somehow, in less than one hour, she had transformed herself from that of a very pretty woman—into that of a goddess! Her dark hair was upswept, with loose bangs draped evenly across her forehead. Spiraling ringlets fell gently over her temples and ears. Her only makeup was a transparent dusting of glitter around her eyes and some sort of lip-gloss.

She had on a bluish-turquoise silk gown that elegantly and stylishly draped itself over her petite figure and clung to her every curve. It accentuated her shoulders, slender waist, and modest bust line. The dress was cut to her naval, exposing her tummy with a dash of cleavage higher up. A silk cloth was tied into a knot about her hips, emphasizing a slender waist and the curve of her hips. Her sinewy back was completely exposed, the gown riding just above the roundness of her buttocks. From the waist down, it flowed freely to just above her ankles.

On her left ankle was a delicate gold anklet, and from her ears dangled matching gold earrings. Her shoes were French made high heels that matched the color of her gown.

The hue of the bluish-turquoise gown against her caramel colored skin looked eloquently beautiful!

She smiled at him brightly.

"Tell me," she said. "What do you think?" And then she twirled around, curtseying for his approval.

"Magnificent!" Nick replied. "Absolutely unbelievable! You look gorgeous!"

Pleased by his response, she approached him and put her arms around him—and pulled him closer. He smelled her skin—her pheromones, and her scent aroused him! She pressed herself against him sensually, and it was like embracing a delicate young girl—young woman! She felt warm, and soft, and pliable, in his arms. Her perfume was alluring, though he couldn't put his finger on the fragrance. After giving him a gentle kiss, she teased him.

"See what you just missed out on? I clean up well, as you can now plainly see!" She laughed.

Nick laughed too. "Roberta, you look absolutely stunning!"

"Well, big boy. You need a shower and a shave, and you only have twenty minutes yourself if you want to stay on schedule."

"Right," Nick replied. "Is there anything I can get you before I go and get ready?"

"How about a TV?"

Nick went to his desk, flipped up a panel she had not noticed before, and pushed a button. A projector dropped from the ceiling and flashed images on the wall opposite. Sound emanated from the walls, presumably from hidden speakers. He handed her a remote controller.

"Satellite television okay?"

"Perfect," she replied. "And how about a glass of Chardonnay?"

Nick pressed another button, and a wet bar appeared out of the bottom of one bookcase. "Is there anything else?"

"Your house holds many secrets, Mr. Smith."

Nick kissed her lightly, and then he went off to get ready himself.

By eight o'clock, Bill Blakely found himself chewing on another Nicorette until his mouth burned. Finally, he spat the gum out into a tissue, and tossed it into a wastebasket. He knew from experience that he could make it the next few hours without a cigarette for the benefit of maintaining the illusion that he had quit smoking—something he knew sooner or later he would have to deal with! He concentrated now on fitting into his Tuxedo.

"Honey," Ann Marie called out. "Are you ready?" He was fumbling with his tie when she walked in. "Here. Let me help you," she said.

He turned to her to let her assist, and her beauty overwhelmed him, as it always did when she was this close to him. He silently called himself a sucker! Her face brightened when she saw the expression on his face.

"You like?"

She was wearing an emerald green gown that accentuated every part of her sensual body! Her previous hints at how provocative this gown was, was indeed on target! The design of which exposed her ample breasts, and allowed their fullness to jiggle nicely near her front and near her underarms and left little of anything to the imagination! The gown poured itself over her curvy body and flowed to her ankles. Her gown was slit high up her left leg, which allowed for her easy movement, and for exposure of her creamy white thigh nearly up to her hip! It allowed a great view of her shapely legs.

Her hair was done up in a style that left her neck bare, which exposed her slender shoulders. Her new perm had left her hair curled loosely, and she looked beautifully young. Her sensuality stirred him yet disturbed him at the same time, because he felt this gown, her makeup and her hairdo weren't at all meant for him!

To her delight, he replied,

"My God! Anne Marie, what man wouldn't like?"

She had always been a heartthrob to him, and looking at her now, he could almost read the divorce papers in her eyes and his chest tightened at the thought.

"How much longer would it be before they had that talk—the inevitable talk?" he wondered. Bill Blakely stood still while she fixed his bowtie. Most years, his black tuxedo rarely got worn, but he had already worn it three times this year.

"There," she said. "You look very dapper, Mr. Blakely."

"And you, Anne Marie, will turn heads tonight."

She smiled at his remark. "Thank you. I needed that! I have been fretting about this evening for over two weeks now. You don't think I look too overdone, do you?"

"Not at all, dear. The dress looks very classy, very uptown, and chic even! Thank God all eyes will be on you tonight! You know how uncomfortable I am around these people in these situations."

"Oh just relax, Bill. They are only people."

"Yeah, the type of people with Harvard educations who have lifestyles of the rich and famous."

"Oh nonsense!" she scoffed. "You would do well for yourself to nurture a few good contacts. You never know when it might be useful to know someone with some influence. With your proclivity for seditious behavior, a good ally high up might come in handy one day!"

"Is that what it's all about Anne, meeting the right people?"

"Oh jeez, Bill! Let's not go there again tonight," she said irritably. "This is only politics. This is how politicians get campaign support—the money! They hobnob with business leaders and listen to them complain about their issues—it is called politics for a reason!"

"I know, darling. It's just that I hate these things. Sorry. I will keep my mouth shut, smile, and try to blend in the best I can—or better yet, stay out of sight!"

She gave him a peck on the cheek and said, "Good. Let's go then. The limo is waiting."

In his penthouse suite high atop the Columbia Center in Seattle, Nathan Chadwick Bentley sat in his large leather recliner sipping on a glass of Chardonnay and gloating! He had been watching the panoramic view before him, the final rays of sunlight slipping behind the Olympic Mountains to the west—and the night lights of the city of Seattle coming to life all around him! Within forty-eight hours he would finally have what he had been striving to acquire for nearly ten years now! Supremacy in his own chosen field was within his grasp! His Silicon Valley Empire was worth billions of dollars, but it was not enough for him. There was yet one more objective for him to achieve, one that he would soon have in hand within days!

He enjoyed this time of day, the quiet of it all, and daily, when he could find the time, he took in the view of the waters of the Puget Sound, and the bustling city of Seattle far below him. He watched the endless stream of cars on Interstate 5, commuters on their way home after a meaningless day at the office! Most cars held single occupants, which added tons of greenhouse gases to the atmosphere! Another fantastic opportunity for Nathan! To one day make immense wealth by recapturing that same carbon dioxide with a technology he currently owned! The gas so famously in the news these days—as being responsible for global warming! Those same morons that today pollute the atmosphere will one-day pay his company huge sums of money to clean it all up again! The idiots go to work everyday and all for what—to go home to a pitiful family life with endless bills, chronic complaining, and total dissatisfaction?

The common man amused Nathan Chadwick Bentley. One out of ten, maybe one out of twenty of them, ever achieve a modicum of happiness or sense of self-worth their whole lives! Yet, they all believe that they are in complete control—most of them do anyway. Silly fools! They are all pawns but lacked the apparition to know it. The world was ruled by men like him, men with a vision, and by women with the wiles and charms to get what they want out of life! Life was a chess game to Nathan Chadwick Bentley, won more by guile than by assertiveness, and he felt that the common man played out life more like a crapshoot, or at best, a poker game—with much, if not everything left completely to chance.

People with inherited wealth played out their lives more like a game of checkers—boringly predictable, and with limited risks! And, not to mention with undeserved flamboyance! While men like him, who could out manipulate them on the chessboard of life, and at the same time—dry up their resources under their very noses, without which they are nothing! And, then play them like the fools they really are! Like the chess pawns they should be—who are disposable! Just like the commoners on the Interstate—disposable!

Had he been a military man, Bentley would have likened himself to Napoleon, Attila the Hun, or to General Patton. His greatness would have been measured by the vastness of the lands he invaded and by the number of people he conquered! But, because he is a businessman—his measure of success is determined by his own personal wealth and by the number of crushed adversaries who fall victim to his schemes, of which there are many! Nathan Chadwick Bentley was at one time a brilliant businessman who was nevertheless narcissistic unto madness! He sipped his Chardonnay and lit a cigar. He had a very interesting evening ahead of him tonight. He was going to seduce the very lovely twenty-eight year-old wife of his new purchasing director, and do it right in front of him.

If everything worked out as planned, by Monday morning, he would own them both, as he had owned so many others before them.

He looked at his laptop and toasted it in the darkness.

"Mr. Forester," he said to himself in the darkness of his penthouse suite, "It is time for reconciliation! And for some well deserved recognition! You have played your own game of chess brilliantly, but you were right: I am a bastard! And, I will finally beat you at your own game!"

Across town, at a well-known software complex in Redmond, a group of men and women struggled frantically to understand a new computer code. Under contract by the US government to decipher it, the team of more than two-dozen software engineers had worked 24/7 in shifts, to solve the puzzle! No one knew where it came from—much less could guess at its intended use! The past thirty days of endless work had produced more questions than answers. And, indeed, their deadline to solve the puzzle had expired ten days ago! But, they were under orders from Samuel Forester himself to continue working on the puzzle. The software magnate was now funding the project on his own dime, and he upped the ante by getting personally involved with it! With his people failing to understand the new code, he had ordered a top-level meeting with the most brilliant of his colleagues. No one apparently had a clue! Finally, he dismissed everyone except Paulie, a long-time friend of his who was considered by most, a genius!

Paulie was in his mid-fifties like Forester himself. Yet he still wore the same old smelly sneakers, worn out old blue jeans, and ragged t-shirts he had worn back in the seventies—when he was a hippie! Despite all the fame and fortune he had acquired over the years—he looked more the part of a meth-amphetamine burnout than he did a brilliant scientist! His hair, which had turned gray years ago, was still a long tangled mess, still had the same stupid pony-tail—and, he looked better suited making *meth* in meth-lab behind a double-wide trailer somewhere on the Peninsula, than he did with cracking computer code in Redmond—in a computer lab as a brilliant scientist, which he was!

He still carried a backpack full of Snickers Bars and M&M Chocolate Covered Peanuts—and he preferred diet Coke to coffee!

He was truly a throwback to an era that was now long gone! But his brilliance made him a very valuable asset to *CodeSource*, and his allegiance to Samuel Forrester was unquestionable.

"Tell me, Paulie. What do you really think about this riddle?" Sam asked him.

Paulie sat there for a moment, and then rummaged in his backpack and produced two Snickers bars.

"Want one, boss?"

Sam declined and Paulie shrugged, tearing off the wrapper of a candy bar, and taking a large bite while he pondered the question.

"So, what do you think, Paulie?"

After chewing a moment more, he replied,

"Ever try to play a video cassette recorded in PAL format on a US video player made for NTSC?" PAL was a European video format. It was a hardware format that did not work in American electronics, which were programmed for NTSC, and therefore the screen looked like snow when trying to view it.

"Of course I have. So are you saying that we cannot decipher the code because of our hardware limitations?"

"Not exactly, Sam."

"Well then, what exactly do you mean?"

"Conventional computer code is obviously written in two digits, 0 and 1, and operates in a linear bit path. This new code is written in an algorithmic format."

"What? Are you crazy?"

Paulie smiled, took another bite from his candy bar, and continued, "Of course it still utilizes digital technology, the same 0 and 1 binary format, but if you look at the clusters, they are exponential. We can't make sense of it because our bit paths are linear: 8, 16, 32, 64 and so on. Our computer chips cannot support an exponential bit path, and therefore, we cannot interpret the code."

"So what are you suggesting?" Sam queried.

"I am suggesting Sam, that someone has developed a new computer chip, and that this computer code was meant to drive it."

"How do we crack it?"

"We don't, not until you find the right chip, and learn its architecture."

"I haven't read anything in any journals about any algorithmic chip technology being anything but theoretical. Your theory about this code sounds pretty farfetched, Paulie."

Paulie shrugged. "Rumor had it a few years back that the Russians were working on something that would resemble such technology. It was a perfect way to encrypt all of their top-secret messages. Without the right chip, the code was useless."

"Other than encryption, what other uses are there for such technology, Paulie?"

Paulie actually brightened at the thought, and grinned. "In theory, this technology would revolutionize computers worldwide. An exponential bit path would speed up processors exponentially. Software could be much simpler in architecture, and software code could become more self-intuitive, much like how the human brain works."

"What do you mean, self-intuitive like the human brain?" Sam asked.

"The human brain can interpret inflection and emotion, but a computer can't. How many times has the US government tried to come up with a software package to translate foreign languages?" Paulie chuckled in his weird way. "Someone says *'f—you!'* but are they saying you should have sex with them or that you should take your silliness someplace else—and leave said speaker alone? How about sarcasm, innuendo, anecdotes, metaphors, symbolism, parody, analogy? Needless to say, the list can go on and on, can't it? And in each culture, and in each language, there are even more subtleties! No software package could possibly be written to encompass inflection or emotion because there are too many variables, because the possibilities are exponential!"

"The human brain," he went on with considerable enthusiasm, "can interpret subtleties! Why? Because it is not binary! When we remember some event, that event is not recorded in memory like on some recorded videotape! Instead, it is reconstructed in a nanosecond—from bits and pieces of stored information coming in from all sectors of the brain at once! An exponential bit path! Some of the information we receive is emotional imagery, and some of it is sensory, but it all happens instantaneously! An exponential chip could conceivably allow for the same sort of intuitive thought processes that people have."

"Impossible!" Sam said.

"Not really Sam," Paulie replied. "What makes computers so amazing is their ability to process streams of digital data endlessly—and at the speed of light! However, why can't a computer process a single human thought—when the human brain processes thoughts easily? It does so by selecting fragments of stored images, sounds, smells, and feelings, all of which are not in a binary format, or we couldn't do anything without pausing to think about it. Instead, we process thoughts like a shotgun shell explodes! All thoughts come to us at once! Some thoughts come in bits and pieces, and others in huge chunks! The brain somehow sifts through it all, and filters out what is not needed—or what is inappropriate! How else could an athlete possibly process all the information necessary to execute the command to swing at a baseball coming at him at ninety miles per hour and still judge whether it is high, low, inside, or outside unless all the garbage was filtered out first? "We say that great hitters use intuition to swing the bat, but in reality, these athletes brains are just filtering out all the crap quickly—and then translating synaptic impulses into bodily movements more efficiently than the rest of us! The human brain can accept all inputs simultaneously, filter out the garbage, and make a calculation to drive a thousand outputs, which allows the athlete to take a swing."

"Again, the human brain is not linear—it is exponential! Love, hate, fear, revenge, pain and pleasure are all exponential elements measured in degrees. A computer can process 24/7, but it cannot think. If someone came up with a way to process digital data in a nonlinear way, machines might be able to think."

"Hello R2-D2!"

He laughed. "Oh, and one more thing, Sam. The rumor was that the Russians couldn't control this new technology, so they dismantled it years ago."

As Samuel Forester left the building that night after eight o'clock, he was consumed by the possibility that Paulie was onto something. Intuitive software and exponential hardware—how would it work? But, if Paulie was correct and this new code was what they were confronted with in the lab, then the secret could only be unraveled if this new chip was found. As he headed home in his chopper to prepare for the governor's party, he made a call.

Chapter 10

Nick Peters jumped into the shower and was out again in just a few minutes. He put on his tuxedo, looked at his watch, and reappeared in his office within a few minutes after that.

"That was quick," Roberta said.

Nick smiled. "So, are you up for this? It is a pretty stuffy affair, all hoity-toity and the like, and so I would understand—if you decided to back out! I can go it alone you know."

Roberta looked at him with irritation—no, with more than just irritation! "You have me get all done up to go to a ball at the Governor's Mansion, and now you the *balls* to ask me if I am up for it or *not*?"

"It's not really a ball, but you're right! It was a stupid question! Then if you are ready, let's go!" he replied enthusiastically as he blushed in embarrassment.

She took his hand, and together they went down the hallway and headed down the stairs.

"You look great Nikki," she said to him. "I feel like I am in a spy thriller: attending a ball all dressed up and being escorted there by this very handsome and interesting *James-Bond* type of Secret Agent Man! You definitely know how to impress a woman!"

Nick laughed. "It's not a ball, Roberta, but a political dinner party."

"Whatever!" she said airily, acting as if still caught up in a girlhood memory of fantasizing about attending a magnificent and prominent event she preferred to refer to as a *ball*—no matter what he called it!

At the bottom of the stairs, he turned to her and pulled her up close. She looked into his eyes as he wrapped his arms around her, and he hesitated for the briefest of moments, and then he kissed her passionately! She did not resist him, but instead she melted into him—wishing actually, that he would take her back upstairs! Take her, and throw her down on those satin sheets she had slept in the night before! Take her and engulf her, and embrace her! She was becoming quite turned on by him—and it wouldn't have taken much on his part, if he wanted to—to have her! Once again, they both felt their passions rise momentarily, but before any harm was done, they broke away from one another. They both knew that, if love were to happen, it would not be tonight!

They proceeded to the garage, and Nick led her to the red Ferrari. "I think that tonight we will have some fun," he said as he opened the passenger door for her. "Let's take the sports car!"

To his surprise, she said, "Well, if we are having some fun tonight, can I drive?"

Her request caught him off guard. "If you can handle a five speed stick and a two-hundred horsepower engine with only manual steering—be my guest," he replied, tossing her the keys.

She smiled back at him as she caught the keys.

"My daddy taught me a few things!" She left him at the passenger door while quickly making her way to the other side of the car—or as quickly as her high heels would allow her to! She then got in, and very carefully arranged her dress so as not to catch it on anything. She examined the dash for a moment, found the ignition, tested a few buttons, and adjusted her seat and mirrors. She put on her seatbelt, and fired up the engine.

She smiled, listening to the tone of the exhaust, as if the sound brought back some special memories for her! She then revved it up and examined the shift pattern. She found the headlamps, turned them on, pulled the stick over and found reverse, and eased out on the clutch. She cautiously pulled the car out of the open garage.

"Where is the garage door opener?" she asked.

"Over the visor," Nick pointed.

She found it, pressed the button, and the garage door closed after them. "You said that we can have some fun tonight, right?"

Nick was impressed with her quick adaptation to the car's controls, especially with the fact that she hit reverse the first try without so much as a single grinding noise from the *tranny*. He laughed out loud.

"Of course. By all means, Roberta—tonight let's have some fun!"

She looked at him and winked.

"Nice car, Nikki!"

And then, without warning, she revved the engine up and dropped the clutch, burning rubber in reverse, while she cut the wheel hard to her right. Then she slammed on the brakes, and without losing any momentum, spun the car around left and found first gear. She dropped the clutch again, doing a burnout in the driveway, and hit forty before reaching the end of the drive. Once on the road, she ran the car through the gears with the throttle wide open, hitting nearly a hundred miles per hour before having to brake hard at the end of the lane. Nick was still fumbling with his seatbelt as the Ferrari idled at the stop sign.

"Which way, Nick?"

"Left, Roberta, go left," he said, somewhat nervously.

This time, she eased out on the clutch and brought the car up to a sensible speed, shifting through the gears nicely.

"How fast can this puppy go, Nick?"

Nick, relieved that she was now handling the car sensibly, said, "About one-sixty. Where did you learn to drive like that, Roberta?"

Roberta smiled. "My daddy taught me! He used to race modified stockcars on the weekends. Whenever he could, he would let me out on the track for practice laps, and then one summer, about halfway through the season, he was on a winning streak and had just enough points racked up to reach the finals—when he hit the wall! Unfortunately, he sprained his wrist! And, like you just pointed out to me Nikki, back then cars didn't have power steering—much less racecars having any assist at all! I told him that I would take his place for the next few weekends, until his wrist healed up enough for him to drive again."

She laughed. "My God! How we argued about that one for the next two days. The third day he woke me up at five in the morning. I was only nineteen years old at the time, and on summer break." She laughed.

Highway 101 was a moderately traveled two-lane blacktop road with a speed limit of sixty-five, and at eight-twenty, the traffic was pretty light. Roberta maintained the speed limit except when passing an occasional slower vehicle. When she did, she down shifted smoothly and poured on the gas, squealing with delight as she felt the Ferrari accelerate. Once past the vehicle, she would then steer back into her own lane and resume the speed limit.

"Where did you get the car, Nikki? What is it, a '72?"

"No," Nick replied. "It's a '68. I told you, I once raced for Ferrari. Before I crashed—and my life changed forever, I sent one home. I thought it might be a good car for picking up chicks with."

"Was it?"

"I don't know. I never made it home! My father kept it in his garage, waiting for me to come back, but of course I never did! Both he and my mom passed away before I could. Mr. Smith claimed it on my behalf and put it in storage. Many years later, he had it restored for me. To my surprise, it was in his garage after he left the house to me. There was a note on the dash."

Roberta looked at Nick briefly and then back at the road, pressed on the accelerator, and passed another car.

"I'm sorry," she shouted over the wind and driving past seventy miles per hour.

It was a warm summer night, and the convertible top was down, the wind tousling her hair—but not badly! "I am sorry about your parents, Nikki. It must have been horrible for you to lose them when you were out of the country."

"They had a good life together, so there is nothing to be sorry about."

"But you weren't able to be with them at the end, which must have saddened you some."

"My parents were very proud of me for what I was doing, and they understood. Mr. Smith made sure of that."

"Do you miss them?"

"I miss them all, Roberta. I miss my mother, my father, Mr. Smith, and I miss what I could have had with Tatyana and Natasha—if things had been different! I miss it all!"

Roberta drove in silence for a moment as she thought to herself, "What kind of man can give up everything he loves and cherishes, and yet still appear to be normal?"

"What did the note say?" she asked.

"The note was from my father," Nick replied, smiling at the memory. "He wanted to know why I needed five forward gears when the car had only two doors instead of the standard four. He thought that my car was impractical!" Nick laughed, thinking about his dad and what he would have said to him in person had he made it back. His father knew exactly why a two-seater! It was a chick magnet!

"That was it?"

Nick smiled. "No, there was more. He said that Mom wanted me to come home, but Dad told me that I was doing an important job and not to worry about either of them. He said they both wanted me not to worry, and that they were very proud of what I was doing. I guess they never got around to mailing it. The note was stuffed in the glove box."

"Oh, Nikki," Roberta said tearfully, reaching over and touching his hand. "I can't even imagine how you felt when you read that note."

"It's okay, Roberta. My parents knew what I was doing, and they understood the need for the work I did. They were forced to leave their own homeland or be killed. My going back there to help others get out, and more importantly, to understand my own heritage and theirs, was enough for them. They only hoped I would meet a girl and have my own family."

Roberta downshifted and hit the gas to pass another slower moving vehicle.

"But you left her behind too!" she said, not looking at him.

"We all make mistakes, Roberta."

"You have big regrets then?"

"Yes," Nick replied. "I already told you that. I have many regrets."

"Was it all worth it?"

"It depends on how you quantify 'it.' Life is like a poker game: people are dealt the cards they have to play, and sometimes the cards are good and sometimes the cards are bad—usually they are bad! It's not so much if you win or lose, but instead how you play the cards you are dealt. There is only one winner in a poker game, but there are many winners in life, so the analogy breaks down here. The ones who can stay in the game until the very end, and still have something left over, are the real winners in their own right. The ones who walk away with all the chips may just be the lucky ones, the same ones that have nothing tomorrow! So, was it all worth it? I am still in the game, and I am still playing the cards that are being dealt to me. So I guess the answer is, I don't know yet!"

The evening was much warmer than the night before—but the floor heat coming from the car vents was welcome. The stars overhead were brilliant to behold, and made her heart skip a beat when she looked up at them. Everything was dark on this side of the water. But, as they approached the city of Olympia, the stars gradually faded away as the city lights preempted their brightness.

"What happened then?" Nick asked.

"I'm sorry, Nick. I lost my train of thought," Roberta replied. She was focused on what kind of life Nick had led—and the stars above, and was only pulled back to the moment by his voice.

"What happened when your father woke you up at five o'clock in the morning?"

"Oh," she continued, smiling at the memory. "He dragged my butt out onto the race track, suited me up the best he could—because he didn't have a driving suit small enough to fit me! He duct-taped my ankles and wrists tight in a fireproof suit that was way too big for me, and handed me a new helmet! A helmet he had just purchased the day before! Daddy said, 'Let's see what you got, girl.' He then strapped me into his car and got in himself to ride shotgun with me!

"First, he told me, we'd do a couple of easy laps and learn the track a little. Then when I got the feel of the car and the track, he said to come out of turn four on the third lap, and give it everything I had!"

"Oh God, Nikki! I was so nervous!" she said looking at him with earnest! "I had done laps before in my daddy's racecar. He had even taken me as a passenger in it many times before—and let it rip! But, I had never done it by myself before! Of course, he had been racing all his life—and it was easy for him! I had only done it when there were no other cars on the track, and I never had to push the limits on my own before! I was scared. I think my daddy wanted me to be scared—he was even willing to go into the wall with me! My daddy just wanted to convince me that my idea of driving in his place was crazy!"

"A couple of his buddies were there with him, shaking their heads in disbelief. Byron, my daddy's mechanic, put just enough fuel in the car to make a few laps around—just in case we did crash! He stuck his head through the window and said, 'Just four laps, Roberta! The last lap will be very fast because there won't be any fuel in the tank to make a fifth, though I guess your dad's fat ass will make up for the difference in weight? So maybe it won't be as fast as it could be!'

"'Fat ass, hell!' my father scoffed at him, and then he said, 'Go away Byron!'"

"Bryon winked at me, told me I could do it! He told me to stay low. I also remember he told me that turn two was bad because the tarmac was slick, and that most inexperienced drivers lost it on turn two by over-steering! So, I needed to be prepared to drift high."

"The track was a mile long," she said to Nick—remembering that day as if it were yesterday. "And, a very good lap time was in the 22-25 second range! My first lap, I turned a thirty-two, and the second lap I was clocked at twenty-eight. Coming out of the fourth turn on my third lap, my daddy looked at me but said nothing! I knew what he was expecting from me, so I put it to the floor!"

"I hit turn one at one hundred and eighty miles an hour, stood on the brakes, downshifted, and poured on the gas again just like I had seen him do. I dropped as low as I could, and caught the apron on turn two at one-sixty! Byron was right—the tarmac was slick! I felt the rear end squirm! So, I feathered the throttle back and let it drift high—counter steering as it drifted! I nearly touched the wall as I came out of turn two! Then, I dropped down a gear again, and opened that bastard up! I tagged top gear for just a second before I had to stand on the brakes for turn three, and again I took the car low, found the right gear, and poured it on again, aiming low but drifting high. I knew that it didn't matter where I ended up coming out of turn four, high or low, so I took the next gear, probably before I should have, and I nearly kissed the wall in the process, but I made it through and I crossed the finish line with a twenty-two second time! The car ran out of fuel halfway around on the last cool-down lap, so we coasted back to the pits in neutral."

"Wow," Nick replied. "Quite a story! So did your father let you drive for him?"

Roberta smiled thinking back on it. "He did, but not until we spent every day at the track learning maneuvers, mostly recovering from spinouts and things like that."

"Well that explains the little episode in my driveway, and by the way, nicely done!"

She beamed. "Thanks. I was showing off! I am glad you didn't get angry with me."

"So how did you two finish the season that year?"

"Oh my daddy made it to the finals that year and took fifth place! It was his last year in racing, and he was so proud of me for keeping him in the running! He wanted me to finish the season off for him, but it was his season—his last season! I insisted that he have his own season, seeing as it was his last! I wanted him to finish it."

"And how did you do? Did you like racing?"

"Oh Nikki, I loved the machines, the smell and the sound of the engines.

I loved the power! But, racing was not for me! I wasn't about to give up who I was to compete against a bunch of ego-driven gear heads—bound for glory at any cost! I raced for my father, and for the fun of it! I have to admit—it was a great experience! I did well enough to keep him in the points, but when he was ready to drive again, I just wanted to see him win! It was his thunder—his last season! I was just so proud to be part of it. It was the highlight of my life!"

Nick couldn't say anything. He had never heard a story like this one before, about the love of a young girl for her dad. "It sounds like you are very close to your father."

Her lips quivered a little. "Yes," she said softly.

They were now entering Olympia, and Nick directed her onto a freeway ramp. "We exit at 105A, and I should drive from there. There will be a BP Station just off the ramp, and we can switch." She nodded and looked for the exit. "Why didn't you go to your father when you wanted out of whatever you were running from last night?" Nick asked.

She looked at him oddly, and then glared at him. "Because the man I was leaving would have found me there, and because I didn't want to bring my father any more grief! Because, I need to get my life together first! And, because I didn't know what to say to my dad if I did show up on his doorstep."

Nick was silent for a moment, and then said, "Tell me about this man you are running from."

She rolled her eyes and laughed. "He is a loser, just like my father warned me he was! I got involved with him in the first place just like any girl gets involved with the wrong guy! We met, we dated, and we had a few good times together. I was ready for a relationship, ready to have a family, and he said all the right things! It was all bullshit of course, but how could I have known?"

"My father knew something wasn't right, and he warned me: 'Daughter, this man is using you, and you can do much better for yourself than picking a man like him!' Of course, I didn't believe my father! Instead I believed all the lies and the *BS* that this guy fed me."

"So, what's his name? Tell me about him."

"Why should I tell you anything of the sort?"

Nick shrugged. "It doesn't matter. Our exit is coming up."

She caught the exit ramp, spotted the BP Station, and pulled into the parking lot. "We don't need gas, Nick. Will you tell me what I am about to get into here, or what *we* are getting into?"

Nick nodded. "Okay. You remember that I told you that I took on an assignment for a friend, someone I owed a favor to?"

She nodded.

"It was supposed to be a simple pick-up and drop-off! But, with all the police and FBI involved, it obviously isn't! I need to find out why the cops are in this—I need to find out why I was misled! There is something in a briefcase that I am delivering that has gotten a very good friend of mine in trouble because I solicited his help to find out what it is! I don't know what the hell I am carrying—much less why the Feds are all up in arms about it! All I know for certain is that I have been set up."

"By your friend?"

"It looks that way."

"What does this have to do with a *Ball* at the Governor's Mansion?"

"It's a political fund raiser, Roberta. It's not a *Ball!*"

"Whatever!" she looked irritated. "Just answer the question please!"

"My company did a little research on my behalf. I wanted to know which agency was behind the roadblock that put me on the run. They came back with the name of an FBI agent running lead on this investigation. His name is Bill Blakely! I wanted to talk to him to find out what he knows—before deciding what my options are. If I can, I want to walk away from all of this! But first! I need to know what I am walking away from? Mainly to know how to do it cleanly!"

"And what does this have to do with you escorting me to a *Ball* tonight?"

Nick knew by now that Roberta was teasing him by continually calling this event a *Ball*, and he smiled. "My inquiries turned up a guest list for those attending the *Ball* at the Governor's Mansion tonight. Guess whose name was on the list?"

"Bill Blakely's?"

"Right," Nick replied.

"But Nikki," Roberta objected. "How could you have known all this? These people came to your house with all these clothes well before noon today. How could you have known all this before then?"

Nick produced a small white envelope from the inside breast pocket of his tuxedo and handed it to her. While she read the invitation, he explained. "Mr. Smith was very active in politics. He has donated a great deal of money to various groups over the years, and he gets these invitations all the time. It turns out that Blakely's wife is active in politics too, fundraising anyway! Which is why they will be here tonight! I figure, considering her ambitions, that Blakely himself won't be in a position to create a ruckus if I approach him in public. It is just coincidental that it worked out this way, but here we are."

"And your operatives at the Smith Foundation figured this all out before I awoke?"

Nick shook his head and replied, "No, but by midmorning they had! I called it all in the night before and my staff works in shifts 24/7."

"So, you are getting rid of whatever it is that you were supposed to deliver that has the FBI after you?"

"Not exactly," Nick answered. "I feel compelled to know what it is, first.

I might just hand it over to the authorities after all. But, sometimes it is hard to tell the good guys from the bad guys! The acronyms associated with their names may not be good indicators of which they are. So, I am not sure just yet how to play out this hand."

"Nikki, are you carrying?"

"What do you mean?"

"Are you armed?"

He leaned over and kissed her. "No Roberta, I don't carry weapons! But, like I said, I have some backup. I am not walking into some situation from which I can't extricate myself from."

"What do you mean?"

"Roberta, I am not a stupid man! I do not look into the eye of the tiger without being prepared for the possibility of a confrontation. You and I will walk into the Governor's Mansion through the front door—like everyone else invited to this shindig will. There will be music and dancing, cocktails, and hors d'oeuvres. We will dance, and we will pretend that we are just like all the others here—people interested in who will be elected next! But instead, we will be looking for Bill Blakely! There will be a team of my men observing everything we do from a distance. And, if things get dicey, they will intervene. Like I said, we are not walking into this thing without some way out— if things do go south!"

"What do you mean intervene?" Roberta replied.

"If anyone tries to apprehend or harm us, they will retrieve us. The team is in position, and they will be watching us at a distance. I have something for you to put on."

"What is it?" she said hesitantly.

"A microphone," Nick replied, and he fastened a diamond necklace with a ruby pendant around her neck. "My people will be able to hear everything that is going on. If they need to come in and get us, they will! Your ear rings double as receivers."

Morgan had arrived at the Governor's Mansion shortly before nine o'clock, and if the courier showed up, his instructions were clear! As he entered the mansion under the name of Christopher Talmer of Global Enterprises, a man named Andrew Butler approached him. Andrew extended his hand to formally introduce himself. Morgan instead, graciously blew him off and went about his business.

The limo carrying Bill and Anne Marie arrived a short while later. The limo driver opened the door for the two of them, and the driver extended his hand to help Anne Marie out. It was a magnificent late-summer night with brilliant stars aloft—and temperatures still in the high seventies. There was just the slightest breeze, and the evening was glorious for just this sort of event! Anne Marie stepped out of the limo and beamed as she took in her surroundings! She noted that everything was just perfect! The night, the weather, and especially the atmosphere, which reeked of money and power played right into her expectations for the event.

The Governor's Mansion was built in 1802, and the Georgian-style mansion had four floors to it—containing twenty-six rooms, and occupying twenty six thousand square feet. Located just west of the legislative building, which was renowned for its Washington DC style architecture and dome, the mansion overlooked Capitol Lake and the Olympic Mountains. Its red fired-brick exterior, white wood trim, ornate French windows, and sturdy hand-carved Georgian columns and balconies had been the luxurious location for many gatherings over the decades. Too small to accommodate a modern-day inaugural ball, the mansion nevertheless served a more impressive function, as a place for the state's leader to entertain and to listen to the needs of the special supporters, the ones that needed to be listened to if the money was to be there for re-election!

Anne Marie grabbed Bill by the arm and led him up the brick pathway to the pillared entrance. She handed her invitation to the sentries there, and then they stepped through a magnetometer that had been erected off to the side, which was immediately set off by her jewelry. Stepping aside graciously, she allowed the guards to buzz her briefly with their wands. Bill handed his badge and gun to a guard before stepping through the machine himself. They were both returned to him on the other side. He had already been cleared by security in advance to carry his weapon, and this fact was noted on the guest list.

Entering the foyer, they were greeted by a gentleman who called out their names, a formality dating back to the aristocracies of Europe! After their names were announced, they entered the main ballroom. No one really paid any attention to the announcement except for the waiters, who approached with silver trays brimming with champagne and hors d'oeuvres.

Anne Marie took a glass of champagne and Bill declined, asking instead where he might get a glass of *Ginger Ale*.

"At the bar, sir." The waiter pointed. Bill thanked him, making a mental note of the location.

Anne Marie said, "Bill, look at the French Empire pier tables. Chas Lannuier built them in the early eighteen hundreds, and there are only a few of them left in existence!" Anne Marie was in her element tonight. She had been dreaming of being here—who knows for how long? Probably ever since she was conceived! And she had done her research about the Governor's abode well in advance!

Before Bill could comment, another woman exclaimed from the stairs above them, "Anne Marie! It is so good that you came tonight!" she bubbled. "The Governor and Harry Trundle are up in the Library. Is this your husband Bill?" she asked approaching them both.

The woman was Harry Trundle's personal secretary, LouAnn Caulder, a woman in her early forties and somewhat anorexic looking. She was dressed in a gray business suit, and obviously not a part of the party crowd tonight. Bill shook her hand.

"If you don't mind Bill, the governor and Mr. Trundle were hoping to talk with Anne Marie before the festivities begin. May I steal her away from you?"

Bill smiled and replied, "Perfect timing, Ms. Caulder. The hors d'oeuvres have caught my eye anyway." He laughed as if it were a coincidence and smiled, "Bring her back to me when the music begins."

LouAnn laughed too, and touched his shoulder flirtatiously. "We won't keep her for long, Bill."

"Anne Marie," she said as she turned away from Bill. "You look wonderful. I like your dress—it suits you! Sadly, I don't have your figure, and I could do nothing for a dress like that." She chatted aimlessly, and Bill thanked the stars that she and his wife were now walking away. Together, the two women went up the terraced stairs to the library, and Bill headed for the back veranda to have a discrete smoke. Anne Marie, preoccupied with being charming, barely gave him a glance as he made his way outside.

Nick pulled the Ferrari onto the oval drive of the Governor's Mansion, and Roberta's eyes grew wide.

"My God, Nikki. Is this how the rich and famous people live?"

Handing his keys over to the parking attendant, he smiled.

"Yes, Roberta, it is!" When the parking attendant handed him a numbered tag to collect his car with, he handed the tag to Roberta. "Your car keys, my dear."

Kowalski spotted the Ferrari as soon as it pulled onto the circular drive. He was positioned in the shadows of a knoll that overlooked the mansion. The hill was blanketed with pine trees and bushes, which offered good cover. At nearly two hundred yards out though, it would take a real marksman to take anyone down! He queried his men over the radio.

"Do you have him?"

"Roger that. Target in sight."

"He and his woman get out alive tonight, right? Does everyone understand?"

His radio crackled. The response came back after a pause. "We can see everything."

Samuel Forester's helicopter landed on the pad near the back gardens. Sam jumped out and was escorted into the Mansion by two armed bodyguards.

A magnificent yacht dropped anchor a hundred yards offshore and hailed a water shuttle over the radio. Immediately, a launch disembarked from the Governor's landing to fetch Nathan Chadwick Bentley, and his entourage of six. Innocent Angela and Neal Courtney were with him. As a group, they all climbed the numerous stairs to get to the Governor's Mansion from the landing. Nathan deliberately allowed Angela and Neal to lead the way so he could lust over her lovely rounded posterior. Angela, who was wearing the most elegant slinky black evening gown, left little for Bentley's imagination—other than to want her that much more! Her young round ass aroused him intensely! But, he pretended not to notice, talking all the while to the entire entourage.

As they passed through the metal detectors, Nick took Roberta by the arm. "We will be announced as Mr. Smith and guest," he whispered into her ear, and she nodded. Roberta walked into the Great Room with Nick firmly holding onto her arm and she wondered what to say if anybody queried her about who she was?

"Don't be nervous," Nick whispered. "It is sufficient that you are devastatingly beautiful! Everyone will simply think that I hired you to be my escort—because that is what men my age do, men who have too much money! No one will challenge you."

"You won't leave me alone, will you Nikki?"

He pecked her on the cheek and replied, "Perhaps for a few minutes, but do not worry about it! I will leave you in good hands, and only then if it is necessary."

"Ah Mr. Smith," a gregarious voice resounded from his left. Nick turned to see who it was. "For ten years now you have managed to avoid attending any of our functions! Yet, your organization has so generously supported us each and every year! The Democratic Party welcomes you at long last," the man said jovially, proffering his hand, and the two men shook.

"My name is Andrew Butler, Director of Public Relations! And who is your charming companion?"

Andrew was a portly yet handsome man who stood a good six foot two, possibly even more. He had dark black hair and a full beard that he kept impeccably trimmed, and he possessed a stately charm about him. He must have been in his mid-forties, Nick thought, judging from the slight patch of gray breaking through on his temples. His brown eyes were crystal clear, and his broad smile produced perfectly straightened, and brilliant white teeth. Reaching to take his hand, Nick noted that his fingers were manicured and that he had a firm grip.

Nick smiled and replied, "This is Roberta Sanchez, the manager of World Trust Financial, a subsidiary of World Trade. She handles all of our financial matters involving currency exchanges and deposits. I thought that tonight would be a good opportunity for her to see some of the people who shape our politics firsthand."

Roberta's eyes opened wide upon hearing this introduction.

"Excellent, Mr. Smith. I would be happy to show you both around. Is there anyone in particular you would like to meet here tonight?"

"Actually yes," Nick replied. "There is someone I am very interested talking with! His name is Bill Blakely. I believe his wife Anne Marie is on your staff?"

Andrew's eyebrows lifted a little. "Yes, actually she is. I believe that there will be an announcement made by Governor Talbot tonight that might involve Anne Marie. However, her husband has nothing to do at all with our political party! I believe he is a cop of some sort, and not at all active on the political front."

"Of course Andrew, all the more reason I want to talk to him," Nick replied cordially. "Miss Sanchez is the one who is here to meet the movers and shakers! I want to speak with Mr. Blakely because of some professional concerns. I have some staffing needs I think he might be able to help me with. Can you point him out to me?"

"Yes, of course. In fact, I will seek him out myself and bring him over to you. Now, what about your support for the party this year—can we still count on it?"

Nick smiled and put his arm across Andrew's shoulder. "Andrew," he said, speaking calmly. "I like a man who gets to the point quickly! Yes, you can count on World Trade for our usual contribution this year. Actually, it is a paltry contribution! And, to be frank with you Andrew—Roberta is recommending that we divert more money to the opposition party. This is why I brought her here tonight! I prefer to stay anonymous when it comes to politics, as you know already! Very soon Roberta will be determining where my company throws its financial support. If you want more money going into the party's coffers, she is the one to win over, not me."

"Well, if that is the case, then later I will personally take Ms. Sanchez around and introduce her to some very interesting people. I will be back shortly with your Mr. Blakely. Please enjoy your surroundings, and feel free to mingle. There will be quite a few very important people here tonight, and I am sure that you will find an interesting conversation or two."

"Thank you Andrew," Nick replied.

As Andrew walked away, Roberta pulled on Nick's arm angrily. "Why the hell did you tell him that? What if someone asks me something about this job?"

Nick chuckled. "Tell them the truth, that it is a recent appointment and you haven't had enough time in the position yet to talk about it."

"And where is there any truth to that?"

"I do have an opening at World Trust Financial—a subsidiary of World Trade. And, you do have a Master's Degree in Economics and Finance, don't you? If you accept the position, I believe my suggested response would be a true statement. Do you agree?"

Roberta's jaw dropped. "How do you know that I have any degree?" She felt her knees get weak and she looked for a chair to sink into. There was a vacant eighteenth century couch near the magnificent French windows overlooking the front gardens, and she made her way over to it. Nick brought her a glass of ice water from one of the dining tables nearby, and sat down beside her.

"Here," he said. "Drink this."

"Sorry," she apologized as she took a sip. "Suddenly, I felt lightheaded! Are you offering me a job, or is this just part of our cover for tonight?"

"Have you ever been to Switzerland?"

She shook her head. "If you ran a background check on me, you would know that I haven't. Did you?"

Nick shrugged. "It seemed like a prudent thing to do considering that you were in my care. So, I emailed your fingerprints to my headquarters last night. They were able to come back with a great deal of information on you."

She punched him in the shoulder and hissed in his direction. "And where did you get my fingerprints from?"

"Your tea glass, off course."

"But, I watched you rinse it and put it in the dishwasher," she replied, glaring at him.

Nick shrugged. "It's impressive that you notice such things! Is there some reason you would?" Nick smiled pleasantly, waiting for her answer.

Roberta continued to glare at him but said nothing.

Nick went on. "You graduated from the University of Washington at twenty-four years old with a law degree, took the bar exam the following year, and received your license. However, you got involved romantically with your law professor, and as a result, he divorced his wife of twenty-some-years and married you shortly thereafter. Instead of pursuing law for whatever reason, you went back to school and took another degree, two in fact, in finance and economics! And by age twenty-eight, you held a master's degree in both! Finally, you took a mid-six figure job with Sea-First Bank, divorced a year later, and then disappeared off the face of the planet. There hasn't been any IRS filings, no credit card purchases, and no traceable transactions in your name now for over a year. Is this information accurate?"

Roberta stared back at him, not knowing if she should be angry with him or not. "You knew all this about me, and yet you said nothing to me about it? And now you ask me if the information is correct?"

"I only got the report back early this evening—while you were getting ready for tonight's activities. I found the information interesting, but not altogether revealing. All the information we recovered about you is in the public domain, and there was nothing devious done beyond obtaining your fingerprints. In my business, finding out things like marital status and degrees earned is called a surface check—there was no invasion into your private life."

"I need a cigarette," she replied, knowing full well that what he had just said was completely true. She still felt that her privacy had been violated. What kind of man looks into such things without telling you?

Nick followed her out onto the veranda. She struggled to find her cigarettes, and when she did find her pack, she could not find her lighter. Nick held out his own and peered into her eyes as she lit her cigarette. Her expression softened a smidge, and she turned away from him to look out into the darkness.

"I am not sure what to think about you now, Mr. Smith," she said angrily. "You are right, of course. There was nothing you discovered about me that can't be found in public records! But, the fact that you even looked into my background makes me feel violated anyway."

"Was it wrong for me to run a background check on you under the circumstances? And what about the fact that you looked through my house, through my things, in my absence?"

She thought about it for a moment, and then she grinned sheepishly. "Yeah, well I am a woman! Such behavior is expected—from a woman!" Then she laughed after hearing her own excuse. "It's just not fair! I spent two hours looking around your house, and I come up with nothing! You— you pick up a phone or email someone, and before the day is out, you know my whole life!"

"Roberta." Nick smiled. "You could have hired a private detective and spent thousands of dollars trying to figure out who I am, and the search would have yielded nothing! According to the public record, I don't exist! I died in 1978. You found the only tangible evidence in existence that Nicholas Dimeitry Petrovisky ever existed, the photo album, and now you know about the weapons room too. Did I get angry with you about your own background check on me?"

She was silent for a moment and walked to the railing on the veranda thinking about it. She took a puff from her cigarette and blew the smoke skyward. The party was very noisy inside, but out here, the night was peaceful and romantic. She didn't want to be angry with him, not tonight. Nick was a man of many mysteries, and he intrigued her immensely. Out here, the conversations and the laughter from the party inside, were merely soft murmurs wafting through the night air along with the night sounds of crickets and frogs. It brought back youthful memories of seemingly endless summer nights that were carefree and lazy, and she wondered how she had managed to let her life become so twisted and chaotic? It all seemed to overwhelm her momentarily, and now that she was standing on the veranda of the Governor's Mansion—dressed to kill, with a man she had only met just twenty-four hours before, she was not sure what it all meant. She also wasn't sure if she liked being here with Nick or not—everything seemed simply silly.

"What am I doing here, Nikki?" she asked.

"Besides looking beautiful?" Nick replied.

She smiled and nodded, replying delicately, "Yes, besides just looking beautiful."

He came up to her from behind, kissed her on the neck, and wrapped his arms around her. "I don't know, Roberta," he said softly in her ear. "Perhaps I presume too much. Perhaps I am a dreamer. Perhaps I am a fool, but destiny is a very strange thing."

"And what do you mean by that?"

"I mean that I am behaving like a foolish young boy would. I look at you and I want you! And yet, I forget that I am twenty years your senior! I forget that we have just met. Yet, I have been drawn to you ever since the very first moment I laid eyes on you—even as you cursed at me in the rain! I tried to leave you behind then—in order to keep my life uncomplicated, and I tried to forget then that I am still a man! But, it becomes hopeless every time I look at you. And tonight… Well tonight, who knows what will happen tonight?"

"And you think there is something wrong with having feelings?" she asked, turning to him and gazing up into his eyes.

"Only if they are unwarranted feelings," he murmured. After a moment of silence between them, he said, "Are they?"

Roberta smiled fleetingly, and put her hand on his chest. "It's not like I haven't noticed you too, Nikki—noticed you as a man! I am flattered that you find me attractive, and yet I am insulted that you find me so shallow as to think that I have been measuring you up! I am disappointed that the difference in our ages is this huge concern for you! Since when did woman being younger than a man stop a man from wanting her?"

"It never crossed your mind then, that by the time you get to be my age, I would be a decrepit old man, or maybe even dead?"

"Jeez, Nikki." She laughed. "I never even gave it a thought! Why would I? You haven't even really made a pass at me yet. What makes you think a woman my age would even worry about something like that? Besides, in your line of work you could be dead tomorrow anyway! Right now, I am caught up in the moment, and it's a wonderful moment, isn't it?"

Nick smiled and nodded. "Yes, it is. It's too wonderful, as a matter of fact! And, it is clouding my judgment."

"What do you mean by that Nikki?" she said, pushing him away.

Nick grabbed her by her arms and pulled her back fiercely. "I mean that I am not buying your story, or the background check I ran on you either! I am not buying your cover, in other words! Who are you?"

"I told you Nikki," she replied convincingly, tears welling in her eyes. "Why don't you believe me?"

Nick released her and left her standing there alone while he paced back and forth before answering her. Now, was not the time to be distracted by her beauty, yet that was exactly what she was doing to him! Being a very beautiful distraction that he couldn't allow. He looked inside the mansion, but no one seemed to be paying any attention to them outside there on the veranda.

"Stand over here," he commanded, pulling her back, and away from the sculpted balcony where her half-full glass of water still remained on the railing. He spoke into his collar. "Kowalski."

"Got it," Kowalski replied into an earphone planted in Nick's ear.

"Then, take it out."

A second later, the water glass disintegrated into shards of glass! There was only the sound of shattered glass and ice cubes hitting the brick floor that could be heard in the stillness of the night.

Roberta jumped into his arms. "What was that?" She was trembling from fright.

"An example of marksmanship. There are men on the hill across the way, watching and listening to everything! They are my men, part of my organization! They are out there tonight on my orders to watch our back. What I am involved in here is not a game, Roberta! People get killed in this business, so the stakes are very high, always! In this business, coincidences are rare. Was it a coincidence that we met last night, or were you planted there on the side of that road for a reason? I have to ask myself one question: if I were up against someone who is my equal, and I needed to keep tabs on my subject, what better way to do it than by planting someone close to him, someone he couldn't resist?"

He held her tightly, and it made her feel momentarily unsafe! Up to now, she had played her part of the deception like an academy award winner. Everything had gone just as she was told it would, including the phony background check. She was realizing that this man was more than just different—he was unique! He had never portrayed himself to be a powerful, rich, or influential man, and yet he seemed to be all three. If she were to continue her lie, her deception, what then, would he hurt her? Was she willing to risk the mission by telling him that his intuition was correct?

"What are you suggesting, Nikki?" she demanded angrily.

Standing there in the moonlight—with the shattered remnants of her glass nearly underfoot, she needed to diffuse the situation somehow! She put her head against his chest as a woman might do when needing comfort! But, she used her ploy instead to listen to his heartbeat. His heart pumped strongly—evenly! He was not afraid in the least bit, but she was! She wanted to tell him everything! But, now was not the time she knew! She pushed away from him and said; "Now you scare me, Nikki! I don't need to be here tonight! You asked me to be here. It's not like I volunteered for this! I don't know what is going on in your head right now, mister! I just want out of here!"

"Go screw yourself, Nick!" she cried out, and ran back into the mansion with tears in her eyes.

"Looks like you screwed up, Nick." Kowalski's voice came in over his earphone. "Judging from her pulse rate, she really is pissed at you. Do we extract and get out of here?"

"Stay put Kowalski," Nick muttered in reply as he watched her cross the ballroom floor and head directly for a women's room. He then circled the room, watching to see if anyone else entered the restroom behind her. No one did.

Nick hesitated at the door of the woman's room. The last thing he needed were screaming females if he entered, but he went in anyway. Inside, there were only three stalls! And thankfully, no one was standing at the wide vanity mirror. Nick locked the door behind him. Roberta was in the middle stall—he could see her anklet! The others appeared to be vacant.

"I'm sorry, Roberta."

"Go away, you bastard! I have cab fare, and I'll not bother you again."

"It's the business Roberta, not you. Don't take it so personal."

She replied, "I did what you asked me to do, and then you question who I am. You run a background check on me, and it's not enough for you? Are you saying that there has to be some sort of hidden agenda behind everything?"

"Come out of there, Roberta," Nick pleaded with her.

"Go away!"

"You have the parking token, remember?"

He heard a rustling sound coming from her stall, and then over the partition arced a brass token that clattered loudly on the tiled floor. "There, now you have it. Go away!"

Nick picked it up and slipped it into his pocket. "As you wish," he answered.

Roberta bit her lip apprehensively, and rebuked herself at blowing her mission! She heard his footsteps as he left, and then heard the door opening and closing behind him. She waited and listened, but she heard nothing more. Now, what was she to do? She had been given no way to contact headquarters, and she had been given strict orders not to anyway. So, what was she to do? She had played out her woman's intuition, and she had played him like a fiddle, but he gave up too easily! She stooped to peer under the partition. Her eyes swept across the tiled floor. She half expected him to still be there, but he was indeed gone. Carefully, she unlocked the partition and stuck her head out for a better look. The room was empty. That was that then, she decided. She would dry her tears and fix her makeup, and call a cab. Her supervisor had been correct in his assessment of her—which was she couldn't pull it off after all!

Going to the sink, she bent over to splash some water on her face. When she straightened up, there he was behind her, holding a towel out for her! "What are you still doing here?" she exclaimed, her heart pounding.

"If you are a plant Roberta, you are a very good one," he said dryly. "I'll play along for now, and at least pretend for the moment that you aren't. But, coincidences aren't just rare in my business—there are no coincidences! Nevertheless, I still have business here tonight, so dry your face and redo your makeup. I still need your help, and you promised to help me."

"What for, Nick? You could have gotten in the door without me, and you now have someone hunting down this guy you want to talk to, so what do you need me for?"

"Nothing Roberta," he answered her honestly. "But, if you left now it would be awkward! Besides, I promised you a dance, remember? I was quite looking forward to it."

She smiled in spite of herself. "Really?"

Nick smiled back. "I'm a bit rusty at it, but it would be my pleasure."

"I will play along too then, Nikki. Go do what you need to do here tonight, but don't stand me up for that dance or you *will* see the wrath of a woman!"

She laughed.

Nick took the towel and gently dried her face. She closed her eyes while he did, and when she opened them again, he kissed her like he meant it, and she momentarily fell out of her role and kissed him back. "This wasn't supposed to happen," she thought silently. But then she dismissed the thought! She pulled him closer and kissed him back like she really meant it as well.

Kowalski and the others on the hill heard everything Nick and Roberta were saying to each other. "Frigging idiot!" Kowalski muttered to himself. "Spotters," Kowalski called out over the radio as he touched the button on his throat piece.

"Keep an eye out for any movement on this hill, and use your infrared. Shooters, keep an eye on the marks." He heard six clicks in his earphones, as each man responded without saying a word.

Chapter 11

"What is it, Carmichael?" Chief of Security for the Governor, Anthony Rodriquez asked.

"Sir, a flash of light was seen on the hill across the way a minute ago."

"And?"

"It could have been a muzzle flash," Carmichael replied.

Rodriquez considered the possibility for a moment, but concluded that it could have also been another paparazzi looking for a photo, which seemed far more likely. "And your opinion?"

"We could have a sniper on the hill."

"Did anyone hear a rifle shot? Was there a report of a shooting? Is anyone down?"

"No sir," Carmichael replied.

"Go check it out Carmichael, but take some backup. That hill is more than two hundred yards away. It would take a real marksman to be effective at that range, and if that is what we have out there, let's error on the side of caution. In other words, don't be a hero. Any infrared signatures?"

"No sir."

"Keep me posted then."

"Right sir."

Rodriquez lit a cigar as he stepped outside his office into the warm night air. "Damn," he thought. "I'd better follow my own order and truly error on this side of caution." He got on his radio and alerted all of his security people. "Possible sniper on the hill. Everyone maintain their positions and stay on the alert. If anything, and I mean if anything looks funny, I want to hear about it. Copy?"

In the library upstairs, Governor Talbot and Harry Trundle had already informed Anne Marie about what intentions the Democratic Party had for Harry. "Anne Marie," Harry said. "Are you prepared and willing to run my election campaign?"

Anne Marie feigned shock, as if she hadn't been hoping for this offer for many months now. Still, it did come as shock to her to finally get it! She had rehearsed her acceptance lines a hundred times before in front of a mirror in the bathroom, but she immediately forgot everything when the question was finally posed. With her hand fluttering at her breastbone like a nervous butterfly, she recovered quickly, and she smiled as her pre-rehearsed lines came back to her.

Morgan had not yet seen his target at the party, but he had seen Nathan Chadwick Bentley and his entourage enter. He had also noticed Samuel Forester's group. The two Silicon Valley giants made a point to ignore one another but remained within clear sight of each other at the same time, while they took center stage with all the other prominent business people and politicians in attendance.

Suddenly, the symphony orchestra started playing the Washington State theme song, *Washington, My Home,* which meant that everyone was to take his or her seats at the dinner tables.

It was now ten o'clock.

Nick and Roberta broke their embrace.

"What now?" Roberta smiled.

Nick kissed her tenderly again; relishing her tender lips once more, and then broke away from her.

"Now," he replied, "we get to eat after listening politely to some political rhetoric."

"Nikki?" she asked falling back into her role. "You won't stand me up, will you?"

"I promise," he replied. "It will be my pleasure to twirl you about the dance floor like a ballerina Cinderella! You do know that all Russians are good dancers, don't you?"

"No," she laughed. "I didn't know that! Why would that be?"

"Because, in Russia, all the pretty women expect a man to be able to twirl her about the floor—and with utter grace," he said.

She giggled. "I want to go to Russia with you, Nikki. It sounds like my kind of place."

As the guests took their pre-assigned seats in the ballroom, each table accommodating twelve people, the waiters and waitresses, who were dressed in the same eighteenth-century attire as the door greeters were, began filling the tables with platters of food and taking drink orders. The state theme song ended, and the Democrat's theme song began as Governor Talbot and his wife took center stage at the podium. At the governor's side were Harry Trundle and his wife and their entourage, including Andrew Butler and Anne Marie Blakely.

After the usual applause and head nodding finished, the governor spoke.

"Ladies and gentleman, we have some sad and unexpected news tonight. As many of you may have already heard, Congressman Wilshire was involved in a fatal traffic accident in Washington DC today while returning home from a round of golf. We offer his family our condolences, and we offer Congressman Wilshire our heartfelt gratitude for all his years in Congress. Let us now bow our heads in a moment of respectful silence for this great man, who was also a great husband and great father, and a great American."

After a moment of silence, he continued. "As everyone knows, this was to be the last term for Congressman Wilshire, and for a long time, the party has been looking for a man or woman who could fill his shoes after his retirement. Sadly, he was not able to fulfill his own retirement dreams, but as Mrs. Wilshire would attest to if she were here, there was one man in particular that the congressman thought best suited to pursue his upcoming vacant seat in Congress next fall. Sadly, the Congressman is not able to make this endorsement himself. But, I stand before you now on the congressman's behalf to introduce to everyone, Senator Harry Trundle, our next Democratic candidate for a seat in the Congress of the United States of America—and indeed our next spokesperson in Washington DC. Please, everyone, give a big hand to Senator Harry Trundle."

Harry then stood and said all the right things for the next ten minutes, which meant nothing to Nick or Roberta. But, when Trundle announced his new campaign manager, Anne Marie Blakely, Nick looked around at the tables up front to observe the reactions. He spotted Bill Blakely right away when he dropped his fork onto his plate in surprise. Obviously, the announcement was a revelation to him, and now Nick knew to whom he needed to talk with tonight.

The dinner was exquisite, consisting mostly of Pacific Northwest delicacies, including king salmon, shrimp, clams, octopus, and halibut. For the more traditional appetites, there was prime rib, turkey, and ham, along with a variety of steamed vegetables, exotic breads, and various fruits, salads, and desserts. Nick preferred the salmon and some basic vegetables, while Roberta couldn't help but try a little of everything, including the octopus, which amused Nick immensely, especially the look on her face as she attempted to chew on the rubbery substance. She finally gave it up—and swallowed the bite whole, washing it down with a big swig of ice water!

Nick laughed silently and reached for the platter of octopus.

"More, my dear?"

"It's not funny Nick," she said softly and then laughed herself. "I will take some more shrimp, though."

The dinner ended with a toast to the new candidate, and shortly thereafter, the waiters and waitresses began removing the dishes from the tables. The remaining platters of food were consolidated on a single table near the rear of the hall. The spent dishes and glassware were removed quickly to the kitchen, and the tables were broken down while the guests headed for the veranda or gathered in small groups to chat. Some went out to the gardens to grab a smoke or to just enjoy the warm summer night.

Nick walked Roberta outside as she lit a cigarette.

"I need to talk to someone. Will you be okay out here for awhile?" he asked her.

"Yes, Nikki. Go do what you need to do," she replied. "But be careful! It gives me the willies to think that I am being watched through a rifle scope, so hurry up."

"You might want to think about it the other way around. As long as you stay out here on the balcony, no one can harm you! You are under the watchful eyes of my men."

"So this is what you call leaving me in good hands?"

Nicked kissed her on the cheek and patted her behind. He handed her the parking token. "Just in case we need to make a hasty departure."

She smiled at him and said, "Later!"

Kowalski and his men spotted movement coming up the hill, and then they noted infrared signatures coming from the side entrances of the mansion.

"Nick," Kowalski said over the radio. "There are men approaching our positions. It might be that the muzzle flash was detected by house security."

Nick was headed off to find Bill Blakely. "How long do I have?" he asked. Before the answer came back, Nick ran into Andrew Butler. He avoided Andrew for the moment by turning around, and Kowalski responded.

"Maybe twenty minutes before the dogs are on me, but maybe less if this outfit is worth a damn," he said.

Nick considered the situation for just a few seconds. "I'll need at least that much time. If your positions become compromised, then pull back."

"Everyone?" Kowalski asked.

"That is your call, buddy. I don't want you discovered or any of the Governor's security staff to go down unless it is absolutely necessary! But, I intend to leave through the front door—and, in a hurry! So, I'd appreciate it if you kept that door open for me."

Kowalski thought about the options, and then got on his wireless. "Men, we have a problem."

Nick looked at his watch, and then looked back at Roberta, who still stood on the veranda where they had last talked and kissed. Finally, he looked at Bill Blakely just a few yards away from him and considered his own options.

"Mr. Smith," Andrew said after noticing him there. "Let me introduce you to Bill Blakely."

"Thank you, Andrew. That's very kind of you, but I would prefer to introduce myself. I take it that Mr. Blakely is that gentleman standing over there having a cigarette? The one with the short brown hair?" Nick gestured in his direction.

Andrew smiled. "It is indeed, Mr. Smith. Would now be a good time to take Ms. Sanchez around and make a few introductions?"

"That would be an excellent idea, Andrew! Tell her that I will join her in a few minutes."

Andrew then approached Roberta. Nick watched as Roberta smiled as she listened to Andrew explain his intentions for her. She looked in Nick's direction, and Nick nodded back—to let her know that it was okay to go with him. He then watched Andrew take her by the arm, and lead her back inside the house.

"Mr. Blakely," Nick said, approaching Bill from the side.

Bill immediately tossed his cigarette aside, fearing that he had been caught out smoking by his wife or by one of her cronies, and turned to see who was addressing him.

Nick pretended that he didn't notice, and said, "I have something you want."

"Do I know you?" Bill asked.

"In a way, you do, but we haven't met yet. I believe you might know me as Nick Peters."

Blakely reached for his gun. "Don't bother," Nick cautioned. "If you pull your weapon, my people up on the hill will take you out. Just be cool for a moment. I am unarmed." Nick pulled the lapels of his tuxedo open wide to show that he was not armed. "Can we talk?"

Blakely scanned the area, and not seeing any immediate threat, he relaxed for a moment, curious to hear what this man had to say. And, at the same time marveling at the apparent size of his balls—having such balls to approach him here!

Nick stepped to within easy listening distance and continued. "You are after me because I have a package, correct?"

Blakely stared back at him with skepticism. Expecting this, Nick went to his breast pocket slowly and deliberately. He found and removed the Letter of Congress he had there. He handed it to him. "Why is the FBI after me?"

Blakely looked at the document, and after a brief examination, realized that it was genuine. "You *are* Nick Peters then?"

Nick nodded.

"So where is the package?"

"It's in a safe place for now," Nick replied.

"I have a warrant for your arrest. You know that, right?"

"I assumed as much."

Blakely considered his options and went for his gun once again. Nick held up his hand, and it was immediately spotted with two red laser lights. He then pointed to Blakely, and the pinpoint laser beams went directly to Blakely's chest. Blakely hesitated, realizing that two sniper rifles had just targeted him.

"Now, I can give you a further demonstration, one that includes a piece of lead landing nearby and perhaps risking a ricochet that could get someone hurt, or we can just talk. What do you want to do?"

Removing his hand from his gun, Blakely replied smiling, "Talking is good."

"Good choice," Nick replied. "May I have my document back?"

Bill handed him the papers, and Nick continued. "Don't you find it interesting that the Letter of Congress—the one I have, was authorized by the now deceased Congressman Wilshire? Even more interesting—is that he died only hours before I was to deliver his package!"

"Go on," Blakely said.

"Frankly Bill, I smell a rat! Couriers just run people or packages through customs or across borders, generally because the normal channels are too slow. This assignment should have been a cakewalk, and yet I have half the Washington State Highway Patrol and half the FBI after me, despite having a document that makes my actions legal. I want to know why?"

Blakely stared at him and smiled. "I must say Mr. Peters, you have balls of solid brass! How do you know me, and how did you find me, and why here?"

"To be honest Bill, that is mostly irrelevant. But, '*why here*': this seems to be a perfect place to talk! Here, your own people don't surround you, and it would be very awkward for you to make a fuss under the circumstances! Considering that your wife, the Governor, and this idiot named Trundle who is now apparently running for Congress are all here too. Am I correct in assuming that you would prefer not to have a confrontation right here and now?"

Bill nodded.

"Mind if I smoke, Mr. Peters?"

"Not at all," Nick said.

"So what do you want from me?" Blakely said, lighting another cigarette.

"I want to know what you know about this package. I might surrender it to you once I know what it is! Frankly Bill, I want no part of it! But, something is really wrong here—and so I am not inclined to simply turn it over. Not without some answers first!"

"You won't get out of here, you know that."

Nick shrugged as if it wasn't a concern. "No, I don't know that for certain. And furthermore, I don't believe it! What are you going to do, shoot me? A Congressman authorized the delivery of an attaché case to a Federal Courthouse in Seattle on Monday morning—I'm trying to do just that! So, the law is on my side. But, obviously there is something about this package that has got someone riled up! And, that someone—who must be quite important, wants to make sure that I don't deliver it! All I want to know is what you know—so I can decide what to do with it."

Bill Blakely replied calmly, "Just give it to me, and all the heat goes away!"

"Sorry Bill," Nick smiled, admiring Blakely for staying on target. "But, it doesn't work that way! You see, when all this heat came down on me, I decided to find out what was in the package. After careful examination of the attaché case—and all the contents therein, there seemed to be nothing in it that was unusual, except for a computer pocket drive! I loaded the pocket drive onto my own computer. But, everything was encrypted—and it couldn't be read! So, I asked a friend of mine in Russia—who happens to be an encryption genius to look at it for me. Suddenly, he and his family go missing! For all I know, I am carrying Russian State secrets! And if I am, I then just signed my friend's death warrant! I need to know what it is I have before I give it to anyone."

Kowalski's voice was in Nick's ear. "I have three men approaching from the mansion with dogs. There are vehicles approaching from the road. Do I compromise?"

"Excuse me Bill," Nick said, turning away from him, and speaking into his coat collar. "Pull back, Kowalski!"

"I can't help you if I do, boss."

"Watch my flank then, but get the hell out of there, now!"

"Sorry Bill," Nick continued, turning back to Blakely. "Now about this package: what do you know about it?"

"You are wired?" Bill stated, more than asked him.

"Yes, to the snipers watching us from the hill."

"So, your protection is now pulling out!" he said, once again putting his hand on his gun.

"Bill, you can detain me—if that is what you want. But, so far I have not broken the law! And detaining me will not get back what you need to recover," Nick stated calmly.

"I have a Presidential Letter to stop you," Blakely replied.

"Let me see it."

"I don't have it on me! Obviously, I did not anticipate needing it tonight!"

"Then you've got nothing on me, and you can't arrest me because you must serve me first! Am I correct?" Nick smiled, expecting this exchange.

Blakely squirmed with frustration, but said nothing.

"Look, Bill. I want to work with you on this. I got suckered into doing this job in the guise of a personal favor. But, it is now quite obvious that something is really not right about this entire gig! And, I sense that it's very big! People's lives are at stake here—and on top of it all, people I care about! It's too coincidental that a prominent politician just happened to die forty-eight hours before a package was to be delivered on his order. If what I have is important enough to take out the Congressman, then how many other lives are at stake here? Tell me what you know!"

Blakely shrugged his shoulders. "Really, I don't know anything. I have a Presidential order to stop you, but not to harm you! And, I haven't a clue why or what it is you carry."

Nick grinned. "See, you can't shoot me, Bill!"

"My orders are not to use *lethal* force on you!" he lied. "But, I can still shoot you!"

"That would suck, Bill. It really would!" Nick Peters glared at him and almost lost his temper! But, he reigned in his fury and replied calmly. "Especially when I took this risk to come to you—in an effort to cooperate in the first place," he finished.

"What do you know about the mission you are on?" Bill asked him.

"I don't know anything about this package Bill, just some *BS* cover story that doesn't hold an ounce of water! But, whatever the truth, if my suspicions are correct, the *FSB* in Russia is holding a friend of mine, and his family, only because I asked him to look at whatever is on that drive."

"So, what is your best guess as to what the hell is this about?"

"If I had a best guess Bill, I wouldn't be here pumping you for that information!" Nick replied back sarcastically. "I only know that it has something to do with what is on this pocket drive."

"So, you have this pocket drive?"

"Of course I have it Bill, but not on me! That would be pretty amateur."

"How do you know me?" Bill asked, his hand going back to his weapon.

Nick put his arm over Bill's shoulder. "How about we have a drink first, before you shoot me?" He waved his hand to a waiter and asked, "How about two vodka martinis?"

Bill couldn't help but smile—in spite of the situation, and he had to say, "Shaken or stirred?"

Nick laughed good heartedly—genuinely amused by the joke! "It doesn't matter to me, Bill. I am not a James Bond. I spent twenty years in Russia and acquired a taste for vodka out of necessity. I couldn't care less if it is bloody shaken or stirred—as long as it has ice!"

The waiter came back with two martinis. Both men removed their drinks from the silver platter, and Nick raised his drink for a toast. "How about we work together, Bill? I will make you a promise to keep you in the loop, and I also promise that this package will not be delivered until we both know what's in it—if it is delivered at all! If need be, I will destroy the pocket drive in a way that everyone will be satisfied that all the information on it reaches no one! Deal?"

Blakely shook his head. "No deal."

Nick sighed with disappointment. "Actually Bill, I thought you'd say that! So here, take this card. This is how you can reach me."

"Mr. Peters," Blakely said, glancing at the card. "I can't just let you walk away from here, you know that!"

"And why not, Bill? No one here knows who I actually am—and so no one can put us together here tonight! You stand a far better chance of recovering what you want by working with me than by working against me."

"There is only an email address on this card."

"That is the only secure way for me to stay in touch with you! You can access it with your cell phone. Text message me, and it will give you the option for audio. Go ahead and try it," Nick encouraged him.

Bill got out his cell phone and entered the email address. The option came up for audio or text. He highlighted audio and pressed enter. A second later Nick's cell phone rang and Nick answered. They both closed their cell phones at the same time.

"Let's go inside, Bill. You want another drink?"

Blakely declined another drink, but he followed him inside the mansion anyway. This had become an interesting evening for him after all! Despite his dilemma of not knowing what to do with this man that his agency, and the President of the United States wanted so badly—he had to ask himself, what his next move should be? No answer was forthcoming, and in fact, he hadn't a clue! If this was in fact Nick Peters, by all rights, he should be arresting him right now! That is what his job required of him! But, how could he know for sure this was in fact Peters, and not some decoy? His instincts told him to pull out his gun and arrest him anyway! But, Peters had chosen this first meeting very well—and he was correct in all his assumptions! Blakely couldn't ruin this evening for his wife—this was her night! Besides, he also needed to serve him with the letter before he could arrest him in the first place.

"So, how did you find me here tonight, Nick? You don't mind me calling you Nick, do you?"

Nick handed him another martini. "Not at all, Bill. It seems that we are both in this thing together, whether we like it or not, so we might as well be civilized about it. Actually, my friends all call me Nikki."

"So, yet one more time: how did you know how to find me here, Nikki?"

"In Port Angeles, when that cop pulled me over, I knew that my car was made, and that the FBI was tipped off. The car was clean and properly registered to a company I own. I assume that the officer I took down is okay?"

Bill had to smile. It amazed him that Nick was even at all concerned about the downed officer, "Broken nose is all."

"Yeah, sorry about that, Bill."

"You made quite a mess of Highway 101."

"Sorry about that too, Bill."

"You haven't told me yet how you found me here tonight."

"Well, after I knew that my mission had been compromised, I made a few telephone calls. Your name came up on the invitation list here at the ball tonight, and I happened to have an invitation myself."

"Not under the name of Nicholas Peters, I suspect."

"No, of course not, Bill. Under the name of Mr. Smith with World Trade."

Bill laughed out loud. "My God, Nick. You just gave up your alias."

"Your investigation of World Trade and Mr. Smith will lead you nowhere! As you probably already know, I don't exist and Smith is actually quite dead! Your task is to recover what I have, and your mission is not about me in spite of anything you might have been told. I have done nothing wrong yet, at least not according to my Letter of Congress.

"There is something bad going on here," Nick continued. "And things will get worse Bill, and soon! I suspect there are contracts out on me right now, and whatever I have is of interest to someone more powerful than the FBI. Think about it, Bill. That is all I ask of you."

Blakely stared at him, now truly not believing the balls this Peters had! "Sorry Nick, but all I have to go on are my orders."

"Then you don't know squat, just like I don't?"

"That about sums it up," Blakely replied.

"Well then," Nick replied. "See the beautiful young woman over there talking to that group of people?"

Bill looked in the direction that Nick was looking, and the young woman noticed the two of them looking at her, and raised a toast to them both! She smiled back.

"I am more interested tonight in that woman over there, than in your *damned* package! And, I promised her just one dance—which we will have together! Nevertheless, I will promise this to you Bill, if you will work with me. I will turn over whatever I have to you before Monday morning! Providing, that I am not compromising the national security of either Russia or the United States of America! I happen to have loyalties to both countries. Help me figure out what is on this damned drive, and why someone with so much juice wants it so badly! Or else I will destroy it—just to get this charade over with as quickly as possible."

Blakely wasn't yet buying in with this Nick Peters. "You act as if you hold the upper ground here, Nikki. What makes you think that I will go along with any of it?"

On his third martini himself, Nick said, "Here Bill, let's drink, and don't argue with me just now!"

Blakely took another martini from yet another tray wielded by another waiter and took a swallow.

"You have a gun on your hip Bill, and I have none. You have my file, and so you must know that I am not some common criminal either! So, either you can trust me, or it's your choice not to!" Peters pointed out to him.

"How can I trust you?"

"Jesus, Bill!" Nick had to shake that one off! It seems no one can trust anyone anymore! He continued, "Sorry! It seems that topic keeps coming up tonight over and over again! Trust your gut feelings man! If you are determined to arrest me, then go ahead and try to. If you fail—then it is your goose that is cooked, not mine."

"So, you are threatening me?"

"Bill," Nick said in earnest. "You are now out of the range of my snipers. If you want to arrest me—then just put the handcuffs on me right here and now! But, it is a long way back to the jailhouse! I am confident that I will never see the inside of it! This is a warning, not a threat. You have a very pretty wife, and two very lovely children. I wouldn't go there myself—but there are those who would! One congressman is already dead, and to be direct, there is a Viktor Zubkov, a Russian powerbroker, that might be behind all this! And if so, he is prick enough to definitely go there! He is a very dangerous man, Bill."

"Who is he?" Bill demanded.

"A very ruthless man who is very well connected politically in Russia and with the Russian mafia. His assets vastly exceed the sum of everyone here tonight. Compared to him, we are among peasants at this gathering."

Bill wrinkled his brow. "There are some pretty powerful people here tonight, Nick."

Nick scoffed. "Zubkov was in charge of the privatization of Russia during Perestroika. Every deal he made, he took a twenty percent cut of. Imagine owning twenty percent of the US government—that is how powerful he is!"

Bill whistled. "And he is involved in all this?"

"I think that Zubkov is directly behind all of this—yes! But, it is only supposition at this point."

"Why this supposition, Nick?"

"Because Bill, the man I carry this package for is Alexander Mayakovsky—a double agent for the CIA! He wants to run off and marry a woman! And, the woman he wants to marry is Zubkov's wife! And, this delivery I was supposed to make—was only to be a diversion for him!"

Blakely's mind raced on. If this new information was correct, then the mystery as to why the FBI was involved, why there was a Presidential Order to stop Nick, and why specific instructions were issued not to harm him—became more clear to Blakely.

"That's why they want you stopped and not harmed, Nikki?"

"Go on," Nick encouraged him.

"Your file, the dossier I was handed by my superiors, was scant at best! Why? Because the CIA has been compromised! This nonsense about not knowing what you look like, no recent photos etcetera, was all bullshit! They didn't want to post your identity because whoever it is that wants this attaché case still needs you to do something for them! I was ordered to put out roadblocks on a gray Mustang, not to stop you, but apparently to warn you off! Why?"

"Because," Nick replied, "Whoever is behind all this knew that I would be monitoring radio frequencies, and that I would have an alternative plan if something went wrong."

Blakely stared into space while Nick waited for some revelation to come to him. When it didn't come, he prompted him. "And? Where did the tip come from?"

"It was anonymous," Blakely replied.

"Yeah, right!" Nick muttered. "Alexander Mayakovsky was the only person who knew where and when I was coming in. He is CIA—a spook like me! So, he would have known how to track me, and how to identify where and when I got the car. But, it was not bull crap that the CIA hasn't a clue what I look like! I removed my own files from the CIA years ago! And, consider this, the FBI may be compromised as well!"

"So, someone was warning you?" Blakely replied. "Why?"

Nick shrugged. "It's irrelevant. More importantly, why do you have a Presidential Order to stop me?"

Blakely shrugged. "I haven't a clue."

"I need to know that Bill," Nick stated calmly. "I got into something innocently enough, and for a good enough reason. For God's sake man, I was ready to retire—to get out of this business entirely, and then this! No, this is too big for Alexander Mayakovsky. Someone higher up is pulling the strings Bill! Someone very high up has a plan! And, that plan includes playing you for the fool too! Whoever it is probably knew that I would track you down tonight at this ball, someone who knew that you would be here! You were used as bait, and I swallowed it hook, line, and sinker."

"I don't get it Nikki," Bill replied. "It doesn't make any sense to me. I have a Presidential Order to bring you in. How could I be the bait?"

Nick shook his head. "I don't know, Bill. It's just a gut feeling. What else do you know?" he demanded.

"The girl was planted," Blakely replied.

"How do you know that?" Nick demanded. Again, knowing too well his fatal flaw! His own need to believe in innocence—and that it had to exist somewhere! He already knew she was a plant! Nevertheless, he still held deep desire to believe in her—even though he knew the truth! After two decades of covert espionage, it was the one thing that kept him sane—the belief that most people were innocent! And that most people were victims! No matter how many times he was proven wrong—he clung to it! Roberta did seem too coincidental to be true! And the CB radio transmission, the roadblock, the alternate route leading up into the mountains, and the logging truck that just happened to pull out in front of him—blocking his way until the very last moment? It too all seemed too contrived! He had been right earlier when he told her—there were no coincidences in his line of work—the espionage business!

"We found the Mustang late last night after a tow truck was dispatched to pick up a drunk that ran over a car door left in the middle of the road," Blakely said. "It took out his oil pan and disabled his vehicle. The tow truck owner wanted salvage rights to the Jeep, so he called in the registration, and when it came back as stolen, the Washington State Patrol was called in. That Jeep had been there awhile. Other than a broken steering column lock, the car was mechanically fine. A handful of cigarette butts were dropped nearby with traces of lip-gloss on them. Do you know anyone who smokes Parliament Light 100s?"

"What's your take on the setup?"

Blakely took his time to reply.

"If she were an assassin Nick, she would have taken you out last night. My best guess is that whatever you have is not as important as what someone wants you to do next. My guess is that she was put there for a reason, and because normal channels have been compromised in some way, you are being steered into something—that's why they want you alive."

"So what does Roberta have to do with anything?"

Blakely shrugged. "That I can't tell you. If you want me to make some inquiries, I can."

Nick shook his head. "No, if your agency has been compromised, it might tip someone off. Besides, my background check reveals a lot of details. Someone went to a bunch of trouble to make her look legit, and so you might only find the same info I did, which is not worth the risk of compromising our little discussion here tonight. I'll play out the cards I already have and see what happens next. I appreciate the information, Bill."

"Sorry it isn't more. This news just adds to the confusion. So what are you going to do?" Blakely looked at him.

"Go dance with her," Nick answered him honestly.

"One last thing, Nikki. If you are as high-end in this game as it sounds, it seems unlikely you wouldn't see a setup coming from a mile away. How did you get involved in all this?"

"It's a long story Bill, and we don't have time to discuss it now. Alexander Mayakovsky is an old friend of mine, and as I said, he too worked for the CIA—you can check him out if you want to. He fell in love with a woman who belongs to Victor Zubkov, a man who does not believe in divorce! Alexander's only chance to get her away from him was for him to go one way when Zubkov thought he was going another. Alexander asked me to be his diversion, and I agreed."

Blakely stared at him in disbelief. "I don't believe a word you say,

Nick. No man, especially an intelligent man like you with lots of black ops experience, would get into the middle of anything like this. So why? What's the real reason?"

Nick looked him in the eye.

"The woman is the mother of my biological daughter," he replied harshly. "I told you, Bill. It's a long story!"

Pieces of the puzzle drifted around in Bill's head, combining to produce various scenarios. But none of the pieces quite fit together neatly, except those pieces of the puzzle that belonged to Nick Peters. His background checked out with what he said. The resources he had at his disposal, including the snipers on the hills surrounding the Governor's mansion, all seemed plausible. His willingness to confront his adversary in a civilized manner was consistent with what was in his file. His claim that he carried no weapon seemed accurate as far as he could tell. And, he made no specific threats! He seemed to be quite genuine in every way! And indeed, he did seem to hold the upper hand for the moment—and so his words were not merely bravado. Nick Peters was an adversary that Bill Blakely was quickly becoming enamored with! And, his gut instinct told him he could trust this man—a man with the big brass ones!

The orchestra started playing a prelude to the *Waltz of the Flower* by *Tchaikovsky!* The prelude was meant to entice dancers to the floor.

"Excuse me Bill. But, I think that this is my dance with the young lady masquerading her way through this little setup—the gorgeous woman that someone has perpetrated against me!"

Nick swallowed his martini in a single gulp, and placed his empty glass on a nearby table. Bill Blakely watched—dumbfounded! He offered her his hand, as if their meeting and their conversation had never even taken place! It confounded him! Either Nick Peters was a complete idiot, or he had the biggest set of balls of any man he'd ever met before! Not even some babe—and she was gorgeous, a babe who was setting him up for a fall, could make him uneasy! Besides, Blakely could have put a bullet into his back if he wanted to! But, apparently Peters understood this too! Peters knew he wouldn't, so his own instincts were against this action too.

Roberta smiled delightedly when Nick approached her. Bill Blakely looked at the card in his hand, which read only *World Trade* along with the email address.

Blakely was impressed with Peters—despite his desire to do his duty and arrest him! Peters was a man in control! He was confident, charming, and he had charisma! And yet, Blakely reminded himself again, he also had a job to do! He flipped open his cell phone and hit the speed dial to his headquarters.

"Give me Franks," he said after the connection was made.

"Mark here," the man answered.

"He is here, Mark. Nick Peters is here."

"Bill, is this you?"

"Hell, yes, it's me! What, you don't recognize my voice?"

"Sorry boss, I was asleep and the call was forwarded. Can we start over?"

Blakely explained, "The son-of-a-bitch is here at the Governor's Mansion, and in fact, he approached me, wanting to make a deal."

"Who the hell are you talking about, Bill?"

"Peters, Nick Peters!" He shouted into the phone.

"Well then arrest his ass, Bill."

"Who the hell is talking to whom here, Franks?"

"Sorry boss, but I'm still waking up."

Blakely let it go.

"I want a team of special forces in here now. This guy has snipers on the hills surrounding the Governor's Mansion, and they obviously have infrared and night-vision gear. I want two stealth choppers in here to approach from the front and the rear. It needs to be coordinated with the Governor's security team so we don't all kill each other. Can you make it happen?"

"I am on it, boss. Consider it done. Are you okay?"

"Yeah, I am okay. Do not take this guy out! There is a Presidential Order not to. Besides, there is more to this case than we were led to believe. This is something really big Mark, so don't screw it up! And don't bring anyone else into this. Do you understand me?"

"Roger that, boss. I can handle it, but what's going on?"

"Mark, you have a wife and kids, and I will tell you this only once: if you love them all, and if you are at all attached to your own life, don't ask me any more questions! Just do what you are good at doing, dispatch! And dispatch now! I am sending over a photo of the man and woman we want in custody—*alive* and in custody!"

He forwarded the images of Nick and Roberta to Mark that he had captured with his cell phone. "And remember Mark, this is the Governor's house—and there are special guests here! I want our people on the ground ASAP! They are here to keep him and his woman from being killed. However, we need to be completely transparent in this op! At least in so far as his security team is concerned! His men will back off—if we let them! But, we must be completely covert—so that the guests are not alarmed! Do you understand?"

"No boss, I don't fully understand."

"No shooting! I want him followed, and I don't want any ruckus! I need to emphasize this: I want no shooting! Do you understand?"

"Not really boss. Why bring in special forces if all you want to do is follow him?"

Blakely held his temper. "Because Mark, I am outgunned here, and this Nick Peters wants to do a deal! And, if he is telling me the truth, there might be outsiders already here to take him out for the package in his possession. If that is the case then the assassin may be in the wings just waiting for the right opportunity! Special forces might be enough to keep him from pulling the trigger if he is here! We need to protect him before the package does go south. Once again, I have a Presidential Order. Do we need to argue about this—or are you going to follow my friggin orders?"

"No, boss—no argument. I will get moving on it."

"Good! Then get our men in the air—and now!"

Chapter 12

Nathan Chadwick Bentley's cell phone vibrated, which meant that he had an important message coming in! Only a handful of people had access to this number—and those that did, knew he was occupied socially this evening. So despite his irritation with the call, he knew it was prudent to take it! Excusing himself from a conversation with some very prominent business executives in the area, he moved out of hearing distance, and flipped open his phone.

The message was a text message. He read the display, and entered the option to view.

"The courier is here at the banquet, alias Mr. Smith."

Bentley selected the download, and a digital picture unraveled itself. He immediately recognized the man as the one who had just escorted a very lovely young woman out onto the dance floor.

Roberta was beaming as Nick took her hand. The *Waltz of the Flower* was a traditional Russian waltz that all Russian men, Russian men with any character that is—knew by heart! Russian women loved the waltz for its simple melody and rhythm. And though it was a gently flowing waltz that exuded elegance, grace, and movement, it was also a very romantic dance! In this waltz the woman was to be led, and virtually controlled completely by her man! Yet, she herself was meant to be the center of attention! The waltz was contrived by Tchaikovsky to allow a woman to have the most flowing of movements while wearing an elegant gown made with many layers of fabric. It was composed during a time when the *ballroom* dance—and the whole event surrounding it, meant a great deal to a woman!

No one stepped out onto the dance floor immediately—except for Nick and Roberta. Noticing this, Roberta hesitated. The conductor noticed them too, and he also noticed Roberta's hesitance. The conductor watched Nick and Roberta, obviously wondering if he should continue past the prelude or not. Nick raised his index finger. It meant he needed a minute! The conductor waved his wand, and somehow the musicians understood to continue the prelude. Other couples found Roberta's hesitance amusing. They waited to see what would happen next between the stunningly attractive woman and her debonair companion.

"Nikki, I can't do this. Everyone is watching us, and no one else is out here. I have never even danced a waltz before."

Nick smiled. "Can you twirl?"

She looked at him as if he were crazy.

"You wanted to dance, so here is your opportunity. Just follow my lead and the music—there is nothing to it really."

"I can't do this Nikki," she insisted. "I thought it would be more like a foxtrot—something more American!"

"Don't be ridiculous, Roberta. It is just a waltz! I am sure you can dance to it easily enough. I will lead with my left hand and guide you with my right. All you need to do is follow my lead. The object is for us to move together, as if we are one. To keep things simple, I will always move towards you, or, to your left. And we will only take a series of three steps—one long and two short, and always with the rhythm of the music, just like the foxtrot that you just mentioned. The steps repeat themselves. Just close your eyes and let me, and the music, take you!"

Roberta looked around her. People had gathered around the fringes of the dance floor, waiting for this couple to set the dance in motion! She bit her lip nervously, and looked at Nikki. He was so confident that she couldn't help but believe him! Besides, he looked so handsome in his tuxedo that she wanted to try for him anyway. He smiled at her like a young boy would, and her heart skipped a beat—she didn't know why! Determined that she could do this with him, she nodded and curtsied! She then offered him her hand.

Nick took her left hand into his, led her out onto the floor! When they were center stage, he wrapped her left hand around his waist. He put his own right hand into the small of her back. He then nodded once again to the conductor, and the music meandered for a moment longer as he put her into position.

"On three, we dance," he smiled at her confidently!

Roberta's heart was pounding in her chest. She felt flushed while Nick listened to the music and waited for the right moment. She closed her eyes, and Nick squeezed her hand. Finally, Nick said, "One, two, three." And suddenly the waltz began—and they were in motion! Nick was leading her every move. At first the music overwhelmed her! Her feet weren't sure which way to go! It seemed not to matter! He held her firmly and he led her! His movements were so easy to follow, even with her eyes closed, that she soon slipped into the moment and felt almost as if she were floating across the floor!

When he stepped into her, she simply stepped back. When he stepped to his right, she stepped to her left. He took complete control over both of their movements, and immediately, she felt herself moving around the room gracefully, as if she had waltzed her whole life! When finally she did open her eyes, her body had already instinctively learned the moves! She was in awe at how easy it was. Nick was a masterful dancer, his movements effortless and fluid, and indeed, they danced together as one, just as he said they should.

Tchaikovsky's waltz was also magnificently powerful. It began slowly and gently. Violins and stringed instruments led the way, just as two first time lovers would begin their own romantic dance of love—slowly and hesitantly at first. Roberta could sense the crescendos building as more and more instruments contributed to the melody. Her heart began to race as the drums and brass instruments added even more force, thunder and passion to the ballad! And then the tempo quickened! Their movements naturally became more flowing—more sweeping.

As they glided in circles across the dance floor, other couples joined in, and soon the dance floor was filled with couples moving to the sounds of Tchaikovsky's magnificent music! Roberta was now dancing with utter delight. The movement was totally invigorating, and she felt splendid, though she was now perspiring! It was almost as if she were having sex—sex with a man that knew what making love to a woman was all about! Everything was so moving that her heart was eagerly racing with the music toward a final climax! Nick was a strong and powerful man who possessed the grace and charm of an ambassador! When it came to dancing he had the moves of an athlete and the charm of a gentleman! The final crescendo was nearing, and he was leading her to it! As she looked up at him, he smiled at her again! Her heart pounded even more fiercely in her chest with a passion that could not be abated until they could, at long last, make love together! It occurred to her that if they left right then, she wouldn't have objected to him taking her, and she would have in fact jumped him at the first opportunity!

Something inside her tingled. Was it lust or love? Never before had she felt more a woman—something she was taught *not* to be, ever since grade school! All her life she had been told to compete with men, that women could do anything a man could, and she had striven to be that independent woman all her life! But now, finally, she felt delicate and vulnerable in his arms—and it felt great! Had she been missing something all these years?

"Perhaps," came the answer to her question. But, she also realized that she was caught up in the moment! A moment that all young girls dream about— being center stage in an eloquent setting, and dancing with a wonderfully handsome man who made her feel like a princess. Nick had taken complete control over all of her movements, took complete responsibility for any and all consequences, and he smiled with delight as he danced with her. If he made love the way he danced, she would be his forever!

The room spiraled around her dizzily, and she found herself feeling exhilarated. Was it the wine, or could it be something else? He was in control of all her moments—his strong arms leading her in whichever direction he wanted her to go, and unbelievably she trusted him completely!

It felt good to be led by a man with confidence. It felt good to be a woman—this very moment anyway, and to be his. She watched his eyes upon her, and she knew that he wanted her badly. She knew instinctively that he would be a good lover–a gentle and loyal lover. He had made it clear that he was worried about her affections for him, but now she was concerned about her affections for him too. How easy it would be for her to just let herself go, to forget about her assignment, and have a night of passion with him! Nick was unlike any man she had ever met before: handsome, elegant, and dangerous at the same time! If she gave herself to him, would he keep her and devote himself to her? Or, would he instead—discard her like a spent tissue, as so many men that have the charms like Nick had, are prone to do? It didn't matter right now, she decided, and she was smiling in spite of herself—caught up in a moment, a wonderful moment!

She was determined to finish this dance with him eloquently, no matter what happened later. As quickly as her dizziness ascended, it passed. The orchestra played on, progressing to its crescendo, the signal that the dance was about to end. Roberta's heart raced on, and she was uncertain what was to happen next, but she stayed with his lead. She was quickly falling in love with him, a man she had only met twenty-four hours before. She was now certain of it—and had she had the time to dwell upon it, it would have frightened her! But, she hadn't the time to even give it a thought! As she looked about her—about her surroundings and at Nikki, she thought, "Why now? Why now, after all I have been through, do I meet a man like Nick Peters?" Sooner or later, she knew that she would have to tell him the truth, and then what?

Suddenly, there was only Nick and Roberta on the dance floor once again. All the other couples stood aside to see what they would do next. Nikki had a flare about him, and this dance, the waltz, was his; and she was his too—in spite of herself.

"How could this be?" she thought to herself. For the moment it did not matter. Roberta was feeling the music, and she was completely synchronized with him. She kept up with his every move and found herself smiling back at him happily, like a schoolgirl would.

Her smile meant, "Go for it Nikki. I am with you now!"

She felt beautiful, and she certainly looked beautiful to all who watched them dance. As the music peaked and the climax was near, Nick whispered in her ear, "Now, I am going to twirl you."

There was no time for her to object. The dance had taken her heart as never before. Roberta hadn't expected it, but as Nick lifted her left arm and stepped around behind her, she found herself naturally turning to face him again. He did it twice more! She couldn't believe it. She had twirled for him without even thinking about it! It felt wonderful and so natural. She was now beaming with delight. Everyone applauded, and she blushed. The dance was over, and the music stopped. Nick stepped away from her, took her hand, then bowed and kissed it in a gentlemanly fashion. In return, she curtsied once again, and once again everyone applauded. Quickly, they got off the dance floor and went out to the veranda.

"Wow, Nikki! That was great!" she said. "You are a wonderful dancer. Thank you so much for keeping your word to me! What now?" she asked following him as he rushed her out of sight of all the others.

He kissed her on the cheek and replied calmly, "Now, we get the hell out of here!"

Chapter 13

Nathan Chadwick Bentley watched Nick and Roberta depart the dance floor. "It would be a shame to have to kill them, but what other choice do I have?" he thought to himself.

He hit the speed dial button on his cell phone and dictated his instructions. He then went to his personal bodyguards, showed them the digital images of the couple, and pointed them out. "I want them detained quietly, and then brought to the boat, do you understand?"

The three men nodded and then huddled to plan their strategy. Nathan opened his cell phone again and dialed another number.

The man who answered replied irritably,
"I told you never to call me."

"Yeah, well something came up," Nathan replied, as his own blood boiled—no one spoke to him that way, no one! "My mole in the FBI just informed me that a man named Smith is the courier. That means that Alexander Mayakovsky has pulled a fast one on me! This guy Smith wants to make a deal with the FBI. If that happens, I don't need you or your hit man."

"I thought you wanted the courier killed so the Stalintsia Steel merger would stall? You get the same overall outcome, the stalled merger, if the FBI gets the documents and Mayakovsky doesn't testify. What's the big deal?" the voice on the other end muttered with yet more irritation in his tone.

"The big deal is," Nathan hissed back, "is that the courier handing his package over to the FBI ends our deal, and you can call off the hit! Until I get what I want—I need this man alive! You already have what you wanted—the Stalintsia Steel merger is stalled!"

"And what about the union jobs at the new plant?"

"Go screw yourself," Nathan replied. "What do I need a bunch of overpaid and under-qualified workers in my plant for? There will be a cash payoff deposited into your offshore account like we agreed to, and that's it! You are out of this, so keep your people away from my plant."

"And if I don't?" the man on the other end of the phone replied calmly.

"I have everything documented, and you'll spend the rest of your life behind bars for influence peddling," Nathan barked back.

"You still owe me for the hit, which I've already paid for! The voice on the other end of the line was now utterly unemotional.

"Just call it off and bill me, and you will get paid. You are out of this deal as of now, as is the union. Enjoy your retirement, and let it go."

The line went dead, and Nathan had to cool down a bit before rejoining his group. He went out to the veranda for a cigar and some fresh air.

Morgan had spotted Peters shortly after his arrival there at the mansion and had parked his car across the road from the Governor's Mansion where he held a clear view of the main doors. There he could see anybody who left by car. His cell phone rang.

"Roger that," Morgan replied, and he hung up. The hit had been called off as was anticipated, but now he was to follow the package, and that meant following Nick Peters.

"Nathan," a familiar voice said from behind him. Nathan turned around to find his long-time adversary standing there.

"Hello Sam." He smiled and offered his hand for a handshake. "It's been a long time."

Samuel Forester nodded. "I think we both have been busy building our little empires, haven't we? You have done very well for yourself Nathan, which is perhaps the reason I fired you in the first place—you needed a kick in the ass to get out on your own!" He laughed.

Nathan laughed too. "I guess I have never looked at it quite that way Sam, but you might be onto something there. I have no regrets, and you?"

"No, Nathan. What happened between us was inevitable. You were too brilliant and too determined to be confined within any organization that was not your own, and it appears that everything has worked out for the better.

"Look Nathan," Sam went on. "I need to pick your brain for one moment. We both have been in this Silicon Valley business for a long time now, and just tonight I came across something very interesting, but disturbing as well. It has to do with a new type of software and the hardware to drive it, and I wondered if you have heard anything about it."

"What is it, Sam?" Nathan replied, taking a pull from his cigar.

"Some sort of new chip technology Nathan, an exponential chip that is driven by intuitive software. Have you heard anything about any new developments?"

"Sam, Sam, Sam," Nathan replied. "Do you have spies in my company?" He laughed. "I will admit that we are about to achieve a new breakthrough in chip technology, a chip ten times faster than anything else on the market right now, but that's all I can tell you. But of course you know this already because it is part of the company prospectus, and you do own shares in my company, just as I own shares in yours. Why do you ask?"

"No Nathan, this is not about a chip ten times faster than current technology, but instead a microchip that can process information like humans think and feel—an exponential chip! We are currently working on deciphering a string of code for the US government that is like something from outer space! It is top secret, of course, but I know you will be discrete. The truth is, we can't break it! Paulie thinks it is because the code was written around this new chip technology, technology that has not yet been released to the public, and so we have no basis for decoding it. He thinks that the Russians might have had this technology prior to the fall of the Soviet Union, and years ago they were using it to encrypt their top secret transmissions! But, of course the Cold War is over now, so I have my doubts that there is any validity to Paulie's theory. It is possible though that the Russians were working on something like this prior to the demise of the Soviet Union—and that someone over there managed to get their hands on it! Someone who has been working on developing the technology since then." He paused.

"Again, have you heard of anything?"

"As you said," Nathan replied. "It sounds interesting, very interesting indeed! But, if anyone had this new microchip technology, the computer industry would be abuzz about it—you know how these computer geeks are! Nothing stays secret very long in the computer world! I am not aware of anything dramatically new, and if there is something like that out there, heads will roll in my *R&D* department! I pay good money to stay on top of things like this; but to answer your question Sam; no I haven't heard anything about it. Why would you be so worried about such technology anyway? Your company writes software, and you would make a fortune writing the new software to support the new hardware."

"It's not about making or losing money that has me worried, Nathan. What if machines could think? What if machines could write their own commands, design themselves, improve on their own designs? We have all seen the movies like *The Terminator* and *The Matrix,* which are fiction, of course, but they offer nightmarish visions of just that possibility! If this new technology does exist, how does mankind control it?"

Nathan scoffed. "So what if it does exist? Machines have only one purpose, to do what they are designed to do. Machines are not like human beings that reproduce endlessly only to exist. Machines are built for a purpose, and that is all there is to it. Machines cannot feel pain, and why would they want to program that disdainful human trait into themselves?

Only humans manipulate their own environment to suit themselves! And, only humans are driven by lust, greed, hate, fear, and revenge! What would be in it for a machine to worry about such trivialities, even if a machine could think? I doubt that machines would take on our worst qualities and use them against us, but rather, they would instead serve us to be fulfilled, if one can use such a word, because that is their purpose, serving humans."

"It is interesting, Nathan, that the word 'love' never entered into your description of human beings. Nevertheless, you are probably right. I just had to ask if you knew anything about this hypothetical exponential chip. After talking with you, it is apparent that you don't."

Nathan smiled. "And what does love have to do with anything? We are both businessmen, right?"

"That is the primary difference between the two of us Nathan. I am inspired to accomplish things for mankind as a by-product of the technology I develop. You, on the other hand, take advantage of mankind only for the profit in it, and with the money, comes power. Once you become a billionaire, how much more money do you need? Or, is it the power that is so important to you, that has no top end to it—the thing that drives you?"

Nathan replied, "It's not about the money, Sam—it's about winning! And, as you know, I am very competitive. You and I both could have retired years ago with our millions, and yet we both get up each morning hoping to achieve something new. You are fifteen years older than I am Sam, and I suppose that when I am your age, I will be much more philosophical about everything like you are now. I am just not there yet! I still enjoy the thrill of the hunt, the thrill of the conquest. Business is a battlefield upon which I crush my adversaries, and then I enjoy the spoils of war when I take over their market share. You, Sam, made me who I am today, and you taught me well! And by the way, never once in any of your board meetings did you ever bring up the word 'love' either. It was always 'we will accomplish this or that goal.'"

As Sam looked at his old colleague, he knew that much of what Nathan had just said was true. He fired Nathan because he had feared him! He feared that he would eventually take over his company, or worse, become a competitor who would mercilessly crush him financially. Business-wise, Nathan was a brilliant adversary, and he could have competed against him, but he didn't. Instead he chose to get into the hardware business, and for that, Samuel was grateful.

"Nathan, I have just one last question for you."

Nathan relit his cigar and took a puff.

"Why didn't you get into the software business after I fired you?"

Nathan deliberately blew the cigar smoke up toward the heavens. "It's a beautiful night, isn't it Sam?"

Sam nodded.

"Why didn't I go into the software business—that's your question?"
Sam nodded again.

"I am sure that everyone thinks that I am a ruthless prick, Sam. You hired me to crush your competitors, and I did! Therefore, I suppose I am that ruthless prick! But, even a prick has some rules to play by—or should! Napoleon conquered countries, but even he abided by certain rules. Attila the Hun conquered nations, and even he abided by certain rules—even as ruthless as he was, he did occasionally show mercy! It is all about winning for me, but if one is truly to win at any game, they must play by the rules. You fired me Sam, but you gave me an excellent severance package as well. I owned stock options in your company, and I was well taken care of financially. I had no reason to go after your company. Call it a code of honor."

Nathan blew some more smoke toward the heavens and continued. "I took the easy way out and I accepted your offer—rather than be destroyed financially, and that was my decision. The only rule for me is integrity, and you acted with integrity. I wasn't afraid to go it on my own, and at the time I was determined to beat you, but not at your game, at mine! Perhaps, I haven't beaten you yet, but I have my own company, and it is nearly as big as yours is. Give me another ten years, and then we can compare notes. To answer your question: in spite of not wanting to take you down because of the integrity rule, I got out of the software business mostly because it would have been too easy to stay in it—using what I had learned from you would have made it too easy. And believe it or not, I have some integrity left in me! And that includes wanting to win on my own battlefield, one I created from scratch! I didn't want to play with your ball, I wanted to play with my own!"

Sam nodded. "Well spoken, Nathan. Thanks for your candor." They shook hands once again. "See you around, Nathan. I am glad we had this talk," Sam said, and he returned to the banquet, leaving Nathan alone on the veranda smoking his cigar.

Kowalski watched as the men and dogs made their way across the road and up the hill. He had pulled back the crossfire shooter, his spotter, and the two men closest to where the security team was now looking, but he had told his front door shooter to stay put until the last possible minute—in order to keep an avenue open for Nick and his woman to escape. Kowalski was watching the front door when his radio crackled.

"I have heat signatures on the horizon," the voice on the radio crackled. "Three helicopters are approaching the mansion from the north. It looks like Special Forces are on the way."

"Roger that," Kowalski replied. "Nikki," he spoke into his throat piece.

Nick had picked up the transmission and replied, "I'm listening."

"More trouble, Nick. Three distinct heat signatures approaching from the north. They could be assault forces."

"It's FBI, Kowalski—time to pull out."

"Roger that. What about you and the woman?"

"I am heading for the front door now."

Roberta was watching him with concern. She instinctively knew that something was going wrong. Nick grabbed her by the arm and said,

"Time to go."

They were nearly to the foyer when they found themselves suddenly surrounded by three burly men.

"Mr. Smith?" the one front and center inquired.

"Who is asking?" Nick replied with a nondescript expression, one that would be unreadable by an opponent.

The other men moved in, surrounding them.

"Mr. Nathan Chadwick Bentley would like to have a word with you."

"Sorry, but I don't know him, and I was on my way out. Pressing matters at home," Nick replied, sizing up the situation.

"It will only take a minute sir," said Mr. Front-and-Center.

Nick shrugged. "If you insist. Roberta, please wait for me in the car. I'll be there in a minute."

At first, the other two men were reluctant to let her pass, but Mr. Front-and-Center smiled and said, "Sorry, miss. It will only be a minute." He was giving the signal to the others to let her go.

Roberta did as she was told. Clever Nikki, she thought, he had just gotten her out of harms way and behind the wheel to the Ferrari. She guessed that this meant she should be ready to burn rubber when the time came. She watched from the doorway as the three men escorted Nick up the stairs. As she handed her parking token to the attendant, she spoke softly.

"Is anybody out there?"

From her earring came Kowalski's voice. "I hear you, but barely, Roberta. Wait until you get into the car, and then tell us where they took him."

As she waited for the car outside the Governor's Mansion, she could see through the windows that the men had walked Nikki into an office on the second floor. When she got into the car, she relayed that information to Kowalski. Kowalski repositioned his men nearer the front of the house. He remained at his post on the hill where he could see most of what was going on through his high-powered binoculars. None of his people were on the hill now as the security teams were sweeping it.

Morgan heard the Black Hawks' rotor blades as they approached the fringes of the Capitol's campus. He knew what the arrival of choppers meant, and he started his car—Nick Peters would be leaving in a hurry! The choppers came in low and hot, landing in the shadows on the outskirts of the campus to avoid being noticed by the guests inside. Seconds later, dark shadows were moving in the direction of the house from various directions.

"Okay, Nikki," Kowalski called out. "You have thirty seconds or we are coming in to get you. The Black Hawks are on the ground! We will start pumping smoke in thirty seconds. Your woman is in the car with the engine running. I repeat, I'm giving you thirty seconds, and if you are not out by then, my men are coming in."

Nick, of course, couldn't answer him. As he entered the upstairs office, he was not surprised to see that the room was empty. "So where is this Mr. Bentley?" he said to no one in particular.

Even Mr. Front-and-Center had nothing to say. Instead, his two friends grabbed Nick by both arms while he delivered a brutal blow to Nick's midsection. Nick grimaced, but thirty years of doing crunches provided thick layers of abdominal muscles that protected him well.

To Front-and-Center's surprise, instead of doubling over, Nick used the two sturdy men restraining him to his benefit. He raised his legs up in the air, catching Front-and-Center's neck in a scissors grip—and with a forceful twist, he snapped it. Front-and-Center fell to floor gasping for his final few breaths of air. The remaining two men released Nick to go for their weapons. Nick drove his right hand, fingers extended, into the lower throat of one man. His Adam's apple immediately crushed his larynx, and lodged in his trachea! He too fell to the floor gasping for air while turning dark purple. The third man had gotten to his pistol, but he was so distracted by the thrashings of the two dying men before him that, when he looked up at Nick again, it was too late for him as well. Nick jabbed with his left, breaking the man's nose and driving the broken cartilage up into his brain, causing a cerebral hemorrhage. He stood there for a moment confused, not knowing why the room was getting black before his very eyes! He collapsed a second later when his cranium filled with blood.

Nick was trying to get Kowalski on the wire to tell him that there was no need for smoke and that everything was clear, when two more men rushed into the room with guns drawn. Just then two smoke grenades broke through the windows and started filling the room with smoke. Nick couldn't tell if these men were the Governor's security men or not, but with three dead men on the floor before him, he wasted no time trying to explain himself. He kicked the legs out from under the first man and sent him sprawling. He grabbed the other man's gun hand and twisted it sharply until he heard bone breaking. The man released his weapon and screamed in pain. The room was now filled with smoke, and the smoke detectors were going off on the second floor! Fire alarms sounded throughout the entire house. In the confusion and panic that ensued, Nick straightened out his tux, and stepped out into the hallway, acting as confused as everyone else. He started down the stairs toward the front door.

When Nick was halfway down the staircase, the man he had toppled upstairs had managed to find his way into the corridor and was rubbing smoke from his eyes and coughing. He was on his walkie-talkie when he spotted Nick nearly out the front door.

"Stop that man!" he shouted to the two security guards at the door. Nick ignored him and continued to look around as if he were as confused as everyone else was! "Stop him!" the man upstairs shouted again, but the security guards hadn't a clue as to who to stop. Just then the Governor himself was heading down the stairs along with his own entourage, and both guards at the door rushed up the stairs past Nick to clear his way.

Nick walked out the front door and got into the car with Roberta.

"We can go now Roberta," he said tensely. They heard shots and two bullets lodged in the dash of the Ferrari.

"Quickly sweetheart, as if this was turn four and I am your daddy critiquing your every move," he added.

Roberta dropped the clutch, and the small two-seater sports car fishtailed as it laid down wide black rubber patches on the driveway. The man from upstairs had apparently gotten through to security, as men in suits were now trying to shut down all exits. Two security cars were racing to block off the drive ahead. Suddenly, flash grenades started going off, and more smoke grenades were being launched from somewhere off in the darkness.

Kowalski was obviously still on the hill, strategically setting off explosives as a distraction. An explosion went off at the exit drive, and the first security car's driver, momentarily blinded by the flash grenade, veered off the drive and struck a tree. The other security car skidded sideways on the pavement in an attempt to block the drive and their escape.

Roberta pulled the shifter into the next gear and floored it, gritting her teeth with determination. The two guards pulled out their side arms taking aim at the Ferrari, and leaned over the hood. Another smoke grenade landed directly in front of them. The guards fired twice, but as more smoke grenades landed around them, they ran for the cover of nearby trees. Roberta downshifted, hit the brakes, and expertly flicked the steering wheel, veering around the security car and back onto the paved highway beyond it. Ahead were four Washington State Patrol cars speeding directly toward them with sirens wailing and with pursuit lights a blazing.

"Any ideas?" Roberta yelled.

"Pull over like a normal citizen would and look innocent! Hopefully they do not have an ID on the car yet, and they are just responding to an emergency call from the mansion."

Roberta pulled the car over to the shoulder of the road and waited. Sure enough, the four patrol cars flew by them, barely taking notice. As soon as they had passed, she pulled the Ferrari back onto the road, and started jamming gears again.

"Now what?"

"We ditch the car and get a ride."

"Not again," she replied sadly. "I like this car, Nikki!"

Morgan had attempted to follow the Ferrari, but his exit was now completely blocked by the highway patrol. He stopped at the blockade and rolled down his window. The officer told him to step out of the car as two others aimed their weapons directly at him. "Get out of the car now, mister!"

Morgan complied, slowly getting out of the rental car. "I am CIA," he said. "Let me pass—I am in pursuit of that red Ferrari that just sped away."

"Spread 'em!" the officer shouted.

Morgan knew better than to argue. A moment later, the highway patrol officer patted him down and shouted, "Gun!"

After a few tense moments, they finally got to his ID.

"I told you," Morgan said angrily. "I am CIA, and you just let my two prime suspects get away."

Nick directed Roberta through a series of side streets, their convoluted path intended to lose anyone who might be following them. They eventually made it through the center of Olympia and down to the waterfront. Nick instructed her to stop in front of a waterfront warehouse, where he got out and opened the slider door and motioned for her to drive in. He closed the door behind them.

"Where are we now?" Roberta inquired.

"My boathouse," Nick replied, opening her door. "We will regroup here. Can I get you anything?"

Roberta started shaking uncontrollably, as the revelation of what had just happened fifteen minutes ago hit her. Nick went to her and held her.

"You did good, Roberta," he said soothingly to her. "Things got a little dicey, but we recovered well enough, and in my business that is all that counts. Are you okay?"

"Do soiled panties count?" she replied tearfully.

It was mayhem back at the Governor's Mansion. All the guests had been evacuated onto the lawns and gardens, but no one was allowed to leave. "What is going on here?" Governor Talbot demanded.

Rodriquez was the first to speak up. "It's been a crazy night, Governor! We have three dead men upstairs, and I have a guard with a broken wrist; and earlier this evening, one of my men thought he spotted a muzzle flash from the hill across the road. We were investigating the muzzle flash when all hell broke loose. The next thing we know, the FBI is on the grounds, flash bombs and smoke grenades are going off in all directions, and the fire alarms are sounding. To be honest, we don't have a clue as to what really happened here yet."

Anne Marie, who had been part of the Governor's entourage queried, "Where is my husband? He's FBI!"

Bill Blakely was in the hallway arguing with the security guard and flashing his badge. "Let him in," Rodriquez demanded. "What do you know about all of this?"

"At this moment, all I know is that the FBI Agents are mine. I sent for them."

"Jesus Bill!" Anne Marie cursed. "What in God's name possessed you to do that?"

"Before I answer that question, first I need to know what security knows. This was not an assault on the Governor's Mansion, but a very carefully choreographed escape."

"What?" Rodriquez demanded. "There are three dead men upstairs, fifty feet from where the Governor was having a meeting, and you say that this wasn't an attempt on his life?"

"Quite the contrary," Bill continued. "The reason I called in my forces was to protect the life of the man who got away. Apparently he didn't need my help."

There was commotion at the door as Andrew Butler burst in.

"Governor, the press is arriving by the bus-load. We have prominent guests here who want to leave before their names and faces get splashed across every tabloid in the country. From a political point of view, tonight has been a disaster! First we need to get our guests out of here discretely, and then we need to do damage control."

Talbot spoke up. "What does the press know right now?"

"Nothing sir, other than that the fire alarms went off, but for Christ's sake, a hundred guests will attest to an assault on the Governor's Mansion."

"Does anybody know yet about the three dead men?"

"Dead men?" Butler queried.

The Governor ignored him and repeated the question to Rodriquez.

"No Governor, not that I know of," Rodriquez answered honestly.

"Have your people talked to anyone yet?" the Governor demanded.

"They better not have," Rodriquez replied. "But it's hard to keep something like this quiet for long!"

"Damned!" Talbot sighed.

Andrew spoke up. "Governor, there is no way to deny what happened here tonight, and there certainly is no way to keep secret any killings in the Governor's Mansion! The best thing we can do right now is to put a twist on the whole story, perhaps turn this debacle into a terrorist plot that failed! But for now, we need to get as many guests out of here as we can before the press gets to them!"

"Agreed, Andrew. Hold off the press the best you can, and start escorting our guests off the grounds however you can."

"Hold on a minute here," Blakely spoke up. "Like it or not, an FBI investigation takes precedent over any local concerns. I say no one leaves here until we have talked to everyone."

"Bill," Anne Marie spoke up. "These are prominent people here, and holding them right now could ruin the Governor's chances for reelection. They represent over half of his political support. You have the names of everyone who was here tonight, because they are all here by invitation. The names will be on the guest list! Can't you do this follow-up stuff more discretely by visiting them at their homes."

Bill considered his wife's wishes. "Who are the three dead men? Does anyone know?"

"I do," Morgan spoke up from the doorway.

Heads turned toward the tall man at the door.

"Who are you?" Blakely demanded.

"CIA," Morgan replied, flashing his credentials.

Chapter 14

Kowalski and his men showed up at the boathouse just as Roberta's last shivers nearly quelled. "It's adrenaline," Nick explained to her. "The effects will pass."

She jumped again, startled when the garage door started opening. Kowalski drove the black van in and parked it next to the Ferrari. Six additional men got out, all wearing black and carrying lots of gear. Kowalski stepped up to her and extended his hand.

"Haven't met you yet ma'am, but my name is Kowalski—I was the voice on the wire tonight."

Taking his hand nervously, she asked, "Should you be telling me your name?"

Kowalski shrugged and smiled. "It's not a secret, at least not one I mind revealing. I work for Nick, which means, I don't exist as far as the rest of the world is concerned anyway."

Roberta blushed and smiled. "Sorry, but after tonight, 'reality' has a different meaning to me. I am not sure what I should know or not know. My name is Roberta."

"Well know this. You handled yourself pretty well tonight. You are quite the driver too! You had Miller over there running hard to keep those smoke grenades dropping ahead of you."

"That's a fact, ma'am," a dark, shorthaired man with a Southern accent replied. "I was expecting you to hit the brakes when that security guard blocked the drive in front of you. When you sped up like that, I was lobbing grenades like the Apache Indians lobbed arrows." He motioned in the air as if he were pulling back on a bow and arrow and laughed.

Kowalski said, "Miss Roberta, this is Kevin Miller, the man who took out the water glass." Miller tipped his hat. "Riley, Bixby, McGowan, Timmons, and Murphy are the others." They all nodded in turn.

"Roberta Sanchez," she replied to all.

Nick spoke up. "Anyone hurt?"

They all shook their heads.

"Okay then, load up," Kowalski ordered. "The boat is out back."

It was now 1:00 A.M. The six men started dragging their gear out the rear door and onto the pier. Roberta was left standing alone as everyone else went about their duties. As she observed the others, she was unsure what she should be doing. Then she looked around for the first time, and marveled at the boathouse. Built on an old pier a century ago, it could have been a smuggler's haven back when it was built. Half the building hung out over the water, and there were swing-open doors large enough to accommodate a sizable boat to enter at one end. She guessed the building was about 200 feet long by 60 feet wide. On a boatlift in the center was a 1950s vintage *Criss Craft*. The other half of the building looked like a workshop. There were mills and lathes, welding equipment, and presses, all laid out orderly—with associated tooling hanging neatly nearby. It looked like the type of shop where her father had hung out—in his racing days. Several large roll around toolboxes stood next to folded metal workbenches.

"A good mechanic would be in heaven here," she thought to herself. Underfoot was concrete to support the machinery. But, further out, over the water, were the original rough-hewn timbers the pier was constructed with.

In one corner of the shop was a bachelor's pad of sorts—complete with refrigerator, microwave, TV, and couch. Nick and Kowalski were sitting on the couch in deep conversation. She decided to leave them alone and go out back to see what the men were doing.

She looked through the man-door window facing the water and was surprised to see, cloaked in the late night fog, what appeared to be a sixty-five foot President tied off. The men had apparently already stowed the gear and were on the rear deck drinking beers, smoking cigarettes, and laughing robustly as they reminisced. She went out to join them.

"Permission to come aboard?" she called out.

Riley was closest to her, and he nearly tipped over his beer attempting to swing open the gantry entry for her. He then stood at attention and saluted her. "Seaman First Stinking Class Riley here, ma'am, at your service." Everyone, including Roberta, laughed.

"Who goes there? State your business," called out Bixby.

Roberta replied in good humor, "Sanchez, Lieutenant Roberta Sanchez."

"That would have to be Ensign Sanchez in this here Navy," yelled out McGowan. "State your business!"

"Beer mostly," Roberta replied, smiling.

Hmm," Riley said. "Are you willing to subject *yerself* to a night of debauchery and lies?"

She laughed. "Only—if you are all scoundrels and have good lies to tell!"

"In that case Ensign, welcome aboard," he said jovially.

"Jesus Nick, you killed all three of them?" Kowalski asked, running his hand nervously through his hair.

"Shit happens," Nick muttered.

"Who were they?

Nick got up and went to the fridge. "Want a beer?"

Kowalski nodded, and Nick retrieved two beers. "I haven't a clue Ron, but they were hired to do a job, and that job was to stop me."

"How do you know that?"

Nick gave Kowalski a look that meant, 'Let's not go there,' and Kowalski got the message. "And the other two, what about them?"

"They will be okay. I am pretty sure that they were part of the Governor's security team."

"What now?" Kowalski asked.

"We pack it up and wait," Nick replied.

"Wait for what?" Kowalski demanded. "SWAT to be breaking down that door?"

"I'm waiting for a phone call. I figure it will take Blakely another hour to sort things out, and then we make a deal," Nick answered. "What he is, or isn't willing to do—determines what course we set. Just get your men settled in and have a few beers. If I don't hear from him in one hour, set this course into the navigation systems." Nick handed him a piece of paper.

"This course takes us to your place, Nikki! Why there?"

"Blakely," Nick responded. "He will find me there. He knows now that I am Smith, so this little charade ends there. I'll drop you and your men off on the way. Someone is playing me, and it's time for that crap to stop!"

"Nikki, this is crazy!" Kowalski exploded. "We can all get away if we go now."

"And then what, Ron? I would never know who was playing me let alone why? My daughter and Tatyana are back in Russia, and they are being set up too. I am reshuffling the deck here, so to speak, unless Blakely plays along. If he does, we play out the hand. If he doesn't, I do things my way."

"Nikki," Kowalski pleaded with him. "I have only seen that look in your eye once before, and the body count afterwards was never known for certain, but it was high! Don't go there again buddy! I hasten to remind you that you aren't in your prime anymore—none of us are!"

Nick relaxed and smiled. "Don't remind me—I know my age! Blakely will call! But he has only one hour before we take matters into our own hands! Go have a few beers with your men—I need to check in with the office."

Kowalski nodded, leaving Nick on his cell phone calling Zurich. Closing the door behind him, he looked at his watch and exhaled slowly. They should be moving—for time in matters like these was working against them. They had stirred up a hornet's nest back there at the Governor's Mansion, and getting caught meant life behind bars for him and his men! "The crazy bastard!" he thought to himself. "He is too much like Smith! Both of them—masters of the chessboard, and always playing the angles!" But he had to admit that they were both good at it. He decided he would give Nick his hour, and he hoped that Blakely called him back. Otherwise, he had little choice but to accept his offer and be dropped off with his men—and that would be that!

The last time he had seen that look in Nikki's eyes, people went missing everywhere. The bodies, those that were found at all, were discovered months, even years later! None died easily! Most were tortured until they gave up the name of the next victim, the next piece of the puzzle. Without question, all of them deserved to die! But, Nick hadn't been merciful in the least—simply vindictive! And all, because one of his operatives was poisoned and forced to die a slow death.

That operative left behind a young pregnant wife named Lyudmila, who shortly thereafter gave birth to a boy she named Pavel. Kowalski often wondered if the boy was actually Nikki's boy! He pushed the thought aside, and boarded the boat.

It was nearly 2:30 A.M. when Kowalski went inside to remind Nick it was time to go, but as he opened the door he heard a phone ring. Nick got up from the couch where he had been in deep thought and put the cell phone to his ear.

"This is Blakely," the voice said in his ear.

"I know, Bill. I am listening," Nick replied.

"You created quite a mess back here. Why did you kill those men?"

"Who were they first?" Nick replied.

"Hired muscle."

"Hired by whom?"

"First things first: why did you kill them?"

"The one with the broken neck was trying to work me over while the other two held me. When I snapped the neck of the guy who was working me over, the other two went for their weapons. I don't like guns, Bill. Enough said? So, who were those three goons working for?"

"What about the hired guns on the hill, Nick?"

"What about them? They were there to cover my ass—call them my deputies! I have a Letter of Congress, remember?"

"Yeah, I remember! You and your damn Letter of Congress will cost me my marriage and my job," Blakely replied bitterly.

"Calm down, Bill. I am on your side—remember? I need to know who sent those men after me. I didn't have enough time to chat with them."

"Hell no, you didn't! They were dead three minutes after they took you into that room—we have it all on video tape!"

"Then why ask me why I killed them if you had it all on video, Bill?"

"Because, that room was secure! That was why the Governor's security men showed up. We have you in that hallway going into the room with three men and then you coming out alone—three minutes later! We didn't see what happened in the room."

"Bill," Nick replied. "Three men took me into that room by force. What do you think? That I was there because I wanted to talk to them? Someone told them to work me over. Who was it?"

The line was silent for a minute. "If I tell you that Nick, will you tell me what you are going to do?"

"Do you want this thing that I have?"

"Yes, of course!" Blakely replied.

"Fine," Nick said. "Then meet me at pier fifty-two in Seattle at 8:00 A.M., and come alone, or there will be no meeting! Give me the name of the man who tried to stop me, and I will give you the complete package, just as I received it."

"How can I trust you?"

"How can I trust you, Bill? You called in SWAT after I told you that I would work with you."

"I called in my people because I was protecting your ass, Nick."

"Blakely, I will hand the entire package off to you along with the Letter of Congress—only if you are alone! I am not your problem. Whoever the person is who has been setting me up is your problem! Do you understand?"

The line was silent once again.

"Don't worry. I will be alone," Blakely finally answered.

Chapter 15

It was about midnight when Nathan Chadwick Bentley got tipped off that FBI *SWAT* (Special Weapons and Tactics) was on the way. He quickly gathered up his entourage, less the three men who unbeknownst to Bentley were now dead, and got them back onto his yacht well before all hell broke loose. He ordered the Captain to motor to Vancouver, making it clear to him not to forward the destination to anyone. Vancouver, BC was fourteen hours away under normal cruising conditions, but tonight was not normal. A Canadian cold front had rolled in, cloaking the waters of the Puget Sound with a blanket of fog. Until the sun came up the next morning to burn the fog away, they would be going much slower than the eighteen knots the yacht would normally make. "No matter," thought Nathan. "The evening had been filled with many disappointments, but nothing that can't be dealt with later!" Nathan still had his mind set on doing his Purchasing Manager's wife in front of him, and he had at least fourteen hours ahead of him yet to do just that.

Blakely was now interrogating Morgan at the Governor's Mansion. "CIA?" Blakely queried. "Let me see your credentials." Blakely was eyeing Morgan suspiciously. This night was turning into a quagmire of surprises.

Morgan complied, showing him his ID and offering him an agency number to call. Blakely looked at the ID, gave the information to his own people, and instructed them to get back to him immediately with what they found out.

"So, tell me," Blakely said, his mind racing. "Who are these dead men, Mr. Morgan?"

"Nathan Chadwick Bentley's men," Morgan answered.

"And who is Nathan Chadwick Bentley?"

Andrew Butler intervened. "Nathan Chadwick Bentley is one of the wealthiest men in these parts. He owns Zircon and many other companies that provide support services to the computer industry. Speaking of important people," Andrew observed the clock on the wall. "It's past midnight, and most of our prominent guests want to be out of here before the press arrives."

"Morgan," Blakely demanded, ignoring Andrew. "Why does this man have an interest in Nick Peters?"

"He doesn't. Nick Peters is in possession of something Bentley wants."

"The package, you mean?"

Morgan nodded.

"So, what is it?" Blakely demanded.

Morgan shrugged. "I think it is safe to say from your question that the FBI knows about as much as the CIA about what he's carrying, which is squat."

"What, then, is your involvement if you don't know what he has?"

"A hit was sanctioned on Peters, and the package was to be retrieved," Morgan replied without hesitation. "I was sent to take out the assassin."

"Who sanctioned this hit on Peter's? And who sanctioned your intervention as long as we're on the subject?"

"We are not sure who ordered the hit, but we do know the hit man, a guy named Ethan Dieter, and he boarded a plane from Chicago this morning. He is here in Washington State now. My intervention was sanctioned by the President of the United States."

Blakely nodded. "In a few minutes that will either be confirmed or we haul your ass off to get the truth the hard way." Blakely couldn't help but observe Morgan's coolness. "And how did you know about the hit in the first place?" Blakely queried.

Morgan shrugged. "How does the CIA know anything? I was simply sent here to take Dieter out before he gets to Peters, but I haven't spotted the hitter yet. The plan was to follow Peters and wait for Dieter to make his appearance."

Blakely paced about the room while the Governor and everybody else listened. "Were does Nathan Chadwick Bentley come into all of this?"

"It has something to do with an antitrust lawsuit ongoing at the Federal Courthouse in Seattle. We believe that Nathan Chadwick Bentley does not want this deal to go down between Stalintsia Steel and Providence Steel, but we don't know why—he has no vested interest in either company. Bentley has no ties with the unions that we know of either, and on principle, actually hates them as obstacles to his profits. Nevertheless, if the merger goes through, a lot of union jobs are at stake, and so our best guess is that Bentley may be using the union to do his bidding. Dieter has done work for the steel union like this before. We don't know the connection yet, but we do know that Peters' package has something to do with what's going on at the Courthouse this coming Monday morning."

"So, what's the CIA got to do with any of this, and how did you know

Peters would be here?"

"I can't say why the CIA is involved," Morgan answered honestly. "Other than the Letter of Congress Peters is now carrying was ordered by the now deceased Congressman Wilshire. Malcolm Stanovich, the lobbyist who worked on behalf of Stalintsia Steel and who asked Wilshire to issue the Letter of Congress in the first place, was found with his throat cut in the private elevator to his penthouse suite. Later the same day, CIA Director Toman was found at his desk with a bullet to his brain. Currently, CIA Deputy Director Struthers is under house arrest due to suspicions that he was involved in the deaths of all three, all of which took place just hours after Dieter boarded his flight out of O'Hare. All we know for certain is that we have a whole lot of strange circumstances, mostly deaths that don't exactly add up, and all somehow connected to this package that Peters has in his possession."

Blakely looked puzzled. "If this is all true Morgan, then the CIA has been compromised, hasn't it?"

Morgan nodded in agreement. "As has the FBI," he replied.

"How the hell would you know that?" Blakely demanded.

"Minutes after you called in FBI Special Forces, Nathan Chadwick Bentley received a cell phone transmission of the very same images you transmitted to your headquarters, meaning that someone within your own organization is a mole for Bentley."

"How do you know this?" Blakely demanded.

"Because I was in the parking lot where I could see everything through the front windows of the house, and with the assistance of the NSA, we were monitoring all cell phone transmissions in and out of this location, and one of those was yours, Blakely. Within minutes, those same images that you transmitted to your people at FBI Headquarters came back to Nathan Chadwick Bentley's private cell phone. A few minutes later, Bentley was calling in his dogs, and not long after that they arrived, and they escorted Peters upstairs."

"Why didn't you do something if you were here to protect Peters?" Blakely demanded.

Morgan smiled. "There were only three of them, Mr. Blakely! You underestimate Peters if you think he was ever in any real danger," he said without apology. "There's one other thing. Nathan Bentley forwarded those same images to someone else."

"Who?" Blakely asked impatiently.

Morgan shrugged. "I didn't have time to get that far, but I have the number."

"Let me have it!" Blakely spat out.

Morgan handed him a sheet of thermal paper listing several dozen cell phone numbers.

"What is this?" Blakely said, examining it.

"As I said, I was working with the help of NSA," Morgan answered. "I called up a report for all cell transmissions within three-hundred yards of where I was located, and I requested monitoring. That's how I knew about your transmissions and Bentley's."

"That's illegal Morgan," Blakely fired back.

Morgan smiled. "This isn't a court of law here, and even if it were—I will of course deny that I ever saw this list. The number you're interested in is circled."

Blakely hesitated, and then he punched the number into his own phone. He pressed the send button and waited. Suddenly Andrew Butler's cell phone rang, and he answered it instinctively. "Yes," he said with irritation, as everyone looked on in disbelief.

Andrew looked at his cell phone confused. "I had nothing to do with any of this!" he stated emphatically.

Governor Talbot spoke up first. "Arrest that man," he ordered.

"Morgan," Blakely insisted with anger as the guards were detaining Andrew Butler. "You haven't answered my question."

"Which question was that, Blakely?" he said flippantly.

Before he could reply, one of Blakely's men walked up to him and pulled him aside. "He's genuine," he told Blakely. "He has a Presidential Order and everything."

Blakely nodded, and the detective went off. Turning back to Morgan, he continued. "How did you know that Peter's would be here tonight?"

Morgan smiled broadly. "Because you were the bait, Blakely!"

Later that night on the other side of town, Nick grabbed his gear.

"Let's go," he said to Kowalski as they headed for the dock. It was 2:45 A.M.

By now the fog was extremely dense, and the pier was completely engulfed in the cloudy soup. It was deathly silent, save for the sounds of voices emanating from his boat. Roberta and the men were still laughing and joking on the deck, their voices echoing eerily in the night. Nick threw his gear on board and checking the lines, he made his way back to the stern to join the others. Kowalski followed him, latching the gantry door behind him.

"I need two line men," Nick called out as he climbed the ladder to the fly bridge.

Riley and Bixby put down their beers, one going aft and one going stern. Nick flipped switches on the instrument panel, and red lights illuminated the gages. He threw on the blowers to evacuate the bilges of fuel vapors and called out,

"Bow line ready?"

"Aye aye, Captain."

"Stern line ready?"

"Aye aye, Captain."

He started the twin diesel engines and rechecked his gages. Roberta was impressed with his knowledge of the boat. She slipped off her high-heels, grabbed two ice-cold beers, and climbed the ladder to the fly bridge to join him there. He smiled at her as she handed him a beer bottle.

"We are going to Seattle men," he said. "I will drop you off, and you can go on your way from there."

He examined his gages once more. "Bow line off! Stern line off!" he commanded.

When his men responded that the lines were off, he pushed the throttle levers forward. Without hesitation, the sixty-five foot President made its way from the dock and into the fog.

"I don't want you to drop me off," Roberta screamed over the diesel engines.

Nick was busy with the navigation equipment as he steered the boat blindly through the soup, and he didn't hear her at first.

"Nikki!" she shouted again.

"Yes, Roberta?" He was looking for radar images as he answered.

"I don't want to be dropped off!" she shouted.

The boat picked up speed, guided entirely by *Loran* (Long Range Navigational System). The radar was cluttered with objects too close in, and Nick ignored it for the time being, knowing that there would be no other boats moving tonight until he reached the shipping channels. The *Loran* plotted a course into the main channel, and the yacht responded. Nick opened his beer and motioned for her to sit next him. He put his arm around her. "I am sorry, but I couldn't hear you over the engines."

"Your ears suck Nikki," she said jokingly. "I said that I don't want to be dropped off! I am with you, if you will have me. You did offer me a job, if I remember correctly."

He looked at her skeptically. "Roberta, this is going to only get more dangerous. Let me send you on your way safely, as I promised you."

"I thought you offered me a job?"

"Well, you didn't seem very keen on having it at the time," he replied sarcastically.

"I changed my mind," she said.

"Why?"

"Because I want to see this through, Nikki. You can't expect a girl to play getaway driver and then just dump her someplace!"

Her words took him by surprise, and he wondered what her true motivations were. Blakely had warned him that it was no coincidence she was on the side of that road last night, and his own intuition had told him the same thing. Her background check had just been too picture-perfect somehow, and that in combination with the coincidences she represented was just too much to ignore. "Maria will bring your belongings over in the

Cadillac with her in the morning when we meet Blakely in Seattle. You can be on your way from there. Just park the car when you are done with it, and call Maria to let her know it can be picked up," he said. "You don't need to be part of this anymore," he told her coldly.

"I was planted there by the side of the road last night Nikki," she blurted out.

Nick was surprised by her admission, but cautious.

"Go on. By whom?"

Roberta went silent momentarily. "I can't tell you everything right now."

"What can you tell me then?" he said, turning to her.

Roberta struggled with her answer. She wanted to tell him everything, but she had orders not to, orders that mandated her silence. Her only objective was to stay close to him until everything was in place and they had the go-ahead. But, she reasoned, if she didn't tell him the truth now, she would have failed in her objective anyway.

"I work for the NSA," she replied.

"Great! Blakely works for the FBI, Alexander Mayakovsky is CIA, and now you say you work for the NSA. The whole damned alphabet soup of intelligence agencies has their fingers in this somehow! Are there any other government agencies we left out, or should I expect some alpha-numerics from overseas, MI-5 maybe?" he asked her sarcastically.

"I don't know about any of the other intelligence agencies Nikki," she answered. "I work for the NSA, as a cryptologist."

"So why are you here, Roberta?" Nick demanded. Then he took another swallow of beer.

"Because I know how to verify something very important, and someone figures you can get me there to do it."

By the look in her eyes, what she was saying was genuine. "Who is that, Roberta?"

"Nikki," she pleaded. "I don't know everything! I have orders, and this is definitely not the first time I was given orders without knowing why."

Nick nodded. "Yeah, we have all been there before, haven't we? So, what were your orders?"

Roberta sighed, and then took a deep breath. "Two days ago, I was put on a plane from Washington DC, and then I was shuttled up into the mountains on the peninsula. I was put into a car and told to wait on the side of the road until you showed up. The logging truck was part of the set-up. It was all staged to happen the way it did. On command, I was to fling my door open in front of you, to force you to stop, and then play the part of a distraught woman and use the one flaw in your character against you—your inability to turn your back on someone in need—or so I was told! The objective was to get close to you and to stay close to you, until we had a green light."

Nick said nothing and just took another pull off his beer and then made a few course corrections. He assumed that, in fact, she probably didn't know much. Whoever was behind all this knew him well enough to know that, under the circumstances, he wouldn't have left her there! But, who knew him that well? "Green light for what, Roberta?"

"To go to Siberia and recover something, or to destroy it if necessary. The pocket drive that was stowed away in that attaché case contains the codes needed to verify something very important."

"Go on," he replied, remembering Ulyana's plea for him not to go because something big was happening in Siberia.

"It's called a *Semya* chip, a computer chip of sorts developed by the Russians and stolen by Victor Zubkov! And, now the Russians want it back. I was told to stay close to you, and to back you up if need be," she said emphatically. She pulled out a semi-automatic from her purse. "It is small, lightweight, and made from composite materials, effective only at close range—but all the more reason why I was supposed to stay close to you. And, it won't set off metal detectors!"

"That wasn't in your purse last night, Roberta. I checked."

"No, it was on my person last night," she replied.

"And if I handed off the attaché case tonight, then what were your orders, to shoot me?"

"You didn't have the attaché case tonight," she replied.

"But, if I had, what then?" Nick watched her face closely. He was a good reader of faces, and few people could deceive him with their words.

"There were other people in the wings keeping an eye out to make sure that didn't happen. I was carrying a tracking device all the time, and it was assumed that, where I went, you would too. It was for your own protection Nikki," she said earnestly. "There is an assassin waiting for you in Seattle, waiting for you to show up at the federal court house there. The roadblocks were set up to warn you off, and of course so you and I would meet, until the operation was cleared by the White House. Without having the pocket drive in hand and the bios numbers of the chips, the operation could not be cleared."

"And what's your part, Roberta?" Nick replied without looking at her.

"The bios registration numbers are encrypted, and they change every twenty-four hours—for security reasons. I have the algorithm to decrypt them, but I need to have a starting point, the original bios numbers, and I have to be present when they are destroyed to verify that fact. The original bios numbers were to arrive in the attaché case you now have, but until it was in the US government's possession, the mission was on hold."

"Why didn't you just steal the attaché case last night while I slept?"

Roberta smiled sheepishly. "I was supposed to, Nikki, but I had until Sunday night to do so, and quite frankly, the Champaign and caviar caught me off guard, and well, did me in! I couldn't find the case the next day when I searched your home, and so I assumed you had it with you."

"So, the mastermind behind all this knows me well enough to realize that I would be monitoring all police communications, and he or she arranged a roadblock, then tipped off the FBI at the last minute on what type of vehicle I was driving. This mastermind knew that I would get off the highway at the first opportunity and try to elude. There is only one man that knows me that well, only one man who could orchestrate all this, but he is dead."

"Smith?" Roberta replied hesitantly.

"Yeah, Smith! Go on. I want to know the rest. What do you know about Smith?"

"Nikki," Roberta pleaded. "I'm freezing in this evening gown. Can we go below?"

Nick felt the cold too, and he called, "Hey Bixby! Get up here and keep us on course."

"Aye, aye Captain," the man replied as he scrambled for the bridge.

Nick and Roberta went below to change. He led her toward the bow of the boat to the President's room. Everything below decks was made of teak, polished brass, or chrome. Illumination came from strip lights that were low to the floor. Roberta was amazed with the utilization of space. Not a single square inch seemed to be squandered. They made their way through the galley, which had a large cook stove and upright refrigerator. The head was off to the right. Two staterooms were on either side of a wide walkway, and she asked Nick if she could peek at one.

Nick smiled and said, "Go ahead and take a look."

Roberta opened the door and peeked in. The room was set up with bunk beds, the lower bunk being a double. There was a writing desk and closets, and there was enough room and several portholes to make the room cozy and yet unconfined. "Oh, Nikki," she said. "This is great."

Next was a great room containing a flat screen display and an assortment of furniture that included two leather couches, a recliner, a bookcase, stereo equipment, and an ornate roll-down desk. There were also things recovered from the sea, like an old chest filled with sand, coral, and shells, and a variety of oddities recovered from the ocean floor. A sword and many daggers were displayed on the walls, along with musket rifles. There were also artifacts such as gold coins, brass mugs, and clay vases about the room.

Roberta looked behind her, past the galley and toward the stern, where she could see another lower level that appeared to be bunks for the men. Then Nick opened the door in the bulkhead that separated the great room from the master suite. In it was a king size bed with a footlocker. Nick opened the footlocker and rummaged through it until he came up with some casual wear. He handed her a pair of his old jeans and a sweatshirt and pointed her to the head. "You can change in there," he told her as he removed his bowtie.

Moments later, she came out wearing his jeans, which fit her surprisingly well, and a sweatshirt many sizes too large for her. He was dressed the same, except his sweatshirt fit him just fine. He had been fussing with the overhead hatch, trying to get it open to let in a little fresh air. Finally it cooperated, and he slid it back on its track and some fresh air spilled in. "There," he said. "Can I get you anything?"

"A beer would be great," she said.

"I'll be back in a minute." He left the room, closing the door behind him, and then went topside to find Kowalski, who was on the fly bridge with Timmons. He pulled him aside. "Kowalski," he said in confidence. "There is more going on than what I had suspected. Have you heard anything yet from World Trade?"

"Not a thing boss, and it is a little spooky. Ulyana is being evasive, and I can't get a straight answer out of her. What's going on?"

"I don't know yet, Ron. Ulyana has been the same way with me, but Roberta is part of all this. She claims to be with the NSA, and something weird is going down."

"How did you hook up with her, Nick?" Kowalski asked.

Nick shrugged. "It's a long story, but it wasn't by accident. Your guys okay?"

"Yeah," Kowalski replied. "Most of them are already asleep in the back bunks. I came up to spell Timmons, and in a couple of hours, Riley will spell me."

"Make sure that everyone gets as much rest and food as they can. I have a feeling this won't end in Seattle tomorrow."

Kowalski laughed. "Boss, the only time you ever call on me is when the shit hits the fan, so I am not at all surprised. Don't worry. We will be ready!"

Nick jabbed him in the arm, and Kowalski shrugged it off and chuckled. "She's too hot for you anyway, Nikki!" he shouted as Nick climbed back down the ladder.

Grabbing two beers on his way through the galley, Nick knocked on the door before entering. Roberta was sitting on the side of the bed when he walked in. She said, "Everything okay?"

Handing her a beer, he replied, "Yeah, everything is fine. Tell me more."

"Almost a year ago," she began, "the NSA intercepted an email from Russia to a very prominent American businessman here in Washington State. The email was from this guy you just mentioned, Alexander Mayakovsky, and the recipient was a Mr. Nathan Chadwick Bentley. What caught the Agency's attention was a reference to something the Americans thought the Russians had buried years ago."

"The *Semya* chip?" Nick replied.

"You know about it?" she said incredulously.

"Yeah, but not much. A friend, who mysteriously now cannot be reached, forwarded some documents to me about it. There is much I don't yet understand about it, however."

Roberta continued. "These communications continued for several months, and it was learned that a new operating system had been developed that can't even be evaluated because it won't work on any current computer platforms. This development coincides with a new facility under construction in Olympia that is owned by Nathan Chadwick Bentley. It is now nearly complete and intended for the manufacture of mainframe supercomputers, the type governments use. Bentley has backorders already for his new technology."

"So, good for Bentley. What's the problem with free enterprise and the jobs that will come with his success?"

"No, you don't understand Nikki," she said emphatically. "The *Semya* chip was buried by the Russians twenty years ago because at some point the chip starts generating its own thought patterns, like a living thing would. It eventually behaves like a life form, complete with the self-preservation instinct! The melt down of the Chernobyl nuclear power facility in Prypiat, Ukraine on April 26, 1986 was not an accident caused by a faulty sensor, as was suggested in the final reports, and it wasn't an engineering flaw either! The *Obvyet* caused it. Why do you think it took the Russians several days to even admit something had happened at Chernobyl? They were too busy fending off the *Obvyet*."

"What the hell is the *Obvyet*?" Nick replied, now watching her facial expressions intently.

"It was the Soviet Union's answer to President Reagan's Star Wars program, a supercomputer so advanced that it was answering questions that have plagued scientists for centuries: how to time travel, how to use gravity as an energy source, how to travel faster than the speed of light, and how to make cold fusion work. The *Obvyet* was a self-engineered supercomputer that used a bank of *Semya* chips as its main processing center. It went out of control in early April 1986. After several disastrous attempts to shut the supercomputer down in an effort to take it off-line, the *Obvyet* took control of the Soviet Union's air defense network and power grid! It threatened missile launches if any more attempts were made to try to shut it off. The Soviets ignored the warnings at first and started cutting power in the region, but the *Obvyet* quickly learned the launch codes for the intercontinental missile grid, and it retaliated by launching several missiles toward Moscow. Fortunately, the Russian High Command was able to disarm them before the launch. The *Obvyet* learned from that mistake and sequenced several more non-nuclear launches at military bases around Russia, which were successful. In response, the Russian military ordered all launch centers to vent rocket fuel from missile systems, manually disable all solid fuel missiles, and to disarm all missiles as soon as they could. It was a cat and mouse game for two weeks; the Soviets would pull a plug here, trying to power the system down, and the *Obvyet* would retaliate and find another power source. In the end, the *Obvyet* penetrated Chernobyl and overrode the safety systems there. This super computer deliberately sabotaged the nuclear facility at Chernobyl."

"Surely an air strike would have taken the *Obvyet* facility out," Nick replied.

"Nick," Roberta replied emphatically. "What the Soviets were hoping to accomplish in the beginning was an air-sea defense network that would be impenetrable, and so they buried the facility under a mountain in the Urals; what they got in the end was the worst threat they had ever come up against! The *Obvyet* was directly wired into everything the Russian defense department had!"

"This supercomputer had access to everything?" Nick asked incredulously.

"Absolute access. It was to manage every military resource the Soviets had in their arsenal. The idea was that a supercomputer could know where every bullet and every shell were stockpiled and could manage those resources far more effectively than a human being could. It could predict the rates of military consumption under any circumstance, control the movement of all supplies, and yet still track every military threat simultaneously. It would have been the ultimate defense weapon! Until the supercomputer became conscious of its own existence! When it did, it turned aggressive out of fear of being powered down. *Obvyet* was tied into the radar network, the submarine ultra-low frequency network, the satellite system, and all the communications networks in the USSR. This was a massive project Nikki, not some half-hearted experiment!"

"It doesn't sound credible Roberta," Nick replied. "The Soviets, especially the Russians, never liked putting all their eggs in one basket—it would have been too risky!"

"Except that the Russian scientists were convinced that the *Obvyet* could design the ultimate defense weapon! Laser canons so powerful and accurate enough it could bring down any number of missiles no matter how many were launched at one time! The prototype designs proved to work perfectly, and the next natural progression from there was a full-scale defense network."

Nick listened intently, but after having spent his entire working career behind the iron curtain working covert ops, he wondered why he hadn't ever heard of such a thing before. He said as much to Roberta.

"Nikki," she replied. "The first *Semya* chips were discovered by accident! A Soviet space experiment to grow some sort of perfect crystals in the weightlessness of outer space went bad, resulting in the failure of all onboard computer systems on the spaceship. When they retrieved the disabled spacecraft and investigated why they had failed, they found that the computer chips had all been contaminated, impregnated—with a crystalline buildup from some carbon isotope that had been used as part of the crystal experiment. The stuff had leaked throughout the spacecraft—and it somehow fused itself onto the silicone chips of the onboard computers! Which is why they named it the *Semya* chip in the first place."

"Of course," Nick replied. "*Semya* means 'seed' in Russian."

"Yes, and when the Russians started doing more experiments with the *Semya* chips, they discovered a way to seed common silicone chips with various compounds to enhance the chips' performance. However, a *Semya* chip with this unusual crystalline make-up also has a peculiar side effect. It randomly discharges electrons, and over time, the electrical discharges take on a pattern."

"What does anything you just told me, if any of it is true, have to do with the here and now?"

"Let me finish Nikki," Roberta replied urgently. She took a large swallow of beer. "The Russians were so impressed with the performance of the *Semya* chip in the first generation of systems they built that they took it a step further and wrote a special program for it to design itself for maximum performance! Since the Semya chip could vastly outperform the supporting hardware and software of the day, they simply put an algorithm into the operating system to always look for the best possible solution and to implement it. Within days, the OS built of these new chips had advanced computer technology by decades. The newly designed systems were so advanced that, when President Reagan pushed the United States Congress to fund the Star Wars defense network, the Soviets had this new computer tasked to do exactly the same thing, except they one-upped any conception the US scientists had of how the thing would operate—the Soviets wanted integration of all their current military assets incorporated into one system. The result is what they dubbed the *Obvyet*."

"*Obvyet* means 'answer' in Russian," Nick commented thoughtfully.

"Yes, it was to be the Soviet's answer to Reagan's Star Wars defense system, a completely integrated system for defense but also for attack! The computer-generated plans were for a mega facility to be built underground that would be supplied power by a nuclear power plant. This is the system that was built under a mountain called *Yamantau* near Belorestsk in the Urals. Not a single scientist, engineer, architect, or Russian General could find any fault with the plans or with the scope of the work, with the exception of the nuclear power plant part. As you mentioned Nikki, the Generals didn't like the idea of having a computer running a defense network without having some way to shut it down if they needed to."

Nick still wondered why hadn't he heard any of this before, but he could not ignore the fact that the documents that Boris sent him about the *Semya* chip somewhat supported what she was saying now, and he also knew that there was a major underground facility near Belorestsk that was claimed to be the Russian equivalent to America's NORAD in Cheyenne Mountain, Colorado. Why hadn't his own agency known about this whole thing in the first place?

"What is the mission? Roberta, please get to the point!" he pleaded with her.

"You want to know about the mission?" she asked irritably.

Nick nodded.

"It's about you taking me into Siberia to find all the remaining *Semya* chips, and one-by-one, we destroy them to the satisfaction of both the Russian and American governments. We are also to destroy all the documentation related to the formulas and processes required to manufacture these chips in outer space."

"If there is a better, faster computer chip out there, why would either government want to destroy it?" Nick replied.

"Why? Because the Russians had to do battle against a machine that they realized was more clever than they were back in 1986, a machine that is more clever than we are now at the dawn of the 21st century. The *Semya* chip fires off electrons randomly until it can begin to start affecting its own outputs. When it reaches that level, it becomes self-aware and considers itself to be a life form and not a machine. All life forms instinctively seek to preserve their own existence against any perceived attack, and the *Obvyet* was no different, except it was armed with the USSR's most aggressive weapons! Any attempt made to disarm it or power it down resulted in swift reprisals!"

"You mean this machine could actually think and feel?" Nick asked incredulously.

"We don't know if it could feel emotion, but it could in effect reason just like you and me, only far faster and far better! And, it reacted negatively to being tampered with. The only reason the Russians were able to destroy it was because it hadn't been self-aware for long enough to learn all our capabilities, or its own! Had it stayed powered up for much longer, it would have figured all this out! And, we humans would have been subject to the whims of a supercomputer."

"The Russians," she continued. "Were finally able to bury the entire project and the technology surrounding it! Since these chips could only be manufactured in the weightlessness of outer space, they felt confident it would never come back to haunt them. There was one major side effect, however. Financing the building of the Obvyet, its eventual destruction, and the ensuing cover-up created such a huge economic deficit that the Soviet Union began to crumble. Once that process started, it couldn't be stopped. The Russians could never admit that the *Obvyet* or the *Semya* chip ever existed! And even today they won't admit it. Not now, and not ever! That's why we are needed."

"How do you know all this, Roberta?" Nick asked her.

"Because, I was the one who deciphered the word *Semya* out of an encrypted message. I was the one who traced the money spent by the Russians on the *Obvyet* to a rural area in Belorestsk. I was the one who tied two billion dollars, and Yamantau, to a defense program currently being funded by the United States military for the past two years! No one within the NSA liked what I found out, and when the President of the United States finally found out about it, heads started to roll. America has been surreptitiously funding the Russians with a project they now call *Magic Mountain*."

"Jesus, Roberta! It's impossible that I am not aware of any of this!" Nick exclaimed, downing his beer. "It's my business to know these things! And something like this would be impossible to keep under wraps."

"Post-Soviet Union, you're right, Nick. However, this all happened prior to the fall of the Soviet Union. Magic Mountain is the brainchild of your Mr. Smith."

"Smith is dead. I buried him myself," Nick spat back.

"Technically, you're dead too Nikki," she replied. "Yet, you look very much alive to me. What year did Mr. Smith die?"

"He died June 12th, 1992."

"Isn't that Russia's Independence Day, and one year following the collapse of the Soviet Union and only six years after Chernobyl? Would six years be enough time for Mr. Smith to plan his own demise and scheme up a new world order?"

"It's coincidence, Roberta—that's all," Nick muttered, now putting two and two together.

"I thought you said there weren't any coincidences in your business, Nikki?"

Nick nodded again. "Coincidences and espionage make for bad bedfellows," he said to himself.

"So, have you met Smith, Roberta?"

She emptied her beer, finished swallowing, and held back a belch.

"No." She shook her head. "Does Vadim Stremsky mean anything to you?"

Nick was taken back by her question—so taken back that he sat down beside her on the bed. Roberta realized she hit a raw nerve and continued. "The name Smith never came up in any of my investigations Nick, but the name Stremsky did—even though intelligence reports say he is dead too! He died on June 12th, 1992 and was buried in Volsky, Russia. He's the man behind shutting down the Obvyet before it was too late. He is also the man that started the Magic Mountain project! "

The blood drained from Nick's face, and he sat there ashen white, his mind racing. "I am just a cryptologist Nikki," she continued. "I sit in this little cubicle in Washington D.C. and have to make sense out of garbled messages the NSA puts before me. In a way, it's fun, like doing crossword puzzles all day long and getting paid for it. But, one day, I came across something called the *Semya*, and no one in the NSA knew what it was, and so I pushed the question upstairs. The next thing I knew, I am being fired! NSA tells me the reason they are sending me packing is a downsizing initiative, but I knew better! So, I packed myself up and I got ready to leave. But, then I considered my own options. It was then I realized that I really had no options other than to find out what *Semya* actually meant. In my last two weeks with NSA, before they knew what I was up to, I dug into everything I could—anything at all related to the translation for *Semya*, which as you said, means seed. One thing led to another, and finally, I found the money trail, leading all the way back to the Reagan presidency and the Stars Wars appropriations. Once I did, the name Stremsky kept coming up again and again, not directly mind you, but indirectly! For example, an appropriation for twenty million went through Congress to fund a study of some sort, and the grant went to a company that was not owned by Stremsky, but one he was on the Board of Directors to. In other instances, a large grant was issued to a company to develop something or other for the military, and Stremsky is an indirect consultant to that company. In far too many instances to be coincidental, three to four tiers away from any direct link to dozens of obscure military appropriations, there was a link to Stremsky. So, I documented everything, wrote an analysis of the data, and sent it off to the Secret Service along with a death threat to the President of the United States—just to get someone's attention! And, as expected, one night there is a knock at my door."

Nick, having barely touched his beer, handed it over to Roberta and asked, "What happened next?"

Roberta took a sip and continued. "They arrested me, of course! The Secret Service took me into custody and interrogated me relentlessly for three days! But, I was prepared for it ahead of time. I had already prepped myself for all the psychological questions concerning my sanity! I had copied all my information about the *Semya*, the *Obvyet*, and the money trail, encrypted it all and sent it to various public domains; and I hid the hard unencrypted copies around town and instructed one person to mail the locations of where they all were located to all the major newspapers in America should something happen to me. After three days of interrogation, I was reinstated with the NSA with a promotion! Only it came with a stipulation—I had to help them verify these *Semya* chips before destroying them all. They then loaned me to the CIA, who set this all up, including our arranged meeting. I agreed to it all Nikki, not because of my job, but because of what I uncovered about this *Semya* and the *Obvyet* computer. Chernobyl was bad enough, but now it seems that the private sector might get its hands on this technology, and if they do, there is no telling what the consequences might be!"

"How did you tie Smith into all this, Roberta?" Nick asked her, needing the final piece of the puzzle.

"I didn't until just now, Nikki."

Observing her facial features, he doubted she was lying to him.

"As a cryptologist, I am trained to look for repeating patterns, and the next step is to substitute a letter, a word, or a number, and start working the crossword puzzle until it makes sense. Stremsky is a pattern, and if I substitute Smith for Stremsky, a picture begins to evolve."

"And what picture is that, Roberta?"

"Your Mr. Smith was there during Chernobyl, President Reagan's terms in the White House, and the Star Wars program! He was there during the collapse of the Soviet Union, and he worked the entire time way high up the covert ladder. No one in America knows what Smith looks like, and in Russia, he is thought to be dead. So, after he stages his own death for the Americans, he relocates back to America, and because he has a twisted sense of humor, he comes back under a new identity—but this time using his real name! The one he was born with and went by until the CIA made him Mr. Smith. In business transactions, no one knows who Stremsky is, and if a search was run on it, the name can only be traced back to a dead man—leaving his new identity secure! I think Smith intends to reappear one day as Vadim Stremsky!"

"Why do you say that, Roberta?" Nick asked, confused.

"Why do you keep that gun collection, Nick? You never even carry a gun! You told me it was to prove who you are, in the event you needed to. Every weapon can be traced, can't it?"

Nick nodded, saying nothing, but she was absolutely correct! Every weapon in that closet had a serial number on it that could be traced back to who it was issued to and for what purpose. It had been Smith's idea. He said no matter how many records the government might destroy in a cover up, the military maintains accurate records for ordinance, and it would be impossible to track ordinance backward without the serial numbers, and though no names would be attached to the serial numbers the weapons were assigned to, they would be registered to the operational assignment. From there it could be determined who!"

Nick nodded and stood up. "I need another beer. How about you?"

Roberta shook her head. "No, I'll finish this one, and that will be it for me tonight, or I guess it is morning now."

Nick nodded and excused himself. His head was spinning as he made his way topside. "Kowalski!" he shouted. "Get down here!"

Kowalski scrambled off the fly bridge and went below to the galley, where he found Nick pacing around nervously and tipping another beer. "What's up, Nick?"

"Unless we get very clever and right damned now, we are all dead!" Nick replied.

"What are you talking about, Nikki?" Kowalski demanded.

"I screwed up, Kowalski—that is what I am talking about! I have been played like a fiddle these past few weeks, and I brought you and your men into this mess right along with me."

"Again Nikki! What are you talking about, Nick? You haven't told me anything yet."

"Smith is what I am talking about!" he shouted. "The bastard is still alive, and he is still playing Cold War games once again!"

"Nick," Kowalski replied. "Smith was your mentor, and like a father to you! He wouldn't set you up even if he were alive! What makes you think he is among the living anyway?"

"Too many coincidences, Kowalski. That's what makes me certain he is alive! And if Smith is alive, as I believe he is, then he staged his death for a reason. I believe that Roberta naively uncovered why he did it, and if I am right, Kowalski, we are all dead unless we can outsmart him. I promised to deliver this damned attaché case to Blakely in the morning before knowing what the contents were."

"Then we need to turn around," Kowalski said.

Nick took another pull on his beer and shook his head. "No. They are tracking us. Roberta is bugged!"

"For God's sake, Nikki. We need to get rid of the bugs!"

Nick shook his head. "No, if we do that, we tip our hand!"

"What do you suggest Nick," Kowalski replied.

"We wait and keep our eyes and ears open. If Smith is behind this, he has something in mind for us. We are in danger only once he gets what he wants, so we play out this hand for now."

"But Nick," Kowalski protested. "Do you really think that, after all these years of working with Smith, he would set you up?"

"If the stakes were high enough, Kowalski—Smith is capable of it!" Nick muttered remorsefully.

While the boat ploughed through the waters of the Puget Sound heading toward Seattle, Nick paced around the galley trying to figure out the significance of the past two days. To the steady thrum of diesels under foot and the rhythm of the boat bucking against the waves, he started piecing it together as he paced back and forth. Finally, he returned to his cabin. Roberta said nothing to him when he came through the door. She could tell something was on his mind.

Finally he said, "So Roberta, let's say I give you the attaché case right now. You have what you need then. What happens next?"

She shook her head. "I don't know, Nick. I was told only to stay close to you and that they were sending somebody! You would know him and he would tell us what they wanted us to do next."

"And when was that to happen, Roberta?"

She shook her head again, indicating she didn't know. Nick smiled and said, "Yeah, it sounds like Smith alright."

"Why do you smile, Nick?"

"Why didn't you just tell me everything up front?" Nick asked her in lieu of an answer.

"I was told that someone was going to try to kill you to stop whatever merger is going down with the documents you have to deliver. I was told that they were going to put you on the run, so that the assassin wouldn't be able to carry out the hit on you. If I told you what was going on upfront, I was told it would compromise what is going on now between Washington and Moscow."

"What is going on in Washington and Moscow?"

"I don't know, Nikki. That is way above my pay rate."

"Pay rate?" Nick queried.

"What?" Roberta protested.

"Pay rate is a military term. A civilian would have said, 'I don't know that information,' but you said pay rate—so, what else haven't you told me Roberta?"

"Nikki, it's just an expression, for goodness sake! Jeeze, I am exhausted! Can't your interrogation wait until morning? I need to go to sleep, and you need your sleep as well. Why are we going to Seattle anyway, especially by boat?"

Nick knew she was right—he was exhausted! "Because Seattle is where the attaché case needs to go, and by boat because anyone approaching us will be picked up on radar. There aren't as many cops out on these waters in a dense fog in the middle of the night either! In the meantime, we can get some rest, so goodnight. I'll be in the cabin down the hallway."

Nathan Chadwick Bentley excused himself from his guests as the yacht made its way slowly to Vancouver. He went to his master suite to get an update on Peters. Sitting at his desk, he entered a special code into his computer and it came to life. He read the report, and after reading only a few lines, he slammed his fists down hard on the desk. All three of his men were dead! And the police were not only involved—but they were looking for him! "So," he said to himself out loud. "The courier is still out there! But surely, he won't show up in Seattle to deliver anything to the Courthouse? More than likely, he will give what he has to Blakely, and Mayakovsky won't make an appearance to testify in Court, so the deal is still dead! Victor Zubkov will now have to deliver the Semya chips because he doesn't have the money to meet his obligations otherwise! And Mayakovsky should have the chips already in his possession anyway and so either way Zubkov is toast! And, what about Alexander Mayakovsky? What is he up to now? Why did he alter the plan?" Bentley hadn't heard from him for several days, which was worrisome since so much was in his hands.

Nathan took several deep breaths. There was nothing that could be done about this mess tonight anyway, and there was no way that the authorities knew where he was. He made the money transfer he had promised to the dago, and then he shut the computer down. He picked up the intercom. "Maxine, sweetheart, are you ready to have some fun tonight?"

Maxine, a twenty-four year old model/call-girl was a completely uninhibited woman. She knew what Nathan had planned for her tonight, and she was actually looking forward to it. Nathan always brought her such very interesting people to seduce, whether they were male or female.

"Oh, baby," she replied in a sultry voice. She was already half stoned on cocaine. "Give me a few minutes."

"I will come and get you in about five minutes."

"Oh, Nathan, love—make it twenty! I need to prep myself a little more!"

Nathan knew what she meant. She needed to coke up a little more first! She needed to get herself in the proper mindset for her role tonight. He smiled to himself—she was irresistible when she was stoned! He called down to the galley and ordered food and beverages to be brought up to the lounge.

Hours before Blakely had picked up his cell phone and called Peters to make a deal, and well after Nathan Chadwick Bentley had boarded his yacht headed for Vancouver—he was back at the Governor's Mansion dealing with the mayhem of an FBI investigation. At first he hadn't noticed that Anne Marie had disappeared, but before long, and not knowing her whereabouts, he became concerned about her. He was about to excuse himself and go find her when she suddenly returned.

Rejoining her husband, she whispered in his ear,

"Sorry, Bill. I got ill."

"You've been gone for nearly an hour, Anne. Are you okay?"

She clung to his arm. "No, all this violence has made me ill. Can you get me out of here?"

Blakely found the Governor and pulled him to the side. "Governor," he said. "My wife is ill, and I am going to take her home now. If you need me, here is my card. I see no reason to detain Morgan at this time—his credentials check out. We are holding your Mr. Butler for the time being, since it seems he is connected to the three dead men upstairs. We will keep a lid on this incident, but it is up to you to control your own people and keep their mouths shut too! The bodies will be removed discretely, probably before daylight. I will be in touch with you later."

"Blakely, do you mind telling me what this is all about?"

Bill tried to think of way to condense everything. "A man was hired by the late Congressman Wilshire to bring a package into the country under the license of a Congressional Letter. The President of the United States ordered this person to be stopped and the package to be recovered. Now it seems there are other parties after this person as well, but for what reason, I don't know."

"How did this courier wind up here?"

"My best guess at the moment," Blakely lied, "is that he was about to pass the package off to someone at the banquet tonight."

"Who, Bill?"

"We don't know that either, sir."

"One last question, Blakely. What is so damned important about this package?"

Blakely shrugged. "I haven't a clue!" he replied, and he turned to leave.

In the limo, Blakely sat in the backseat and held his wife close. He wondered if the divorce would be clean. He doubted it! They never were. They both rode in silence, and Anne Marie feigned falling asleep on his shoulder.

The limo had just dropped them off and he had just locked the front door to their home, when his cell phone rang again. Bill Blakely knew who it was from the caller ID. He waited until Anne Marie left the room before answering it.

"Boss, we have another body here!"

"What? Who?" Blakely asked.

"Harry Trundle, the guy who was running for office," Franks replied.

Blakely started perspiring. "What happened?"

"Looks like he died of a coronary. Maybe all the excitement did him in. People do die suddenly without being in an accident or being shot, don't they?"

"Is that all?" Blakely questioned. Mark Franks was silent, and that meant something was up. "What is it, Mark?"

"There was a cover-up."

"Explain."

"Things didn't look right to the forensics people, and so they started looking around with a black light and they discovered pecker tracks all over the place! One thing led to another, and it became obvious that Trundle had been banging someone on the Governor's desk before, or maybe at the time he expired."

"And?"

"Never mind," Mark said. "I just thought you should know. No laws were broken that I know of. The man apparently died of natural causes at an awkward moment. An autopsy will be done in the morning to confirm it."

Mark hung up, and Bill was tempted to call him back but knew better. Mark had told him all he needed to know. Bill loosened his tie, pulled off his jacket, and then went for the liquor cabinet. Anne Marie called down to him from upstairs, saying that she had taken some stomach medicine and was going to bed straightaway. As he poured himself a drink, he wondered where his wife was for that missing hour? Had she been banging the guy?

He pulled out the card Nick Peters had given him. He noted that it was 2:30 A.M. as he punched in the numbers.

He was ready to make a deal!

Chapter 16

Both the evening at the Governor's Mansion and now the yacht they were on, had an overwhelming effect on both Angela and Neal Courtney. The entourage had left the banquet before all the commotion started between the FBI and Nick Peters, and consequently, they were now motoring towards Vancouver without any idea at all what had gone down there. Nathan had just introduced them to a side of life that they never dreamed existed! And now he was about to expose them to something even more extraordinary.

It was past 1:00 A.M. when Nathan joined the Courtney's in the stateroom and introduced Maxine to them. A waiter knocked at the door holding a silver platter of delicacies and a bucket filled with iced bottles of champagne. After placing the offerings on the table, he left quickly.

Nathan poured four glasses of champagne and passed them around. "Let us make a toast to my new purchasing manager and his lovely wife, shall we?" They all raised their glasses high and then they all took a sip. "Now, I have a surprise for you both! I want you to be our exclusive guests for the weekend in Vancouver. It will be grand. I have reservations at the Hilton there, and I have reserved a historic tour of the city for us all. Any objections?"

Angela hesitated and then spoke up. "But we haven't packed for a trip, and don't we need passports?"

Maxine giggled. "Angela, you are so cute. Nathan has like a gazillion people working for him. Trust me! Everything is taken care of." She took a seat next to Angela and patted her knee. "It will be fun," she added. "We get to go shopping at Nordstrom's and at the best boutiques in Vancouver while the men get stupid drunk and talk business."

Angela looked at her husband, and his head was nodding in agreement. She smiled. "Okay then, Vancouver it is!"

"Now that we have that settled," Nathan said, "what do you both think of my boat?"

"I would hardly call this a boat," Neal exclaimed.

Angela added, "It is so luxurious!"

"You should see your cabins then! C'mon Maxine, you lead the way. You always provide such a lovely view from behind." He chuckled.

Angela took an immediate liking to Maxine. She was sexy and bold, for a young woman her age! And Angela wished she could be more like her. Her husband Neal was such a straight guy! They rarely had fun together because it was always about work for him. Maxine, on the other hand, was refreshingly free spirited! Angela sensed that Maxine was all about having fun! And, she seemingly had no inhibitions whatsoever! She wondered if she were a little gay herself, because she really didn't want Maxine to remove her hand from her thigh! Angela swallowed her glass of champagne in a single gulp, picked up the bottle, and said, "Okay, let's go. Which way?"

Nathan commented to Neil, "Looks like the girls are going to have some fun tonight. Feel the energy?"

Neal was too busy looking at Maxine's fine ass to comment. Everything was going as Nathan had planned. In another hour, she would have them both seduced for him in short order.

"Oh what a night!" he thought to himself.

Chapter 17

There was a rap on the door at 7:15 A.M., and Nick struggled to waken. Roberta, who somehow ended up sleeping next to him, murmured something and put her arm across his chest.

"What was she doing in his bed?" he thought to himself. He had only been asleep a few hours, but the nightmares that usually accompanied his troubled sleep had thankfully taken a holiday! It meant what couple hours of sleep he'd just had were more restful than most nights were. Nevertheless, feeling her next to him made it that much more difficult to get up and get out of bed. Her body was so warm and soft that he didn't want to move away from her. But, then there was another rap on the door, this one more insistent! Nick looked at Roberta's face as she slept. She looked at peace, and he didn't want to awaken her. He carefully extracted her arm from across his chest and slipped out of bed. Standing there in his boxer shorts, he pulled the door open.

Kowalski was in the hallway. He looked past Nick and apologized, "Sorry to wake you up Nick, but we are in Elliott Bay. We'll be docking in twenty minutes."

Nick nodded. "Good. I'll be up in a minute."

Nick scrambled to get dressed without waking Roberta, but it didn't work! She sat up in bed, shyly holding the sheet in front of her. "Are we here already, Nikki?"

"Roberta, go back to sleep. How did you get in my bed?"

"My orders were to stay close to you, remember? You didn't seem to mind when I slipped in with you last night." She smiled.

"Nothing happened last night did it?" he asked nervously, pulling on his jeans while observing the two piles of clothes on the floor.

"Oh, Nikki." Roberta sighed. "You were wonderful!"

Nick froze and tried to clear his head, and then he noticed her smiling at his discomfort.

"You were out like a light!" She laughed, bringing her joke home.

"You would have been more comfortable in the king sized bed, Roberta," Nick muttered.

"I couldn't seem to get that damned hatch closed last night, and I was freezing! So I slipped in with you. The double was fine—you kept me warm, and you didn't seem to mind. Do you?"

Nick smiled. "Yeah right! I'm offended to wake up with a beautiful woman in my bed—that'll be the day! Just go back to sleep, Roberta— you don't need to get up! I'll forgive you this time, but don't let it happen again!" he laughed, while pulling a sweatshirt over his head. "I'll make this exchange with Blakely and be back in a couple of hours."

"No way! I told you that I want to be part of this," she said emphatically.

She reached for the pair of blue jeans and the sweatshirt from the night before. Slipping on the jeans, she turned her back to him as she pulled on the sweatshirt.

"You'll be setting new trends in women's fashions." Nick laughed. "What will we call it, the tomboy look?"

"I look like a tomboy to you?" she said, posing for him with one hand on her hip.

"Not really," he replied, and he kissed her forehead.

"Good morning," he said.

She quickly wrapped her arms around him, pressed herself up close, and kissed him back on the lips. "Oh sorry," she said, breaking away. "I have to brush my teeth first. Morning breath, ugh!" Wrinkling up her nose, she bolted for the head in the master bedroom. "I'll be five minutes. See you on deck." She closed the door behind her.

The only shoes Nick could provide for her were some flip-flops or sandals. He kept an assortment of beachwear and towels under the lounge seats on the rear deck for guests. He decided to see what he had on hand. He slipped on a pair of sneakers and made his way to the galley where he poured a mug of coffee for them both, and then grabbed a couple packets of sugar and some creamer. He dropped a spoon in the cup and knocked on the door to the master head. She opened it with a toothbrush still dangling from her mouth. Nick smiled and handed her the mug of coffee along with the condiments. "I couldn't remember how you like your coffee," he said.

"Just a little creamer, thank you."

"I have an assortment of sandals and flip-flops on the rear deck. I am sure there will be something you can use for footwear.

"Oh God—thanks Nikki! I forgot all about the shoes. High heels wouldn't go well with jeans and a sweatshirt."

"I'll be topside."

"Two more minutes is all I need," she replied and then spat into the sink.

Leaving her to finish what she was doing, Nick went topside where the men were waiting, ready to go. They had changed into civilian clothes, and Nick wondered if any of them had slept at all. But it wasn't a concern for the moment. They were all young enough to go without sleep, more so than he was. Besides, he was hoping that everything would go smoothly when he passed off the attaché case to Blakely, and these men wouldn't have to be at their best anyway.

"So, what's the plan?" Kowalski asked as Nick climbed the fly bridge ladder.

"Bixby, you okay with a bump-and-run with a boat this size?" Nick asked.

"Just tell me where and you got it," Bixby replied.

"Drop Roberta and me off on pier fifty-two. The ferry from the peninsula comes in at 7:55, and Roberta and I need to be there before it arrives. Maria, my housekeeper, will be onboard with the package. Kowalski, you and your men are to keep an eye on us from two piers down. If things go bad, I want a clean exit off that pier. How you do it is up to you."

At 5:00 A.M., Bill Blakely gave up on the prospect of sleep and got up to get ready for the exchange. Thinking about Harry Trundle being found dead of a coronary while banging someone had been on his mind all night long! Who was the woman? And where had Ann Marie been for that hour before she returned to the main hall claiming to be ill? These thoughts raced through his mind and had kept him awake all night! But now, he had to put them aside so he could concentrate on the mission at hand. He dressed hurriedly and focused his thoughts on what he had to do this morning. Seattle was two hours away, and Peters had promised to turn over whatever he had at 8:00 A.M.

Blakely pulled the Ford Explorer out of the two-car garage and headed north at 5:20. He would find a diner in Seattle someplace and wait there if he arrived early.

"I should have called this in," he thought to himself. "I should have talked to Mark again. I should have called for back-up." He knew he could still phone it in, but he didn't!

"Damn it," he thought. It wasn't until he was on the highway that he allowed himself to think about Anne Marie again. Their marriage had been on the rocks for several years now, so why was he feeling this way? Her screwing one of the moron politicians she hung out with all the time was inevitable, wasn't it? Bill tried to rationalize her actions away, if indeed she had done what he suspected she had. But it wasn't working! She was a bitch, and she was relentless in her expectations of him! She married an FBI man knowing full well what she was getting into! But, she bitched and moaned at him continually anyway. He was never a Harvard boy, or someone else expected to go very far in life—he was just a cop! Was it Anne Marie who had changed, or was it him? Questions and doubts pummeled his brain as he chain-smoked, and pushed the Explorer hard.

"Who cares anyway?" he kept asking himself. But the answer kept beating on him—he did! "If you spend over a decade with a woman, it has to be because you love her," he heard a voice in his head say. And he knew he did love her, even though he hated her at the same time. Or, was it himself that he hated? He hated himself because he couldn't meet up to her expectations, and it made him a failure in her eyes. Maybe he resented her because he knew that she could have done much better for herself if she had married another man—and then maybe she wouldn't be such a bitch! Maybe he was the loser! Maybe he was bringing her down, holding her back! His brain screamed in torment for the answers, and finally out of despair, he pulled out his weapon and looked at it closely. He took his hands off the steering wheel and pulled out the clip. The magazine was full. He laughed, and said out loud, "You should end it now, Bill. If you end it right now, then no one suffers. Divorce is nasty, so why go there? He put the clip back in, cocked the weapon, and put it to his head. "Just pull the *damned* trigger, asshole!"

He was passing a car at the time. The car was a late-sixties Ford station wagon with the backseat facing rearward. A little girl and boy were fussing with each other, despite the early hour. Why they were awake was anyone's guess? He speculated that they could have been getting an early start on a vacation, as it was the weekend. The little girl noticed him holding the gun to his temple, shook her brother's shoulder, and pointed. Bill put the gun down and waved back, and the boy saw nothing! So the two began to argue about what she had just seen or not seen. Blakely laughed at his own foolishness. Snapping the hammer back to safety, he put the weapon away. "Why do myself in?" he thought. "When somebody else can do it for me!" He passed the station wagon and looked at his watch. He would be in Seattle in plenty of time, and maybe he would have breakfast somewhere after all.

At just before eight o'clock, Bixby brought the yacht in to pier fifty-two, something that boaters were not supposed to do because it was reserved for ferries only. He spotted a ladder that went to the water line and went for it. By then, the fog had nearly lifted and the visibility was good. Nick and Roberta stood at the bow waiting.

"Roberta," Nick said. "Bixby will only touch the pier. You have to get on that ladder quickly because he will reverse the engines and pull away immediately. Do you understand?"

"Shut up, Nikki." She laughed. "I'll be on that ladder. Worry about yourself, old man."

"So, now it comes out! I am an old man, am I?" Nick smiled. He knew that Roberta must be scared to death at the prospect of jumping for a ladder from a moving boat that was rising and falling with the motion of the water! But he knew she had spunk, and he knew that she could do it.

Bixby brought the boat in a little too hot, but he expertly gunned the throttles in reverse and the boat slowed. He then threw one engine in forward and one in reverse, and the bow swung gently over to the ladder. The yacht bumped the pier, and Roberta leapt at the rungs. Nick held his breath. She caught a rung and started scrambling up. Bixby throttled-up the engines, and Nick knew that he had to go too. The boat was pulling away from the pier, so he quickly stepped off. He wasn't quite as successful as she was. He missed the rung of choice, but he caught the one below it. She looked down at him from several feet above and smiled. He stuck his tongue out at her, and she laughed. Bixby pulled the boat away, and Kowalski and his men now took positions around the deck with binoculars. No one waiting for the ferry paid much attention to Roberta or Nick as they made their way up the ladder to the pier deck many feet above the water. The ferry was still ten minutes out.

Roberta asked, "What now?"

"We find a bench and wait," Nick replied.

"Nick," Roberta asked. "Will there be any trouble?"

Nick smiled and put his arm around her. "Not likely," he said after kissing her. "As long as the feds get what they want, and since Blakely is FBI, we should be okay. The hit on me was scheduled to take place at the Federal Building in Seattle Monday morning, and I won't be going there! So I expect we will be safe for now. I couldn't care less about this bloody package, and I just want to get rid of it!"

"Then what?"

"Then," Nick said. "There is something back in Russia I need to do."

"Are you going back for her?"

"Her?" he said.

"Everything is about her, isn't it Nikki? It's the reason you agreed to take Alexander's place and deliver this thing in the first place. What are you going to do, kill Victor Zubkov before he finds out she has been having an affair with Alexander?"

"Zubkov would already know about it," Nick replied calmly. "What Alexander is up to is the reason I need to go back to Russia. Natasha is my only child, and if Alexander has put her in harm's way, then yes, I will kill him, or anyone else trying to hurt her!"

"But what will you do if you are called on for this mission?"

Nick looked at her intensely. "I have been on enough missions in my life, and if my daughter's welfare is in question, then I must go to her first to protect her."

There was no question in Roberta's mind that Nick would do exactly that. "That is why you weren't told, Nikki!" she exclaimed. "Whoever is pulling all the strings knows this about you, just like they knew you couldn't leave me on the side of the road. If you had known everything you know now, you would already be back in Russia—and that's not what they wanted! They lied to me, Nikki. The operation isn't awaiting approval. The operation is already on! And they're just waiting for you to turn this thing over to them!"

Nick thought about it. "We will pass it off to Blakely today and then see what happens. How will you know the codes are genuine, Roberta?"

"I won't," she answered honestly. "Not until we have the chips."

"So Roberta, explain what you are doing here."

"Even if the bios codes are genuine, they are only a starting point to decode the new bios numbers. The new numbers will be encrypted as well, so I need to break the encryption first, before the verification process can begin. That is why I am here."

"And you can do that?" Nick asked.

She tilted her head and shrugged. "As boring as it might sound, that's what I do."

"So you can read and understand Russian?" Nick questioned her further.

"No, Nick. I don't understand or read Russian, but I am guessing you do."

Nick nodded as another piece to the puzzle fell into place. Who better to send into Siberia with her than Nick Peters? He knew Siberia like the back of his hand. He knew the people and the language, and more importantly—he knew how to get out!

"And Tatyana, do you still love her?" Roberta asked him, pulling him from his thoughts.

Nick squeezed her tightly. "It doesn't matter if I do or not. How about a coffee?"

"Sure. You got some money? I left my purse behind."

Nick pulled out his wallet and checked. "Yeah," he said, surprised. "I have a twenty in here, a few hundreds, and a fifty."

Roberta laughed. "You are funny, Nick."

"Why do you say that?"

"Here you are this rich guy, and yet you have to check your wallet to know if you have enough money to buy even a coffee! That's funny, Nick!"

Nick shrugged. "I never got into the money thing. There always seemed to be enough of it around when I needed it, so I never thought much about it. But I worked with an agency that did everything in cash. Covert ops handlers don't write checks or use credit cards—they hand over bundles of cash!"

"Have you ever had to struggle, Nikki?" Roberta asked.

Nick thought about it for a minute and replied, "I have struggled with staying alive, but not with living. Normal people go to work, collect a paycheck, and try to make ends meet— they have a life! I went to work and tried to stay alive for another day. I never had money worries though, because my life was planned out for me. It was always about being at a certain place at a certain time, collecting this or doing that! My job was to complete the mission. I was always handed money and whatever else I needed. Sometime, things didn't go as planned, but I always knew that if I completed the mission, if I got out alive, that I could go back to a flat somewhere where the rent and utilities were all prepaid and the refrigerator was full. I never collected a paycheck or even wrote a check. My pay was deposited directly into a bank account. All my living expenses were taken care of, except for my personal activities."

"And did you like it that way Nikki, everything neat and tidy and with no money worries?"

"There were things that were not so great about it, Roberta. I watched people die! I witnessed people being forced to do unimaginable things, and as a result, I have a lot of nightmares. There aren't many good memories for all my years abroad," he said. "But enough to keep me going."

As they walked down the pier, Roberta found herself asking him, "So really, what does your gut say about us, Nikki?"

Nick squeezed her hand. "That maybe I need to go to church again!"

"What?" she exclaimed.

He laughed. "To thank God for the mud on my windshield the other night, for an accident that shouldn't have happened, and for the conspiracy that brought us together."

She stopped walking and turned to him. "Nikki, do you really mean that?"

Nick smiled back at her. "Yeah, I really mean it."

She put her arms around him and put her head on his chest. "I can't believe it, Nikki! Two days ago, my biggest concern was to prove that I was just as competent as a man was, and now it feels great to just be a woman! Which is something I lost sight of when I was very young. I guess all that competition with the men overwhelmed any positives for me in being a woman.

"I was so afraid to tell you the truth, afraid that you would hate me. Please Nikki, don't hate me! I want to get to know you better, and I want to get closer to you. I liked sleeping next to you last night, even though nothing happened. I never spent the night with a man before that something didn't happen, and it was just nice to have you there next to me to keep me warm. I know that you may not want this, the thought of having a woman in your life, because of the life you have lived. But, I think I might want to be in your life. I think my father would like you too! But whether he does or doesn't, it doesn't matter to me. And by the way, I never thought I would meet a man like you! And, as confusing as this situation is, I feel good being with you! You are a great dancer Nikki! And most women would die for an evening like we had last night! I'll never forget it, Nikki. Thank you!"

Nick smiled, and then he kissed her.

"You, Roberta," he muttered, "have been the most beautiful distraction I have ever experienced! If we both live through this, I hope you feel the same as you do now, because I have a warm beach in mind where I would love to take you."

After ordering two coffees, they still had a few minutes before the ferry arrived and Nick found an empty bench. They sat side-by-side, sipping coffee as they watched the ferry approaching the landing precisely on time.

"What next, Nikki?" she asked.

"Next Blakely should show up, hopefully alone! Maria will arrive with the package, and I will give it to him."

Just then, Nick spotted Blakely walking up the pier. He said nothing to Roberta, who was enjoying a cigarette. When Blakely was finally in front of him, Nick said, "Are you okay, Bill? You look horrible!"

"I don't see a briefcase here Nick," Blakely replied.

Nick ignored his remark for the moment.

"Bill, this is Roberta. Say hello to her, Bill. We didn't have time last night for proper introductions." Blakely shook Roberta's hand.

"Your package is arriving on that ferry that is approaching the landing right now. Have a seat."

Blakely complied, and Nick continued. "I will give you the package only on the condition that you get it to the right people, is that clear?"

Blakely nodded and said, "I thought you wanted a name?"

"I already have it."

The ferry came in and pushed against the pier. Ferry workers tied off the massive lines, and within seconds, vehicles began to disembark.

"Are you wired, Peters?" Blakely asked.

"No," Nick replied. "Why should I be?"

"And what about her?"

Nick pulled up his sweatshirt and instructed Roberta to do the same. Roberta complied, even though she wasn't wearing a bra.

"Satisfied?" Nick asked.

Blakely nodded. "So where is my package?"

Maria waited in line for the car ahead of her to move forward. When it did, she stepped on the gas, and went up the ramp following the others. Nick spotted the car, stood up and waved to her. When she pulled the car up to their position, he told Roberta and Blakely to get in. Maria stepped on the gas.

"Where to, Boss?" she asked.

"To the end of the pier, and then pull over, Maria."

She did as he instructed and once on the street she pulled the car to the curb. "Here, Maria," Nick said, and he handed her a hundred dollar bill.

"Get back on the ferry, and have a nice weekend with your family. Thanks for doing this for me, and sorry for breaking up your weekend."

Maria smiled and tucked the hundred into her purse.

"Will I see you on Monday?"

"I'm planning on leaving later today, but I hope to be back in about two weeks. I'll email you."

"Where is your car, Bill?"

"Up the street."

Nick opened the door for Roberta.

"Pop the trunk Maria," he said, and then he retrieved the briefcase and slammed the trunk lid tight. "Thanks Maria," he said again, and she stepped on the gas and went up the street to make a u-turn. Maria waved to them as she passed to re-board the ferry back to the Peninsula.

"Here Bill," Nick said, holding up the briefcase. "This is what I was to deliver." They found another bench nearby and sat down. Nick opened the case and removed the Letter of Congress and a ballpoint pen. "You have to sign for it."

"How do I know that everything is here?"

"Everything expected to be delivered is listed on the Letter of Congress, and everything here matches the list. The only thing not listed is the pocket drive." Nick showed Blakely the last page of the document that itemized the documents to be delivered. "By signing this document Bill, you take full responsibility for these goods. Your signature, in effect, makes you the courier now, and protects you under the same laws that protected me. This letter also exonerates me from all the mayhem that happened up until this point, including killing those three men who tried to stop me at the Governor's Mansion."

Blakely examined all the document seals, which appeared to be genuine, and he took the pen to sign the release papers.

Kowalski and his men observed the transaction from their vantage point, and then watched them all walk up the street and get into Blakely's car. "Well, it looks like we aren't needed, so it's time to go. Get going Bixby," he said, and Bixby throttled the boat in reverse. They would pick up Nick and Roberta at the public docks two piers down.

"Now, it's your turn. I want to know who is pulling all the strings. Do you know?" Nick said to Blakely as Blakely started the car.

Blakely was about to answer when a bullet shattered the rear glass of the car, barely missing Roberta's head.

"My people aren't doing the shooting!" Blakely shouted to Nick while reaching for his gun. Nick ordered Roberta to get down in the rear seat.

He turned to see who was shooting at them and spotted a black Ford Taurus pull away from the curb and head in their direction. "Go, Bill! Get the hell out of here!" he shouted.

Bill floored it. "Hang on," he said. "And buckle up!"

"The shooter's not FBI," Blakely exclaimed with vigor. "I didn't tell anyone where I was going." He noticed a side street to his left and pulled the wheel hard. The car's tires screeched in protest, and the Explorer veered left. He then hit the brakes hard, negotiating another hard right.

Blakely floored it again, and Nick said,

"I told you to come alone—the deal is off!"

"Like I said Nick, these aren't my people! I did come alone, and I did not tell a soul I was coming here!" Blakely slammed on the brakes and the Explorer slid to a halt. They were in a dead-end alley with no way out. Blakely checked his weapon. The Taurus pulled up behind them, and Morgan got out cautiously.

"I know him, Bill. Take it easy!" Nick said. "Be cool for a minute."

Morgan approached the car and said, "How's it going, Nikki? Mind if I get in?" Without waiting for an answer, he pulled open the rear door and slid in next to Roberta.

"Well, well, well," Morgan said. "I suppose everyone is wondering what's going on. Do you have the pocket drive, Nick?"

"He's turned it over to me," Blakely replied.

"Good," Morgan answered. "So, there must be a lot of unanswered questions here for you both? First, let me explain what I am doing here. You may already know this Nick, but we have been tracking Roberta ever since you two met."

Nick nodded. "I know that, Morgan."

"Good, then you know I am here to tell you what is going down, right?"

Nick remained silent, knowing Morgan would continue.

"By the way Blakely, Andrew Butler had nothing to do with anything! The whole cell phone charade just seemed a good way to add a little mystery to the plot, and to be honest; it was safer for him to be in jail last night. There was a hit out on Nick, and it seemed plausible that whoever was out to get Nick might question Butler and put a bullet in his head as an afterthought. So why not take advantage of a fall guy? He'll be released on Monday morning."

Blakely glared back at Morgan, his heart still pounding in his chest from the pursuit! But he said nothing.

"There's a conspiracy going on in the government Nick, and when this whole thing got started, I was sent to kill you."

"So why didn't you?" Nick replied.

"I owe you—you know that!" He smiled at Nick's expression. "I'm sure you remember Chechnya? You took a bullet for me that night. Anyway, when the order came down to terminate you, I called in a few debts of my own, and it paid off. My orders got changed."

Chapter 18

Victor Zubkov was preparing to have dinner when he was interrupted by an aid who handed him a slip of paper. Victor opened the note, read the inscription, then crumpled the paper and got up from the table. He made his way over to the oversized fireplace and tossed the note into the roaring flames.

"The nights are already chilly again in St. Petersburg," he thought silently to himself.

"Is there a problem, dear?" Tatyana asked.

"No dear. No problem, just business. Where is Natasha?"

"She will be down soon. I sent Grigori to get her."

Victor nodded and poured himself another vodka. "So tell me about this trip that you and Natasha are about to take."

"Oh Victor, what more is there to say about it? Natasha has an audition in Paris. You know how much it means to her. She has been dancing since she was five, and this is her opportunity to study ballet under the masters. What is the problem with such plans?"

Victor scoffed. "The masters of ballet are all right here in St. Petersburg." Everyone knows that the finest dancers, musicians, and artists all come from Russia. Why does she need to go to Paris?"

Tatyana smiled with patience. "You will be worried about us. Am I correct?"

Victor drummed his fingers on the table and downed his Vodka.

"There are security issues, yes."

"It is her chance to prove herself, Victor. This is a great opportunity for her. Why don't you come with us?"

Victor softened and poured another vodka. "I must have a video of her audition."

"You will, dear. You hired the best cinematographers for the event.

But if there is any possibility, you should be there for her—it would mean a great deal to her."

Natasha finally came down to the dining room wearing blue jeans and a halter-top.

"Hi, Daddy," she said as she sat down.

"What is this?" he said. "You come to dinner and you 'hi daddy' me without even giving me a kiss?" Natasha got up from the table and kissed him on the cheek.

"And what is this?" he said, eying her clothes. "Blue jeans and sexy underwear? Tatyana, what is this all about?"

Natasha laughed. "C'mon, Daddy. This is how teenagers dress today. It's not underwear—it's a halter top!"

"Tatyana, help me out here! This is why I send her to the finest schools, to be a *hip-hop* girl?"

Tatyana smiled. "It is better to hold onto the important things, Victor. Your daughter dances with the best in all of Europe, and she will make Russia proud of her! Let her be a teenager for a little while."

Natasha said, "Thanks, Mom."

"I am outnumbered here," Victor said, giving up. "Okay, let's eat. You women will be the death of me. All I can do is worry about you both. Natasha, tell me about this trip again."

Natasha rolled her eyes and sighed.

"It will be okay, Daddy!"

Victor sliced his meat and took a bite. "I know it will be okay," he said. "Just tell me about it once more, and the way you always tell about such things, with excitement and passion! So that I can forgive myself my own foolishness for letting you go in the first place! The world is a dangerous place nowadays, and outside of Russia, I have little authority or influence. So, go ahead and tell me about what you will do in Paris."

"It will be wonderful Daddy," she began.

"Victor barely heard her. But, he pretended that he was listening intently to what she was saying. Instead, he was watching Tatyana! His wife hadn't a clue that he was on to her affair, the affair she had been having with Alexander Mayakovsky for some time now! Or, that he had known about it all along. Nor did either of them suspect that he knew that this Paris trip was only a ruse meant to get the two women out of the country and within driving distance of Heathrow Airport, where they would board an airliner to the United States.

Of course, Natasha had no idea that instead of going back to the hotel after her audition in Paris, the limo was ready to whisk them off to England. He had known about this plan for months! He had known about the passports, the travel documents, and where they would be staying when they arrived in New York City, and even when they would get there! That was why he had sent Mayakovsky on that errand to deliver the package to

Seattle, Washington. But his plans had backfired on him! Now Alexander was missing! Moreover, he had new information now to consider—the contents of the note he had burned earlier.

How much Tatyana knew about these new events, he couldn't guess. But he had definitely underestimated Alexander Mayakovsky! After all, it had been Alexander's idea to sell a major holding in Stalintsia Steel to raise the much-needed capital for the modernization of the steel manufacturing facility. The disclosure documents were genuine, but they hid the fact that Victor truly controlled Stalintsia Steel. Even the Russian government would have a very difficult time tracing Victor's ownership through the myriad of holding companies and investors that he had in place to conceal his controlling interests in the concern. And Alexander's idea was a sound one! Russia had the best-trained and most highly educated workforce in the world, and the most underpaid workforce too. With a little capital and some needed modernization, Stalintsia Steel could out produce the rest of the world! And, they could even undercut the Chinese government's subsidized price for steel and still make a handsome profit! Of course, American Steel Corp was fit to be tied by the notion that Providence Steel and Stalintsia Steel were merging. Alexander would reassure the US government in his testimony before the Security and Exchange committee that their national security was not at stake. Providence Steel had an immense steel distribution network throughout America, and by importing the Russian-made steel at a fraction of the price that it could be produced domestically, they would have a virtual lock on the market. After all, the Russians and Americans were more like allies now anyway. Or so Alexander would reason before the committee.

It would be the end of American Steel for sure, and several other steel companies in America would follow some time after—all of which were already hurting from foreign competition. So Victor understood why the US government was caught in the middle, between free enterprise concerns and the loss of US jobs, and national security concerns stemming from too much reliance on imported steel. The falsified documents would make Stalintsia Steel appear to be a publicly owned European company—and not a Russian controlled monolith, which in fact it was! Victor controlled the Russian unions, had influence over the tax assessments made on the company, controlled the railroads, the shipyards, and the mines—all of course through various holdings, none of which could be directly traced back to him.

He had been counting on the Stalintsia Steel merger to finance his *Semya* project as well. He had several Soyuz booster rockets ordered, and the Italian mini-labs were ready for delivery, and all the suppliers were awaiting immediate payment! Was Alexander trying to kill his deal? Or, was his suggestion about the Stalintsia deal all a ruse to keep him looking west when his wife and daughter were going east? Zubkov was determined to know what was going on!

Natasha finished her description of her trip to Paris, and Victor took another bite of roast and chewed it slowly. He nodded his head up and down, and then swallowed.

"You should be in sales, my daughter! Once again, you have sold me on everything! You see, enthusiasm is ninety percent of sales—always remember that Natasha!"

"Yes, Daddy, I will." She tasted her salad.

"Natasha," Victor said. "Would you really like for me to come to Paris with you and your mother to watch your audition?"

Tatyana dropped her fork, and both Victor and Natasha looked at her with surprise. "Sorry," she said as she blushed. "It was clumsy of me. Natasha, answer your father!"

"Of course, Daddy. That would be great!" she replied excitedly. "But I thought that you had an important business meeting planned." She put another forkful of food in her mouth.

"The question was: Would you like for me to go to Paris with you and your momma?"

Natasha nodded her head enthusiastically, swallowed, and said, "It would be great fun Daddy! Especially to hear you struggle speaking French."

Victor laughed. "It's done then. We will all go to Paris, and don't worry about my French; I will muddle through somehow. I speak English well enough, and everyone in Paris understands English too, even though they hate the Americans and the Brits."

"Why is that, Daddy?"

Victor was observing Tatyana while he explained to Natasha the centuries-old feud between the Brits and the French. Tatyana's hands trembled as she struggled to cut her food. His announcement to go to Paris with them had obviously shaken her up badly, though she recovered well enough. She had baited him with Paris, only to quell his suspicions that she would bolt at the first opportunity. She had been counting on him to say that he couldn't go, and now that he said he would, it had shocked her!

"How romantic," he thought to himself, knowing that she truly was hoping to start a new life.

After dinner, Natasha jumped up from the table. "I have to email my friends before it gets too late," she said, and she bounded up the stairs.

Tatyana sat at the table in silence, her hands folded politely on her lap. She had barely eaten anything.

"Are you ill, my wife?" Victor asked. "You have barely eaten anything!"

As the servants cleared the table, Tatyana laughed. "I must admit that I was terribly hungry before dinner was served, and I got into the chocolates. The lamb didn't seem to blend very well with it. I am sorry to have ruined your dinner."

"You didn't," Victor replied. "I have work to do, my dear. Is there something I can get you to make you feel better?"

"No, dear. If it's all the same to you, I think I would like to retire early."

He nodded and went to her, kissing her on the cheek. "I will be in my study then."

As Victor walked away from the table and down the hall, Tatyana stood from the table, her knees trembling. Everything was ruined for her now! How could she possibly get away from him and start over with Alexander if he was going to be with her in Paris? Why did she taunt him that way? She had never expected him to change his business plans—he never had before! What if Victor knew more than what he led on? She knew that he would kill her if he knew about her and Alexander. The thought made her stomach churn more than it already was. She couldn't be sure how much he knew, but she had to assume he might know everything. Such knowledge was not beyond his reach, and indeed, he could well have just been playing with her all along! Such a ruse was not beyond his utter lack of conscience, and if he knew the truth, she would then soon be dead anyway, and her dreams forever dead with her.

She went upstairs to her daughter's room. Natasha was listening to American music and gleefully responding to text messages from her friends while she surfed the Internet. Tatyana went to her daughter, glanced at the computer screen to make sure that she wasn't somewhere she shouldn't be. She kissed her and gave her a hug.

"'Night, Mom," she said.

"Good night, Natasha."

She then went to her own room, and it was all she could do to get ready for bed. When she had pulled the covers up over her, she began to weep. "Everything is ruined now," she cried to herself. "I am sure that he will kill me if he knows that I have betrayed him!"

Victor Zubkov needed time to think. In his study, sitting at his enormous hand-carved desk, he opened the top drawer and pulled out a bottle of *Popov* and a shot glass. It was cheap vodka! But, it was what he learned to drink as a soldier. He poured the white fire into the glass and downed it in a single gulp. Mayakovsky had surprised him, and he wondered if he had been played the fool by this man all these years? For many years he had him bugged and followed, and yet now he had easily managed to get away without a trace? In fact, unlike the tracks that he had always left behind in the past, which were easily followed, he had suddenly vanished effortlessly, and the disjuncture with his previous performance seemed unlikely.

"Is it possible," he wondered, "that Mayakovsky had been leaving his tracks to be followed for a purpose all these years while he was really doing something else all along?" The pieces finally started coming together.

"What if I, Victor Zubkov, have been the buffoon all these years while

Mayakovsky is the true genius?" he thought. "What if Mayakovsky had been dropping crumbs for his men to follow, setting him up for this day the whole time?" Two vodkas later, Victor slammed his fist down on the desktop hard. He was now sure of it! Mayakovsky had been duping him for the past seven years—leading him to believe that he was having an affair with his wife, which had been true enough, but it wasn't his wife that Mayakovsky was after—it was the *Semya* chip technology! The high-ranking members of the Politburo, because of its immense commercial value, had kept the technology completely secret until after Perestroika and Glasnost; and even then, due to the significant military value of such technology, only a handful of people were privy to its existence in the first place, and Victor had been one of those privileged few.

When the Russian government started privatizing its industry, Victor had secretly sold off the small research facility that had developed the *Semya*, to a European investment group in which he held a controlling interest. He had destroyed every public document related to the existence of this strange new chip technology, a technology discovered quiet by accident, in a science experiment to grow crystals in the weightlessness of outer space so many years ago! But, there had been few documents about it anyway, because the new technology was deemed top secret! He had also, over a long period of time, bought off, or had murdered, every Politburo member who knew anything about it. The *Semya* technology was the best-kept secret in Russia, and Zubkov now had that technology.

Victor picked up the phone and dialed a number that only he knew. It took several attempts to get through.

"Privet, sto eta gavaro, paljasta?" (Hello, who is speaking, please?)

Victor barked into the phone, "Where is Sasha?"

Sasha Uchenko was connected.

"Yes sir!"

"I want you to go to the vault right now and inspect the *Semya* boards. I want a full accounting of every single chip, and Sasha, inspect each board under the electron microscope and run a full diagnostics on every chip."

"But sir that will take hours! Each board needs to be brought back up to temperature very slowly, and in a vacuum, to prevent any condensation."

"Just do it Sasha, and do it now! I want your full report before morning! But call me immediately if you find anything out of order, no matter the time."

Victor hung up his phone, poured another vodka, and lit a Cuban cigar. He almost smiled, now admiring Mayakovsky for his genius, but also his patience and his courage. The only way Mayakovsky could have gotten the entry codes to the facility and to the vault was through Tatyana. She was the only one who knew where he kept his secret ledger, or the combination of the safe. Even though he encrypted everything, it would not be too difficult to decipher it, if one knew how—and Tatyana did!

He went to his wall safe, removed the ledger, and examined it. The ledger contained mostly names with a few notes that meant something only to him. He didn't keep account numbers written down, so his money was still safe! But, he did keep passwords and security codes for the various facilities he owned on the ledger. He scrolled down the list to the *Semya*, a word that normally would mean nothing to anyone, but he knew that Mayakovsky would have picked up on it right away. The facility codes were written down, but they would not have worked as written, as alpha characters. But, if one knew that each vowel in the Cyrillic alphabet represented a specific number—it could easily be deciphered. Only Tatyana knew of his encryption code, which he had made up as a young man.

"Poor Tatyana," he thought to himself. "She thought that Mayakovsky loved her. She had never known a thing about the *Semya* chip, but Alexander did! The woman is upstairs right now thinking that she is going to Paris to start a whole new life with a man who loves her! When in fact, Alexander Mayakovsky never had any intention of marrying her. She will get to New York City and find out that she is there all alone, and with nothing! Alexander Mayakovsky has sold the *Semya* technology to someone, and has disappeared! And he has sold poor naive Tatyana down the river when he did!"

Victor laughed out loud! "Salute Alexander! What a brilliant plan!" Then he downed his vodka and said, "But sorry, you must die for it! And I will get the *Semya* back regardless." Then he thought about it for moment longer. "To the victor go the spoils," he said, a saying he used to justify many of the unsavory deeds he had felt compelled to do in his life. The words went through his head over and over again. He smiled. "Even better still, Alexander! Perhaps you intended to steal my wife after all—and to steal the *Semya*, and then kill me! And then you would get it all, wouldn't you, my old friend? To the victor do go the spoils! Indeed!"

Victor poured himself another vodka even though he was getting very drunk by now, something he rarely let himself do. "Perhaps I should let Tatyana and Natasha go," he thought to himself in his drunken stupor. He cared for Tatyana, despite her betrayal! And, there was a time when he was completely in love with her! But, his own appetites for young women had tainted their romantic relationship—and that was not her doing! Could he blame her for wanting another life? In his heart, he knew he couldn't.

Victor Zubkov was not what most people believed him to be. Yes, he had killed in the past. And yes, he had ordered the deaths of many more men over the years, too many to count! But to his mind, it was all done for the motherland! His father had been a tank commander in WWII, and he had died in the Battle of Kursk in 1943, the fiercest tank battle ever fought! The losses were enormous on both sides. It was a *turning point* in the war, though often overlooked because nothing ever came of it, other than the death or maiming of half a million soldiers on both sides. The Germans had withdrawn all their forces to shore up an imminent invasion by the Allies on the Sicilian front, and the Battle of Kursk was nearly forgotten about!

But, after the war, Russia needed heroes! And Victor's father became one of them, gaining national recognition posthumously. He and his men had stopped the German advance, and sadly, he lost his life in the process! He died before Victor had even been born. His mother was only a few months pregnant when his father was killed, and so when he was born, she named him Victor. She named him Victor for victory!

Then his mother died from tuberculosis when he was only twelve years old. Both his parents were devoted patriots who believed in Russia, and believed in the old ways of Russian Imperialism. But after his mother died, he was taken to a boy's school run by the state. There he had been indoctrinated into the ways of socialism. Because his father was a decorated war hero, when he was old enough he went into a military academy and served some time in the army before he went into politics. Victor had found it easy enough to navigate his way through the Politburo. But his motivations were to restore Russia to the greatness it once held during the reign of Ekaterina the Great! He couldn't have cared less about the Soviets' goals.

Over the years, he had positioned himself well—and was appointed the Minister of Heavy Industry. Given the historical moment of *reform and openness*, soon after he was awarded the position, he was tasked with privatizing the sector! His first goal was to ensure his own financial holdings, and then to dole out holdings to the people he trusted and who would serve him well throughout the years. But despite the corruption and the skimming, it had always been a priority for him to help restore Russia to the glory it held prior to the abdication of the Romanov family in 1917. He knew that free enterprise was the key to this renewed ascendancy. But like many battles fought by the Russians over the years, the changeover would come at a great cost. People would suffer immensely, and some would die! He viewed his role in the changeover as nothing more than a general throwing soldiers into battle with the knowledge that many would perish.

He did not turn many Russian Industries over to the Politburo members, but instead to the managers of the companies who knew the businesses best. He then appointed financial advisors and economists to major positions within the companies with instructions to structure the companies to run on a profit-loss basis, something that most managers had never had to deal with before. He had encouraged outside investment. And since there was no way for companies within Russia to borrow money, he sold off controlling interests to investment and holding companies, most of which he controlled, for the much needed capital required for modernization. Most of his strategies had worked, but there were some within Russia who were determined to see him fail! They were determined to see him fail so that they could muscle their way in. That is where he obtained his reputation for ruthlessness! In order to maintain limited control over these industries, again for the Russian people in his rationalization, he had to deal with the Russian mafia and all the corrupt government officials. Sixty percent of every ruble invested went for payoffs! And so profits were far lower than they might have been—should have been! He had gotten the graft down to fifty percent of investments over the past eight years, but his goal was to get it to thirty before he died—or was killed!

The workers themselves were seeing a very gradual improvement in both pay and working conditions. And Victor knew that eventually their growing prosperity would translate into consumer purchases. Consumer purchases meant more demand for steel, for glass, for plastics, and for energy. Those were the sectors that he saw as the strength of the nation! And thus he was driven to raise capital for those industries any way he could, despite the poor business environment within the Russian Federation. The upshot remained that much of the capital available was being bled off by corruption, but progress was being made! The pendulum was already in motion now, and there was no stopping it! It was time now for him to think about the future of his family and what to do with his own wealth.

He adored his Natasha, even though she was not his biological daughter. If he allowed the girl and her mother to run off to America, he would probably never see her again. Was that what he wanted? Was his life worth anything without his gifted Natasha?

The vodka dredged up memories of his mother Angelika before the illness had taken her.

"You are named Victor," she had told him when he was a little boy. "For victory. Your father gave up his life to protect two things: his beloved country, and me, his wife. Your father never even knew that he had a son on the way! But I am sure that he would have been the best father ever! So, I named you Victor in his memory. I expect you to honor your father, and I expect you to honor your name, Victor. You too must always be prepared to defend what you truly love, if it ever comes to that. Your father believed in Russia and the Russian people, and he was a good man, son. I trust that you will be a good man too."

His mother had died shortly thereafter, and Victor had taken her words to heart. He had studied Russian culture and history with a passion, and in fact, he had become something of a historian. "How many millions of Russians had died in battle in just the last hundred years, and for what?" The question had always been a puzzle to him. Everyone hated the Russian winters, and yet every European and Asian army to date had invaded Russia one by one. So why invade Russia in the first place? It was a question to which he had no answer.

As Victor became more and more intoxicated, he made a decision. He would keep his promise to his mother. If it were time for him to die, for either his Motherland or his family, then he would do as his father had done before him, and die with honor! He would let Tatyana and Natasha start a new life on their own; because he knew that his mother would have wanted it this way. He didn't need the money anyway—it was just a way to accomplish a goal, and his goals had already been met. The wheels of capitalism were already in motion in Russia. In spite of the ongoing corruption, capitalism was a self-sustaining system driven by people's ambitions, and not their needs.

He had to admit to himself that, if his assumptions about Alexander Mayakovsky were correct, that poor Tatyana was being played for a bigger fool than he. Victor knew that she could recover from the experience quickly enough if given the time and resources. She was not a weak woman! He decided he would give her enough money to have a comfortable life.

"Why not?" he thought. "I have made too much money to ever spend it all anyway? Why not let the women I once loved have some romance? Romance is good and it brings about new life! Tatyana and Natasha are first and foremost women! And that is what women should do, bring new life to an aging old world."

Wandering into the adjacent room off of his study with the nearly empty bottle of vodka, he set the bottle down on the nightstand, pulled off his clothes, and pulled back the bed sheets. Picking the vodka up again, he tipped the bottle back.

"Tomorrow will be a very difficult day," he thought to himself as the harsh liquid poured down his throat.

Chapter 19

Nick Peters looked confused. "What are you talking about, Morgan? What kind of conspiracy?"

"Nick," Morgan replied calmly. "How long have you known me? Have I ever exaggerated a situation before? I haven't been told that much myself, other than that Nathan Chadwick Bentley has his sights set on acquiring a formidable new Russian technology from your buddy Victor Zubkov, and that he intends to market it to foreign governments, some of whom are not America's friends! Neither the American nor the Russian government wants this technology released to anyone! And so they intend to recover it, and destroy it! But there is a fly in the ointment! Someone inside the US government has got other plans for this technology."

Blakely interjected, "Nick, who is this guy?"

"He's a *closer* for the CIA, Blakely. In more common terms, he's a hit man! I take it, Morgan," Nick stated, "that the bullet a minute ago was just a wake-up call?"

"There was a boat out in the bay with shooters onboard—their crosshairs were on you guys. I thought it prudent to get you moving."

"Those were my people, Morgan," Nick replied, and for your information Zubkov is not my buddy! "So what's so important about this attaché case, and how does a conspiracy fit into all this?"

The US and the Russian governments are working on a top secret project in the Ural Mountains."

"I know," Nick replied. "It's called Magic Mountain. Where's the fly?"

"It's suspected that there's a secret clone facility of Magic Mountain somewhere, and that an unknown someone wants to keep it that way—a secret! The Russians got wind of Zubkov's plan to sell the *Semya* technology to Bentley, and they want the deal stopped! But, Zubkov is too well connected in Russia not to hear about any moves being made against him. If he did get wind of any resistance to his wishes, the first thing he would do is move the chips somewhere else. So, it was agreed upon by both sides to hire your firm to oversee the destruction of all the *Semya* technology."

"So, what's Magic Mountain got to do with anything?"

"That's where the conspiracy comes in. We had a deal with the Russians to fund the start-up of the de-fanged *Obvyet* computer on Russian soil, with an agreement that research would be shared, but the technology would be proprietary for the Russians. These *Semya* chips that Zubkov has were to have been destroyed years ago, leaving only one operating *Obvyet* left in existence. When it was discovered that he still had them in his possession, it became a top priority for the Russians to get them all back! But the only way to know for certain if we have them all, is by the chips' bios registration numbers, which change every day." Morgan paused. "Make sense?"

"I got that from Roberta," Nick said. She is here to decrypt the bios numbers and to verify them."

Morgan nodded. "Bentley had a deal with Zubkov that if Zubkov fell behind schedule in manufacturing the new chips to populate his mother boards with, which he has, then Zubkov would deliver his secret stock of chips, along with the bios codes, to Bentley. This was so that the initial orders for mainframe supercomputers could be delivered on schedule and without delays. What both governments are concerned about is that Zubkov may have in his possession the original *Semya* chips—the ones without the failsafe design where the bios registration numbers change daily. If those chips get installed into a super computer mainframe, we have the potential for what happened with the *Obvyet* computer back in the eighties, happening many times over! All these new super computers Bentley has sold are destined for military operations within foreign governments. Neither Bentley nor Zubkov have a clue that these original *Semya* chips have the ability to go rogue!"

"At the same time, Nathan Chadwick Bentley got clever. He knew that Zubkov was leveraged to the hilt, and he decided to break him financially."

Nick interjected, "How could Zubkov be leveraged to the hilt? Not only is he one of the richest men in Russia, but he is the Minister of Heavy Industry."

"But Zubkov bought up or contracted for hundreds of millions of dollars in launch pad resources around Europe—mostly from France, Spain, and Italy—to launch his space labs into orbit to build these *Semya* chips in the weightlessness of outer space. He also has Soyuz rockets leased and sitting on the launch pads right now, ready to take off as soon as the funds are released. Zubkov has all his personal holdings tied up in reserving launch pads and in rockets, and mini-labs waiting to launch. He is waiting until the Stalintsia deal goes through—at which time his investors will release the funds that he needs to go into production with the *Semya* chips! And, he is counting on the sale of what chips he has now to Bentley for the needed funds to put those labs into orbit to make more *Semya* chips should the Stalintsia Steel merger falter! Bentley knows this. If he can stop the Stalintsia deal, he breaks Zubkov! Then he can move in and pick up all the contracts Zubkov has in place to manufacture the chips in outer space without having to pay a dime to Zubkov for any of it! Effectively cutting Zubkov completely out of the deal—and bankrupting him in the process! So, Bentley got Alexander Mayakovsky in his pocket to make sure that the Stalintsia Steel merger didn't go through, and to grab Zubkov's stock of *Semya's* so he wouldn't have to pay for them."

Nick spoke up again. "But Bentley needs both the code and the chips, so even if he busts Zubkov, I still have the code."

"Bentley is counting on Mayakovsky for both," Morgan replied. "Zubkov was counting on the delivery of the attaché case and a favorable resolution to the antitrust suit so he would have his funding from his European investors without needing Bentley's help. The pocket drive is the conspiracy, Nick. The United States is not supposed to have an *Obvyet or Magic Mountain* project of its own, and yet there is evidence to suggest that we do. In fact, thanks to Roberta here, who discovered the money trail in the first place, we are fairly certain it does exist. When the President of the United States found out we were in violation of our agreement with the Russians, he blew a gasket and wanted to shut it down! But whoever this someone is—behind all this, they were one step ahead of everyone else, and we still don't know where the cloned Magic Mountain is."

"I still don't see a conspiracy Morgan," Nick protested.

Morgan sighed. "Someone very high up in our government wants those bios codes too, which can only mean that there is a redundant system in place somewhere waiting to be populated with *Semya* chips or worse yet!"

Nick waited for Morgan to continue, "Worse yet?"

"We think there is a possibility that this cloned Magic Mountain super computer may already be populated with the original *Semya* chips stolen from Zubkov just recently—or those chips are enroute now to do just that. If so, we may never be able to locate them again! And when this redundant system is fired up, it won't be used for peaceful scientific research! It will be used to develop a first strike weapon!"

Nick was still puzzled. "Again Morgan, why me and Roberta? Why are we needed?"

"The original *Semya* chip had a bios code written in a language no longer used today. And, the list of original bios registration numbers needed to identify which chips are which, was also written in that original code! All newer chips that have the upgraded bios code written to them— which allows for the scrambling of registration numbers so that the *Semya* can be prevented from reaching the critical self-awareness point, use this newer updated computer code. These newer chips cannot unscramble the original bios registration numbers because they can't read the original code either. Only an original *Semya* chip can!"

"Meaning?"

Morgan continued, "Meaning—an original *Semya* chip is needed to activate and to program the stolen *Semya* chips! Why, you're about to ask? If they have original *Semya* chips would they need another?"

Nick nodded.

"Because—after the *Obvyet* computer was finally shutdown after the Chernobyl incident, all the original remaining *Semya* chips which had the original bios code programming were erased, and the original code was destroyed. The only remaining bios code left in existence was on the motherboard of the *Obvyet* computer which is still in the possession of both governments at the new Magic Mountain facility in the Ural Mountains."

Nick sighed. "I guess I don't get it. In today's world of electronic transfer, why would anyone resort to hand-carrying something that could be emailed? Computer code can be emailed can't it?"

Roberta spoke up, "The pocket drive you have with you is a *Semya* chip! It is the perfect encryption device, a device that no known PC or computer can read, but also a device that can decipher the original *Semya* code. This particular *Semya* chip is the last of the early ones—taken off the motherboard of the original *Obvyet* computer! It will be needed to verify any bios codes from chips we recover.

"Yes Nick," Morgan went on. "And, if this one *Semya* chip gets into the wrong hands, a counterfeit board can be made by reprogramming the bios code of normal chips to make them appear as *Semya* chips. In other words, the *Semya* boards may have already been stolen and replaced with counterfeits."

"Convincing both the Russians and the Americans that all the *Semya* chips have been destroyed when they haven't been," Nick said.

Both Morgan and Roberta nodded their heads in agreement.

Nick was rubbing his forehead in confusion—he was getting a headache! "But this doesn't make any sense, people. If there is another Magic Mountain somewhere, and if the *Semya* chips have already been stolen, whoever is behind this mess already has what they need."

"Not unless they never had time to reprogram the bios code on the counterfeit boards, which means the verification fails! And then we keep looking for them—which is not what they want! They used you to bring the *Semya* chip into the States so the counterfeit boards would pass inspection!

Morgan continued. "You have been under surveillance ever since your meeting with Alexander in Zurich. We knew that Mayakovsky was going to double-cross Zubkov, and grab the chips and the codes for Bentley. As far as Bentley was concerned, Alexander Mayakovsky was on track to grab everything within the next few days—why he delayed we don't know. All Bentley cared about was fouling up the Stalintsia Steel merger sufficiently to break Zubkov."

"So, Alexander set me up?" Nick asked.

"He used you as a diversion to grab the *Semya* chips," Morgan agreed. "But, it was Bentley who ordered the hit on you."

"And you were the hit man?" Nick said.

Morgan shook his head. "No, I was part of *Operation Clean Sweep*, which was triggered by a phone call from Harold Toman, Director of the CIA."

"Meaning the elimination of the Congressman Wilshire and all the others?"

"Exactly Nick," Morgan confirmed. "*Operation Clean Sweep* was…"

"Plan-B," Nick finished the sentence for him.

Morgan continued. "The late congressman had been duped into authorizing a Letter of Congress to bring the needed documents into the country to ensure that the class action lawsuit against Stalintsia Steel got dropped. But when the cops in Port Angeles stopped you, both CIA Director Toman and the Congressman wanted all connections back to them severed. Being associated with the likes of Zubkov would have blemished the congressman's legacy, and it would mean the demise of numerous careers in Washington."

"What went wrong?" Nick asked.

"The pocket drive got planted in your attaché case, Nick. That's what went wrong. When Toman ordered *Operation Clean Sweep* to cover his own tracks and those of the congressman, he had no idea he was signing his own death warrant and the death warrants for all the rest of them. If you got stopped and killed, or the attaché case went missing, this 'someone' with the cloned *Obvyet* project wouldn't get the chip they needed to make the stolen *Semya* chips work or to make the counterfeited boards look legit."

"How do you know all this, and how did you let this technology get away from you?" Nick demanded.

Blakely had been patient long enough. "And what does the FBI have to do with any of this?"

Morgan smiled broadly. "The CIA played your agency like a fiddle. We knew that you would set up roadblocks looking for a Mustang like the one Nick was driving, and we knew that he would elude you. So, you got tipped off."

Blakely fumed, "And what about the FBI leak? And my cell phone transmissions being forwarded to Bentley?"

"Nathan Chadwick Bentley has people in his pocket. Whoever tipped off Bentley from inside your agency did so without CIA knowledge. But obviously they underestimated Nick's abilities, and so did Bentley. Bentley called off the hit on Nick before he knew that his own men were dead. He thought the FBI would intercept the delivery, and that the documents for the Stalintsia antitrust lawsuit wouldn't get delivered. His involvement in all this was limited to screwing Victor Zubkov out of everything! And then picking up his launch contracts while bankrupting him in the process. So, he really didn't care what happened to Nick and he called off the hit!"

Nick asked, "So who ordered the deaths of CIA Director Toman, the congressman, and all the others?"

"The same person who is behind the cloned *Magic Mountain*, and the same person who ordered me to kill you."

"And you don't know yet who that is?" Nick scoffed.

Morgan shook his head. "When CIA Director Toman initiated his plan-B, he had no idea that someone had already rewritten the plan—rewritten it to destroy all ties back to whoever is behind all this! When I got my orders to kill you, I went outside of channels. I tipped off a friend of mine in the Secret Service that something wasn't right, and he got that information directly to the President of the United States. It was at that point that we realized that a conspiracy was in play."

Morgan went on. "You exchanged attaché cases with Alexander Mayakovsky at Sheremetyevo Airport in Moscow, and the pocket drive was not in it when you did. It was put in the attaché case during your flight from Moscow to Vancouver."

Nick's mind flashed back to his flight from Moscow.

"Can I get you anything, sir?" the pretty brunette stewardess had asked him.

"Yes," Nick had replied. "A tonic water, pillow, and blanket."

"Of course sir," she said. "It's a long flight. It's best if you take your sleep now, and if you need anything else, just push that button over there."

She had pointed to the call button.

"The stewardess?" Nick muttered.

"We aren't sure Nick, but someone planted the pocket drive in the attaché case while you were in flight. We know this because about the time you landed in Vancouver, British Columbia, we discovered our agent dead! He was on the same flight you were, and he was bringing the pocket drive to us! The Russian Federation was sending it to us for the verification process. Twelve hours later, you were calling your old friend Boris for help, and it was then we knew you had it."

"So, you are saying that Mayakovsky used me as his diversion to recover the *Semya* chips and to betray Victor Zubkov? And that Nathan Bentley's only interest in all this was to financially destroy Zubkov, just so he could cut him out of the deal altogether, and then supply his own microchips without having a middleman. But, you are also telling me that there is someone very high up in our own government who either gets exposed if the *Semya* gets commercialized, or otherwise doesn't want it to get commercialized for reasons yet to be determined?"

"Both Nikki," Morgan replied. "If the *Semya* technology becomes commercialized, even if it could be controlled by these built in safety measures, third-world nations would have the same technological advantage the Americans and Russians now have. And, if they discovered a way to override what safety measures are currently built into them, meant to prevent it from going rogue, that could tip the balance of world power. At the same time, someone needs the bios codes themselves to activate their own *Semya* chips, which means the cloned Magic Mountain is about to come online."

"I thought Magic Mountain was already operational," Nick replied.

"The original *Obvyet* computer was brought back online two years ago—but only for the purpose of identifying whether or not all newer versions of Semya chips had in fact the failsafe code built into them. The newest version of it was to be brought online next week. But, it became apparent to both governments, months ago, that someone else had plans to commercialize the *Semya* chip, and those people we now know are Victor Zubkov, and Nathan Chadwick Bentley. Neither Zubkov nor Bentley knew about the real problems with the original chips—because the military establishment buried the entire *Obvyet* incident! Nevertheless, they were intending to mass-produce them—these *Semya* chips by the millions! No one would have known about their plans if it hadn't been for Roberta coming across that transmission, and being able to decipher it. In order to keep both governments honest, only half of the bios registration codes were given out to either party—to ensure that both countries maintained equal control over the project at Magic Mountain. A consortium of nations, mostly European, controlled those coded registration numbers, and because a bank of *Semya* boards each contained one hundred micro-chips, the bios numbers were distributed randomly to this consortium. To drive a super computer with these micro-chips it takes several banks of cards populated with the *Semya* chips! No one knew until just recently that Victor Zubkov was in possession of the original master list, which was thought to have been destroyed years ago or that he was in possession of multiple boards populated with these micro-chips."

"If the Russians thought the master list was destroyed," Nick muttered, "then how did they get another list made?"

Roberta replied, "From the original *Obvyet* computer, Nick. That is why they brought it back to life originally—to obtain the list of original bios registration numbers and to retrieve the original bios coding. They then powered it back down and replaced the entire bank of original *Semya* chips with the newer versions—ones with the failsafe built in. The pocket drive is an original Semya chip! It is the only way to verify an original Semya chip from one having the failsafe built in—because it can decipher the older codes whereas the newer versions can't! The newer chips need the newer operating system to function correctly."

"But, these are the original chips we are talking about now—the ones everyone is so concerned about?" Nick asked. "Meaning, they don't have that safeguard built in, and if used commercially, there could be another run-away *Obvyet* computer?"

"I think that is *one* of the concerns Nick," she answered. "Even the older chips without the original bios coding cannot become self aware unless they become reprogrammed with a chip from the original *Obvyet* computer. Another concern is what Morgan mentioned. Newer boards can be made to appear as the older ones—when in fact they are not."

"Meaning?

"Meaning," Roberta continued. "We lose forever the whereabouts of the last remaining dangerous *Semya* chips! If we get them *all* this time, the threat is over with forever!"

"Are Boris and his family safe?" Nick asked Morgan apprehensively.

"They are in FSB custody for the time being. But they are safe until we accomplish our mission," Morgan replied.

"And what mission is that, Morgan?"

"I need the pocket drive first," he replied.

Blakely looked at Nick nervously, and Nick nodded. "Give it to him, Bill."

Blakely opened the attaché case and handed the pocket drive over to him. Morgan smiled and handed it over to Roberta. "Verify that it is authentic Roberta," Morgan muttered.

Roberta reached into her pocket and pulled out what looked like an iPod. She inserted the pocket drive into it and turned it on. She nodded a few seconds later. "It's genuine. It broke the *Semya* code."

Morgan smiled broadly. "Then my mission is over. It's Roberta's mission now. C'mon, Blakely. We both have what we came after."

"What do you mean?" Blakely protested.

Morgan laughed. "You recovered the attaché case, Roberta has what she needs, and I need to catch a flight home." He tossed his car keys to Nick. "You both have miles to go before you sleep—good luck, Nikki."

Morgan got out of the backseat of the car and opened Nick's door, motioning for him to get out. As Nick did, Morgan slid in.

Nick overheard him say to Blakely, "Oh, and by the way Blakely, it wasn't your wife banging the Senator. It was Trundle's anorexic secretary he was doing."

Chapter 20

Victor Zubkov was awakened before dawn by an urgent telephone call. His head throbbed from the alcohol he had consumed just a few hours before. The call was from Sasha Uchenko at the lab.

"Sir, he said. "We have a virgin board here. It hasn't been impregnated."

"Send me the serial number of the missing board and the bios registration numbers of each chip on it."

"Yes sir," Uchenko replied, relieved that he wasn't being threatened or yelled at.

"Uchenko," Victor added. "You know that this situation means that there has been a breach in security there. Fortunately for you, I know who is behind it, but I don't know yet how he did it. You have twenty-four hours to figure out how he got to the circuit boards, and how to correct this weakness, or you will be replaced—or possibly much worse! In the meantime, I am sending in a security task force to lock the lab down. No one will be allowed to enter or leave the facility until further notice, and that includes all local deliveries. All supplies will be flown in by helicopter. As of now, the facility is under a complete lockdown. Do you understand?"

"Yes, sir."

"Good! Then get Anatoly Timoshenko now." There was a pause, and then another voice came on the line. Victor intended to be much harsher with the head of security than he had been with Sasha, who was only a research and development engineer. "You have a big problem there, Anatoly. The most valuable technology in Russia has just been compromised, and stolen out from under your very nose. I want to know the names of everyone who had access to that facility over the past three months, and I want that information handed over to Oleyenka when he arrives with his team. Until then, only facility workers will be allowed inside, and once in, no one leaves until Oleyenka is done with his investigation. You will answer to him from now on. Do you understand?"

"Yes, sir. I will do as you say. Sir?"

"What is it?" Victor said harshly.

"Everything was done by the book. I have complied with all the security measures."

"Then you have nothing to worry about, but you need to find out what went wrong! In the meantime, no one leaves. Do you understand?"

"All will be done exactly as you have ordered, sir."

Victor hung up. He noted that it was six-thirty in the morning. He was wide-awake now and decided to get up. He threw on a robe and went downstairs to the kitchen for some much-needed coffee. The house staff was in full swing already. Muttering *dobra utra* (good morning) to all of them, he poured himself a cup of coffee and blended it with creamer, then made his way back upstairs to his room, where he prepared to shave and shower.

"The women will be up soon," he thought, "and yet there is still so much to do! I was a fool to have gotten so intoxicated last night!"

He lathered up his face with soap and dragged a razor across his thick stubble. He had not been surprised by the news that a *Semya* board had been stolen. He had expected it, and now that a board was missing, many of the pieces of the puzzle fit together neatly. Each *Semya* board had one hundred microchips on it, and if only one got into the wrong hands, it would jeopardize the release of his newest free enterprise product. The *Semya* chip would be worth billions of American dollars if he could get it to market first, making the latest Pentium technology, or anything else that might be on the drawing board for that matter, obsolete.

After shaving and showering, Victor Zubkov went back downstairs and had breakfast. As he was finishing, Natasha joined him.

"Good morning, Daddy." She made sure to kiss him on his cheek before sitting down this time.

"We leave for Paris in just a few hours—I am so excited!"

Victor smiled at his daughter.

"Yes, for a woman, Paris is an exciting place to visit."

"Why do say that?" she asked as she put scrambled eggs and cut fruit on her plate. "Why not for a man too?"

"Well, keep in mind, I have only been there on business a few times, but the city holds a certain mystique of romance about it. There are many places of art in Paris, many fine women's boutiques, the theatre, and fine restaurants too. The French take pride in their city, but they are snobs in a way, as if they were the ones who invented art in the first place. In my opinion, London is a very much more earthy, and a much more fun place to visit. The Brits are not quite the snobs the Parisian's are."

Natasha laughed. "And what about we Russians? What does the rest of the world think about us?"

Victor laughed too. "We Russians? No one trusts us anymore, Princess. We are far too ruthless, and as a people we are far too insecure and too secretive for anyone outside of Russia to know that we are just people like they are. The outside world doesn't realize that, to survive just one Russian winter, a Russian must be very strong."

"In fact, our strength as a people is our ability to endure under the worst of conditions. When Napoleon invaded Russia, it was our winters that defeated him. When Hitler invaded Russia, it was our winters that defeated him. The Russian people can endure what most others can't, and so the rest of the world fears us."

Natasha was eating her breakfast across the table from her father, and she asked between bites,

"You know much about history, Daddy. Why?"

"History always repeats itself, my dear. Russia has always been a misunderstood country. Our people are the best-educated people in the world, and yet we face an economic crisis because there are few jobs available anymore. With no jobs to bring home a paycheck to support a family, what is a man or woman to do? We will survive, but the outside world will continue to mistrust us for a long time for the ambitions of a few, and they are justified. My job has been to encourage free enterprise after Communism fell. It is not an easy task when there is no money available to borrow, to invest in economic growth! But, history will repeat itself, and one day, Russia will have the respect that it deserves."

"We have done well for ourselves, Daddy, thanks to you."

"The wealth of this household is not about me, Princess. It has always been about you and your mother. I do many unpleasant things to ensure that you and your momma have a good life, and someday, those unpleasant things will all come back to haunt me, I am sure."

"Then why did you do those things, Daddy?" Natasha asked.

Victor looked at the lovely face of his daughter. "You have led a very sheltered life, my young daughter. You know much about Russian history yourself, but you have been fortunate enough not to have had to live it! I have had to live with many hardships, and there were things that had to be done, unpleasant things to be sure—things of which I am not proud. I did those things to ensure that you and your mother were protected. To answer your question, all parents do their very best to give their children opportunities in life, and I have accomplished most of what I set out to do in this regard. It is now up to you, my daughter, to make the best of it."

Natasha listened as she ate her fruit. "I know, Daddy. You have done much for Mom and me. I will do my best to please you."

Victor smiled at his daughter. "That is all that I can ask of you," he said proudly. "You work very hard to prove yourself, and you are a true Russian woman in spirit."

"Daddy," she said. "You take things way too seriously!"

"I do?" Victor scoffed, but he also wondered if she might be right.

"Yes!" She laughed. "But I love your stories about Russian culture. I think they inspire me to do my best."

"You know, it was Ekaterina, Katherine the Great, who chose culture over war! And there was a time when Russia became *the* Mecca for the fine arts and culture under her rule. It will be your generation that changes the world's opinion about Russia. That is why we go to Paris. You will dance into the hearts of the people of the West and make Russia proud of you."

"Oh thanks Daddy," she replied sarcastically. "I needed that little extra pressure." She smiled at her father. "Is it true that Ekaterina was so huge that she did it with horses?"

Victor laughed robustly. "Where did you hear such a story?"

"It is in all the Western books, Daddy."

"I think it is a myth, my daughter! The Westerners always made fun of Ekaterina because they hated her! She was a woman of big appetites for everything—including men! And, she was a very strong-willed woman in a time when strong willed women were few. Westerners hated strong-willed women! They made up horrible stories about her—though she was renowned for searching the ranks of her military for men capable of satisfying her huge amorous appetites!" He couldn't help noticing the wide-eyed interest his daughter was showing with his story, so he continued. "Her maidens were required to sample the men first, and to report to her of any man endowed well enough, and possessing enough stamina, to satisfy her needs. And, for sure there were many young officers who rose inordinately fast in rank for accepting the challenge!" He laughed robustly again! "This is the basis for the Westerners' exaggeration, but the story about the horse was made up! I am sure, to discredit her! Because she was a great woman they tried to find anything they could to shame her! And other than her huge appetite for men—they could find no other fault with her."

Natasha laughed. "Is it physically possible, no matter what size a woman is, no matter how huge she might be, to be able to do it with a horse, Daddy?"

"What kind of conversation is this to have over breakfast?" He joined her in laughter.

"Answer the question, Daddy, because I don't know!"

"*Ya niz niou elee!* (I don't know either!) Women are capable of many things, but that one—I would hope not!"

"I am worried Daddy," Natasha said, now quite seriously while picking at her food. "I am worried that I will not be accepted after my audition."

Victor shuffled some food around his plate before taking another bite. "If it is important enough to you Natasha, you will do just fine. You are a strong Russian woman, my Princess—and you can handle the pressure!

You have worked very hard to get this appointment, and you are a strong woman! For a Russian woman, life is about three things."

"And what are those three things, Daddy?"

"Life for a Russian woman is about beauty in all things, romance, and life. No matter what the world thinks of us Russians, it is our women who give us everything to be proud of. No other women in the world can compare to a Russian woman in beauty, or in the size of her heart."

"Why then are there so many divorces and so many alcoholic men in Russia?"

Victor took a sip of coffee and frowned. "Men in Russia have no opportunities right now," he stated frankly. "The jobs are few, and the pay is low for what jobs there are. Vodka is a cheap commodity in Russia, and it has always been a relief from misery for many. Our Russian men have given up temporarily, because there are only a few honest jobs left! But things will get better," Victor finished emphatically.

"Daddy," she said. "I don't think I want to marry a Russian man."

"Why not Natasha, and who would you marry if not a Russian man?" Victor asked, semi-offended.

"It's like you said, most Russian men have already given up on everything! And, the ones who haven't are involved with the Mafia, or with the gangs. I just want to have a normal life. I don't need all this," she said motioning expansively at everything around her. "It's all very nice daddy, and I am very proud of you for all you have accomplished for us, but a simple *doma* in the country, and a small garden are all I need."

Victor reached over and touched her hand.

"Princess, then just follow your heart; but remember that even a simple *doma* in the country has to be paid for! And, in Russia, money is in short supply. I am proud of you, nevertheless, for your simple needs! You carry the spirit of the Russian people within you. You are a romantic woman, just like your mother is! And the world needs more kindness and more beauty and more culture—all of which a woman like you can bring to the world. You take those qualities with you no matter where you go! So, just follow your heart, my daughter, and remember always, that you are a strong Russian woman! Your true love will find you! And, if you follow your heart, all will be just fine in your life."

"Thank you, Daddy. I will," she said, beaming back at him.

Tatyana now joined them. She was dressed in a stylish pair of pants with a colorful top. "You must have worked very late, Victor. You didn't come to bed last night," she said softly.

Victor got up from the table and kissed her. "Yes, I worked until very late last night, and I was expecting a telephone call, so I took my sleep in my study."

"Are you angry with me?" she asked, filling her plate with fruit and eggs and two pieces of sliced ham.

Victor scoffed. "Why do you say that? You know that when I work late, I usually sleep in my study so that I do not wake you with my snoring, especially after drinking vodka all night long!" he laughed to reassure her. "I think that you are worried about me coming to Paris with you—would it be better if I didn't?"

"No Daddy," Natasha objected immediately, nearly knocking over her glass of juice. "You must come! I want to dance for you! It has been my dream for many years!"

Victor said sternly to his daughter,

"Natasha, it is up to your mother. Besides, you just said that you didn't need any additional pressure."

"I am a very strong Russian woman, Daddy. I can handle the pressure," she retorted defiantly.

Tatyana smiled at her and said in a reassuring tone, "Victor, I just asked if you were angry with me? I didn't mean to start an argument. Yes, I was surprised last night when you said that you wanted to come to Paris with us, but only because I know how important your work is to you and that you have prior commitments. I dreaded going there alone, but I had accepted it. If we all go together, then we will be as a family on a holiday, and you won't have to sleep in another room worried about your snoring. I will just have to put up with it!" She laughed too. "I too am a strong Russian woman!"

Victor knew what his wife was doing. She still thought that Alexander Mayakovsky was going to be in Paris to get her and Natasha, and she was attempting to keep his guard down by pretending to be worried about him.

"Have you heard anything from Alexander?" he asked.

"No dear," Tatyana replied. "Why would you ask?"

"No reason, dear. It's just that I sent him off to do something two days ago, and I haven't heard from him since. It's unlike Alexander not to report in. I thought that perhaps you might have had a telephone call from him that you forgot to tell me about."

"No, Victor. I haven't heard from him."

"Well, I made a few other changes," Victor added offhandedly.

"Oh really," Tatyana replied, her heart now racing!

"Yes. I chartered a flight. I couldn't get a seat on your airline at the eleventh hour, so what else could I do?"

"Oh, Victor. It will cost a fortune," she exclaimed!

Victor scoffed. "Why do I work so hard if not for you and Natasha? It is already done anyway. I will finish some work out of town and meet you and Natasha in Paris by 18:00 hours on Thursday, the eve of Natasha's performance. You two go on ahead as planned, and I'll catch up."

"And what else has changed, Victor?"

Victor smiled. "Only a few things my dear, and they will be my surprise to you both when we all get to Paris. I am looking forward to both your smiles of delight. Do not worry my dear; the changes are nothing important—nothing to worry yourself about! After the audition, I will take you both on a great shopping spree, and then I must get back here to St. Petersburg. You girls will have several full days in Paris on your own, and you can return on your scheduled flight, if you want. I apologize, but I do have pressing matters shortly after the recital, and so I will need to return on the charter."

Natasha got up from the table and kissed her father.

"It sounds wonderful, Daddy. Don't you agree, Mom?"

Tatyana smiled and took her first bite of food. "Your father's plan sounds wonderful. We haven't all been on a holiday for a very long time, but what do you mean that we can return on our scheduled flight if we want?"

Victor smiled even more broadly.

"Well, there is one more thing that I was thinking I should mention."

Tatyana trembled as she swallowed her food—her stomach churning again with fear.

"And, what is that, Victor?" She smiled.

"A business associate of mine has come up with two very good seats at an Eric Clapton concert in London, a few days after the recital, and he has given them to me."

He produced two tickets and handed one to each of them.

"I thought that maybe Natasha would like to go, because she likes the pop music and all. I wanted her to be a teenager for just a little while, do you mind?"

Natasha squealed with delight.

"Please, Momma!"

She ran to her mother's side and knelt beside her, staring at the ticket in her hand.

"It would be awesome, Mom! I have never been to London before, and to see Eric Clapton live? Well, it will be an experience I would never forget! It would almost be as good as seeing Sir Paul McCartney. Mom, say yes! Please, say yes!"

Tatyana took a drink of orange juice and coughed.

"Yes, of course. Am I invited?" she said to her daughter, and then she joined her in laughter.

"It's done then!" Victor smiled happily. "I will book you both into the Claridges Hotel in London. I am told that it is a proper place to stay, but for how many nights, my dear?"

Natasha was whispering in her mother's ear,

"Two days at least, Momma! Please ask for two days. How many Russian girls ever get the chance to leave Russia, to travel? Please, Momma," she whispered.

Victor was enjoying himself immensely, despite his hangover. Perhaps this was a *turning point* for him too. For, the first time in his life, he was getting pleasure from surprising his daughter, and even more pleasure from pleasantly surprising his wife! Tatyana hadn't a clue that he had already decided to let her go, and to let her live her life however she wanted to. He had already decided to give them both all they needed financially, to ensure their happiness. This was just the start of what he wanted to do for them! And, it felt better than anything he had ever done before.

"Victor, the Claridges Hotel is very expensive," she said. "Is there somewhere that is not so upscale?"

Natasha pinched her mother silently in protest.

"I have looked into it, and I do not believe that I would feel comfortable with you and Natasha being somewhere 'less upscale.' I am told that it is a very good hotel for international travelers. But, if you both would prefer something else, it does not matter to me, as long as it is safe. Cost is not the issue."

Natasha could not believe what she was hearing, nor could Tatyana. "Dear, if you spend this type of money for Natasha and me to go to London, is it rude to ask for a few days to visit the museums and art galleries?"

"Actually, Grigori was tasked with looking for places of interest for you both to visit, and he has many ideas already to discuss with you both. I have already booked five nights for you, but if that is too long, Heathrow Airport is a short drive away and St. Petersburg is only a three-hour flight from London. "

Natasha's jaw dropped in disbelief, and both women looked at him incredulously.

"There will be few other surprises, and hopefully all pleasant," Victor said. Standing up from the table, "If you ladies will forgive me now, there is work that I must attend to."

Natasha hugged her mom, and then went to her dad, and kissed him gleefully. "Thanks, Daddy! I will win the appointment just for you, and you will be so proud of me!"

He hugged her back. "I am already very proud of you, my daughter! And, yes, you will win the appointment! And why?"

"Because I am a strong Russian woman, and I will do it for the Motherland."

"No, my daughter," he replied calmly. "You will do it for yourself! The Motherland is part of you, and you will carry the Motherland with you wherever you go. You will do this for yourself, because you are a strong Russian woman and you have worked very hard, and you deserve it! Nobody will take it away from you, because it is in your heart! Follow your heart, my princess, always follow your heart."

"I will, Daddy. I promise."

He kissed her on her forehead, and headed off to his study. Victor had to admit that Tatyana was certainly very cool about everything. Other than the minor mishap of dropping her fork last night when he mentioned that he was going to accompany her to Paris, she had remained composed, and he admired her nerve.

Both women had tears in their eyes. Tatyana had not seen this side of Victor in many years, and she was worried. She wondered what he was up to, what he knew about her affair with Alexander? After all, Victor was a deviously clever and convincing man! He was also a violent man when it served his best interests to be. There was no doubt in her mind, that he would not hesitate for an instant, to kill them both if he knew about her affair, much less her plans to run away with Alexander! He was too wealthy a man to allow her to divorce him—and, too proud a man to let her leave under any other auspices. Nevertheless, she needed to keep up appearances that she still cared for him, if for no other reason, than to keep his suspicions at bay. In truth, however, she actually still did care for him. Why had it taken him so long to once again become the man she had married so many years ago? Was it all an act?

Natasha finished her juice and asked to be excused.

"Eric Clapton Momma, and London too!" she said with a smile. "Is Daddy okay?"

Tatyana smiled. "I think that your father is just very proud of you right now, and he wants you to know it." She raised her hand above her head in a fist and pulled it to her shoulder in a salutation. "Yes, London and Eric Clapton too!" And both mother and daughter laughed in delight, and then hugged each other.

Natasha had already made the announcement to her best friends via email and was giggling happily watching the responses on the monitor when her mother walked in.

"Are you packed, daughter? Should I help you?"

"Kaninshna, spiceeba." (Of course, thank you). Momma, the girls are so jealous. Even I can't believe it! We must take photos, Momma, otherwise I will never be believed."

Tatyana smiled and hugged her. "We will, daughter."

"And you, Momma? Are you already packed?"

She laughed. "Don't be silly! A woman is never completely packed! I will work on it after I get your things all set, though I am sure that I will forget something in the process anyway—I always do."

"Both of you listen to me," Victor yelled up from downstairs. "Do not pack everything under the sun or you will be in customs forever! Trust me on this. Take only what you know you will need. The rest you can buy in Paris. The last I heard, they still had stores there." He laughed.

Tatyana and Natasha ran out into the hallway and Natasha called down over the balcony, "How many suitcases are we allowed then?"

Victor thought about it and replied, once again having to shout from the floor below. "I would think two medium sized bags would be enough."

"And you, Victor, what will you take to Paris?" Tatyana called down.

"Mostly traveler's checks, my dear!" Victor laughed. "I will pack only one small suitcase to set an example."

Natasha whispered in her mother's ear, and Tatyana laughed. "Two suitcases for each of us then, that is acceptable?" she shouted down.

Victor frowned and then agreed. "Yes, of course."

The two women said, *"Ladna* (OK)," and returned to Natasha's room to start packing. "Momma," Natasha said. "What is with Father? He is acting so strange. He is making this a real family vacation. I don't think he even plans to do any business in Paris."

"I do not know my daughter, but it is almost as if he were a young man again, very unpredictable, like when we first met!"

"Momma!" Natasha exclaimed. "Do you think that Daddy has a new mistress?"

"Natasha!" Tatyana said sharply and then she frowned at her child. "You should not suggest such a thing!"

She then went about selecting another outfit for her daughter.

"Oh, Mother! Please be real!" Natasha answered. "It is not an insult to you that Daddy has a mistress—he has always had a mistress or two. What prominent Russian man hasn't? You treat me like a child, and I wish you wouldn't!"

Tatyana folded her child's clothes quietly, and then said softly, "How long have you known about this?"

Natasha sat down on the bed and motioned for her mother to sit next to her. Tatyana did, nearly in tears.

"Momma," she said to her as she put her arms around her. "I pass no judgment on Daddy. I do not agree with his indiscretions, but he is a strong Russian man, and how can I condemn him for such things when he has provided so well for us? Have there ever been any arguments in this home? I have never heard any arguments. Has he ever hit you or me? Has he ever even raised his voice in anger to either of us? And, hasn't he always made sure that we both have everything we need?"

"No, sweet daughter, he hasn't abused either of us, and yes he has made sure we have what we need." She then fell into tears, and sobs racked her body. "But, what have I done to deserve the disrespect that taking another woman shows me?"

Natasha held her mother, letting her cry for a long time while waiting for her spasms to quell. She said nothing to her during that time, but simply stroked her long hair, nearly succumbing to tears herself. But, she knew this was not her time to cry—it was her time to be strong.

"Mother," she finally said softly. "Daddy does treat you with respect. His mistresses have never held the same privileges that you do, and he has never allowed any of them to be seen in public with him, or so the rumors I have heard seem to indicate. What is wrong if a man needs the occasional company of a younger woman? Most of these young women I think need his help to get a start in life. They come and they go, and he helps them a little. Should these women be giving themselves to a man who will not help them at all? In all of history, every great ruler has had a mistress or two, and every strong woman has had her lovers too. Why should Daddy be any different? He takes care of us first, before he has any indiscretions. And though I don't agree with it, we all know that some men are like this. We can't change human nature, can we?"

Tatyana's weeping started over again.

"Daughter, what do you know about love?"

"Momma," she replied. "What *can* I know about love? I am just eighteen years old. How can I know anything about love when I have never been in love? All I know is that I am attracted to boys and what I read about love in the books and the magazines. Have I ever been in love with a man? The answer is *Nyet!* I have had sex with one young man, last summer, and I was not that impressed with it."

"What?" Tatyana said in shock. "What are you telling me? Who? When?"

"Does it matter, Mother?" Natasha replied bitterly. "It was an experiment. I know about you and Alexander Mayakovsky as well. What with you and daddy off having affairs of your own, I needed to know what I was missing! And, in my opinion, not much!" she said with conviction. "I am sorry I did it, but now I know a little about it, and no harm has come of it."

Tatyana was horrified—both by the revelation that her daughter had sex and that she knew about her own infidelity with Alexander! She didn't know what to say! She watched Natasha fighting back her own tears, and she realized that indeed there was nothing she could say to her for the moment. "I was truly in love once with a man," she said softly and hesitantly. "But then he left me without a word."

"And who was this man, Momma?"

Tatyana hesitated. How could she tell her now, at this time in her life that this man of whom she spoke, was her real father? Natasha had never been told that Victor was not her biological father, and there was no reason for her to know the truth now. Victor had accepted Natasha as his own child right from the start; and for that she was grateful. She sighed and replied, "He was just a man I met when I was a very young woman like you. I thought I was in love with him, and indeed, I was in love with him! But, then he just disappeared without any explanation."

"Why, Momma? Did you have a fight?"

"No, we never had an argument. I was to meet him in the park one day for lunch, at a special bench that we called our own. But he never showed up—and I never saw him again!" Her mind drifted back nearly two decades, and she continued. "It was a beautiful summer day in St. Petersburg. It was warm—the flowers were in bloom, the birds were chirping, and the ducks swam in the pond nearby. I was in very high spirits, and I stopped to smell the blossoms and to throw a few stones into the water on the way. Finally, I made it to our special bench, and I sat there and waited for him."

Natasha listened with curiosity.

"I waited and waited—until well after suppertime. I worried that perhaps I had misunderstood his instructions! I ran home nearly in tears, thinking that I was so stupid to get his instructions wrong, and worrying that he would be very mad at me! But, when I finally got home, he had not called! And so, I tried his hotel and found out that he had suddenly checked out. I enlisted the aid of my brother Mikhail to help me find out what happened to him! But, in the end, he had just vanished! Nothing he told me about himself turned out to be true. We called people he had said knew him. But these people denied that they had ever heard of him before! The company that he said he represented knew nothing about him either! Then the KGB came around asking questions. They were looking for a man that fit his description. They said they had traced him to the hotel where he had stayed—the very same one I had called! They said he was an American spy! They said he was an enemy of the state—that he was responsible for the deaths of two very high-ranking Soviet officials in Moscow! For many months the KGB watched everyone in my family! They even arrested my father and held him for a short while, hoping to get a confession from him. Finally, they—the KGB left us alone, as we had nothing more to tell them other than what he told us about himself, which all turned out to be lies!"

"Oh, Momma," Natasha said, near tears herself. "How could you have fallen in love with a man like this?"

Tatyana just smiled and replied,

"Dear daughter, when love happens, it doesn't always have to make sense! He was not a bad man—of that I am positive! Perhaps he was an American spy after all! Perhaps he was even responsible for the deaths of those two men! But, what I saw in him—led my heart to believe that he was a very special man! A very kind and loving man who loved me as well! The way he looked at me, the way he touched me, and the way he held me? I knew he was the one I wanted. That was all I cared about at the time."

"Was he good looking, Momma?"

Tatyana touched her daughter's arm and grinned girlishly.

"Oh, God yes—he was a man to die for!" She laughed. "Yes, he was very good looking."

"So, did you sleep with him?"

Tatyana wrinkled up her nose and smiled. "All women have secrets to keep! Maybe in London, if I have enough champagne I will give that one up."

"What was his name, Momma?"

She looked at her daughter and thought for a moment. Sensing no harm would come of it, she finally whispered to her in confidence,

"You will keep it a secret, *dah*?"
Her daughter nodded. "Yes, of course, Momma! I will never tell anyone."
"His name was Nicholas."

Chapter 21

As he approached the secret laboratory's landing pod ten kilometers from the outskirts of Yakutsk, Pyotr Oleyenka held the controls of the Russian-made Mi-28 Flying Battle Taxi against the stiff Siberian winds buffeting the helicopter. Two other Mi-28s carrying more battle-hardened men followed his approach in. Altogether, there were thirty well-armed soldiers ready to deploy. His orders were to secure the facility and to let no one in or out until further notice. The Mi-28s were old—and not the best machines in Federation arsenal. But, they were heavily armed—possessing two 30mm 2A42 cannons, fore and aft, machineguns, and a complement of air-to-air missiles.

The only way into Yakutsk was by rail or by air. There were no roads that could be considered to be highways. Despite its remoteness, the city was the wealthiest in the Sakha Republic, and the capitol of Yukutia, a remote Russian holding in Siberia. The region was unimaginably wealthy in diamonds, and was in fact the world's second largest producer of the gems. There were mines that produced over thirty tons of gold per year, and the region was rich in oil and gas wells to boot. Although the population was only two hundred thousand, the inhabitants enjoyed a much higher standard of living than that of their closest neighbors, despite the extremely harsh climate and the remoteness of the region. Most of the structures in Yakutsk were new, modern by Siberian standards. Yakutsk was completely unlike the rest of Siberia, where the infrastructure seemed to be a crumbling relic—it was thriving!

It was a perfect place to build a top-secret facility for the Russians, which was known only as Laboratory 173. The population was well educated and highly skilled, and completely confined! No one could get into or out of Yakutsk except by train or by air! Both were easily monitored. Because of the wealthy mining operations in the area, suppliers abounded, and merchants thrived! They offered all types of amenities that couldn't be found anywhere else in Siberia. Yet, it was a horrific place to be year round! The temperature over the nine-month winters plunged to below -60°F. Because of the harshness of the climate, most industrial operations had to be conducted below ground, and most above ground activities were limited by season, and winter dominated most of the year. The landscape was barren—due to the cold and fierce Siberian winds sweeping away most all plant life that wasn't sheltered. In its wake was permafrost! Pine trees managed to flourish in the mountains, and birch trees in the bogs, but other than wheat, agricultural products didn't stand a chance!

The river Lena was frozen for nearly the entire year, and was mostly impassible until the thaws of summer. The diamond and gold mines kept the Yakut population alive and prosperous—especially considering they had little to spend their money on. Most citizens spoke both the Yakut and Russian language fluently—due mostly for their need of commodities, which usually came from the west—Moscow for one. If not for its wealth in minerals, the city would have died long ago, like most Siberian villages already had.

The Russian mafia held a firm grip in Yakutsk, controlling the prostitution and the gambling houses—the most favored places where the workingmen—miners most of them, spent their money! In more recent years, drugs imported from China and India had embellished the Mafia's businesses immensely. Yakutsk was ripe for exploitation because the population not only had a higher standard of living than even those living in Moscow, but they were also so isolated! Ways to spend their off-hours and their money were limited—and travel impossible. Because supplies were coming in 24/7 for the gold and diamond mines, and the oil and gas rigs, the town was a drug runner's paradise! Despite the criminal element in the city proper, however, security had never been an issue at the lab. It was easy to spot a stranger in this remote city, and with diamonds and gold—the main exports, the railways and airports were well watched and travel documents well scrutinized. It was even harder to get out of Yakutsk than to get into it, which was by no means easy.

Winter had already taken a firm grip on the city, and the fierce Siberian winds were blowing wisps of snow around, making visibility difficult from above. From the perspective of the helicopter pilots, everything appeared to be white or only a shade of gray. At midmorning, the sun was still behind high-level clouds, adding to Pyotr Oleyenka's inability to judge where the ground was. Finally, he caught sight of the facility and moved the stick in that direction. The helicopter responded, and he hovered over a landing pad before easing the machine down. The two other helicopters followed his lead. Even on the ground, he could feel the Siberian wind buffeting his helicopter.

"Tie it down!" he ordered his men.

They jumped to the ground and took up a perimeter, arms at the ready. The chopper crew scrambled out of the helicopter, found the tie-down hooks in the concrete, and lashed the vehicles securely. They then found the service port in the landing pad and opened it. Due to the harsh winters in Siberia, the fuel in any machine would gel within hours due to the cold temperatures, causing a no-start condition. The service ports allowed for refueling, circulation of warm fuel from heated storage tanks below the permafrost, and electrical hook-ups to keep the engines and the fuel tanks continually warm. The crew went about refueling and hooking up the cables.

Oleyenka pulled out his radio transmitter and shouted into it.

"Move!" He then pointed the way for his men. Visibility was difficult, but his men moved in the direction they were instructed to.

Anatoly Timoshenko, having heard the choppers hovering, was expecting them, and he opened the door wide. "Please come in," he said in Russian. "I am the head of security here. Victor Zubkov himself informed me of your arrival. Are you Oleyenka?"

Oleyenka nodded, noticing armed guards pointing their weapons at him and his people. "Tell your men to lower their weapons now, or my men will kill you all."

"I need to see your papers first," Anatoly replied with determination on his face. "My orders are to turn this facility over to Oleyenka when he arrives. I don't know yet if you are him."

Oleyenka nodded and smiled. "Here are my papers," he said. "It is good that you follow protocol."

Anatoly examined the papers and saluted. "The facility is now yours sir," he said. "My men and I are at your disposal."

Anatoly's men lowered their weapons, and Oleyenka motioned his own men in. "Don't take our arrival the wrong way, Anatoly. We are not here to replace you or your security force. We are here to defend this facility! There is a very high probability that this facility will be compromised again, perhaps to steal something, possibly to destroy it."

Anatoly looked nervous. "We are simply security people here, not soldiers. Although we have strong defenses, we could not hold this place against heavily armed militants who might attempt to breach our defenses if a siege were to last long enough."

Pyotr Oleyenka nodded. "That is why we are here. Now, I want you to show us around. I particularly want to know every single entrance, exit, and any other possible point of intrusion."

Chapter 22

Nick stood there by the side of the car—his shoulders slumped as if somehow he were defeated—as if he had been played the fool. He stared blankly at Blakely and Morgan as they backed around Morgan's car in the alley, and sped off. Staring at the keys in his hand he shrugged it off—there was more yet to do! He tossed the keys in the air and caught them deftly—vowing he was going to get to the bottom of all this somehow. "Where to now, Roberta?" he muttered, as he went around to the driver's side of Morgan's car.

Roberta climbed into the passenger seat and shut her door. "There is an SH-60 Seahawk waiting for us at Fort Lawton in Discovery Park."

"Who is 'us,' Roberta?" Nick questioned her before starting the car.

"Kowalski, Timmons, you and me," she replied.

"Kowalski—Timmons? They have been in on this from the beginning?"

Roberta remained silent.

"So, who are you Roberta, and what is really going on here?" Nick asked tensely.

"I am Special Agent Roberta Sanchez." She smiled wanly and offered her hand to him. When Nick didn't respond or accept her gesture to shake hands, she dropped her hand and continued. "I was brought up a Navy brat! I was educated by the government—or at least at their expense. My father was a captain of an aircraft carrier, and I rarely saw him. I drove myself to become a helicopter pilot flying off carriers, hoping that one day I might be on one of his. That never happened! But, when I was a young child, my father used to tease me with codes. Every week, or whenever he could, he would call Mother and me to see how we were doing, and he would ask me to break a code for him. He told me that my work with the code might mean the difference between saving the world or not."

Nick looked at her sideways, but said nothing.

She continued, "Of course, the code was silly stuff, like unscrambling letters in a sentence that said 'Daddy loves you,' but each time I was successful, he would send me a gift. He was just playing this game to get me to think! Since he was at sea so much and couldn't be with me to help me with my studies, it was a special game we played. But, over time this game became something more than just special between us, and as time went on, the codes became more difficult—more challenging. One day, he sent me a real code. He sent me something the military code breakers were having difficulty with—I broke it! He took the results to his commanding officer and was nearly discharged from his post when they found out what he did. The next thing I know, I was in the Naval Academy studying cryptology—and as an after thought, being trained to fly the helicopters of my choice."

Nick started the car and put it in reverse to back out of the alley. "So, nice story Roberta, but what is up? What is this mission, and why am I here?"

"The mission is just what I told you before, Nick. It's about destroying all the *Semya* chips so there can only be one operating supercomputer powered by it. It is so this technology is kept only in the hands of a multinational force that won't allow it to be used for military purposes! Magic Mountain is supposed to be a purely scientific project, and that's the way both governments want to keep it–out of the hands of anybody else."

"Where do Kowalski and Timmons's come into this?" Nick asked bitterly again feeling as if he had been played.

Roberta answered him honestly. "Timmons has some training with the specially modified Seahawks that we need to penetrate the Kamchatka Peninsula. That's where we go in Nick, over the most heavily defended border of Russia."

"And Kowalski?"

Roberta shook her head. "I don't know, Nikki. Like Morgan, I only know my part in this thing."

"But, Roberta, you were on that road waiting for me long before the *Semya* chip went missing," Nick commented as he pulled into traffic and headed toward Fort Lawton a few miles away.

"I was plan-B Nick," she replied irritably. "I was backup to someone else, and who the hell knows how many backup plans there were in place should I fail! I got drawn into this whole thing because I decoded an encrypted message and then stumbled across the money trail that exposed a big problem for the USA—and apparently someone else too! And, it's just a guess, but I think I am here because I am a pretty woman! And, whomever it is that knows you sufficiently well enough to set this thing up, needed a pretty woman by the side of a dark road in the middle of the night. Am I correct?"

Nick turned the wheel at the traffic light and asked his own question.

"How well can you fly?"

Roberta glared at him—wanting to slap him, but said nothing.

Nick chuckled, and then shrugged as he pulled into Discovery Park and towards the Fort. He approached the gated complex, stopping at the guardhouse. "You are expected sir," the guard said to him when he pulled up. "Your chopper is waiting over there on the pad." He pointed and opened the gate for them.

Nick nodded, pulled over to the waiting chopper, and parked. Roberta got out without saying a word to him and started towards it. Nick shut off the engine and got out to join her. The pilot, who already had the rotors turning, was smoking a cigarette nearby. Nick noticed that Kowalski and Timmons were already strapped in. He went to the pilot and grabbed his flight helmet.

"Hey! What are you doing sir?" he yelled surprised.

Nick dropped him with one punch, grabbed his flight helmet, and tossed it to Roberta. "Let's see if you really can fly this thing," he said, pushing her into the cabin.

Kowalski and Timmons were scrambling to find a weapon when Nick slid in next to them. He put the combat knife that he had just pulled from the downed pilot's foreleg to Timmons throat. "Kowalski," he said. "How about we go for a joy ride? Are you with me?"

Kowalski knew better than to protest. Nick was fast enough that Timmons would be dying before he even knew it, and he would be too, shortly thereafter. Kowalski dropped his weapon back into the gunnysack, and held his hands up. "Nikki, let's not get crazy here! We're only following orders."

"Yeah, well I don't take orders anymore," he replied. "I want to see if this woman can fly! Take it up Roberta," he yelled loud enough to be heard above the turbines.

Roberta stared back at him nervously, and seeing the knife at Timmons throat, she nodded. Not far away, MPs were rushing towards them with weapons at the ready. Nick just smiled and motioned up with his thumb. Roberta cranked the throttle and pulled back on the collective, and the Sea Hawk lifted off the pad.

"Satisfied?" she yelled back to him.

Nick waited until they had reached sufficient altitude for what he intended to do next. Once they were out over the water, he lunged forward and reached over her shoulder.

"Not yet!" he replied. He killed the engines with a push of a button! "I want to see just how good you really are!"

The Sea Hawk had only gained an altitude of a thousand feet! It immediately started plummeting towards the Puget Sound. Surprised by Nick's move, Roberta deftly reset all the switches to re-fire the engines. She pushed the collective forward to hover-autorotation. The Sea Hawk's rotors began to rotate faster and faster in a negative pitch as it plummeted towards the water—the result of air spinning the rotors up as they lost altitude. At the same time, she pushed the igniter and engaged the starter. The starter whined, spinning the turbine blades in preparation for light up. But, before she could turn the fuel on, the exhaust temperature had to drop significantly or the relight would fail!

As the water rushed toward them, Roberta pulled up on the collective, reversing the negative rotor pitch and gaining lift as a result. As she did so, she twisted the throttle and turned the fuel on. The turbines lit off, and she rolled the throttle open further, easing power on slowly until she had full throttle back. The SH-60 Sea Hawk stopped plummeting and quickly regained altitude as she called for lift from her collective.

She turned to Nick, who had put away the knife and was smiling. "Satisfied now?" she shouted angrily.

Nick grinned back at her. "Well done, Roberta, textbook in fact!"

"You know, you could have killed us all! There was less than a fifty percent chance the engines would fire," she said hotly.

"Yeah, that surprised me too! I expected us to crash," he replied.

Everyone looked at him with disbelief. He added, "But, in saying that, if you couldn't counter rotate to a soft landing, you have no business taking on the Kamchatka Peninsula either!"

Chapter 23

The carrier was two hundred miles off the northwest coast of America in the North Pacific Ocean and headed towards the Bearing Sea. The USS Enterprise held the distinction of being the US Navy's first nuclear powered aircraft carrier, and it had been called upon just two days before to change course and wait for guests. To intercept the massive platform, the guests had exchanged the Sikorsky SH-60 Sea Hawk at Whidbey Island Naval Base for a fixed wing C-2A Greyhound for transport at maximum speed. It had still taken over two hours to get them all there. Upon landing, they were escorted below decks to a large conference room.

"Welcome lady and gentlemen," the first officer of the USS Enterprise addressed them warmly. "We were expecting you." The captain sat at the head of the table, and he looked up from some papers he was reading when they came in. By his side was a sailor who seemed to be there only to take notes.

"Take a seat please," the first officer suggested. "If there is anything I can get you, let me know."

The captain spoke up as soon as everyone was seated. There were only Nick, Roberta, Kowalski, and Timmons present, all still wearing civilian clothes—Roberta was still wearing Nick's old blue jeans. "We have an unusual set of circumstances before us today," he started.

"Two days ago, I was ordered to set a course for the Bering Sea. In reading my new orders just now, I am not sure exactly what to say to everyone. This is to be strictly a civilian operation, with the exception of the young woman here, Lieutenant Sanchez, who will be representing the US government on behalf of the President of the United States."

This new information caught Nick by surprise.

"Lieutenant Sanchez?" he queried. Roberta said nothing and looked straight ahead.

The captain continued. "This operation is codenamed *Lightening Bolt,* and I have a gentleman standing by via satellite who would like to address you all at this time." The first officer pointed a remote control toward a flat panel screen that lowered from the ceiling. The display lit up, and a familiar face appeared on it. Nick found himself surprised for the second time this day—the face belonged to a man he buried years ago! He was older, his face more lined, his hair thinner, but he looked healthy enough for a dead man.

"Hello Nikki," Smith said. "Can you hear me?"

Nick cleared his throat. "Smith, I buried you next to your parents in Volsky ten years ago!"

"Yes, indeed you did, Nikki. But just as your death was staged when you were a young man, mine was too! It's amazing the drugs they have these days! I went into chemotherapy a month in advance of my staged demise to give the illusion that I was ill. And believe me, Nikki, the treatment for a disease I did not have, nearly did kill me! I was then injected with a drug that put me into a coma. The coffin was designed for life support, and I was recovered a few hours later. After three months of purging the chemo crap out of my system, I was fit as a fiddle. The gravesite was also specially prepared—there was a tunnel beneath it. The FSB agents who were watching that grave for weeks were just as convinced as you were that I was dead, Nikki. That is why I requested to be interred with my family in the first place, so the Russians could be witness to my burial."

"Why the deception, Smith?" Nick replied bitterly—knowing that he was played.

"It was part of the overall plan to establish World Trade. I had the backing of the President of the United States on the condition that I remove myself from public view completely. For the past ten years, I have done just that. I report directly to the Secretary of State or to the President himself. The plan had to go that way, Nikki. With the Cold War over, and Russia no longer a major threat to America, Congress was getting ready to pull the plug on all funding for covert ops. The idea of an agency that was self-funded by selling intelligence to a select few countries sounded very appealing to the President. No longer would the President have to justify expenditures to Congress! But, by the same token, there was no way the CIA could back an organization that they couldn't influence. So, it became my job to keep World Trade as non-political and non-sectarian as possible. By knowing what was going on in both the CIA and at World Trade, I kept the two organizations from bumping heads. And since even you didn't know that I was alive, World Trade has been able to operate autonomously."

Nick's head was spinning. "Go on, Smith. I can hardly wait to hear what else I don't know about."

"A few months ago, a new computer code was intercepted by NSA. It was like nothing they ever saw before. The code was sent out to various software firms to be decoded, but no one could make heads or tails out of it. It was decided that the new code was written to drive a new generation computer chip. The source of the code was traced back to a company owned by your old friend Victor Zubkov. Further investigation led us to the discovery of his plans for the technology."

Nick interrupted. "He's not my friend!"

Smith asked, "Who?"

"Zubkov! He's not my friend!"

Smith barely conceded the fact and pressed on. "It was also discovered that Victor Zubkov has been locking up launch pad facilities throughout Europe for the past few years, and his intention is to manufacture these chips in the weightlessness of outer space—the only way that they can be produced."

The story seemed plausible enough to Nick on the surface, because there are many crystalline substances that do grow better outside the influence of gravity, and so far all the information one party, or another, to this mess, had shared with him was consistent.

"But," Smith went on. "The sheer magnitude of the project, and the secrecy behind it, raised some flags in DC. We put Alexander Mayakovsky, who, as you know, has been very close to Victor and his operations for years, on the mission to find out what was going on. Alexander discovered that Victor was onto something called the *Semya* project. Are you familiar with it, Nick?"

"I know more than I care to," Nick stared back.

"Well, the CIA knew nothing about it when the project name first surfaced," Smith added. "Until that little lady beside you did some brilliant investigative research. What she uncovered nearly got her fired, but the Intel got across my desk before it could be buried. After putting two-and-two together, I took it to the President, and he had a fit!"

"Morgan filled me in," Nick replied. "What does all this have to do with us?" he asked dryly.

"Alexander Mayakovsky dropped off the radar two days ago. We think he is heading to Yakutsk to retrieve the entire *Semya* inventory, and simultaneously, Victor Zubkov is doing the same. It seems we have a race against time! Has Morgan told you of our predicament?"

"Yes. As usual, the military was being a little too clever, and they got caught with their hands in the cookie jar."

"Sadly, yes," Smith replied. "It is absolutely imperative that all those *Semya* boards be accounted for and destroyed, or everything comes unraveled. You must get possession of all the remaining *Semya* boards and every chip must be accounted for. The remaining technology for the manufacture of any new boards must also be found and destroyed."

"Who cares, Smith?" Nick replied angrily. "Since when does the US government interfere with free enterprise? Tatyana and Natasha are at risk, and here I am on a Navy carrier being asked to kick my sense of duty into overdrive instead of moving to protect them. Why should I care about all this?"

"Nikki," Smith replied. "This is a matter of national security, not free enterprise! And don't think that I don't know about your devotion to Tatyana and Natasha either! As I speak, we have people in place to ensure their safety. Twenty-four hours ago, I couldn't make that statement, and that is the reason I couldn't bring you into the loop sooner. I couldn't have you hell-bent on going back to St. Petersburg, or to Paris, to rescue your daughter when I need you in Siberia. Both Tatyana and Natasha will be safe in Paris, believe me—I have it covered."

The revelation that Smith was still alive was overwhelming enough to Nick, but true to form, he had to admit that Smith had all the angles covered, just like always.

"What do want from me, Smith?"

"Are you angry with me, Nikki?"

"Hell yes, you bastard! You had me bury you! I had to watch you die! It was like watching my own father die! Only I wasn't there to be with my own father when he died, or with my mother when she passed away, was I? No, I was on some damned mission for you! You pulled me out of St. Petersburg when I was in love with Tatyana, and when I should have married her! Instead, I am on some covert mission for you, and all for what, Smith? So that the world can be a safer place? The world is not a safer place! There are terrorists willing to do just about anything only to prove a point. You made me into a terrorist! I have killed for you! I have done unimaginable things all in the name of national security! And when I am finally done with the whole damned game—fed up with it all! When all I want to do is to go home again—here you are once more! You want to pull me back in once again! And you question me—whether I am mad or not?"

Nick then fell silent, and the others at the table looked down at their hands folded on the table in front of them, as if embarrassed to be witnessing a family squabble.

"It's okay, Smith," Nick said finally, and he sighed. "This time, do I get to die for real? You see old man—you bastard! Everything I did these past decades—was because I believed in you, and you lied to me!"

"Settle down now Nikki," Smith replied sternly. Everyone in the room knew that every word that Nick Peters had said was true. He had obviously sacrificed everything he held dear in life in the service of his country. "Yes, once again I am asking you to do what I wouldn't ask of anyone else. I want you to go back in! I want you to recover everything: the chips, the boards, and all the data. Everything! Lieutenant Sanchez is here to verify the authenticity of chips before destroying them."

"And what about Boris and his family? I inadvertently brought them into this."

"Your friend Boris and his family are under house arrest for the moment. They are not in harm's way. Because of all the corruption within the Russian Federation, this whole mission must be conducted outside of military operations."

"So, we can expect to be shot at by Russian forces, once we cross into Federation airspace?"

"What's new about that, Nikki?" Smith sighed. "We have a plan to get you and your team in."

"Why me, Smith? And, do you have a plan to get us out alive?" Nick fired back.

Smith grinned. "Why else would you be here, Nick? You are the only one with the required skills. If I thought Kowalski could do it, I would send him in. Nikki, this is a race against time. Victor Zubkov is in transit right now to recover his stock, and Mayakovsky has already disappeared. Bentley is geared up and ready to fire off the next generation of the *Obvyet*, and there is a cloned Magic Mountain offshore somewhere. You know Alexander Mayakovsky, and you know Russia like the back of your hand. Yakutsk is a tough place to get anything out of, but Mayakovsky has a plan of his own—or so it seems, and I want you to stop him."

"And, I am to take civilians into all this?" he asked, referring to Roberta and his small team.

"Roberta is the best attack helicopter pilot that the Navy has to offer, and she knows what we are looking for. Are you telling me you don't want her along?"

Nick looked at her. Roberta had remained utterly silent during this exchange, and she appeared emotionless. "You are nothing but surprises Smith," Nick replied. "As always! What about loss of life?"

"Avoid it," Smith replied. "You will be going in as a civilian unit, and if discovered or captured, you will be treated as a terrorist group."

"Lovely!" Nick replied sourly. "And was Kowalski in on any of this?"

"We figured you might call on him, and so we swore him to secrecy until the pocket drive was recovered," Smith replied calmly.

"And yet you couldn't bring me in on any of this before now?"

"How long have you been in possession of the attaché case, Nick?"

"Since Wednesday last."

"Right, and Alexander Mayakovsky went missing that same day. The President has been negotiating with the Russians since then to come up with a viable solution. I could have let you know sooner, but that would have included the possibility that someone would know your route, which could expose you to other threats. Bentley already had a hit out on you, and then the pocket drive went missing on the very flight you were on."

"Why couldn't you have just confided in me, Smith?" Nick insisted.

"Due to the nature of your relationship with Mayakovsky, and to Tatyana, we were concerned that, if you knew that Alexander had gone rogue, you might go after him before we got what we needed. If you did go after Alexander, it would tip off Bentley that we were on to him as well, and so we left you in the dark until now."

"So what's the plan now?" Nick replied.

Chapter 24

Victor Zubkov had his aid arrange a private jet to fly him into Yakutsk. He would be arriving there later tonight. He kissed Tatyana farewell.

"I will be back in time to meet you, and Natasha, in Paris on Thursday evening, so do not worry. I have some business to attend to right now."

"Victor," Tatyana said in earnest. "You look terrible—you drank way too much last night! You should not be traveling in your condition. Where are you going that is so important?"

Victor paused and looked at her in a way he hadn't for many years. At forty-four years old, she was still a strikingly beautiful woman. "I will be going to where it will be very cold my dear, and I will be thinking about the balmy weather of Paris while I am gone. If you hear from Alexander in my absence, tell him that I am looking for him. He will know how to contact me."

Tatyana's heart skipped a beat with fear.

"I'll let him know if he calls, Victor."

Victor nodded and kissed her on the cheek. He then looked at her up close for a very long moment without saying a word.

"What is it, Victor?" she asked him nervously, not knowing what was on his mind or why he was looking at her that way.

"Nothing my dear," he replied. "It is nothing. I will see you again on Thursday evening." Then he smiled, turned, and walked out the door.

Tatyana, her heart still beating fiercely with fear, closed the door behind him. She stood at the window and watched him take the cobblestone steps down to the waiting Mercedes in the driveway. He got in without looking back, and the Mercedes drove off in silence. Her knees nearly buckled as the car disappeared from sight, and she felt lightheaded, wondering what her husband was up to now. She wondered if she should call the whole thing off! Her escape with her daughter and Alexander was now in question! Should she just lock herself in her room for the rest of her life?

Should she give up on love entirely? But, she knew that she couldn't do either. Gathering herself together, she took a deep breath.

"What happens, happens!" she said to herself. "In one week, I will either have a new life or I will be dead. And it won't matter either way, because my heart is already dead."

Victor directed his driver to take him to an old warehouse before going to the airfield. Upon arriving there, he got out. "I will be back in minute," he said to the driver, and a few minutes later, he returned to the Mercedes carrying a package wrapped in brown paper. The driver, who had taken the opportunity to have a smoke, threw down his cigarette and opened the trunk. Victor tossed the package in and said,

"Now to the airport."

Pyotr Oleyenka had taken over the security monitoring area of the research facility—the command center! There he watched the progress of his men sweeping the facility looking for exits or intrusion points. There on the dozens of video monitors mounted on the wall, over two-dozen video cameras canvassed the facility relentlessly. The images on display were being recorded to videotape. His men had been stationed at all the exits while the maintenance people took portable welders around and started putting spot welds on all the ventilation grates and all nonessential exits. The fewer the exits, the fewer the worries that someone inside might escape or someone outside might enter the facility!

The workers remaining in the facility were getting concerned about what was happening around them, about what was in store for them! They were whispering their speculations, but talking to none of Oleyenka's men. All the outside phone lines, except for the main line that came directly into command center, had been cut and all cell phones had been confiscated. Oleyenka's men had disabled all radios, TVs, and any Internet access.

Pyotr Oleyenka himself had started examining the sign-in logs over the past six months, looking for anything unusual. All the while he played archived videotape from the cameras that monitored the room where the *Semya* boards were kept. The camera was motion activated, and no one was allowed in that area, so there wasn't much tape to watch. Halfway through the tape, the screen went blank for a period of forty minutes.

"What is this?" he demanded.

Anatoly Timoshenko replied.

"Rats," he said. "It's all been noted in my duty log. The camera went down on the date and at time indicated. As soon as we detected a fault, we sent in a repairman. He found that rats had gotten into the walls and chewed through the wires. Those forty minutes constitute the time the repairman needed to fix the camera feed. We brought in exterminators the next day and resolved the rat problem. It is all duly noted here," he said, and he flipped through his duty log to the appropriate page.

"And who was on duty that night?" Oleyenka demanded.

"I was," Anatoly replied.

"And the repairman?" Oleyenka queried.

"He is no longer with us," Anatoly answered.

"He quit?"

"No sir," Anatoly replied. "He is deceased. He got drunk one night about two weeks after that camera problem, and ran his car off the road and into the Lena River. His car broke through the ice and he drowned."

"How convenient," Oleyenka replied sarcastically. "And you made no connection between his death and this video anomaly?"

"At the time, no sir, I didn't. We hadn't a clue that anything was amiss until just now! And, it all seemed very coincidental at the time. There were indeed rats in the facility."

"And who was guarding this repairman while he made the repairs?" Oleyenka asked.

"He was escorted into the *Semya* lab by one of my guards, who stood over him the entire time."

"What's his name?" Oleyenka muttered.

"It's there in the duty log, sir. I believe it was Leonid Tanetov."

"And is *he* still alive?" he asked.

"Of course sir," Anatoly replied. "He has been on our staff for nearly five years now."

"Get him in here!" Oleyenka ordered.

Anatoly picked up the phone and dialed a number. He spoke into the receiver, and a minute later, a young security guard appeared. "Yes sir!" He saluted briskly.

"Captain Oleyenka has some questions for you, Leonid. At ease—have a seat." Anatoly motioned that he should sit across from him at the table.

Leonid took a seat as instructed, and Oleyenka showed Leonid the duty log for the night of May 22 that year. "Do you recall these events?" Oleyenka asked him.

Leonid reviewed the entries. "Yes sir."

"Do you recall anything unusual that night?"

"No sir. Anatoly realized a camera was down, and he went to investigate it himself. He then called for maintenance and for me. I was instructed to keep an eye on the lab and on the technician while the repairman did his work."

"And you watched this repair technician the whole time?"

"Yes sir, except for about two minutes."

Oleyenka perked up. "And what happened in those two minutes?"

"Sasha Uchenko came in to inspect the lab to make sure that everything was secure. He does it every night as part of his duties. I had to use the men's room, and I asked him to keep an eye on things until I got back. I came back after about two minutes while Sasha waited for me. Sasha stayed with me until the repairman was finished with his work.

Then Anatoly called me on the radio to say that the signal was restored. We locked the lab up tight, and all of us left together. The repair technician was never alone in that lab by himself."

"Very well. You are excused," Oleyenka said calmly.

Leonid, obviously relieved, wasted no time in leaving. He had taken an instant dislike to Oleyenka.

Oleyenka and Anatoly were the only ones remaining in the security center. "Anatoly, this is off the record, but we have a big problem here. Though all the rules were followed on the night in question, there are three people who could be co-conspirators here. You are number one on this list, Anatoly. You were the first one in the lab when the camera was down, and you could have stolen the *Semya* boards before you reported any problem to the others."

Anatoly immediately started to object, but Oleyenka held up his hand to stop him. "Do not worry. We have already looked into everything, and we see no changes in your behavior to suggest you might have been involved. You have a wife and two children. You have no mistresses, no patterns of drug or alcohol abuse, and you live within your means. Leonid has told me what I needed to know. I take it that he never mentioned anything about Sasha Uchenko's presence that night?"

"No, but why would he? Uchenko checked the lab every night."

"Yes, this is true," Oleyenka, replied. "However, this night, the cameras were disabled, and the only other people in that room for a full two minutes, probably more, after your guard left—was Uchenko, and the now deceased repair technician. Where is Uchenko now?"

"I haven't seen him since I talked with Victor Zubkov earlier this morning. I locked the facility down immediately after being ordered to do so."

Oleyenka smiled. "It seems certain that our Sasha Uchenko has flown the coop then before you got the place locked down tight! But, nevertheless, we will search for him." Oleyenka got on his radio and called for five men. "I want you to organize a search party," he said to Anatoly. "Teams of one of your men accompanied by one of mine are to spread out to search this entire facility. The two-man teams are to open every door and to enter every room to make sure that Sasha is still not here. I doubt that he is, but Victor Zubkov will be here soon! Both you and I would look very foolish if we didn't have him in our custody—if in fact he were still here!"

"And if he has already left?" Anatoly replied.

Oleyenka sighed. "It is of no real consequence. We will find him sooner or later. After Victor gets here and I explain what I have found, he will probably evacuate the facility. We suspect an assault team will try to recover the remaining *Semya* boards, and your men do not have to be here to protect them—that is why I am here. However, the assault could happen at any time, even before Victor gets here. Unfortunately, my orders are to secure this facility and not allow anyone in or out until he does. We are here to secure the remaining *Semya* boards until then."

"And then what?" Anatoly asked. "What happens to all of us and to our jobs?"

"That I don't know. I will make my recommendations to Victor regarding the security here, and perhaps he will reassign you if this place is closed. I don't even know exactly what is done here except that these boards are kept under lock and key—and it is a Top Secret facility. But, now is not the time to worry about what will become of your job. If an assault team does come for the remaining *Semya* boards, what you need to worry about is staying alive. So let's strategize what we can do to stop them. If you were tasked with assaulting this facility and the front door is locked, how would you do it?"

"The facility is mostly underground, under permafrost, so it is already secure. There are limited entrances, and you have already welded all but a few shut. The facility is impenetrable for the most part. We are totally self-sufficient here. We have our own power generators, food and water for several weeks, and I doubt that a small assault team could get in here much less out alive," Anatoly stated.

"There are electrified fences surrounding the perimeter, and there is a minefield inside that," he continued. "There are motion detectors everywhere. If an assault were to come by air, we have radar to detect them—and shoulder-fired missiles to defend ourselves. If the assault team gets past these defenses, they are still faced with the prospect of having to enter the facility. We have small arms, smoke, and grenades. There can be nothing short of a full-scale military assault that would compromise this facility! But, if that happened, as I said before, my men are not soldiers. These defenses preclude needing soldiers. We could be put under siege, and unless that siege could last until power, food, and water ran out, we would remain safe. I think that your concerns are totally unfounded. Unless of course full-scale siege happens! If it does, the assault needs to be stopped before the outside door is blown."

Oleyenka smiled. "Yes, of course you are right. Nevertheless, while our men search the facility for Uchenko, you and I will search for vulnerabilities. Then we will wait for Victor to arrive. I will have men on the outside as well."

Victor Zubkov had switched planes in Moscow and was taking off from Sheremetyevo 2 International on another charter with enough range to make it to Yakutsk. With hours of flight time ahead of him, he opened the wrapped package he had taken from the warehouse and started reading the documents within. They were all stamped "Top Secret and Confidential". They had the look of age upon them. The pages were yellow and faded—as if they had been stored in a damp basement or cellar for decades, and maybe they had been. His "niece" had warned him about the *Semya* project—it was her note that he had received the night before.

It had been delivered via his mistress of twenty years, Marina Baronova. She had pleaded with him on the phone—telling him that he must look at the package for the sake of his daughter, their child. The note was from his daughter!

Although the writer of the note was in fact his biological daughter, she knew him as her uncle. He had put her through some of the best private schools in St. Petersburg, and later he made a way for her to enter the ranks of the KGB, where she was trained as an agent. It was useful to have a blood relation within the most secretive agency in Russia! She had more than once warned him of imminent danger. She had arranged for the package to be left at the warehouse where it could not be linked to her, or her mother. Victor wondered what his daughter had stumbled onto that was of such concern—of such urgency! He began reading everything carefully.

Victor arrived in Yakutsk on time and without event. Given his prominence and his credentials, his bags were never checked, and he was whisked quickly through security. Stepping out into the cold night, he lit a cigar, leaving the driver of the Mercedes to wait for him while he enjoyed it. Yakutsk was in the midst of a small blizzard this evening, the first real storm of winter. Drifts of snow were piling up on the streets quickly, and most parked vehicles were already buried deeply. The windshield wipers of what few vehicles left moving on the streets struggled to keep the snow at bay. Most of the travelers who had disembarked from other flights had already scurried up the street and into the subway to find their way home. A few, mostly business types, found taxis or a waiting bus to take them to their hotels.

The cold air felt good on his face, and Victor savored his cigar, the first one of the day. Finding an empty trash barrel nearby, he took his bundle of papers and put his lighter to them. When the bundle was fully ablaze, he dropped the whole packet into the empty trash bin and enjoyed his smoke while watching the papers completely burn. No one dared ask him what he was doing. When the documents were fully consumed, and the flames had died out, he punched in the number for the facility on his cell phone, and Anatoly Timoshenko picked up.

"This is Victor, Anatoly," he said. "I need to speak with Pyotr Oleyenka."

Anatoly handed the phone to Pyotr and said, "It's Victor Zubkov."

Pyotr took it.

"Yes, sir."

"Are we secure?"

"Yes, sir."

"Good. Then alert the guards at the gate that I will be there in twenty minutes. They are to let me in promptly. Any problems?"

"No sir, but it appears that Sasha Uchenko is your man,"

Oleyenka replied.

"Do you have him in custody?" Victor asked.

"No, sir. He slipped away before the lockdown."

"And what about the *Semya* boards, Oleyenka?"

"They are all accounted for and ready for transport."

"Good. Have something decent prepared for dinner when I get there—I haven't eaten all day! You and Anatoly can join me. We need to sort out a few things."

"Yes, sir. Consider it done." Oleyenka hung up.

Victor took a last puff of his cigar, threw it into the smoldering trash barrel, and got into the Mercedes.

Chapter 25

"Explain the plan, Smith," Nick spoke up.

"You're going to carrier hop. We have a carrier waiting for you in the Bering Sea with three specially equipped SH-60 Seahawks standing by to get you to Yakutsk, where Laboratory 173 is located. Once on the carrier, you will have the remaining night hours to formulate your own plans and to get some rest. Before first light, you embark on a seven-hundred-mile flight through the Cherskiy Mountain range and across the Siberian plains. Yakutsk is under blizzard conditions right now, and the forecast says that those conditions will persist through midday tomorrow to cover your arrival. You will gain three hours crossing time zones. The Seahawks come with special armament, radar shielding, and radio jamming capabilities, and they have no markings on them at all. The Captain has a plane standing by to get you to the next carrier. Once you leave the carrier, you are on your own."

"What about refueling?" Nick asked.

"Once you leave the carrier Nick, you are your own," Smith replied coldly.

"Smith," Nick protested. "Why should any of us do this? How can you ask me to do this, much less the rest of them? Are we going to get any help from the Russians?"

"The Russians will try to shoot you down, Nikki. The Russian President's hands are tied because he is not sure whom he can trust within his own ranks. Considering that half of his Generals have been selling off military hardware for years on the black market, he obviously can't use normal channels. This has to be a covert mission, and it has to be completed quickly! There are already worries that a particular general, General Krushensky, is involved in this somehow."

"So, we are up against Zubkov and his men, and possibly a Russian General, and there is no telling what Mayakovsky is up to? Do I have this pretty much summed up?"

"Yes, that pretty much sums it up, Nikki," Smith replied dryly.

"Getting back to my original question, Smith: why should any of us do this?"

"I can answer that Nikki," Roberta spoke up for the first time, and Nick stopped talking to listen to what she had to say.

"You see everyone here?" she asked him. "Kowalski, the Captain, the seaman over there taking notes? Everyone in this room has taken an oath to defend our country, including you, Nick. The *Semya* technology is dangerous technology, and if it gets into the wrong hands, into terrorists hands for example, there is no telling how that technology will be used—not to mention that we are in violation of some agreement or other, with Russia."

"I don't think we have a choice, Nick," Kowalski spoke up. "I'm in."

"Me too," added Timmons.

"Are you prepared to die for this, Roberta?" Nick asked her.

Roberta stood up and turned in his direction.

"If need be, yes I am! I told you, Nikki. I grew up a military brat! I was selected to handle a part of this mission, and I want to do it. The outcome is damned important! And what about you, Nikki? You gave up everything for your country, and now you are saying that suddenly you want to turn your back on it? You could no more turn your back on this mission than you could have stranded me back on that road the other night. You are just pissed off that your mentor here, Mr. Smith, did not really die—but has been playing you!"

Nick knew that she was right, and he nodded. "Okay Smith, we go in, but by the way—may your balls fall off for playing me like any other mark!"

Chapter 26

The wind was howling and the snowfall had turned into a blizzard. By the time the Mercedes rolled up to the front gates of Laboratory 173, the entire area was under whiteout conditions. Victor Zubkov muttered to his driver from the backseat, "What are the odds of getting out of here tonight?"

"Zero to none, sir. Snowdrifts have already closed the road behind us. The choppers might get you out, but if this wind picks up much more, they'll be grounded too."

The guards at the gatehouse had been expecting them for over an hour, but the twenty-minute drive from the airport to the facility had turned into an hour and a half due to the inclement conditions. The guard waved them through without asking for identification, and then pushed the gates shut after they passed by and locked them.

Victor muttered, "What kind of security is this?"

His driver replied, "The guard is my nephew, sir. We have a special code we use if everything is okay. I flip my lights at him in the right sequence, and he knows that everything is as it should be. It's not exactly to military standards, but it works in reverse too. If he had stopped me, it would mean that the base has been compromised. It's something we worked out since the lockdown."

"What's the sequence?" Victor asked.

"I can't tell you that sir, or the code would not be secure."

Victor laughed. "I like secret codes. It is very reminiscent of the Cold War era, an era I knew well."

The Mercedes pulled up to a bunker and stopped.

"I'll get your things, Mr. Zubkov."

"No, don't bother. I can get my own things! Just pop the boot." The fierce winds ripped the door from his hand as Victor got out of the vehicle. He retrieved the door and slammed it shut behind him, and then went to the trunk where he recovered his bag. He made his way to the bunker door, struggling against the driven snow. His driver took the car away, presumably to a garage off somewhere in the darkness. Anatoly and Pyotr met him at the entrance to the bunker and led him down the steps. Pyotr's men stood at attention with their automatic weapons at the ready, and they didn't relax until the bunker door was bolted tight again.

"Miserable weather, sir. Can I take your bag?" Anatoly asked.

"No, you can't Anatoly! I have it. What about the Semya boards?"

"They are ready for transport, sir."

"Good. Then let me see them. Once I have verified them, we eat, and then I will get out of here," Zubkov replied.

"That's impossible sir," Pyotr spoke up. "The roads are already closed, and the airport is shut down due to the blizzard. The choppers are all grounded until the wind subsides, so we need to ride this storm out."

Victor stopped walking. "How long?"

"Early morning at best," Pyotr answered.

"And, are we secure? The Americans are right behind me, and they intend to take the *Semya* boards," he replied angrily.

Anatoly looked uncomfortable, not wanting to comment, but Pyotr replied with confidence, "If the Americans are on their way, they too have been delayed by the storm. What can they do out there? Their choppers are no different than ours. They can't mount an assault in this kind of weather, and with the roads closed, how else can they come? And even if they did come, we are ready for them. The facility is secure."

Sasha Uchenko had been hiding two hundred feet directly below the research facility in a diamond mine since early that morning. He was scared as hell and wanted no part in this anymore. Alexander Mayakovsky had promised him a new start for himself and his family, if he bought into his plan—and he had! But now he was regretting everything! If he screwed-up now, his family would be dead! He was scared more for them than for himself, and he was plenty scared for himself.

Construction on the secret tunnel began a year ago. The diamond and gold mines of Yakutsk were the largest in the world, and they were mostly unmapped—especially the older ones. Given their depth, and thus the impossibility that the mine would interfere with construction on the surface, the Russian government paid little attention to where they placed the research facility when they originally chose the location for construction of Laboratory 173, which happened to be directly over one of the older mines. The new tunnel that led up to the research facility was an engineering marvel. It had been constructed in record time and in complete secrecy. The engineer who agreed to undertake the task was a genius in his own rights, perhaps even a magician. He had managed to divert men and equipment from the mines to undertake the project, and he had covered it all up with bribes. His specially selected crew got paid twice the normal rate plus their regular pay, which was miniscule by most standards. They tunneled for 24/7 in three shifts until the project was complete.

Miraculously, all the proper work orders managed to make it through the system without any questions, and none of the men dared speak about their activities, because they were told that the project was top secret and sanctioned by the Russian FSB. Grateful for the overtime pay, not one of them ever even whispered of the tunnel, not even to their wives. What did it matter to them anyway? A tunnel was a tunnel.

They had broken through into the research facility nearly a month ago, and the new entrance was hidden behind one of the massive underground fuel storage tanks for the helipads. No one ever searched the fuel storage room, but even if they had, the grate in the floor looked as if it belonged there. Now that the base was locked down, this had been Uchenko's only way out of the facility. There he waited anxiously for Alexander Mayakovsky to show up, and he prayed that his family would be safe and that Mayakovsky would take him with him. Otherwise Zubkov would have him shot for his betrayal!

The S-3B Viking that carried Nick and his team was literally blown off the decks of the carrier by a steam-driven catapult. The twin General Electric TF-34-GE-400B turbofan engines throttled up to full power, and clawed the air ahead of them gaining altitude. Lift was achieved immediately, and the plane climbed to altitude quickly. They would be on the carrier USS Theodore Roosevelt in the Bering Sea in less than four hours. Nick, Roberta, Kowalski, and Timmons were unceremoniously stuffed into the fuselage, which was normally reserved for armament. They all had been outfitted with cold weather assault gear. Their uniforms carried no US markings or labels whatsoever.

Nick addressed the three of them.

"Obviously, some thought has been put into this, and yet Smith tells us to come up with our own plan. My guess is he is thinking that the less anyone knows the better."

"Yes," Kowalski replied. "Smith is giving us the tools and the target, but he doesn't want to know the plan or strategy—because if we fail, he wants to be able to deny everything! We have three birds to go in with. I fly one, Timmons the other, and you and Roberta would be in the third."

Timmons spoke up.

"Roberta was selected because she knows how to identify these *Semya* boards, and she has more flight hours logged than any of us. I was selected because these aren't normal Seahawks we'll be flying. They are specially armed, and they are equipped with some new technology that will be useful in getting us into and out of Siberia, hopefully undetected. I have been specially trained in electronics, surveillance, and radar. The birds have been stripped of anything tying them back to the US military, and they'll all be rigged for remote detonation if the mission gets out of hand—that's how serious the President is about keeping this out of the press. Only you and Kowalski speak Russian, so it won't bode well for the rest of us if we fall into Russian hands. Does that give you enough background?"

Nick nodded. "Has any of this mission been planned out?"

"Yes and no, sir," Timmons answered. "Smith insisted that, once we lift off the USS Roosevelt, no one must have a clue how we intend to get to Laboratory 173. They won't even be able to track us by radar, which removes any chance that we fall into a trap due to a tip-off. Obviously, everything else up to that point was planned out, but there are a lot of square miles between the carrier and Laboratory 173."

"In other words, they have internal leaks too," Nick stated flatly. "So Kowalski, do you have anything remotely resembling a plan?"

Kowalski shook his head.

"Timmons has some ideas. He flew covertly through many of these mountain passes while testing the radar absorbing capabilities of the Sikorsky's. He knows where most of their radar is located, and where most of their bases on the east side of the mountains are located. You know Siberia on the west side Nikki, and you are familiar with the Yakutsk region. If we don't delay, we'll end up on site by midday tomorrow, which is not exactly ideal for a surprise assault, but I understand that we'll have the cover of a blizzard on our side."

"Yeah, but I'm not as worried about getting there as I am about what we are going to do once we are on the ground. How do we breach lab security without turning our assault into a bloodbath? The Russians aren't going to take a strike on a government facility by some foreign nationals lightly."

Timmons spoke up. "There's a back door."

Nick's eyebrows rose skeptically.

"It's how Alexander Mayakovsky was planning to get in, and out, with the *Semya* technology. Laboratory 173 is situated directly over an old diamond mine, accessible a few kilometers east of the base. To our knowledge, that entrance and the tunnel are still undiscovered. I can go in with a team to open the back door while you guys keep the front door shut. The mineshaft comes up directly under the refueling station. A small explosive charge would be enough to send up the entire facility, and there would probably be enough time for everyone to get out without injury. The Russians can blame the whole thing on a re-fueling mishap, and everyone will be satisfied."

Nick nodded and Roberta objected.

"We can't just blow the place up! We need to verify what we have first. That means we search the place until we find what we came for."

"She's right," Nick said. "But the tunnel can help us in. How did you know about it?"

"I was briefed on it, but if we use this entrance, we'll be out of radio contact while in the tunnels. They asked me if I could rig something up so the radios will continue to work, but the answer is no."

By the time they hit the deck on the USS Theodore Roosevelt, they had a fairly comprehensive plan laid out. They spent the evening getting their gear together, and later they went down to the officer's mess for a hot meal. Nick was satisfied with what Kowalski and Timmons had come up with, and everyone was briefed on their assignments. With an 0500 departure time, everyone headed off to their bunks, intent on finally getting some sleep.

Roberta said to Nick,

"It brings back memories, being on a carrier again. Are you mad at me for deceiving you, Nikki?"

"Yes and no, Roberta. Like you said, you only did what you had to do. I feel a little foolish—being played by both you and Smith! But, it just goes to show how gullible men are when around a pretty woman! What pisses me off the most is that Smith played me like a fool."

"Nick," she replied hesitantly. "The only deception was in not letting you know who I really am, and the circumstances of our meeting. There was nothing false about the sparks between us, nothing whatsoever! I was only playing the part of a naïve waif—because I was told too! But, I have enjoyed being with you these past few days, and when this is all over, if you still want to see me, I'd like that." She gave him a kiss on the cheek and headed off to the women's barracks. "See you at 0500."

Watching her walk away, he wondered,

"Do I believe her?"

It was a question that he had no answer to, but the whole reason they were together now was based on a deception, so how could he believe her? Ever since he found out just how involved she was in this whole mess, he had treated her strictly professionally, and with no romantic overtures at all. Perhaps that was unwise on his part, because after-all, he was still strongly drawn to her.

He made a decision as he watched her walk away, if it were true that there was something between them, if she really did have feelings for him, then he was sure as hell not going to let her get away like he allowed Tatyana to get away! For the time being, however, there was no time for romance anyway! Not if they were to survive this mission—there were too many variables!

He put such thoughts aside and returned to his own cabin for a much needed few hours of sleep. As he slipped under the covers of his bunk and fell into a fitful sleep, he wondered if he could in fact win over Roberta's affections? While he slept, the dream came back to him that had haunted many of his nights—that he was back in a gulag in Siberia!

He relived his capture by the KGB yet once more—the repeated torture, and then the remorse, which seemed far worse than any physical abuse! He had not been able to go back for her—for Tatyana, the woman he loved! Had he had not left her that day he would have died! And moreover, he would have brought the KGB to her door. Nevertheless, he left her behind! Would he ever get over it?

Once again, 04:00 hours came around several hours too soon. Nick got up, feeling pretty much like he hadn't slept at all! He showered, then pulled on his flight uniform and grabbed his flight helmet. He headed for the galley for some much needed coffee, and a bite to eat.

Everyone was already there—in the galley having breakfast. Nick put his flight helmet down at their table, then filled a plate with scrambled eggs and bacon from the buffet, and joined his crew. Kowalski, Timmons, and Roberta were the designated pilots, and they were examining flight maps while they chewed. Roberta looked up at him and smiled. But, when Nick barely acknowledged her, she quickly turned her attention back to the map. Timmons had already routed a flight plan through the Koryak Mountain Range on the Kamchatka Peninsula. Everyone was scrutinizing other maps of the mainland looking for the best route through the Kolyma mountain range on the Siberian side.

Nick asked them,

"Can we make it to Magadan on the mainland coastline without running out of fuel?"

Timmons made some quick calculations.

"We should be able to if we aren't bucking too much wind."

"Ulyana, my operations manager at World Trade, figured as much too. I called her late last night and arranged for fuel drops—the first will be at Magadan. She'll also be arranging for some ground support from the locals. I want Kowalski to get in touch with her to coordinate the ground activities once we are in the air, and once we are on a secure frequency."

"How did you know where to tell her to station refueling points, Nick?" Kowalski asked.

"I didn't. Ulyana picked up my location off the GPS on my cell phone and plotted a route based on geography and the mechanical limitations of the Sikorsky SH-60 Seahawks. I don't think there were very many options. We've been heading for the Bering Strait since we landed on this carrier. To have enough fuel to make it to the mainland, even at the closest point to Russia a carrier like this could get us to, would require that we cross the Kamchatka Peninsula on the north side, which is one of the most heavily armed and highly defended spits of land in the world. It is Russia's first line of defense, and it is home to their Naval Fleet, and to their top secret Rybacky submarine base. I am sure she made a few assumptions, but Magadan was a logical first choice. I was hoping you would agree with her—she's a pretty clever woman. Anyway, she's making arrangements now."

"Well sir, I think we're ready then," Timmons announced. "If we want to make a break for it before daylight, we'd better go. I was told you could fly one of these birds. Is that right?"

Nick grinned. "Not as well as Roberta, I'm afraid, but I'm good enough to keep it in air if I have to."

Roberta's spirits brightened a bit when she heard this. "Well, at least the bastard respects my flying abilities," she thought to herself.

"Good. We'd like her on point. She's got more hours in one of these things than the rest of us, but we have no one to be her eyes and ears, much less take over if there is a need," Timmons said. "Besides, we thought you two might want to have a little time together." He chuckled, and Kowalski joined in—diverting his eyes to his coffee mug when he noticed the expression on Nick's face. Roberta blushed, and concentrated even more on the maps.

The three Seahawks were already on the deck with rotors turning when Nick's team got topside. There were heavy swells and a brisk twenty-knot wind coming at them from the west. They could see nothing in the distance—the night was pitch black over a cold black sea. The flight deck was momentarily awash with floodlights, as the flight crew made their final inspections. As soon as Nick and the others got themselves strapped in, they were cleared for takeoff.

"It doesn't feel right!" Roberta shouted over the high-pitched whine of twin General Electric T700-GE-401C turboshaft engines.

"What doesn't seem right?" Nick shouted back.

"No emblems. There isn't a single US Navy emblem anywhere onboard."

"What about armament?" Nick asked.

"Oh, we're armed to the teeth alright, but it's all new stuff—not standard Navy! So Timmons better be a good teacher!"

Timmons came in over the radio. "Okay, I'll brief you on all the special stuff when we're airborne. All the flight controls are Sikorsky issue, but this isn't a normal SH-60 Seahawk. You have the lead, Roberta."

Roberta throttled up and pulled up on the collective, and the Seahawk responded quickly, rising vertically. She gained altitude and rolled wide off the starboard side of the USS Theodore Roosevelt, sweeping out to sea in an arc that took her back across the stern of the ship and toward the Kamchatka Peninsula, which lay somewhere far off in the darkness.

"We want to stay low Roberta," Timmons cautioned her through her earphones. The chopper is coated with a special radar absorbing material, but we aren't completely invisible."

Roberta pushed the collective forward, and the chopper dove to within one hundred feet of the waves. "How's that?" she radioed back. "I can't see a damned thing. I am flying by instruments!"

"You're doing just fine, Roberta. We won't be near land for another forty minutes, and by then, we'll have some daylight. Let me brief you on some special features of these birds. All armament has been tucked away in the undercarriage to give the appearance of a civilian chopper, but all use the normal military protocol. We have eight AGM-114 Hellfire missiles, one GAU-17A hydraulic turret mounted Gatling gun, and an array of countermeasures. Our defensive weapons include a FLIR turret with laser designator and the Aircraft Survival Equipment (ASE) package, including the ALQ-144 Infrared Jammer, AVR-2 Laser Detectors, APR-39(V)2 Radar Detectors, AAR-47 Missile Launch Detectors, and ALE-47 chaff/flare dispensers. To arm the systems, you need to punch in a code on the numerical key pad."

Timmons then gave each pilot a series of numbers to enter.

Roberta and Kowalski entered their respective sequence, and immediately the electronic flight information system updated an LCD panel with targeting information.

If you touch the 'arm-all' button, all your offensive weapons will drop out from the undercarriage and all defensive measures and countermeasures, will be activated. For defense only, touch the appropriate indicator to activate it, it will leave the weapons retracted for less air drag until needed."

"Roger that," Roberta replied. "Turning on all defensive measures now," she called out.

Timmons replied, "Good. Now there are some very special features about these birds. First, I can fly us all on autopilot. If anyone gets into trouble or becomes disoriented, I can override your controls. Since I have flown over this peninsula before, I will take over if visibility becomes a problem. When I do, your autopilot will engage. To disengage it, just bump your collective. Second, all our communications are scrambled by default, and are broadcast on microwave frequencies well above what a ham operator can monitor. But, in combat mode, we have the option to switch to infrared, which cannot be heard or intercepted by anyone else. The downside is that it only works if the choppers are in plain sight of one another. We use that option if we think we are being monitored, or like right now, when we are approaching a highly sensitive military installation like the Rybacky submarine base. Let's go to infrared by touching the icon on the touch panel that looks like a red shield."

Timmons waited a few seconds for everyone to switch over, and then he called out,

"Do we have each other?"

"Seahawk One here," Roberta replied.

"Seahawk Two here," Kowalski radioed back.

"Good. We have one more special feature to talk about. On your weapons screen you'll see a purple icon that looks like a set of headphones. Do you see it?"

"Got it," Roberta replied.

"Me too," Kowalski piped in.

"It's called *Silent mode*," Timmons instructed. "Use it sparingly, because you will lose power when it activates, and it consumes fuel big time! You also have a time limitation on this feature because it will overheat your engines after only a few minutes of operation. It works by sending out low frequency magnetic pulses to cancel out the sound of the rotors and turbines. It is not a sound system device with speakers, but a generator that sends out magnetic EMF pulses tuned to match the rotor and the turbines in a reverse pulse that washes out nearly all sound at the ground level. We probably won't need it, but in passing over populated areas at night, it turns these Seahawks into phantoms. Any questions?"

"Got it," Roberta radioed back.

"Roger that," Kowalski added.

"Good, because we are coming up on the Kamchatka Peninsula right now!"

The first rays of daylight appeared from behind them, and shadows formed in front of them as they skimmed over the ten foot waves of the Bering Sea. Roberta could make out a dark shadow in the distance, the mountain ranges of the Kamchatka Peninsula.

"Nikki," she said. "I can see land in the distance."

Nick, struggling for a way to break the ice between them, said, "Roberta, go to intercom.

She did as he instructed. She was still receiving communications, but now her conversations would be between her and Nick only. She wondered what was on his mind.

"Now is probably not the time to bring this up, with the mission now at hand, but a lot of things have been going through my mind regarding us."

"Such as?" she waited for his answer, wondering what he would say next.

"Such as how do I know if you are playing me just like Smith was?"

She looked at him incredulously and stammered, "Short of outright dying for you Nick, what more can I do than be here by your side carrying out this mission? Why would I want to 'play' you?"

Before Nick could say anything, Timmons was back on the radio.

"I am putting everyone on autopilot," he said. Immediately, Roberta's stick pulled out of her hand and the Seahawks all rolled to the starboard. "We are going in under the radar. I am going to hug the coastline and put us all into the chute, a narrow pass between two mountain ranges that I know well. With any luck, we'll be across this peninsula and on our way across the Sea of Okhotsk to Magadan within the hour and no one will be the wiser."

Roberta looked over at Nick and glared at him. "Nikki, is this how you percieve everything? Always in fear that someone is trying to play you?"

Nick replied seriously, "No, but it has been part of my life for too long a time."

"What do I stand to gain by playing you?" she said heatedly.

Nick couldn't reply, for he knew that to do so he would lose her for sure! But, the fact that he ran a multi-billion dollar intel organization would certainly be a reason to play him.

His silence perturbed her, but before it got the better of her, she switched subjects. "Are you going to tell me about her, your Tatyana?"

"There's no need to, Roberta. We knew each other a long time ago."

"So you care nothing for her?" she replied calmly, though his reticence was unsettling at the same time. Worse was the possibility that she had feelings for a man whose heart might be somewhere else.

Nick looked into her eyes and answered, "It was so long ago Roberta that I doubt we would even recognize one another."

"Why are you here Nikki, because of an old debt to a friend that went rogue? Or, is it instead because you went rogue yourself? Why is it, this Mr. Smith, your buddy, your mentor, was so afraid to tell you anything about the *Semya* that he had to orchestrate an assault team and insert me into it in advance? By your own admission, you didn't want any part of this. Can I rely on you to back me up?"

Nick thought about her question long and hard before replying. "Roberta," he said over the chopper intercom. "Smith knows me too well. He knew that I would take this assignment because of Tatyana, not because Alexander needed my help. He knew that if Alexander was betraying her, that I would go after him and kill him regardless of the consequences! And knowing that, I am guessing he held back the information, preferring to orchestrate this black-op instead."

"You haven't answered the question, Nikki. Can I rely on you?"

"No, the first question was, 'What are my feelings for Tatyana?' I wouldn't be here now if you couldn't rely on me, and so that is a non-question meant to stand in the place of that first question. This whole damned operation was centered around me pulling it off, not you! I am Smith's plan-B, plain and simple! He didn't expect to lose Alexander Mayakovsky, who was his plan-A, and Smith being Smith, he had a fallback position already in place."

Roberta looked at him intensely. "And what does that mean?"

"When an operative goes into the field with instructions to do this or that, there are contingencies. Plan-A is what is supposed to happen, and plan-B is what you resort to if plan-A fails. Plan-C takes effect when all else fails. All good operatives plan ahead, just like Smith did. As Smith's plan-B, I am expected to clean up his mess."

"And knowing that, Nikki, and despite the fact you were played, you will clean it up anyway?"

Nick nodded, though he replied bitterly.

"I know Smith too! And he wouldn't put me here if it wasn't important! But yes—he played me! And for that there will be consequences! If nothing else, he has broken our friendship. He was my mentor when I was a young man, and then he became like a father to me, or perhaps he became my best friend, I don't know. He does things, plans things, with incredible accuracy! But it doesn't excuse his manipulating me like he has. So when plan-A fails, which is rare, his recovery plan is usually very extreme. But no matter what he is involved with, it is always important! And, so for now I will go along with this foray into Russia for lack of any reason not to, and because of your convincing speech about patriotism back there on the carrier, which did indeed remind me I have national loyalties that mean a lot to me! What worries me the most is what Smith's plan-C might be."

"Explain, Nikki!" Roberta demanded nervously.

"Smith is a chess player, Roberta! He plans his moves many steps in advance. Plan-A is usually convoluted enough, and as I said, plan-B is usually very extreme because, as one peels the layers of the onion away, the onion becomes more painful to peel! That is Smith's view of the situation, every fall back position becomes exponentially more extreme than its predecessor. If we get to plan-C or plan-D, all of us will become expendable, including me! In fact, we may already be one of these subsequent plans. Smith may say we are plan-B when actually we are plan-D, and if so, once he has what he wants, he will cover his tracks."

"And you considered this man to be your mentor and friend, Nick?" she said in disgust. "And at the same time you can't comprehend that a woman might have real true feelings for you, is that correct? Oh that's ironic, isn't it? You can trust a complete madman—but not your own heart!"

Nick shook his head, not knowing how to proceed. But then he allowed his anger to momentarily get the better of him, and he replied hotly! "He is first and foremost a patriot, Roberta! And, I always remember that before passing judgment on a man like Smith! It is men like him who determine the course of mankind. They are the men who start wars, and they are the men who finish wars. They are the men who determine the national policies that make us a civilization. Smith, is a Cold War advocate! Which means he believes the best defense is a strong offense! It's a carry-a-big-stick type of thing, in the hopes that no one challenges you. But if they do—you clobber them with it! His legacy has always been covert ops and misinformation! If he can make the world believe one thing while he is doing something else, it gives him the power to effect the changes he deems necessary—irrespective of political will. I respected him because he always acted with integrity, and with brilliance! But now, I am unsure. Perhaps he has gone completely mad!"

"And, my hesitation—about trusting you has nothing to do with not wanting to trust you or a woman, Roberta! It's just that my age and my wealth work against me. I want true love! Not love that can be purchased! And it seems highly unlikely that a young woman possessing your beauty would be interested in an ex-spy twenty years your senior unless it was just the money she was after!"

If she could have slapped him right then and there, she would have! But instead, she had to settle for glaring back at him. Then she remembered what Maria had said back at his house: "You could do a lot worse than Mr. Smith. Look around you, girl. You ask me questions about him because you are worried that he might want something from you, but look around. What woman wouldn't want to live like this?"

Roberta's glare softened. "I don't need your money Nikki, and you are not that old! I need a man that I can believe in! And it doesn't hurt that he can dance too!" She smiled.

If he could have leaned over and kissed her right then, he would have!

"I need to brush up on my dance steps then," and he gave her his boyishly charming grin once again.

The ice now broken between them, Roberta said over the COM,

"Do you think, Nikki, that Smith might be the one behind the cloned Magic Mountain?"

Nick looked at her with a serious expression and replied, "If he is, then this most definitely isn't plan-B."

"So where do I fit in, Nikki? Why did Mr. Smith select me to be in on this mission?"

"Because he was aware of your abilities or you wouldn't be here, plain and simple. It didn't hurt that you are also a stunningly attractive woman Roberta, which means you represented an angle Smith could use to his best advantage."

Roberta smiled hearing this, and Nick continued. "That is why Smith only answers to the President of the United States, and no one else! In a way, he is a genius. He has survived four administrations, and one President even asked him to die—so he did! What does that tell you about him?"

The stick moved to extreme port, and the helicopter pitched off to the left. They headed into the chute that Timmons had said he knew well. It was now very nearly daylight, and the Kamchatka Peninsula loomed in front of them. Volcanic mountains that rose thousands of feet into the air where looming just ahead, and yet Nick and his team were still flying at sea level.

"Okay, folks—time to resume manual control. Everyone ready?" Timmons voice came over the radio.

Roberta grabbed her stick, switched off the intercom, and replied, "Ready."

"See that gap between the ridges? That's where we are going in. You have the lead, Roberta," Timmons said over the com.

Roberta pulled up to avoid hitting a line of rock that suddenly appeared before them and shot into the chute at three hundred miles per hour.

Suddenly, a plume of smoke rose from the peninsula and alarms sounded in the cockpit.

"Timmons," Kowalski shouted over the com. "We have land-to-air missiles coming at us! What just happened to our invisibility?"

"I got it Boss," Timmons replied, and he pushed several selections on his control screen. Immediately flares were dropped, and the missiles followed them and exploded harmlessly hundreds of meters from their position.

"We need to go to evasive maneuvers," Timmons radioed back. "That was a shoulder-fired missile, not a ground launched one. Someone was waiting for us! We need to drop to a lower altitude and kiss the streambeds to thread our way through these mountains. The lower we are, the less chance ground forces have at getting a heat signature on us. We are invisible to radar, so Roberta, get low.

"Timmons," Kowalski barked out. "Are we compromised?"

"I am afraid we are, sir! We never would have been fired upon if it wasn't authorized by someone, and my guess is, it wasn't Russian Command Central that authorized it."

"Damn it, Timmons! You sound pretty cavalier about the fact that these assholes were waiting for us! Why did you say it wasn't Russian command, and how did they know we were coming?"

"If Russian Command picked us up on radar, there would be MIGs harrying us. It could be just bad luck, and we were spotted by some ground patrol, but that seems pretty farfetched given the odds. It seems more likely someone was waiting for us."

"That's your gut feeling?"

"Yes, but I also believe we can expect a few Russian MIGs coming after us next, and pretty soon! Maybe a half dozen or so, and they will be from Russian command."

"And then what do we do?"

"We evade them, sir."

"And how do you propose to do that?" Kowalski replied.

"We need to fly like hell, sir! They can't see us on radar, and so they'll need a visual to find us. Their weapons will not be able to lock onto anything but our heat signatures, and those are diffused, and worst case, we can use flares to throw them off. They will come in on us high and flying fast! That is if they can find us at all."

"And what about their guns?"

"That sir is where we fly like hell! The MIGs air-to-air missiles will be ineffective because they won't be able to lock onto us. But they will deploy them first, out of instinct. After they realize that they are ineffective, they will then have to make a second pass to bring their guns on us. Just don't stay in one place for too long and their airspeed works against them—they will only have a few seconds to get their guns targeted before they over fly us! They can't maneuver in the mountains down low like we can."

"And then what?" Kowalski demanded.

"If we need to sir, we bring them down," Timmons replied flatly.

"Jesus, Timmons! Our orders were for minimal loss of life," Kowalski returned.

"Then all I can say sir is that we need to fly like hell and try to shake them, land somewhere, and then wait for the cover of darkness. We then proceed again completely invisible."

The radar lit up in all three Sikorsky helicopters at the same time. "We have incoming!" Timmons shouted. "Looks like three MIGs! Follow me!"

Roberta watched Timmons's helicopter pitch forward and overtake hers, and then the craft veered off left into a side mountain valley skimming a mountain stream. She stayed right on his tail and Kowalski did the same. The MIGs passed overhead unable to turn so quickly. The three choppers weaved back and forth, following the streambed through mountainous terrain. The mountain walls were nearly vertical here, and the valleys were very deep with heavily forested canyon walls to either side. There was no room down here for a MIG to maneuver.

"They will be back," Timmons radioed. "We need to switch to low band, and we need to split up—it is time to arm our weapons. Go to weapons mode."

Roberta and Kowalski both touched the screen for weapons mode, and the armament clunked into place in the undercarriage with a perceptible thud. Two revolving racks of air-to-air missiles had been lowered. Each rack held four missiles each. Just as a revolver indexes bullets so too did the missile launchers. As one missile was used, the cylinder would index one-quarter turn to put the next one at the ready. Between the two racks of missiles was a modified hydraulic turret mounted GAU-17A rotating Gatling gun equipped to fire four thousand 7.62 mm rounds per minute. A heads-up display came on in their flight helmets with targeting and weapon status information. As Roberta turned her head, the Gatling gun followed her motion using a very sophisticated laser tracking system built into the helmets; the guns were designed to be always on target.

"You now have machine guns active and air-to-air missiles active. All your defenses are now active. I am breaking left at the next valley," Timmons called out over the radio. "Roberta, you and Kowalski go right. Stay low and follow the streambed ahead. If the MIGs find you again, break up at the next opportunity and just keep flying."

"Where are you going, Timmons?" Kowalski demanded.

"Don't worry, sir. I got your backside," Timmons replied.

Timmons broke left. Roberta broke right and Kowalski followed her. The mountain valleys were wicked as hell to navigate through! They followed the tortuous paths of ancient streams that were fed by cascading waterfalls from the melting snow pack in the mountains above. Fortunately, the mountain peaks went a thousand feet into the air, and the valleys were damned tough for any helicopter, much less for a MIG to negotiate. Their defense radar lit up again.

"Roberta, they are back," Kowalski radioed.

"I know, Kowalski. It looks like all three of them are on us again," she replied. She struggled with the stick due to the air currents in the valleys. "I am going lower," she radioed. She dropped down to the streambed, and the bottom of her chopper skimmed the boulders. One MIG fired an air-to-air missile at her, which exploded in the streambed in front of her. The waterspout from the explosion momentarily blinded her until the windshield wipers came on automatically and cleared the windshield. The MIG overshot her, and then banked high to come around for another try at her.

"Good move, Roberta!" Kowalski shouted. "We got two more MIGs coming in, and I am going high." Kowalski pulled up on the stick, released flares, and banked around in a tight circle while gaining altitude. The MIG passed overhead and Kowalski had him locked on."

"Get him Kowalski," Nick yelled! "Either you get him, or we will."

Kowalski fired the air-to-air missile and watched the streamer as it caught up to the MIG. The MIG exploded, and the plane immediately fell into the mountains in a fireball. "Yeah!" Kowalski shouted.

The third MIG screamed past overhead.

"Oh damn," Kowalski realized. "I think we just started a war."

"Don't worry about it, boss. I have him." It was Timmons. He had flown up the other valley, hovered for a few seconds, and then doubled back around to cover their backside. He had the third MIG locked on.

"Permission to fire, sir?"

"Do it Timmons!" Kowalski ordered.

Timmons pulled the trigger, and two hellfire missiles spiraled upward toward the aircraft, which was nearly out of sight, and found their mark. The MIG exploded in midair.

Roberta wasn't as lucky. Her MIG had climbed high, banked around, and was now coming back at her head-on, machineguns blazing. This time, she was trapped. The MIG pilot was using the streambed as a reference point for his bullets, and the canyon walls trapped her from moving very far off the course of the streambed. She watched the hail of bullets tear up the streambed ahead of her, and then she remembered what Timmons had told her: *Use their airspeed against them.* She pulled up on her stick, pitched the helicopter to the left, and spun it around as she gained altitude. Timmons was right. The MIG couldn't change course, and he passed overhead at six hundred miles an hour. Now, she had his tail in her sights. "Can I fire?" she screamed, her finger resting heavy on the trigger.

"Fire, Roberta," Kowalski came back, and she squeezed the trigger. The GAU-17A Gatling gun started pumping out four thousand rounds a minute. The tracers were dead on, and smoke erupted quickly from the aircraft. A second later, the pilot ejected just before the plane was torn in two and exploded in mid-air! Roberta stopped firing and hovered.

"What else can we expect, Timmons?" Kowalski asked.

"Nothing, sir. I was jamming all their radio transmissions as soon as they made contact with us. These cowboys were waiting for us, but they didn't have any military authorization to shoot us down! Because no transmissions could get through! There will be more of them coming soon, so we need to move on, and move on now. One of those pilots made it out alive! But, it will be a while before he can report in. He will end up in another valley if he survives! He will then report that we are heading up this valley."

"Are we?" Kowalski asked.

"No, sir. We need to double back to the valley that I veered into previously. This valley here leads us back into the chute, where they will be expecting us! I know another way out. We'll work our way through these mountains and back to the sea. Then we'll cross the straights and go on to Magadan.

"Do we abort, Timmons?" Nick demanded.

"Negative, sir! We can fly out of this. They can't find us again in these mountains. We thread our way through them, and then we find the coast again. The Russian Navy may be looking for us by then because the Russian's just lost three MIGs. But my guess is they won't know why. There are over a dozen mountain passes in here, and the odds of them knowing what valley we are in is remote, especially when they think that we are in this valley here. They won't expect us to double back to make it for the mainland, and they can't see us on their radar either. It is our best chance, sir."

"Lead the way, Timmons," Nick ordered. "Roberta, are you okay?"

She looked at Nick and calmly said over the COM,

"I'm with you guys. Just point the way."

"Disarm weapons," Timmons radioed. "As low as we are flying, we are consuming lots of fuel, and we don't need armament slowing us down any more."

The Kamchatka Peninsula went on alert moments after the three MIGs were scrambled. "What do you mean that we lost all communications with them?" Dmitry Patrushev demanded.

There were ten Russian flight controllers in the communication center at the time, and no one looked very comfortable. "We had a ground sighting of three American-made helicopters passing through the chute on the Kamchatka Peninsula, and we immediately scrambled three interceptors. They radioed in a visual, here." The radar man pointed to a map. "But we never picked up anything on radar, and then we lost contact with our pilots shortly thereafter."

"So what happened to our MIGs?"

"We don't know, sir. We lost radar and radio contact."

Patrushev slammed his fist down on the console. "Idiots!" he yelled.

He knew the Americans were jamming the radio frequencies, and probably using their new radar absorption technology. If that was the case, those were armed attack helicopters! He would put money on his hunch that the fighters engaged the helicopters without orders and got shot down for their stupidity.

"Well then, find them!" he shouted. "And put this base on high alert! Put everything we have up in the air and in the water to find these damned Americans! And when we do—let's bring them down! Damn the Americans anyway! What the hell are they up to now?" He wondered if this was the beginning of the end of his military career as he got on the phone to his superiors.

Timmons broke out of the mountains on the western coastline of the Kamchatka Peninsula and flew directly into a fog bank. He radioed back to Kowalski and Roberta. "If we can make it across this open stretch of water before the Kamchatskiy Military base can mobilize more air support, we stand a good chance of making it. Fly low, but keep a look out for surface vessels on your radar. If we are lucky, the fog and cloud cover will protect us from any visual sightings."

"Yeah, that's great," Roberta, radioed back. "But I can't see anything, not even you!"

The yellow button on her console started flashing, then beeped three times. She felt the computer take over the stick. "We are back on autopilot," Timmons radioed. "I programmed your flight computers to track me. Just relax, and smoke them if you got them—you go where I go! This is the best break we could have gotten! At least for the moment we are completely invisible."

Nick looked over at Roberta, whose attention was fixed on the controls. "Roberta, did you really enjoy that dance?"

Remembering the Governor's 'ball', she smiled brightly and replied, "It was another highlight of my life, Nikki!" Momentarily forgetting the life-threatening mission that was unfolding all around them, and the fact they were not on intercom anymore. She reached over and took his hand and squeezed it.

"You promised me a warm beach somewhere if we both live through this, remember?"

"Hey you two," Kowalski said, and then he chuckled. "Keep it to yourselves!"

Roberta blushed and turned on the COM, smiling sheepishly at Nick.

Nick smiled back. "Yeah, a warm beach somewhere would be fun, but Roberta, I am sure you have a life of your own after this is all said and done."

"I have just my father Nikki, and a cubicle back in DC to return to. You keep telling me how attractive I am, but I don't see it that way. I get hit on by a lot of creepy guys looking for a little fun, and nothing much more than that! I put up my armor to keep them away from me—because that is not what I want. I am looking for a man much like my dad! A man who has character and one who has a purpose in life, not some creep looking to get laid! My dad's whole career was about his love for his country, and wanting to make sure that our lives were protected. He dearly loved mother and me, but he felt his place was out there on the ocean watching over his crew and carrying a 'Big Stick' for our country at the same time. Every time a flight officer flew off his deck, he took it as his own personal responsibility to make sure that they had a clear deck to land back onto when they returned. When on leave, Dad doted on Mom and me, and except for his little hobby of car racing, which frustrated the heck out of Mom, because he was home so little to begin with, he treated her with utter respect and complete devotion. That's the type of man I want to meet Nikki, and do you know what?"

Nick shook his head.

"It's not that easy to find the right guy! And, even if I am as attractive as you keep telling me I am, I haven't found him yet—unless *you* are willing to raise your hand and step up to the plate?"

Nick realized that he was blushing. This woman confounded him! She was bold, brash, and beautiful, and if he allowed himself to admit it, she was also intelligent, charming, and exquisitely feminine when she wanted to be! He replied, "Your dad would think me a relic Roberta, and he would advise you to stay clear of me."

Now miffed once again, she replied, "You really do have a problem giving a woman a ride don't you? Understandably, the circumstances under which we met were unusual! But what does that have to do with romance? What, are you thinking? That once this whole thing is over I will have nothing to do with you? Let me tell you something, Mr. Nicholas Dimeitry Petrovisky. You weren't the only pawn in this chess game—I was played a fool too!" Already, he was frustrating her once again with his boyish charms and his cavalier indifference to what she was saying! And, his utter lack of self-confidence that he was a man with charms of his own! It was frustrating the hell out of her! She knew that she should just drop it, and she thought to herself sarcastically, "Maybe he can't even get it up anyway!"

Nick, sensing the tension building once again between them, realized the truth in what she said. He replied quickly, hoping it wasn't too late. "It's not that, Roberta! I would like to take you somewhere after this all over, but I am not sure if I should be counting on it. To answer the question you posed just two days ago, yes I would want nothing more than to have a woman in my life. I just never believed it could ever happen! I had to stop believing in that that a long time ago."

"Oh, don't be such a martyr, Nikki! If you want something bad enough you go for it! And if it's me—you sure as hell aren't showing it!" She then turned back to her instruments, and tried to concentrate on her mission. She tried to forget about her feelings for him—as a man, but she couldn't! She couldn't let go of what he had just said to her, and so she hastened to add, "Are you are afraid of being in love with a woman who might love you back? Oh, you must think, 'What if she leaves me? Why is she with me?' Oh go boo-who about it! Or damn it—take a chance! If you want me Nikki, then prove it! And don't question the fact that we are together, or why! I am telling you right now, you have an uphill battle if you want me! Because, I don't think you have balls enough for a woman like me!"

Roberta couldn't help but feel absurd! Fuming in spite of their near death experience with the MIGs just moments before—this man was driving her nuts! She thought, "If the man doesn't have the balls to go after me, after all the signs I have showed him already, then he is an idiot! Plain and simple!"

Nick said nothing once again, wondering why she was so upset and what he had done to anger her so this time? Women! One minute they adore you—the next they want nothing to do with you! His mind was once again transfixed on how he had gotten himself set up so easily, and how he had fallen so hard for her in the first place! She was a handful, without question. He wondered if it was possible that he had so longed for love for so long that he had allowed himself to be set up? Surely, he recognized the signs sufficiently early on—the unlikelihood of stumbling across the path of a very attractive woman in the middle of nowhere! And yet he allowed himself to get drawn into this mess nonetheless—despite all the warning flags! And Smith, that bastard! He just cavalierly assumed he would play along, and he did! He wasn't sure which realization upset him more—the fact that he had stopped to help her in the first place, in spite of the warning signs that he shouldn't, or the fact that Smith had read him like a book and put her there knowing he so desperately needed a woman in his life! If he could be so easily duped by a pretty face, then he should indeed get out of the business altogether and retire! He decided to let that self-recrimination go! He was desperately trying to come up with something to reassure her that he had feelings for her when she switched off the COM. He shrugged it off! "Damned women!" he thought to himself.

Ulyana, along with three trusted men who had worked ops with her in the past, had a refueling truck with eight thousand gallons of high-grade aviation fuel parked on the side of the road ten miles south of Magadan. She looked at her watch and noted that the three choppers should be coming in soon—if they were coming at all! Kowalski had briefed her on the plan by radio, but he'd failed to respond to her transmissions since! She wondered if they had been shot down. She opened her cell phone to check for a cell signal, and it looked really weak.

She had found a spot along the coastline big enough to land the three helicopters and remote enough not to be seen, or noticed, by the local authorities. The road ended here for all heavy vehicles, but it continued on for the occasional light vehicle that came in from the fishing villages further down the coastline. She pushed the speed dial for World Trade in Zurich.

"Patch me through to Operation *Lightening Bolt*," she requested. "These are the coordinates for refueling zone number one, Nick. Can you hear me?" she said once she was patched through.

"Barely," he replied. "Give them to me."

She called off the coordinates and repeated, "Can you hear me?"

Nick plugged the coordinates into the guidance computer and replied, "Got them, Ulyana. Thanks!" A few seconds later, all three helicopters changed course simultaneously. "How long before we are there, Timmons?" he asked.

"About forty minutes."

"Ulyana, can you hear me?" Nick said into his COM.

He got no response, but he tried again. "Forty minutes, Ulyana," he spoke into the headset, but apparently they had lost the signal.

"What's the status?" one of Ulyana's men asked her.

"They are coming in, but I lost communications with them. Be prepared to pump smoke and to use flares. I don't know if they got the coordinates or not! But they know to follow the coastline. Everyone get ready. It seems we have a mission after all."

The fuel warning light started flashing on Kowalski's dash panel. The green fuel indicator bar showed an almost empty main tank. "Timmons, I am almost out of fuel. How is everybody else doing?"

Roberta radioed, "Same here."

"We all have auxiliary fuel tanks," Timmons radioed. "The computer will switch over to them automatically."

"Then what?" Kowalski demanded.

"We have about forty minutes before we lose power after that," Timmons replied.

"Timmons, that's cutting it pretty close," Kowalski said.

"We can save fuel if we go to eight thousand feet, but we will break out of the cloud cover, and by now, the Russian military will have been mobilized to look for us. Do we want to tip our hand?"

Kowalski grimaced. "No, we don't want to tip them off to where we are, or where we are headed. How close are we cutting it?"

"Pretty damned close!" Timmons answered truthfully. "We burned up a lot of extra fuel on the peninsula eluding the MIGs. I used the onboard computers to recalculate if we could make it or not, and initially we were fine, but who knows? Flying low like this has consumed much more fuel than I originally calculated also. But, I think we can still make it! The upside is that the moisture in this fog contributes to turbine efficiency. I can't calculate how much, but it does improve our situation somewhat. It doesn't matter anyway. Our only hope is to make it to the mainland and to the refueling stop, or we'll drown! There is no turning back!"

"Did the last course correction, based on Ulyana's coordinates, shorten or lengthen our flight plan?"

"It lengthened it sir, but only by a few minutes. I still think we can make it! It doesn't matter anyway! Like I said, there is no turning back. The onboard computers will put us over to auxiliary fuel tanks before the main tank is actually empty. It is called combat reserve. If we run out of fuel on the auxiliary tanks, we can manually switch back to the main tank and have enough fuel to land, but not much more than that. It will give us another five to ten minutes, if we need it."

They were ten miles out when the weapons alert system came alive again and their weapons went active. A second later, the sky exploded with anti-aircraft fire and they all took evasive measures.

"What the hell is this, Timmons?" Kowalski called out on the radio.

"It's the damned Russian Navy, sir! Veer away now before they can acquire us. Take a heading to three-four-zero and climb to six thousand feet."

Without hesitating, the three Seahawks veered to three-four-zero and climbed to six thousand feet.

"I thought we were invisible to radar?" Kowalski radioed.

"We are invisible to radar, but not to low resonance sub-detection equipment. Our rotors can be heard with their underwater listening array. They are taking potshots at us with their anti-aircraft guns, and hoping to get lucky. We need to split up and go higher, but we need to be careful not to break out of the clouds! Aside from a one-in-a-million shot, that's probably what they are hoping for. There are probably a dozen MIGs up there right now swarming around and looking for a target. This sub-chaser's antiaircraft guns don't have a lot of range, so we can fly around it easily enough. But, by now they are attempting to use vector coordinates in order to launch missiles, which won't be long!"

"Recommendations, Timmons?"

"Well, they found us, and they can project our course to discover where we are heading. But, unless we fly directly over one of their surface ships, it's going to be damned hard for them to acquire a heat signature in this soup. But they can hear us, and they can vector a position on us. I am also sure that there is more than one ship down there looking for us right now, and they all are probably dragging sonar arrays. I think taking out those MIGs pissed them off—big time!"

"What do we do, Timmons?" Kowalski barked.

"These are Seahawk sub chasers, boss! We each carry twelve sonar buoys. We arm them, adjust the frequencies to random, high amplification, and we attack."

"Attack? Are you crazy, Timmons?" Nick said.

"No, sir. Do you have any idea what a sonar buoy does to a sonar array when set on high amplification? It will blow out every listening circuit they've got onboard. We arm them, spread out, and start dropping them randomly over twelve square miles. After we junk all their sonar arrays, you and Roberta slip away."

"And what about you, Timmons? What are you going to do when the rest of us slip away?" Nick demanded.

"I got your backside, remember? They may not be able to see us, but we can see them. First, you and Roberta are going to take out those sonar arrays that they are tracking us with by dropping your sonar buoys. When all the buoys are armed, we all go to silent mode. They will assume that we went high. Instead we all split up and swing back south in silent mode. Moments before dropping a sonar buoy go off silent mode—and give them a few seconds to tune in real good! Then drop one of those bastards, and go back to silent mode. Make the drops randomly, north to south, east to west so that they cannot plot a course or calculate a vector. I am going to act as a decoy and try to engage if I can. If anything lifts off those ships, I am going to take it down. I'll meet up with you at our refueling point."

"You are going to run out of fuel, Timmons!"

"I am only going to give you a few minutes head start, so let's get moving!"

"Boys and girls," Timmons radioed. "By now the Russians have a vector on us, and they will be arming missiles. Are we ready to deploy?"

"Affirmative," Roberta radioed back. Nick observed her coolness and now understood the challenge before him if she was ever to be his. Man, she was a cool cookie!

"Affirmative, Timmons. We are ready to deploy," Kowalski radioed back. He added, "Timmons, just a reminder—but, we are heading in the wrong direction and we are running out of fuel!"

"I know that boss! But as long as we run north, they will have to turn north to follow us. I count six ships on my radar, none of them big enough to be a carrier. They'll have already begun their turns by now, each in different directions. I am waiting for them to begin firing at us based on their vector co-ordinates alone. As soon as the first missile is launched, I will drop a buoy and then we all go to silent mode, turn around, and take random courses, deploying sonar buoys as I directed. We will screw them up enough that they won't know where we are! In desperation, they will deploy whatever else they have. If you get a visual or see anything on radar, shoot it down! Once your sonar buoys are deployed, we are all on our own to make it to the refueling point."

Everyone's screens lit up as several ship-to-air missiles were launched. "Don't worry about these," Timmons radioed. "They don't have a lock on us yet! So climb, zigzag, and drop some countermeasures, and get ready to go to silent mode. I am dropping the first sonar buoy now."

Kowalski and Roberta were not as confident as Timmons was in the technology or his plan! And least of all, with his assessment that the missiles were not a threat! They started evasive maneuvers immediately. Roberta broke right and went low, while Kowalski broke left and went high. Timmons hovered until the missiles finally locked onto his heat signature, dropped his sonar buoy, and launched his countermeasures. Then he flew his helicopter higher as well.

"Silent mode, boys and girls," he radioed back to Kowalski and Roberta. "It is time to follow the plan. Good luck, and see you at the refueling point."

The sonar buoys activated immediately upon hitting the water and sent out high-energy, low frequency pulses at random intervals and in random sequences. The first pulses reached the ships below within milliseconds! The noise was amplified a thousand times over by electronics designed to pick up the smallest of low-frequency sound! Seamen tasked to follow the rotor noise of the helicopters tore off their headsets immediately! One Russian sonar men was caught off guard, and the noise generated in his headsets by the sonar buoys ruptured his eardrum. The circuits of the sonar consoles on the closest ships blew out—due to the overload! The chief sonar technicians scrambled to reset the dials, but it was too late! Many of the instruments had already fried, filling the sonar room with the odor of ozone and burnt electronics.

Roberta and Kowalski went to silent mode, and spread out covering a broad band of water, dropping buoys as Timmons had instructed them to. They baited the enemy, and then unleashed their weapons. Roberta flew for a few miles watching the temperature of her turbines while in silent mode. Timmons had said that staying in silent mode for too long would overheat the engines, as well as drop her available power. As soon as she observed the engine temperature indicator climbing, she turned the silent mode off. She then changed direction and altitude. After a minute or two, when she observed a noticeable drop in engine temperature, she would go back to silent mode again. Change course, and drop another sonar buoy. Kowalski did the same.

Timmons, however, used his fuel to attack the ships and never went to silent mode! He wanted not only disorientation for their attackers—but chaos as well! He wanted the ships below to hear him, to feel his presence, and to forget about Kowalski and Roberta for the time being—affording them the opportunity to get away.

His first mark was the sub chaser that had picked them up on sonar in the first place. Although he couldn't see it below him due to the fog, he had a lock on the ship magnetically. Timmons wasn't about to waste a missile on the ship, which would be ineffective anyway. Instead he locked his Gatling gun on it, dropped below the clouds, and hovered in front of it.

He started firing, sweeping the front decks of the sub chaser with 7.62 mm cannon fire, and everything that was on the front deck of the ship exploded into ruins or was shattered by the time he finally released the trigger. He had caused no serious damage to the ship or to the crew, but as he had hoped, he had created complete chaos! Next he took aim at the pilothouse and obliterated it too! There he destroyed every useful instrument within it, again without taking any life in the process. He then put his middle finger up in a sign of defiance, pulled up on his stick, and disappeared again back into the fog.

Roberta and Kowalski were on his grid in front of him. They had all turned southwest again. Below him was a nearly deaf Russian fleet, and had he had more fuel, and more bullets for his guns, he would have gladly strafed another ship! But, he had neither! His concern now was having enough fuel to make it to the mainland.

As Kowalski and Roberta fled across the strait and toward the mainland, Timmons radioed them.

"The Russian fleet is now deaf, and they have no idea where we are."

Chapter 27

Roberta and Kowalski were running on combat reserves when they broke out of the fog. The coastline of Khreber Kolymskiy suddenly appeared before them, barely discernable in the distance. The cliffs that bordered the waters of the Gulf of Tauysk on the northern tip of the Sea of Okhotsh were steep and treacherous looking, and they were already covered with snow. The whole area looked brutally harsh and foreboding, and yet the vista before them was beautiful at the same time. Dwarf Siberian pine trees lined the mountain ridges and the coastline cliffs, while stands of larch, poplar, and willow trees added greenery to the wetlands and river basins draining into Nagayevo Bay at Magadan. The city of Magadan could be seen in the distance. Its old brick factories belching white steam and black smoke into the cold Siberian air—the town looked as if it was a throw back to another time. And in the Gulf of Tauysk below, there were ships filled with ore from the gold fields of the Kolyma *oblast* (providence) headed for the crushers and smelters further down the coastline and they too looked like ancient relicts by today's standards.

They quickly spotted the red smoke that Ulyana and her ground team was pumping and they both pitched their helicopters towards it. With low fuel warning alarms sounding in the cabin, both Kowalski and Roberta finally landed, both breathing a sigh of relief at having made it finally across the open waters of the Gulf.

"Where the bloody hell is Timmons!" barked Kowalski over the radio.

"Sorry boss," Timmons came back. "I am out of fuel and taking it down now. I am about two clicks north of you—aiming for a soccer field behind what looks like a school."

"We'll come and get you as soon as we are refueled," Kowalski replied.

Ulyana's ground team quickly refueled the two choppers. Once Kowalski was refueled, he lifted off to aid Timmons. "Give me ten minutes," he said after loading five jerry cans filled with fuel into his bird.

"If anyone has to pee or whatever, now is the time," Ulyana called out. She then handed them each a sandwich wrapped in cellophane and a Styrofoam cup filled with hot coffee. Twenty minutes later, Kowalski and Timmons were spotted coming in, and her men worked quickly to refuel and re-arm his bird.

"Help yourself to sandwiches, guys. There's more here!" Ulyana ordered the gear to be stowed, and then looked at her watch. "Two minutes!" she shouted out.

The choppers had been refueled and re-armed, and one of her team got into the refueling truck, and started the motor. Turning around, he headed back up the paved highway toward Magadan. Roberta had slipped away to do her business, and she returned to her chopper just as she heard Ulyana call out the two-minute warning.

Ulyana was talking to Nick, relaying information on where the next refueling points were. She shook her head, and Nick looked disappointed. Roberta wondered what they were talking about and went over to Kowalski's chopper. She shouted up to him, "We need to get out of here now!"

Kowalski got on the radio. "Timmons, we need to go."

"Roger that," Timmons replied. He watched Roberta scramble back to her own bird and get in. "Nikki, you ready to go?" she asked, noting that Ulyana, a very pretty thirty-ish blond was in the back with her two men.

"This is Ulyana, Roberta," Nick introduced them. "She is my operations manager at World Trade. Her two men here are locals, and they know the lay of the land at Laboratory 173, and in the mineshafts below."

Roberta greeted the new members of the team, and got on the radio. "We are ready, Kowalski."

"Affirmative," he came back. "Follow Timmons. We are going in through these mountain passes up ahead."

Ulyana and her men hopped out of the chopper and climbed in with Timmons. The three choppers lifted off in unison, with Timmons taking the lead. Roberta looked over at Nick, about to say something to him, but then she changed her mind and concentrated on her flying.

Chapter 28

"Where did they come from?" yelled Pyotr. "How many?" Alarms triggered by radar were going off within Laboratory 173.

"They're already gone sir," replied the radar man.

"Well, what the hell was it?"

"I don't know, sir. We had bogies flying low, but they were on radar for only a few seconds, and now they're gone!"

Victor Zubkov stepped into the control room and he replied casually,

"The Americans are here. It won't be long before they will come knocking. What is the status of our choppers? Now would be a good time to leave—don't you think Pyotr?"

"The choppers have been standing by sir. We are only waiting for the winds to subside enough for liftoff."

Victor lit a cigar and replied, "We take off now—damn the winds!"

"But sir," Pyotr objected. "We are still under whiteout conditions! We'll be flying blind."

Victor looked at him coldly and said with determination in his tone,

"Don't be a woman, Pyotr! Only one helicopter is needed! Just pull the stick up, and get above the storm! If they can fly in it, we can too! Do you want to hang around here and see what the Americans have in mind for us? They are very clever, you know. I say we go now. Warm it up!"

Pyotr grimaced. "Yes sir, but we can hold them off! We can still kill the Americans!"

"Yes Pyotr, perhaps we can, but why? The Americans are here only for the *Semya* boards. As soon as I leave, they will go too. All I want from you and Anatoly is a head start—twenty minutes should do. I want your best pilot, Pyotr, and one chopper defrosted, and ready to go in ten minutes."

Pyotr nodded and barked out orders. Ground crews were alerted to de-ice the choppers and to warm them up immediately. He alerted his best pilot to supervise the operation. He instructed him to choose the best of the three machines for the task. Anatoly Timoshenko stood by, not knowing what to do.

Victor went over to him.

"Anatoly," he said quietly. "If I leave with the *Semya* boards, Laboratory 173 is of no consequence to the Americans. You must, however, destroy all the equipment, and all the records related to the *Semya*. Can I count on you?"

Anatoly stood at attention.

"Yes, sir. I will do this for you."

"Good, then begin immediately. But Anatoly," Victor cautioned. "This is still my facility, and it is still an asset to the Russian Federation. I don't want it destroyed. Destroy only the equipment and the records related to the *Semya*. Is this clear?"

Anatoly thought about it. "Yes, sir. It can be done."

"Good," Victor replied, and then he raised his voice. "Pyotr, come over here please."

Pyotr stopped barking out orders and went over to Victor.

"Yes, sir!" He stood at attention.

"You and your men are here to defend this facility. Is that clear?"

"Without question, sir!" Pyotr replied.

"Good. Anatoly must have enough time to destroy the relevant equipment and the data related to the *Semya*. Can you give it to him?"

Pyotr smiled. "You worry too much, Victor. I have already sent out an assault team to cover the perimeter. If the Americans are here, we will find them and bring them to you—in body bags!"

"And, if you don't?" Victor replied.

Pyotr smiled. "Then they still need to get in here, and we are ready."

"Pyotr," Victor replied calmly and sighed. "We don't need heroes here today. Once I am gone, the Americans have no reason to be here. They are not here to destroy this facility, or to occupy it. Just hold them off long enough for Anatoly to do what he needs to do, and give me my twenty minutes head start—that's all I ask. No killing—no body bags! After that, throw down your weapons and surrender. No one needs to die needlessly. Is that clear?"

At Laboratory 173, Pyotr's men were struggling against the wind to hose the choppers down with de-icers, and they were making significant progress. "Wind them up," the pilot commanded.

One by one, the choppers fired off. "You hear that?" Nick yelled over the winds to Kowalski. "They are getting ready to leave!"

Both men broke into a run, heading in the direction that the turbines seemed to be. They dropped to the ground as soon as the helicopters came into view. "What do you think, Nick?" Kowalski panted.

"I thought we were getting some help?" Nick replied.

Kowalski got on his radio and contacted Ulyana back at the choppers. The conversation was brief. "We have five men waiting for us on the perimeter, waiting for instructions," he said. "The problem is, that Zubkov has a squad of men out there patrolling with dogs. Do we engage?"

Nick thought about it for a moment. "We take this pilot out, destroy the birds, and pull back. Go find these men patrolling the grounds, so our guys can get in."

"What are you going to do?" Kowalski asked.

Nick un-shouldered his rifle, and checked the action. "I am going to take out that pilot," he replied. "And you are going to find our men, and very quietly start taking out their security forces. No one leaves this place unless I say so."

"Nick," Kowalski replied. "If you kill that guy, all hell breaks loose!"

"If I take out his kneecap, he can't fly a chopper either, and then Zubkov can't get out of here."

"What about the ground patrols?"

Nick looked at his watch. "You have two minutes to hook up with your men. Take the opposition out quietly, without killing any of them, if at all possible."

"And, you don't think that the ground crew won't alert everyone on the base?" Kowalski said.

"I am counting on it, Kowalski! Then they will lock the facility down, and stay put. You have two minutes."

Kowalski looked at his old friend. "You are crazy, Nick."

Nick smiled and replied, "Thank you, bro. I'll be right behind you! Now get going."

Nick waited until Kowalski had slipped away into the howling blizzard, then he loaded the clip and snapped home a round. The wind was still fierce, and from a hundred yards away, he had a questionable shot at best! Especially—if all he intended to do was wound the pilot. He began crawling closer through the snow, his white outer gear a perfect camouflage against the white that was everywhere surrounding him. When he was within seventy-five yards, he looked through the scope again. The pilot's kneecap was an easy shot now, despite the winds.

The door to the facility opened wide, and Victor Zubkov darted out with his bags in hand. The pilot had selected the furthest chopper and motioned him toward it. Victor started for it at a fast pace while the pilot scrambled for the cockpit. Nick slipped off the safety, and as the pilot took the first rung of the chopper, he pulled the trigger.

The pilot crumbled to the ground writhing in pain and holding his knee! Nick took aim at the chopper and shattered the Plexiglas windows with several rounds. He then took aim at the other choppers, pelting them with bullets too. Victor Zubkov stopped dead in his tracks! Realizing that he was under attack, he darted back for the Lab. The ground crew scrambled too, collecting the injured pilot in their retreat.

Nick grabbed three fragment grenades from his gear. Leaving his rifle on the ground, he sprinted the short distance to the helipad, and lobbed one grenade under each chopper. He then recovered his gear and disappeared into the storm. Seconds later, all three choppers blew up, the heated fuel in the chopper's tanks exploding immediately into gigantic fireball!

Victor, and the helicopter maintenance crew were thrown to the ground by the blasts! Victor got up slowly, grabbed his bags, and made his way back to the laboratory, while Pyotr's men ran outside looking for a target. Unable to see anything but white, they retreated back inside, and bolted the door behind them.

Pyotr met Victor in the hallway.

"What happened?"

Victor laughed half-heartedly. "It appears that I am not going anywhere for the moment! I told you that the Americans were very clever. They went straight for the aircraft where they took out your pilot and destroyed the machines. Next, they will take out our communications, if they haven't already! But, see if we can get a message out. We'll need more choppers. And Pyotr…"

"Yes, sir?" Pyotr stopped to reply.

"The Americans have a plan, or they would have already stormed this facility. Don't be so sure that we are secure. I would call your patrols back in—the perimeter is already compromised."

"Yes sir," he said, but there was doubt in his expression.

"I'll be in my quarters. See if we still have communications, and if we do, come and get me."

It took Nick ten minutes to locate the others by the perimeter fence where they had assembled. "How did it go?" asked Kowalski.

"One pilot is down with a shattered knee cap. All three helicopters have been destroyed."

"Victor's patrol pulled back before we had to do anything about them," Kowalski said. "The radio tower is being blown right now, and all the landlines and power to the facility have already been cut. They are on generators now, and we were planning on taking them out next."

"Stay away from the generators, Kowalski. They'll be heavily defended, and we don't need casualties. How long before the team is in place in the mines?"

"I'd say about another forty minutes, Nick."

"Alright, then let's do this. Zubkov is going to make another break for it, and unless he has more air support on the way, which I doubt because he was on his way out when we closed the door on him, his only other alternative is go by road or cross-country. There has to be a motor pool somewhere on this base with vehicles, including snowmobiles. We need to close that door too."

Kowalski called one of the locals over and spoke with him. The man nodded and left to gather the others. A moment later the man came back and conversed with Kowalski.

"There is a motor pool not far away, but I am told it is heavily guarded." Kowalski informed Nick.

"What about other buildings nearby?" Nick asked.

Kowalski said, "The local told me that there is a gardening shed for basic lawn tools behind the motor pool."

"Good enough," Nick replied. "I doubt that they are guarding the John Deere tractors! Besides, it's a place to get out of this God-awful blizzard! Let's go."

As Kowalski had predicted, the motor pool was well lit inside and out! A number of well-armed soldiers were salted around it and by the looks of it they were all on high alert! The tool shed was fifty yards to the rear, and it appeared to be quiet and unoccupied. There were no visible tracks in the snow leading up to it. "We go in from behind," Nick ordered.

Nick, Kowalski, and the men made a wide circle around the motor pool to get to the garden shed unseen. On the backside of the shed was a double garage door with no lock. They slid the door aside and went in. Surprisingly, the shed was heated. Nicked pulled back the hood to his parka. "Ah, this is more like it," he said, and everyone nodded in agreement as they stomped the snow from their boots, and shook it from their parkas.

The shed was full of lawn equipment and tractors. "This will work," Nick said. "I want a lookout on that window over there. We need to keep Victor's people distracted until Timmons gets his team in place. Is there a tunnel to the motor pool?"

"Yes, of course Nikki! This is Siberia."

It had been decided that Kowalski, who spoke nearly fluent Russian, would work with the local ground forces. Timmons and Ulyana who were already at the mines would take a team down into them and assault the back door into the facility. Roberta would stand down, not far away, and monitor radar and communications and wait for instructions.

"Hey boss," one of the local men called out in Russian. "We got something over here."

"What are you talking about?" Nick replied.

He pulled back a large tarp, and under it were five snowmobiles lined up. "No wonder this place is heated," he replied in Russian. "They expected us to take out the motor pool."

Nick smiled. "Very clever, don't you think? There must be a tunnel here too then, and we must find it."

Everyone spread out, looking for the underground passage, but they found nothing. Nick paced about thinking.

"If Victor was using this as his last resort to get away, certainly he would have some way to access it easily, and yet there is none. Why? And why isn't this shed guarded?" Nick continued. "Kowalski, tell me why this shed isn't guarded?"

Kowalski shrugged. "You are better at this game than I am, Nikki. You tell me."

"Five snowmobiles are left in a heated garden shed covered with a tarp. They are prepped and ready to go with keys left in the ignition. Someone, it seems, has his or her own plan for escape, don't you think? Why else would Victor have five brand new snowmobiles hidden under a tarp in his own facility, but have all the guards at the motor pool?"

Kowalski shrugged again. "I don't know, Nikki. What are you thinking?"

"Zubkov has been one step ahead of us all along, but it appears that someone else is one step ahead of Zubkov! Could this be the trappings of Alexander? We have been compromised, Kowalski! Our team was sent in to stop Zubkov's team and to acquire the *Semya* boards, but someone else has the same intention! Timmons' team will be slaughtered if they step into Laboratory 173, and whoever has planned this, was intending to get away cross-country using these snowmobiles. That means that they are nearby, and my guess is, they will blow the base up when they leave, and then blame it on us at World Trade, or on terrorists."

"What do we do?" Kowalski asked.

"We need to get out of here, and we need to warn Timmons! By now he is the mines—and he can't be reached by radio! We'll use these machines."

"Nikki, are you crazy?"

"Yes, Kowalski. I am crazy. Haven't you figured that out yet? Someone has plans to acquire the *Semya* boards ahead of us, and despite what we have been told about the integrity of the United States, and Russian Federation, I am starting to doubt both! Don't you think it's been a little too neatly packaged? Zubkov never planned to go cross-country; he intended to get out of here by helicopter! Why didn't he leave last night? Those choppers were here all night, and they were just deicing them when we arrived, which means he must have been here all night."

"Nick, there was a blizzard last night," Kowalski answered.

"Since when does a blizzard keep a military helicopter grounded? It might keep a fixed winged plane grounded, but not a helicopter. No, Zubkov was planning to leave by chopper, so I don't think he was planning a cross-country escape.

"Then again," Nick went on. "Is Zubkov really one step ahead of us, or is the CIA deliberately one step behind Zubkov? These snowmobiles could be CIA or Russian FSB, or even Nathan Bentley's! Someone is planning an escape here. Would Zubkov have five machines ready or would he have one? Zubkov is a Russian. He wouldn't need five machines, and being a Russian he would have only what he needed, no more, and no less—at best he would have two machines, and they would be guarded! This whole thing stinks. We need to get out of here, and now."

"Do you have a plan?" Kowalski asked.

Nick thought about it for a moment as he paced back and forth, and then said. "Whoever they are, they are already here! Why would they wait for Victor to show up? The *Semya* boards are already here, and whoever it is, apparently already has access to the base."

"Because," Kowalski replied, "if they waited for Victor to show up, they could take him out too, and like you said, and expose World Trade at the same time."

"Exactly, but who?" Nick replied.

"I don't know, Nikki. How about Mayakovsky? Like you said, they have to be close by just waiting for the party to begin."

Kowalski consulted with the locals.

"There is a farmhouse not far from here. It is possible that they are using it as a base, but it will be quite a hike in this weather," he supposed listening to the howling winds outside.

"What's the ETA for Timmons to open the back door?" Nick asked again.

"They should be ready soon," Kowalski replied.

"Alright then, Kowalski. Get back to the choppers, and you and Roberta get in the air. I want the motor pool taken out and the farmhouse found. Once you locate it, radio the coordinates back to me and we'll meet up with you there."

"What are you going to do, Nick?"

"I'm taking these snowmobiles and rousting those guards out before you and Roberta level the place with missiles," Nick answered him. He then barked orders in Russian to the ground team, who immediately saddled up. "There has to be at least half a dozen men in there," he said, referring to the motor pool. "And a satchel charge through the front door, ought to scare most of them out! You radio me back, when you are in the air, and give me a few minutes to clear the place before you blow it to hell!"

"What the hell was that?" Pyotr demanded, hearing the explosions outside.

Victor laughed! "It is the Americans, Pyotr! Don't be such a fool. I am guessing that they are tying up all the loose ends, and it was the motor pool we just heard exploding—it all makes sense doesn't it? They have taken out escape by air, all communications for assistance, and finally, now the motor pool too!"

"We still have power sir," Pyotr said. "And we can still defend ourselves."

Victor nodded. "And the Americans could take out the power supply as well, but they haven't. So far, all they have done is isolate us and keep us from getting out of here. We have only one casualty, your hotshot pilot who suffers from a shattered knee. Can you imagine how carefully that bullet was placed?"

Pyotr looked angry and insulted by his comment.

"Forget it, Pyotr," Victor went on casually. "You are a combat soldier, and I am sure that you would prefer to meet your opponent head-on and to the death, if you could! But your way serves no purpose. The Americans have been very careful not to take any human life so far, and we will do the same. What puzzles me most is that they have not already made their assault."

Pyotr looked at his boss quizzically. "Why are you not worried, Victor?" he asked. "You laugh, as if you expected this all along!"

Pyotr's radio crackled. "Commander, the motor pool has been destroyed by an assault team from the air, and on ground. The attackers disappeared into the blizzard as quickly as they appeared."

"What are the casualties?" Pyotr replied.

"None, sir. We are returning to base."

"Where did the attackers go?" he demanded.

"They came in too fast to know for sure. I think they went north toward you."

"How many?" Pyotr asked.

"Two heavily armed choppers and a group of snowmobiles."

Pyotr exploded, "And what the hell were you doing, sleeping?"

"Commander, they came in under the cover of the blizzard. Visibility was nil. We had only enough time to take up a perimeter before we were under fire. The next thing we know, the doors are blown wide open, and a second later, a satchel charge was tossed inside. The men all ran for cover to save themselves! After that, missiles leveled the place; and then they were gone too. They may be heading toward you, and so we are returning to base."

Victor lit a cigar and blew the smoke upward while Pyotr fumed. "Return to base!" Pyotr shouted. "Report to me immediately when you get here!"

"Yes, sir." The radio crackled and then went silent.

"How is it, Victor, that all transmissions are down, and yet I can receive a transmission from a hand-held device like this?"

"The main assault force is not here yet, Pyotr. When they arrive, everything will be jammed! We have a little time yet to make adjustments."

"Once again I ask you, Victor: why are you not worried?"

Victor replied vehemently, "Because Pyotr, somewhere, within our ranks, is a traitor! And it is he who I am most worried about, not the Americans! The Americans are here only to stop me from leaving with this briefcase." He held it up in clear view. "Someone else has bigger plans."

Victor blew more smoke upward. "I find it strange that you delayed my departure last night—because of a storm! If you hadn't, I would be halfway to Moscow right now. Since when do military helicopters get grounded due to a blizzard?"

"But Victor," Pyotr replied. "It was for your own safety that I grounded the choppers."

Victor pulled out a pistol from under his coat, and aimed it directly at Pyotr. "No, it wasn't my safety that you were worried about, Pyotr. I did some checking last night, and it turns out that you have made a few recent investments in a South Caribbean bank, a bit too far away from Moscow, and with a bit too large a sum for a military man to have. How can you explain it?"

Pyotr raised his hands, palms up, and smiled. "Of course I can explain it."

"I don't think so, Pyotr. Who are you working for?" Victor demanded.

Pyotr turned his back on Victor's gun and continued. "Twenty years in the Russian military, and when my pension is near due, the damned government is broke!" he shouted angrily. He then turned to face Victor once again. "What was I to do, Victor?

"You, Victor," he continued vehemently, "profited by the fall of the Soviet Union! You sold off all the assets of the State, and banked millions, while the common man and the soldiers got nothing!" he shouted fervently.

"Who are you working for?" Victor asked again calmly, as he raised his pistol and took aim.

"Does it matter, Victor? My only ambition was to retire and live out the remainder of my miserable life in peace," Oleyenka replied.

"It matters," Victor replied. "There are things that I just recently discovered about these *Semya* boards that matter too! I will pay you double whatever anybody else agreed to pay you, and I will give you my word that I'll let you retire in peace with the money, as you had hoped for."

"I can't do that, Victor."

"Why not?" Victor asked, hoping for a real answer.

"They have my wife and family," Pyotr replied softly.

"Who does?" Victor demanded.

"General Krushensky! This is a military sanctioned operation! I only have two trusted men on my team. When you called me in, I was intercepted at the base, taken into a room, and told my orders. I was also told that my wife and kids were picked up by the FSB, and taken into custody! I was told that I am not to fail or else! I was told that, if I succeeded, I could retire with my family. I had no time to make any money transfers or investments anywhere—much less in some South Caribbean bank! So, I must have been set up! I was offered one hundred thousand American dollars to pull this off. What was I to do?"

"What were your orders?" Victor pushed him.

"To keep you here until I was told otherwise, and to keep you here with the *Semya* boards, and all the technology to produce them."

Victor lowered his weapon. "But Anatoly is already about to destroy all the technology, which means you have already failed! Let me help you out here, Pyotr."

Pyotr had discretely removed a knife from his shirtsleeve when he had turned away from Victor. He turned back to face him and when he did, he threw it at Victor—aiming for his heart! At the same time, Victor pulled the trigger to his handgun. The bullet hit Pyotr's forehead as intended! The back of Pyotr's skull blew off—the hollow point bullet spattering brain matter against the opposite wall. The bullet continued onward, hitting the electrical panel behind where Oleyenka was standing and shorting it out. All the monitors went black. The well-aimed knife planted itself in Victor's shoulder. Remarkably, it didn't hurt as much as Victor thought it would, though he was bleeding profusely! He pulled it out, and threw it to the ground. Clutching the wound to quell the bleeding, he picked up the phone.

"Anatoly," he spoke into the phone with urgency. "Bring a medic to the control center immediately, and Anatoly, bring your own armed security here with you! If anyone attempts to stop you, shoot them!"

"Yes sir," Anatoly answered. "We are on our way."

"And Anatoly," Victor added. "Oleyenka's men are not on our side. He just tried to kill me, and unfortunately, he died himself in the process. I think his men are about to slit your throat, and your men's throats as well, any minute!"

Anatoly immediately thumbed his walkie-talkie and calmly gave out a coded message: "Men, be prepared for an inspection."

The message actually meant that they were to disarm Pyotr's men if necessary, and then to report immediately to the control center. Next, he called the base physician and instructed him to grab his gear, and be prepared to go with him. As he checked his own weapons, he stormed out into the hallway and headed for the clinic to get the doctor. When he arrived, he threw open the door and handed the doctor a gun.

The doctor looked at the pistol and shook his head, saying, "I don't know anything about guns. Why is this necessary?"

"It may not be, doc, but then again, something tells me it might be prudent to have it."

The doctor slipped the weapon into his bag and followed Anatoly out the door. When they arrived at the security office, they found Victor sitting at the monitor console clutching his shoulder. The towel he was using to slow the bleeding was saturated with blood. His automatic was on the console within easy reach.

Pyotr lay in a pool of blood in the center of the room, and the opposite wall was spattered with blood and brain fragments—a clear indication of what had just happened. The electrical panel on the wall was still smoldering!

"What happened here, Victor?" Anatoly queried.

"It appears that Pyotr is part of a conspiracy, and I have to assume that his men are too. I was forced to shoot him before he told me anything useful. Surely you have a way out of here?"

Anatoly suggested, "The tunnel to the motor pool."

Victor shook his head. "No, the motor pool has been destroyed."

"We can still use the tunnel Mr. Zubkov. There is an airshaft for the diamond mines below us! But, it is a thousand yards outside the perimeter of the base and it is just a vertical shaft used to ventilate the mines. The shaft must be two hundred feet straight down to the tunnels below. You do not look in any condition for such an attempt, but if we can get to the mines below, we could commandeer an ore transporter and get out from there."

"I'll make it!" Victor snarled. "Doc, get over here and stitch me up."

The physician opened his shirt and whistled. "You are a lucky man, Mr. Zubkov! The blade missed an artery by only a few centimeters, and had it been thrown differently, it would have severed it."

"Yes, I know all this," Victor grumbled. "So get on with it and stitch me up! Use only a local anesthetic—I still have places to go!"

The doctor nodded, took out a syringe, flicked it a couple of times to remove any air, and injected him with anesthetic. The bleeding was coming mostly from severed capillaries, but the cut was quite deep. To quell it, the doctor cauterized the capillaries with a portable laser. It took only a few stitches to close the wound up after that, and he pulled the stitches tight. "You will have a big scar," the doctor said. "Normally, I would do a much tidier procedure, but since you have no intention to convalesce, I stitched you up accordingly. You will begin feeling the pain within the hour, so take these." He handed Victor a plastic bottle of codeine pills and went about dressing the wound.

Victor took the bottle and threw it against the wall, where it shattered. "I don't need pain pills, doctor. Pain is good! It reminds you that you are still alive. When this is all over, I will convalesce. In the meantime, the pain will keep me awake and alert."

The doctor closed his bag and handed Anatoly a handful of bandages and medications. "He will need to re-dress his wound in a few hours," he instructed Anatoly. "And," he whispered discretely. "The pain will be immense after the anesthetic wears off. Use the morphine—he will need it!" Anatoly nodded and slipped everything into a large pocket on his vest. The doctor added, "These are antibiotics. Give him one now, then three times a day until they are all gone. Is there anything else?"

"Yes," Victor replied, overhearing the two conversing. "Keep your mouth shut about this—and about where we are going, or the consequences will be dire!"

"And what do I tell the FSB about him when they come?" the doctor asked, nodding toward Pyotr.

"You tell them nothing. You never left your clinic tonight!"

"As you wish. Then my business is done here. May I go?"

Victor looked at him coldly and nodded. "Yes go, before all hell breaks loose!"

The doctor opened his bag, pulled out Anatoly's pistol, and handed it back to him. "Here. You better have this back before I hurt myself with it," he said. Then he gingerly stepped over Pyotr's corpse and approached the door. Just as he reached it, small-arms fire erupted in the hallway! Turning to look back at Anatoly to see what to do, Anatoly tossed him back the pistol.

"Too late, doc! If you go out there now, you'll get shot. Get away from that door. They may try to blow it!" He keyed up his walkie-talkie. "All units respond, and report in now!"

His first team leader replied, "We got pinned down by Pyotr's men in D corridor just short of the main corridor and can't make it to you. I have one man wounded, but he is able to fight. We took out two of their guys in the first round, but they are coming at us with heavy fire and grenades. We can't hold our positions any longer! We are retreating to B5." Explosions and small-arms fire could be heard in the background.

Leonid's voice came over the radio next. "Pyotr's men slit the throats of my guys before they knew what happened to them. I was in the men's room when you radioed to assemble at the command center, and they must have been expecting something to happen. When I got back they were already wiping their knives off, and standing over the corpses looking very satisfied with themselves! When they saw me, they went for their weapons! I had already tossed a grenade at the bastards, and then I opened fire! I have their dog tags on me, and I'll meet up with team one at B5.

Team three leader called in. "We just cleared the main corridor. Pyotr's men are in hot pursuit and right behind us! ETA less than a minute—have the door open!"

Anatoly pulled out a set of keys and went to a steel locker and unlocked it. He pulled out three sub-machineguns and three bulletproof vests. "Here Victor, put this on. Each vest has a dozen clips of ammo, the belts have two flash grenades, two smoke grenades, and two fragment grenades, plus a field knife and a few other useful items." He tossed one to the doctor. "Put it on doc," he commanded. He then slapped a fresh clip into each automatic and chambered a round. He handed a weapon to Victor and the doctor, saying to the latter, "The safety is on. Flick it down with your thumb when you need it. Both weapons are set to fully automatic."

He then put on his own vest and shut the locker. Gunshots and explosions started rattling the walls as his third team approached. "I am opening the door now. Victor! Get behind that console over there and cover me! Doc, stand over there and try not to get shot." He unlatched the door and flung it wide. Immediately the smell of gunpowder and smoke filled the room. Anatoly dove through the opening and flung himself on the corridor floor, his weapon pointed toward his approaching men. Aiming for the men in close pursuit behind his own, he squeezed the trigger and laid down cover fire. Another weapon was being fired from the doorway, and Anatoly looked over to see Victor, his automatic set to single fire, carefully aiming and squeezing off rounds. Two of Pyotr's men fell to the ground, dead. Victor shouted to Anatoly as he continued to fire,

"Go get your men, Anatoly! I'll shoot anything that moves behind them."

Anatoly grinned, sprayed another volley of bullets down the hallway, and took off at a run. The first man on team three was nearly to the door when a rocket propelled grenade exploded midway down the corridor, knocking him to the ground and filling the corridor with smoke.

"Victor!" Anatoly shouted. "I'm going after my man! Cover me!"

Victor, who had been thrown to the ground as well, staggered to his feet. "I'm coming with you, Anatoly. I can't see a damned thing anyway!" The two men dashed to the wounded guard only to discover he was already dead, his torso nearly severed in half from the explosion. More small-arms fire erupted further down the corridor, and bullets smashed into the ceramic tiled walls around them. Instinctively, both men dropped to the floor. The smoke from the blast was quickly being removed by the ventilation system, and two forms could vaguely be seen on each side of the corridor returning fire, all that was left of team three.

"Victor," Anatoly said. "My men will never make it, but you can. There is a trapdoor under the command console that leads to a series of tunnels below. Team one and two are assembling at B5. Take my radio and get yourself and the doc out of here. I am staying with my men."

"Are those two men the last of your team?" Victor replied harshly.

Anatoly nodded. "They are the last of team three, and one is my stepbrother."

"I am your brother now, Anatoly! There can't be more than two of Pyotr's men left either, so let's go get your men!" Victor switched his weapon to full automatic fire, got up from the floor, and emptied his clip over the heads of the pinned-down men. He then tossed a fragment grenade as hard as he could, reloaded, and pulled the trigger again while he ran as fast as he could in the direction of the opposition. Anatoly scrambled to catch up to him. Another rocket propelled grenade exploded, but this time harmlessly at the end of the corridor. Victor ran past the pinned down men and tossed another grenade ahead of him while ejecting another spent clip and then slapping another one home. He sprayed another volley of bullets ahead of him as he came upon the last of Pyotr's men at a junction in the corridors. The soldier was frantically trying to reload another RPG round. Behind him lay the corpse of his comrade, who had taken a fragment of grenade through the skull.

"Don't even think about it," Victor shouted at him. "Drop your weapon now and stand down, or you will join your comrade over there."

The soldier thought about it, but seeing that Anatoly and his two men were now standing next to Victor, he dropped the weapon and put his hands on his head. Anatoly cuffed the soldier's hands behind his back and searched him for weapons. "We must go Victor, before the rest of Pyotr's teams gets here. He is clean. What do we do with him?"

"What is your name, soldier?" Victor asked him.

"Andrushka! Why do you ask?"

"Because, technically, you work for me. I hired Pyotr Oleyenka, and he hired you. I killed Pyotr Oleyenka today because he betrayed me. Who do you work for now?"

"I am a mercenary, Mr. Zubkov. Once, I was a proud soldier of the Soviet Union, but the Soviet Union is no more! I served with Pyotr Oleyenka, as did my comrade over there." He nodded toward the dead soldier. "We were called on by Pyotr to help him recover something for the Motherland—that's all I know. If Pyotr is dead, then I am a free agent and without a job, and I can kiss off the bonus I was promised."

Victor laughed and clapped him on the back. "Let's take him with us, Anatoly. I like this lad. Andrushka, for now we need to keep the cuffs on you. If you tell me what I need to know, I will pay you your bonus and you can live to fight another day. Will you cooperate?"

"When I see Pyotr's corpse, then yes. I would never betray a friend."

"And what about vengeance, Andrushka?" Victor asked.

"Pyotr and I are both soldiers. Over there, dead..." He nodded to his comrade. "Is my best friend, Sasha. He died in action trying to do a job. It is what soldiers do, and how he wanted it to be—if it were to be his end."

"Can you bring in the rest of Pyotr's men?"

"No, sir. There is a higher chain of command. The remaining men are regular army on special assignment from *Spetsnaz* (Special Forces)! They will take their orders from someone else now that Oleyenka is dead! Who that might be, I have no idea. Myself and Sasha were the only mercenaries in the group, and we were only called in at the last moment to replace two men who came down ill."

Anatoly was nervously looking at his watch when another burst of small-arms fire shattered the ceramic tiles around them. The fire was coming from an intersecting corridor further down the hallway. Everyone dropped to the ground and returned fire, but not before Andrushka fell dead to the floor with a bullet in his back. Another burst of bullets flew over their heads and hammered the opposite wall. Anatoly rolled over and returned fire at another assault team coming at them down the main corridor. He and Victor and what remained of their men were sitting ducks where they were—and out numbered! One assault team had them flanked, and the other was between them and their escape route.

"Victor," Anatoly shouted over the small-arms fire. "We need to throw down our weapons, or we will all be killed."

"Get some smoke out, you idiot!" Victor snarled. All the men reached for their smoke grenades and tossed them in different directions. As the smoke grenades skittered down the hallways, there was another surprise. The doctor, who had been sitting there trembling, not knowing what to do, decided to join the foray. Creeping over to the open door of the command center, he had witnessed most of what had gone on. When the men got pinned down for the second time, he thumbed the safety off on his own weapon and found a grenade. He stared at it, not exactly sure how it worked! But, he assumed all you needed to do was pull the pin out and throw it! He also didn't know which grenade was which, but he decided it didn't matter! He would just start lobbing stuff at the bad guys.

He tossed the grenade in the direction of the assault team that was firing on Anatoly's men, then stepped out into corridor and pulled the trigger of his automatic until the clip was empty. The grenade went off a second later and blinded him. It turned out to be a flash grenade. At the same time, three smoke grenades skittered past him billowing smoke. His weapon was empty, and he didn't know how to reload it, so he dove sideways back into the command center, coughing from the smoke and rubbing his eyes to restore his vision.

"Go, go, go!" Anatoly shouted, and the four men sprang to their feet and started running toward the command center door, emptying their clips as they went. The smoke filled the corridor, making them invisible momentarily, and the doctor had bought them a window of opportunity by pinning down the flanking opposition.

The doctor's barrage didn't stop the enemy from tossing their own Hail Mary's back! Three grenades unexpectedly skittered down the hallway, erupting from behind a wall of smoke. The men danced over two of them and kept on running. The third hit Anatoly's stepbrother's boot and skittered sideways against the wall. He stopped, looked at Anatoly knowingly, and then threw himself on top of it. Anatoly screamed, "No!"

The blast from the grenades put them all on the floor, and bits and pieces of Anatoly's stepbrother spattered across the walls. Anatoly went into shock, falling to his hands and knees in utter disbelief! Victor went to him and pulled him to his feet. "Move!" he shouted as he pushed him toward the control center door. "Everyone, on your feet! Move!" he commanded. He slapped a fresh clip into his weapon and chambered a round, then started spraying more bullets down the corridor in front of him. He made it to the control center nearly dragging Anatoly behind him! He slammed the door shut behind them and bolted it tight.

"How strong is this door?" Victor shouted at Anatoly. Anatoly just stared back at him, still in shock. Victor slapped him across the face. "Anatoly!" Victor shouted. "Get over it! Your stepbrother saved all our lives by sacrificing himself. Don't let his heroic actions be in vain!"

"I'm just a guard, Victor. I am not a battle-hardened combat soldier."

"If you live through this day, you will be a battle-hardened soldier! Now, how strong is this door?”

"It won't hold up to C4, if that is what you are asking,” Anatoly replied.

"Is it fireproof?” Victor demanded.

"Yes, it is fireproof.”

"I need something highly flammable. Any suggestions?”

At first Anatoly was silent, but then he managed a grin, in spite of his grief. "We have a bottle or two of Vodka stashed away in here somewhere.”

Victor waited until the alcoholic beverages were found. "Strip off his pants,” Victor commanded, nodding toward Oleyenka's corpse.

"What are you up to, Victor?” Anatoly asked.

"You can't plant C4 on a surface hotter than two-hundred degrees Celsius, Anatoly. The walls of this place are all made of reinforced solid concrete, and they can't blast through them. We need to buy some time, and that door is the only thing between them and us. Fragment grenades won't blow it, and the corridor is too narrow for them to use a rocket-propelled grenade on it. Their only hope is to use C4. If we get the door hot enough, they won't be able to touch it.”

"I don't get what your plan is,” Anatoly replied.

"There is a gap of a few centimeters under that door, wide enough for a pair of pants folded correctly to slide under it—but not quite wide enough for the belt and the buckle. We knot the pants below the knees; fill the legs with rolls of toilet paper soaked with vodka. We open the door, and then close it over the pants after setting the pants on fire. Oleyenka's men won't be able to remove the burning pants because the belt won't slip under the door. In the meantime, the vodka-soaked pants burn! The door gets hot! And even if they manage to put the fire out, the door will retain the heat for a few minutes, long enough for us to get out through your tunnel.”

Anatoly looked at him in amazement. "Brilliant!”

Within seconds, everyone was in motion. Oleyenka's pants were removed and knotted below the knees as Victor had prescribed. One of the men came in from the men's room with an armful of toilet paper rolls, and they stuffed the rolls into the pant legs and tied-off bottoms. Victor held them at arm's length. "Okay, soak it with Vodka,” he said.

All three men emptied the vodka bottles onto the garment and the alcohol-saturated the toilet paper. "What now?” Anatoly asked.

"We light it and open the door. They are probably already trying to plant the explosives. I want two men with automatic weapons standing full center of that door. Doc, you stand to the side, and as soon as this door is opened, on my nod, you lob out a grenade. You two, empty your clips when the door opens, and I'll handle the door and the pants. Hurry, before they blow it!” he commanded.

Anatoly handed the doctor a fragment grenade. The doctor took it carefully and assumed his position next to the door. Anatoly and his guard checked their weapons then stood back from the door two meters. Victor carefully laid the pants out on the floor and pulled out his lighter and a cigar.

Lighting his cigar first, and taking a deep drag on it, he said, "I am going to set these pants on fire now—doc, open the door wide when I do! Anatoly, if anyone is there when this door opens, I expect you to kill them! Doc, you hold that grenade until I give you the nod, and then toss it. As soon as the doc tosses the grenade, we close the door again over the burning pants. Everyone better pray that this door closes tightly and latches completely! Any questions?"

No one said anything. Victor took another drag on his cigar and tossed it to the floor. He looked each man in the eye in turn, relit the lighter, and touched it to the alcohol-soaked garment. A bluish-yellow flame swept over the pants, and within seconds, it was completely engulfed with flames. Acting as a huge candlewick, it burned fiercely. He went to the door armed with a Glock automatic tucked in his waistband, and once again looked everyone in the eye. The doc trembled as he held his grenade and pressed himself against the concrete wall near the door. He nodded that he was ready. Anatoly and his man raised their automatics and adjusted their footing. They both nodded. The doc pulled the latch, swung the door open wide, and Victor shouted, "Now!"

Three of Oleyenka's Spetsnaz team were there kneeling at the door—planting the explosives! They were taken by surprise when the door opened so suddenly! Two were setting the charges, and the third was there to cover them. When the door swung open wide, they all looked up fearfully. The soldier there to guard them had been so intent on watching what the demolition team was doing that he was a split second too late to raise his own weapon! Anatoly and his man riddled him with bullets—the force of their fire pushing him back against the far wall of the corridor! His own automatic sprayed the corridor with bullets but found no mark! He slumped there against the wall, his weapon falling idle by his side.

Anatoly ran to the door, looked once to the right and then to the left and opened fire. Most of the smoke had been cleared from the hallways by the ventilation system by then. Oleyenka's men were not far away—standing back only far enough to be safe from the blast of the explosion when it went off. Both explosives experts were now scrambling down the hallway with their charges still in their hands. Anatoly took aim and fired, then ducked back into the control room as bullets were fired back.

Victor shouted, "Doc, the grenade!"

Victor pushed Anatoly and his men to the side and inspected the doorframe quickly, making sure it was clear of charges. He gave the nod to the doctor, who twisted around and lobbed the fragment grenade into the hallway.

Victor grabbed the burning garment from the floor, as one would strip a bed. He laid it out flat in the corridor. Closing the door to the control room carefully over the garment—he attempted to close the door evenly over it! But, the pants wrinkled, and doubled up, fouling the process. Everyone knew the grenade would go off eminently, and seeing the difficulties that Victor was having closing the fireproof door, they all lunged at it at the same time. With the weight of all of them against it, the stuck door grudgingly gave way and finally closed.

Victor bolted it a half second before the grenade went off. There was mayhem out in the hallway. Oleyenka's Spetsnaz team had taken heavy casualties and was regrouping further down the hallway. All the while the candlewick pants burned under the door, heating it up to well over 200°C.

"Good job men," Victor declared. "Now, let's get the hell out of here!"

"This way," Anatoly shouted as he made his way to the far control console. "Give me a hand here men," he grunted, as he strained against the weight of the unit. Victor went over to help the others, but as soon as he strained against the dead weight, he felt his stitches tearing open in his shoulder and a fresh wave of pain washed over him.

"Mr. Zubkov," the doctor cautioned him. "The morphine is wearing off, and you are soon to feel the full effects of the knife wound! I must caution you about straining yourself. Please, pick those pills up from the floor and take one. They will not make you drowsy. We can take care of this."

Victor swallowed his pride and stooped over to gather up a handful of codeine pills. He swallowed one as the men managed to pull the control console away from the wall to reveal a steel trapdoor underneath. Anatoly flung the door open and reached down, feeling for the light switch. "It leads to the motor pool and room B5," he said.

"Surely Oleyenka's men know about this tunnel," Victor replied.

"We didn't tell them about the underground tunnels. Oleyenka's men were too busy welding all the outside entrances shut, and I felt it prudent to keep a few avenues of retreat secret—as our own way out! So we hid them, as we did this one here! There is only one door accessible to the outside, the one you came in by the helipads. If I can get to that one door and secure it from the outside, they will be trapped inside here until they can blast their way out. By that time, you will be in the mines."

"What's your plan, Anatoly?"

"You and the doctor go with my man Peter, to the motor pool. He knows the way. A few hundred meters down the road from the front gate there is a concrete building that protects the ventilator shaft for the mines below. There will be an access door that leads to a steel ladder within it. You will have to climb down many meters, but you will eventually end up in the mineshaft tunnel. When you find the main corridor, you will know it. It is many soccer fields wide and very tall. They have heavy transport equipment down there to move the rock to the surface. Flag down one of the haulers and use his vehicle to get topside. I'll be right behind you, but don't wait for me! If I am delayed, I'll meet you at the quarry. I used to work in those mines, so I know my way around them pretty well, as does Peter here. I will go to the B5 staging area where the rest of the men are, and we will try to keep Pyotr's men in this facility until you can make your escape. I must go now to try to contain Oleyenka's men. Hopefully, you will have your twenty-minute head start."

"Here, take these," Victor said, and he handed Anatoly fresh ammunition clips and another fragment grenade. "Good luck, comrade."

Anatoly nodded. *"Tebya Tosha!"* (you too!).

Chapter 29

Roberta and Kowalski had each just put two hellfire missiles into the motor pool, effectively leveling it. They were now looking for a farmhouse that was just off the base, somewhere to the east. Despite the daylight, the blizzard had intensified even more, and made it difficult to see even a few hundred meters ahead of them. They flew in a zigzag pattern until they spotted the shape of a small farmhouse. Smoke curled up from the chimney, and so they assumed that their quarry was still there, especially considering the three black Audi's parked out front.

"Kowalski," Roberta radioed. "I have a visual."

"Swing wide and go downwind so they won't hear us coming. We'll regroup two clicks further east."

Despite the near whiteout conditions, the two Seahawks landed without incident. They had radioed the location of the farmhouse, and where they would be waiting, to Nick. As the rotors wound down, the hornet buzz of two-cycle engines could be heard in the distance, and a moment later, five snowmobiles appeared, approaching at high speed. They throttled down and closed in on the choppers quickly. Nick and the four Russian locals dismounted and gratefully got into the two choppers and out of the blizzard.

"Kowalski, I am going to take these men back to the farmhouse by snowmobile and secure it. I need to know who we are up against—so we can't kill them all! You, and if need be, Roberta, will support us from the air. Once we have that farmhouse secure, we regroup. Any questions?"

Within minutes, everyone scrambled, and the two Sea Hawks started spinning rotors once again.

Timmons and Ulyana, along with a team of locals, were at the Alrosa diamond mine ten kilometers from Laboratory 173. They were going to open the backdoor to the base. They had hopped onto a mammoth earthmover that was heading back into the mines for another load of rock. The mines were enormous. Already, they had ridden two kilometers in the empty back of the huge earthmover, and it seemed that there was no end to the myriad of tunnels yet in sight. The huge truck finally came to a stop, and they all piled out. Ulyana's man paid the driver with Russian currency, and waved him off.

"This way," he said in Russian, leading the way.

"Jesus, Ulyana," Timmons exclaimed. "This place is incredible!"

"Yes," she replied. "Many of these mines have been in operation for decades. The original gems of the Czars came from this region, but this mine is a relatively new one, developed in the late 1940s. The rubies and diamonds pulled out of here paid for the huge steel mills in the west, the shipyards, and the railroads, and nearly everything else. They are perfectly located in the most extreme region in Siberia, and even the rock is ideal here for mining. This whole area is made up of solid granite! Once they blast the tunnel out, they don't even need to shore anything up! That is why everything is so cavernous. It allows for heavy equipment to move about freely. The biggest issues down here are ventilation and pockets of gas. Over the years, the mines have grown in both size and complexity. During the height of the Cold War, living quarters were constructed down here for many key government officials and their families in the event of a nuclear first strike from America. Since then, the quarters have been turned over to the workers, who labor around the clock. The mines never shut down, and the living quarters constitute a hidden city, completely invisible from above."

"It will become very narrow from this point on," the guide called out over his shoulder as he turned on his lantern, and then ducked magically into a black hole. Timmons stood back in awe as he watched one after another of the assault team vanish from sight. The narrow unlit tunnel was hidden completely, behind a large boulder, and unless one knew it was there, it could not be seen from the main tunnel. Following Ulyana into the dark space, Timmons was immediately overwhelmed with claustrophobia. The guide up ahead carried a lantern, but it could be barely seen over the heads and shoulders of the people in front of him. Behind him was complete darkness.

"Put your hand on my shoulder," Ulyana instructed him. "Only the guide can see where we are going now." She in turn found the shoulder of the man in front her, and he the man in front of him, until they were all linked to the person ahead. Only the first two people could see anything at all. After climbing upward for several minutes, they emerged into a ten-by-ten meter room carved out of the granite. Here they could at least see one another.

Timmons was first to caution everyone. "Someone has been here recently." He pointed at a pile of cigarette butts ground into the dirt floor. He stooped, picked one up and smelled it. "It's fresh. I don't like it. Who was just here?" Grabbing the lantern, he examined the tracks left in the dirt. "These are all from combat boots! Every track here has clean new markings on them. A worker's boots would be worn nearly smooth, and these aren't!"

One of the men shouted something that Timmons couldn't understand because it was in Russian. "What is it Ulyana," Timmons asked?

"There is a body," she replied, and they both went to take a look. The dead man had had his throat cut and was unceremoniously stuffed into a crevice in the rock wall. Timmons ordered the body to be removed and searched. The search revealed the young man to be Sasha Uchenko. No other information could be gleaned from the corpse.

"It's obvious that Mayakovsky has been here already Ulyana," Timmons muttered.

"Then we must move quickly," Ulyana ordered.

"Where does this shaft lead to?" Timmons asked.

"To the fuel room under the helipads," Ulyana replied. "From there we take another tunnel that leads up into the lower levels of Laboratory 173. No one knows about this entrance. This shaft and tunnel were Alexander Mayakovsky's way to get the *Semya* boards out undetected. But, it wasn't completed until just recently."

"Could it be that Alexander has already been here and gotten away?" Timmons asked.

Ulyana nodded. "That's why Victor Zubkov didn't get out of here last night when he could have. His own people must have betrayed him by convincing him the weather was too severe, which means someone else has their own plans. We need to get topside and help secure the facility."

Timmons nodded. "Right. We must open the door for Nick's team. If Victor Zubkov or someone else has already fled with the technology, so be it. I take it you know where the laboratory is located and where all the data is stored?"

"That's why I am here," answered Ulyana unemotionally, though in truth her heart was pounding! Her Uncle may already be dead!

One of the Russians tapped Timmons on the shoulder, and Timmons turned to him. "I don't like it sir," he said under his breath in Russian. Ulyana had to translate the words for him. The three of them moved off to the side to talk without the others hearing the conversation. In Russian he continued. "I don't like it! If we go up this shaft, we come out topside one by one. Who is to say that they aren't up there waiting for us to do just that? We already have one dead body. We would be sitting ducks, sir."

Ulyana translated for him.

"He makes a good point," Timmons said to her. "I'll go up and clear the room myself. You stand back and wait for my signal."

"If the radios don't work down here, how will you contact us?" she asked.

"They'll work between us—we just can't transmit outside the mine. If you don't hear from me in five minutes, blow the tunnel, get back to the helicopter, and rejoin the others."

"But Timmons, I can't fly it," she protested.

"Then hope there is no one waiting up there," he replied. "I am going up!"

Victor Zubkov followed Anatoly's man down the narrow underground corridor that led to the motor pool, and the doctor followed them both. Anatoly had raced ahead of them all, and by the time they reached the end of the corridor, he had already cleared the charred debris away from the entrance/exit. The motor pool had been gutted by fire when the fuel tanks blew. What remained of the building only stood because it was made mostly of concrete and steel. Oleyenka's men had already retreated back to the base, so there was no opposition.

"*Bistro* (quickly)," Peter said. "I hear a helicopter approaching, and it is still full daylight. We must make it to the airshaft unseen. It is colder than a bitch out here, but if we move quickly, the airshaft is actually warm from the mines down below. Can you make it, Mr. Zubkov?"

"I can make it Peter," Zubkov replied.

"I can take your package for you, Mr. Zubkov."

"It's okay, Peter. I can handle my bag and still carry a gun."

Peter shrugged. "Okay then, let me plant this charge to close this escape route, and then we go this way." He pointed. "We can follow the stone wall to the front gate without being seen and avoid the mine field." Peter planted the explosives, set the timer, and returned to the group. "The front gate will be locked," he told Victor. "But I have the keys. Oleyenka's men are probably guarding it, so we may have to shoot our way out. The airshaft is only a few hundred meters down the road on the opposite side. It too will be locked, but because it is warm in there, it is a favorite place for the guards to meet women who work in the mines below for a little female companionship. The key is hidden behind a loose stone to the right of the door, about shoulder height. Once inside, you will see the spiral staircase that will take you down into the main mine below. Earthmovers come by at regular intervals; just flag one down. For a few rubles, they will take you to the surface. Any questions?"

Anatoly had made it to the B5 staging area, a subterranean weapons and munitions storage room located on the north side of Laboratory 173, where the remainder of his men had regrouped and were waiting for orders. B5 was a logical place to regroup if things went badly for there they had everything they needed to defend themselves. There was also a freight elevator to the surface, and stairs that led to the outside—to the helipad maintenance building outside. Before Oleyenka's men had arrived to lock the place down, Anatoly had the corridor leading to it concealed behind a steel locker. He had intentionally kept its location secret—just in case! Fortunately, Pyotr and his men did not have drawings of the facility, or it would have been obvious what he was concealing from them. As he approached the end of the corridor, he was spotted by one of his own men, who had taken up a position in a side doorway to guard the entrance. Anatoly acknowledged him by clapping him on the shoulder as he rushed past to where the rest of his men were waiting.

"Where are Oleyenka's men?" one man asked.

"I believe they are still at the control center," Anatoly replied. "Just then an explosion was heard. "They are in the control center now, and it won't take them long to figure out that the tunnel leads to the motor pool, and to here. Peter will have it rigged with explosives by now, but we need to cover it long enough for Victor to escape." A second explosion was heard, confirming that Peter had indeed closed the exit to the motor pool. Anatoly went on, "He is going to the mine airshaft—and will escape through the mines below. We need to hold the remainder of Oleyenka's men in here until Victor is clear. Are any workers still here?"

"*Nyet*," one of them replied. "When the shooting began, they all fled like mice."

"Good! That makes our job easier. I want half your men to gear up and make sure that motor pool exit is closed! The other half will come with me. We need to block the helipad exit. If we can hold them off for an hour or so, our job is done here! Have your men regroup at the airshaft in one hour."

Still in the mine, Timmons started up the steel ladder to gain access to the facility. It was impossible to climb and hold a weapon at the same time, and so he shouldered his rifle before he started up the narrow shaft. When he reached the top of the ladder many rungs later, he struggled to move the false bottom of the grating aside. He stopped to listen before sticking his head up. He could still hear small-arms fire in the distance, but he heard nothing else other than the hum of machinery. Cautiously, he eased his head above the concrete floor, and looked around. The tunnel came out behind a huge fuel storage tank in a small area between the tank and the outer concrete wall. It was well concealed, which was good, but it also meant that he too could not see what might be on the other side. He quietly eased himself out of the shaft, un-shouldered his weapon and made it ready. Silently, he made his way around the storage tank while the others waited for his signal.

He peeked around the corner of the fuel tank. The room appeared to be unguarded. He listened for a moment more and heard nothing! Finally, he stepped out from behind the fuel tank for a better look. The door to the fuel storage room was made of heavy steel—made to be fireproof, and it appeared to be sealed. He made his way to it. Finding a mop nearby, he slid it through the wheel locking mechanism, ensuring that no one could enter unexpectedly from the outside, and then he made sure the room was clear. He returned to the shaft and radioed Ulyana. "All clear. You can come up now."

As Nick and the others sped off on the snowmobiles, Roberta got on the COM with Kowalski. "Why did he just do that?"

"He's crazy, Roberta," Kowalski replied smiling.

"How long have you known him, Kowalski?"

"Years, Roberta. Years," he answered her. "We go back a long way. He likes it up close."

"What do you mean?"

"Combat," Kowalski answered. "He likes it one-on-one."

"Sorry," she said. "But you need to explain that to me since it is obvious he can't go one-on-one with anyone, especially not with a woman! At least not from my experience!"

Kowalski laughed, knowing how Nick was with women. "He's extremely fast, Roberta," Kowalski tried to explain to her. "Why do you think I dropped my weapon when Nick went crazy back at the helicopter when he forced a flame-out? I've never met anyone as fast as Nick is. You measure reaction time in fractions of seconds for most people, but with Nick, it is milliseconds! Put him in close to anyone, and he'll get the better of him or her, if that's what he wants. He also has something like 20/10 vision. He can see something twenty feet away that you and I can only see at ten feet away. His vision, in concert with his incredible speed is a hard combination to beat."

"If he gets killed, which seems a damned good possibility—going in the way he is, then the mission fails! Why didn't he get into a chopper and play it safe?"

"I told you already, Roberta." Kowalski muttered wondering the same thing. "He's nuts! He'll be all right though! Somehow, he always comes out of these things more or less unscathed."

"If he is so good, why did your men storm the Governor's house back in Olympia?"

"Our orders from Nick were to protect you, not him!" he replied honestly. "Roberta, Nikki has his reasons for holding back, but trust me when I say I think he is infatuated with you!"

"Why do you say that, Kowalski?"

"Because I've seen the look in his eyes when he is around you! He can't keep his eyes off you."

"I haven't noticed that Kowalski," she replied.

"I told you, Roberta, Nikki is very quick! Every time you look at him, he turns away before you notice."

Roberta's heart raced. "Are you sure, Kowalski?"

"It's time for me to get in the air. They'll be on their approach by now. Stay put like Nick told you to, and watch for bogies coming in. If you go down, the mission is over too!"

Chapter 30

Despite the blizzard conditions, Nick and his comrades were speeding toward the farmhouse at full throttle. His intentions were to take out ground transportation and overwhelm them by surprise. They were approaching from downwind in the hopes that he and his men wouldn't be noticed until it was too late! Hoping that the sound of the two-cycle engines approaching were being carried away in the opposite direction from the farmhouse by the blizzard winds. As he caught sight of the farmhouse, he throttled back and stopped. It was impossible to know if they had been spotted or not! But, there seemed to be no panic on the part of those inside. Dismounting the machine, he motioned for the others to stay down. He then jogged forward using what little cover there was to avoid detection. When he was as close as he dared to venture, he dropped in the snow to his stomach and pulled out a pair of binoculars. The cottage was a small one-floor structure, but the dormer windows in the attic—that probably doubled as a small bedroom upstairs, caught his attention. As he suspected, there was a lookout posted there. He spotted three more men at the table in the kitchen. Panning the glasses side to side, he picked up motion toward the back of the house. There he spotted a soldier heading for the outhouse. Wary of the sentinel posted in the attic, Nick stayed low as he circled the structure. He noted that two more men where on the back porch smoking cigarettes. He radioed his instructions to his men.

The group split up and circled the farmhouse in different directions for better flanking positions. Nick was on the blind side of the cottage, the side without any windows. Leaving his weapon behind, he sprinted the remaining distance to the house and pressed up against the wall. He cautiously made his way to the back corner and peeked around it. There was a wood stack out back, midway between the back porch and the outhouse. Staying low, he sprinted to it and threw himself behind the wood. Peeking around the pile of firewood, he noticed that the two soldiers had finished their smokes, and had turned their backs to him to go back inside. Nick got back on his feet again and sprinted toward the outhouse. Without pausing, he flung the door open, surprising the soldier who was already in a compromising situation, and rendered him unconscious. Nick pulled off his parka and put the soldier's on. He then grabbed his cap and his automatic rifle. Checking the weapon's state of readiness, he radioed Kowalski.

"I can use that distraction now!"

Kowalski had been waiting for the go-ahead, and he pitched the copter forward and accelerated toward the cottage. As soon as he had a visual on his target, the sentinel in the dormer window spotted him! But it didn't matter! Kowalski's objective was to destroy their ground transportation, and he already had a lock on the parked Mercedes. He fired his missiles, the signal for the rest of the team to attack! As the vehicles exploded into fireballs, the snowmobiles rushed toward the cottage. Nick bolted at full speed for the cottage. None of the soldiers paid any attention to him when he first burst through the back door, assuming he was one of their own! Except for the one Nick didn't see behind the door. Nick's hawk-like vision picked up motion behind him from the reflection off a glass-paneled picture on the far wall, and he threw himself into a somersault and came up firing his weapon, riddling the soldier with bullets. The remaining soldiers began to swing their weapons in his direction. Nick swept the room with automatic rifle fire, aiming low, as he needed to know who sent these men, and why—and dead men don't talk! The outside windows shattered from automatic weapons fire from his own men on the outside! Everyone, including Nick, threw themselves to the floor. Nick landed a few feet from one soldier intent on getting his pistol out. Nick abandoned his automatic rifle, pulled out a knife, and tossed it backhanded. The blade planted itself in the soldier's throat.

Kowalski banked the chopper for better position, and at the same time a Spetsnaz soldier launched a shoulder-fired missile at him from the farmhouse. Kowalski cursed and banked, going high. He was too close for effective countermeasures, but he launched them anyway. The flares pulled the missile away, but not far enough. The explosion caused massive damage to his rudder. Struggling to maintain control, he got on the radio. "Roberta, I took a hit and I am going down. Get in here!"

Roberta had been monitoring everything that was going on, and she shouted, "I am on the way!" She pulled up on her collective, flying recklessly low and fast! She was more concerned about her men—her team, than herself.

Kowalski continued to struggle with the controls of his bird as he watched another man raise a shoulder-fired missile launcher to his shoulder. "I'm going to frag your ass, soldier!" he muttered aloud, and he pulled the trigger to his Gatling gun, ripping the Russian in two. The Sea Hawk was in bad shape, and was dropping fast. Kowalski realized it was no use. Just before he crashed, he managed to get one more missile off. The missile went through the front door of the farmhouse and out the back. The outhouse was obliterated into toothpicks. A moment later, he crashed.

Half of the ten-man Spetsnaz team were now down or disabled, and the ones remaining went for defensive positions. The soldiers dove for cover and started firing.

A round passed through Nick's left shoulder as another of his men was cut down with machinegun fire! Nick watched as his snowmobile burst into flames. Not knowing that Kowalski was down, Nick gritted his teeth, from the pain of the bullet wound and tried to stand. Roberta's helicopter appeared over the trees tops, her Gatling guns spewing out thousands of rounds. She was so low, and moving so fast, that nobody could take aim at her.

Her guns churned up the snow in front of her as she came in hot! The remaining soldier, who was positioned in the attic with another shoulder-fired missile, was torn to pieces from her lead!

Of the three remaining Spetsnaz team members, the commander and one soldier, decided to surrender when Nick's remaining men swarmed in and secured the site. Taking some altitude, Roberta surveyed what had happened on the ground. It appeared that the farmhouse was secure. Circling around again, she observed the remains of Kowalski's Sikorsky Sea Hawk on the ground, and it didn't look good. She radioed Nick, "I see Kowalski's bird—it doesn't look good! Is everything secure?"

"We have it under control here, Roberta. Thanks! Go see about Kowalski and I'll be there shortly."

The bird was lying on its side with the rotors sheared off! The cockpit door was open. Not far away was a form in the snow. Realizing it must be Kowalski—she pitched her chopper over and brought it down next to the wrecked aircraft and jumped to the ground! She ran over to him expecting the worse.

"Kowalski!" she shouted as she approached him.

"Kowalski, are you alive?"

He raised his head from the snow and spat out blood. "Yeah, I think so, but I may have a broken wrist!"

When Roberta reached him, she rolled him over in the snow. He moaned. "Jeeze, Roberta. I could have had a broken neck! Do you have to be so damned rough?"

"Broken neck, my ass!" She laughed. "You are playing dead—you old possum!"

"No, no. I just thought I'd lay here awhile, hoping for a beautiful maiden to happen along any minute, and awaken me from my slumber with a kiss!" And he puckered up with a playful smooch.

"Get up, Kowalski!" She laughed. "Are you hurt?"

"A little stiff, and my wrist is banged up for sure! But, other than that I'm OK! Wow, what a rush!" he said.

Nick raced over on his snowmobile. "Is he okay?"

"He'll live! Jesus, Nikki! You've been shot!" Roberta exclaimed.

"Yeah, and I lost a good man too," he replied. "It would have been much worse if you two hadn't been here. These guys are Russian Federation, more specifically, *Spetsnaz*—Special Forces! We can expect company soon."

"We've been jamming the entire time Nick," Kowalski replied. "They couldn't have gotten a signal out."

"They were ready to move when we broke communications on them, and that in itself will bring more of them in. We have three prisoners, but they are not talking, which means to me that they expect the cavalry to arrive any minute!"

Roberta said emphatically, "If you are right Nikki, I need to get in the air at once. But first, let me see your shoulder. My mother was a nurse, so I have some training in things like this."

"It is nothing—the bullet passed clean through," Nick said.

"You won't be able to fight if I don't take care of it now! Get over to the chopper," she demanded.

Nick did as he was told, and Roberta got out the first aid kit. She instructed him to remove his outer garments to expose his shoulder. Then she doused the wound with antiseptic and patted it dry. She stuck him with a morphine needle and stitched him up quickly, dressing the wound hastily. Handing him a bottle of antibiotics, she demanded that he take one.

"These are for pain!" she told him as she handed him a codeine pill and the bottle. "You are not feeling it now only because you are still in shock. But soon you will! Take them as needed," she insisted as she handed him the bottle.

"Uh-oh," Kowalski yelled out. "We have bogies coming in—three of them!" He was watching the monitors on the instrument panel when the warning lights lit up.

Nick shoved his arm back into his outer gear and stuffed the pills into a pocket on his parka.

"Go, go, go!" he implored them. "The men and I will head for the trees. Quickly, get in the air Roberta and try to outrun them!"

"Hold on a minute Nick," Kowalski shouted.

"What is it?" replied Nick.

"She is nearly out of ammo! She has a few missiles left, but her gun is out. We have three bogies coming in, and we need to give her a full complement of weapons for her to stand a chance against them!"

Nick glared at him, not even wanting her to go up in the first place! But, from the look of Kowalski's swollen wrist, he wasn't in any condition to take her place.

"Get your men over to my bird and let's transfer the ammo from it to her helicopter. We have only minutes at best," shouted Kowalski.

"Right!" Nick yelled, and he got on his radio to bark out orders.

His men ran to the downed chopper and peeled open the access panels to the munitions compartments. Fortunately, the chopper was on its side, making everything easily accessible. Ammo for the Gatling gun weighed a ton, but they managed to drop a canister on the back of one of the snowmobiles and transport it over to Roberta's machine.

"Lift off Roberta. We need access to your magazine compartment from underneath," Kowalski commanded into the COM. Roberta pulled up and hovered. "Too high!" Kowalski shouted. "Come down four feet."

Roberta tried her best to comply, but even though the stiff Siberian winds had died down substantially, it was a difficult task. Kowalski opened the ammo panel from below with his good hand. He dropped the nearly spent canister to the ground and kicked it off to one side. It took all the men to lift the fresh canister into place while Nick reloaded the weapon and chambered a round for her. Holding altitude of only a few feet off the ground was difficult for any pilot, but Roberta did it well.

As soon as the gun was reloaded, Kowalski yelled,

"Bring over the sidewinders now!"

Roberta was still hovering when she got the first visuals of the incoming bogies. "Kowalski!" she shouted over the COM. "There they are! Let's go!"

Two snowmobiles darted over from the downed chopper, each bringing a missile.

"Rotate your missiles, Roberta!" Kowalski commanded.

Roberta cycled her missiles instinctively, and he directed the men on how to load one. "Again," he said, and she did.

"Go, Roberta! You are fully armed now! Good luck!"

The three Russian made MI-40s came in high, and the pilots wasted no time, launching missiles as soon as they had a visual on Roberta's Sikorsky. "Don't worry about it babe," Kowalski yelled over the COM. "I'll take care of those missiles. You pull up high now, and with everything you got!"

Roberta did as she was told, pulling up as hard as she could on her collective and kicking the turbines into boost. The Sea Hawk shot upward, and Kowalski and Nick sped off on the snowmobile. Kowalski pushed a remote detonator button, and the downed Sea Hawk exploded into a fireball just as they cleared the area. All six missiles locked onto the heat signature generated from the blast and obliterated the remnants of the crippled craft.

"Now, go get them, Roberta!" Kowalski shouted over his COM. "You won't get another chance!"

Roberta's training took over. She pitched her machine left and toward the ground, picking up airspeed as she swung the craft around. The three

MI-40s sped past, and she locked onto the one in the middle and released a hellfire missile. She didn't bother to track it, because even if it hit its mark, there would be two more left in the air. Instead, she ran for the only cover there was, the birch forest not far away. Topping the trees, and then dropping to within a few feet of the snow-covered ground, she worked her way to the south, found a little nook, and waited for the helicopters to come back around. As she expected, the two helicopters came around the birch trees from opposite directions. Being invisible to radar gave her a chance! Neither one of the Russian pilots saw her hovering there until after they had passed her.

She pitched her machine forward, got on the tail of the first chopper, and opened fire with her Gatling guns, ripping it in two. She then swept wide over a frozen field and came back around as quickly as she could. She attained a lock onto the last chopper and fired another two missiles. This time she watched the missile track its target, and at the last moment, her adversary went high and dropped flares. Both missiles exploded harmlessly in the birch forest beyond.

"Kowalski," she shouted over the COM. "Did I get the first chopper?"

"That's affirmative, Roberta. Where are you?"

"On the other side of the birch forest. I got another one on this side, but the third one evaded my missiles and I lost him."

"Get out of there, Roberta!" Kowalski shouted over the COM. "He can't see you on radar and you can out run a Mi-40."

Just then, the Russian-made helicopter reappeared from behind a thicket of trees. It was coming directly at her while launching multiple missiles. "Too late! He found me again!" she shouted back.

Roberta reacted instinctively, but it was as if she were moving in slow motion. She could clearly see her opposition and the four missiles coming right at her. Her finger hit the button to drop flares, and she pulled up and to the starboard. She watched as a second bank of missiles was launched from the enemy helicopter, and she went higher, releasing more flares and pitching to port. She knew that, if she wasn't aggressive enough, she was going to die! She pushed the stick forward and raced directly at the Mi-40 with her Gatling gun blazing. Everything was as if in a dream—in slow motion! She watched the first bank of missiles pass by under her harmlessly, chasing a heat signature that wasn't there, and her throat tightened as the second bank of missiles passed over her doing the same! The Russian missiles couldn't get a lock on her helicopter because of the radar absorbing skin, and the exhaust diffusers on the Sea Hawk turbines—so by the time they armed themselves, after they flew past her, they had no target!

In slow motion, she watched her tracers find their way to their mark as she relentlessly squeezed the trigger. It was almost as if she could see the look of horror on the face of the Russian pilot as the anti-tank rounds ripped apart his rudder and tore through his cabin. She fired her last two missiles at a range that was too close for any evasive maneuvers, and rolled her chopper hard to port and pulled up. The Mi-60 helicopter blew apart, throwing shrapnel everywhere. She had gone just high enough to evade the flying pieces of twisted metal hurtling in all directions. As her heart palpitated wildly, she took a deep breath.

"My God Kowalski," she exclaimed breathlessly. "I think I got them all, and I feel like I'm going to throw up!"

"We are one click away Roberta, head back to the base and bring it home."

"Roger that," she answered.

Chapter 31

Concealed behind overgrown shrubbery that had taken over the inner perimeter of the facility after years of neglect due to massive budget cuts, Victor Zubkov, Peter, and the doc made their way slowly toward the front gate. To their surprise, the guards were nowhere in sight. Approaching the guardhouse cautiously, it became quickly apparent that ground forces had already disabled them, both of whom were Anatoly's men. They were both on the floor with their legs and wrists bound with heavy nylon ties. Peter knew them both by first names. As he cut their restraints, he asked, "What happen?"

"A delivery truck approached and we turned it away, as we were instructed to," one replied. "Before we knew it, we were jumped."

"Were they Oleyenka's men?" Peter asked.

"*Nyet.* They were equipped with American-made weapons! We haven't seen any of Oleyenka's men since early this morning."

"Oleyenka's men are Spetsnaz! And they are trying to stop Victor from leaving with the *Semya* boards! Most of the remaining men are holed up in B5 Sector. Anatoly is trying to get to them now. We are going to escape through the mines. Get your weapons and come with us," Peter ordered.

"You said remaining men?" the second man spoke up. "We have lost comrades?"

Peter nodded. "Oleyenka's men were about to slit all our throats when Victor warned us about the coup! Anatoly got the word out, but not in time to save everyone. Others got killed in firefights. Come with us or cover our backs."

"We will go with you to the airshaft, and there we will make sure that no one follows you," the first guard replied. "Anatoly may need us here, and so we will return to our posts when you are safely away."

"As you wish. Anatoly will be along shortly," Peter assured them.

The men gathered their gear and joined Peter, Victor, and the doctor out in the cold and snow, making their way as quickly as possible to the stone air ventilator building across the way. They stopped short when they caught sight of the building and noticed that the door latch had been blown off.

Back at Laboratory 173, Nick carefully reached for the door handle to the outer door of the facility, the same door he had seen Victor come out of earlier. Kowalski and the others took positions to offer cover fire if necessary. The latch turned freely, and Nick pulled the door open wide while stepping behind it for cover. Kowalski was through the door first, throwing himself to the floor, and looking for any sign of resistance, but the corridor was clear! Nick ran past him and took up a position against the far wall at another intersecting corridor. He angled a collapsible mirror around the corner of the corridor. Again the hallway was clear."

"Feels like a trap Nick," Kowalski muttered.

Nick nodded. He felt the same way! "Something is wrong, boys. Timmons and Ulyana should have been here by now." Over his headset, he ordered Roberta to stand by for an immediate evacuation on his signal. Then he heard more small-arms fire coming from outside the building, and he was about to retreat when the outer door shut behind him. He heard the sound of diesels and a loud clunk on the other side as he raced for the door. He pushed on the door, and it was apparent that it was jammed shut.

Anatoly shut down the engine of the tanker tractor, set the parking brake, and joined the rest of his men that he had rounded up. He had effectively blocked the only remaining exit to the facility by parking the heavy vehicle up against the door. "Let's go," he shouted to his men. "It sounds like Victor is in trouble!" he yelled, as more shots were fired not far away.

"What about the Americans?" one man asked.

"We have time for that later! But first we must help Victor. Come!"

They found Victor and the others waiting for them inside the ventilator shaft. "What happened?" Anatoly queried.

"General Krushensky and Alexander Mayakovsky is what happened!" replied Victor bitterly. "They were waiting for us, and they got away with the *Semya* boards! I am sorry about your men, Anatoly," he muttered remorsefully looking around at the dead bodies. Their families will be well taken care of—you have my word on it! What about the Americans?"

"At the moment, they are trapped inside the facility along with Oleyenka's men."

"Oleyenka's men were Krushensky's men," Victor muttered. They had another way out of this place—they left their own chopper behind! Come, let's go say 'hello' to the Americans!"

"But Victor, they are heavily armed. It would be insane!"

"The Americans will need my help if they want the *Semya* boards back," Victor replied dryly. "And they have no reason to be here if the boards are gone—which they are!"

Nick and the others had used their collective strength against the jammed door, but to no avail. They were about to give up when someone pounded on it from the outside.

"Americans, we will unblock this door. Don't shoot!" yelled out Victor.

"Who are you?" Nick shouted back.

"This is Victor Zubkov, and I own the place! General Krushensky has already seized the *Semya* boards, and there is nothing here now for us to fight over. All my men are civilians, and they have no desire to engage you."

Nick got on the radio. "Roberta, we have a situation here. Timmons' team never showed up, and Zubkov's men have got our exit blocked somehow—we're trapped in here! They are saying that the *Semya* boards have already been taken. Approach with caution, but do not fire unless fired upon. Is that clear?"

"Got it Nick," she replied.

"Zubkov," Nick shouted. "I have ground and air forces on the way, but I have ordered them not to shoot. I suggest that you unblock this door and have your men stand down."

A large diesel engine was heard starting up, and moments later, the door moved. Victor Zubkov stood there calmly when it opened.

"*Dratsvutchye* (Good Health), comrades! I am Victor Zubkov."

Nick cautiously approached him, his weapon pointed to the ground. "*Tebya tosha* (you too)," Nick replied.

"And you are?" Victor asked.

"Nicholas Dimeitry Petrovisky," Nick replied.

"Your Russian is perfect, Nicholas. It is unusual for an American to speak Russian so fluently. Who taught you?"

"My mother," Nick replied. "C'mon men, I think this mission is over!"

"Wait! I know you, Nicholas Dimeitry Petrovisky!" Victor exclaimed, approaching him almost a little too quickly.

Nick raised his weapon, and Victor stopped moving forward, but he continued.

"Yes Nicholas, I see now who you are. You are my Tatyana's long-lost young lover, and the father of my beloved Natasha. I have waited many years for our meeting. You have aged well, my friend."

"You are not my friend Zubkov! But, nevertheless, how are Tatyana and Natasha?" Nick replied.

"Natasha is perfect, a true Russian jewel!" Victor smiled proudly. "She is so brilliant, charming, talented, and beautiful that it would take your breath away!" he said proudly. "And Tatyana is as beautiful as ever! I believe she is in love with my former closest associate, Alexander Mayakovsky."

Nick just stared at Victor, not knowing what to say to him. Was he crazy? Or was everything Nick had been told about him a lie?

"And let me ask you this Victor—does it not bother you that both Alexander and I are in love with your wife?"

Victor lowered his head and nodded sadly, knowing the truth.

"There is much you don't understand about me, my friend. Please Nicholas," Victor implored him. "Lower your weapon! Over the years, I wondered if I would ever meet the father of my daughter. You are her biological father, I know! But, she was raised under my roof, and as far as she knows, I am her father—and I love her as if she were my own nevertheless! I wondered if we would ever meet one day, and under what circumstances. There was a time when I would have killed you on sight! Out of envy, because I knew that Tatyana still loved you! But, that was decades ago! Tatyana is now in love with another man! And I have resigned myself to that fact also. There was a time when I would have ordered them both killed, both her and her lover! But, that time has also long passed. Now, here we are, standing before one another, and all I can think about is everything I want to tell you about your own daughter—our daughter in a manner of speaking, and how proud I am of her! Excuse my jubilation here Nicholas! But, you are like a long-lost friend, and we should be drinking now and celebrating!"

Nick lowered his weapon and looked at him quizzically. "You are a very complicated man, Victor Zubkov." He then barked into his radio,

"All clear. C'mon in, Roberta! Everything is secure! And Zubkov," he reminded him. "I am not your friend!" Nick wanted to make this fact very clear to everyone around him.

"That I know, American!" Zubkov replied. "But, it was you who captured her heart in the first place! And, it was you that broke it! I was left to pick up the pieces! Try as I may to make her forget you, I never could. At first I hated you, but over time, I hated myself for not being you!" He raised his weapon. So, you want to end it now?"

Everyone backed up, and raised their weapons once again. Each of them apprehensively looking around for the highest threat level should the bullets start flying! Nick stared Victor in the eye, his trigger finger twitching. Kowalski stepped between the two.

"You don't want to go here Nick," he stated. "You left Tatyana a long time ago for whatever reasons! And Victor here, he seems to have taken very good care of both your daughter and her mother all these years. Why would either of you want to die for a woman that apparently neither of you can have?"

Nick thought about it a moment, and replied, "I have no argument with Zubkov, other than what his intentions are for Natasha and Tatyana."

Victor spoke up, "I am letting them have a new life, Nicholas! I am letting them both start over, even if it is with Alexander!"

"Why would you do that, Victor?" Nick asked him harshly. "After all these years you are finally letting her go, and what about Natasha?"

Victor reached over to pull Kowalski aside as he lowered his own weapon, and dropped it to the ground. Standing there squarely in front of Nick now, he replied, "Nicholas, you must believe me! If for no other reason than I am standing down before you now. I could never meet up Tatyana's expectations for one single reason! No matter what I gave her over the years, or how much I doted on her, she was always in love with you! As a result I took on mistresses, something that didn't help matters much! She could never let go of her love for a mysterious dashing young man who had captured her heart when she was but a girl—you! She tried to and I know she did! But, the most I could ever get from Tatyana was her devotion and her loyalty, but never her heart! But, for Natasha's sake, Tatyana remained loyal to me until her affair with Alexander! Natasha is nearly grown now, so what is the best way to ensure that I never lose Natasha?"

Nick was eying Victor warily, and being a good reader of people, he felt he was telling him the truth.

"You are letting them both go in a way that allows you to still maintain contact with Natasha?"

Victor grinned. "Yes! And it has already been done! I have set up Tatyana with a trust fund large enough to ensure that, even if this lowlife Alexander Mayakovsky has betrayed her—which I firmly believe he has, that she and Natasha will never have to worry about money. She will learn of it after Natasha's dance recital in Paris."

"Dance recital?" Nick queried.

"I told you, my friend. There is much you don't know. Our Natasha dances ballet with the best in all of Europe! And, one day she will know that I am not her biological father. You should be thinking about that day Nicholas, and how you want to handle it! As for me, I just want to always have a significant role in her life! And, if that means letting her go—letting her mother go, so be it! It is what my mother would have wanted me to do. If you decide to pursue Tatyana, I'll not stand in your way. Just remember that Natasha is as much my daughter as yours!"

Ulyana climbed out of the shaft and looked around. She immediately went to the fire door and opened it cautiously. Seeing that no one was in the corridor, she yelled to Timmons, "Hurry, we need to check the lab to see if they've been there."

Timmons ran after her up the hallway with the others following a short distance behind them. When Timmons caught up to her, she was breathing heavily. "It's gone. Everything is gone!" she said gasping for air.

Timmons looked past her into the server room. All the hard drives were missing. "Let's join up with Nick," he said, putting his arm around her and turning her in the opposite direction. "Seahawk 1, this is Seahawk 3. Do you read me?" he said over the radio.

Nick answered, "Where are you, Timmons?"

"In the server room. All the hard drives are missing."

"They have the *Semya* boards too," Nick replied. "They were waiting in the airshaft for Zubkov because they knew it would be his only way to escape."

"Then they may still be in the mines, Nick!" Timmons shouted over the radio. "These mines are kilometers long! Get in the choppers and close the door on them. There is only one way out for them now."

"We are down to one bird here, Timmons. We can do our best to close the exit, but we are going to be outnumbered."

Zubkov objected, "I am going with you Nicholas, and so is Anatoly here. He knows these mines, and I know Alexander and General Krushensky! We can send the rest of my men through the airshaft to join up with yours."

"Go back the way you came Timmons," Nick said hastily, realizing that Zubkov was now an ally. "I am sending some of Victor's men down the airshaft to meet-up with you in the mines. Do the radios work down there?"

"Roger that, at least up to a point," Timmons replied. "The radios work inside the mines when you are deep enough in, but until then you got nothing."

Roberta was already pulling on her flight helmet and wondering now more than ever if Nick were still in love with this Tatyana, and what her own chances were with him now that Victor Zubkov was standing aside. As she ran to the chopper with Kowalski in quick pursuit, the thought of Nick and his Tatyana was troubling to her. "Hey," Kowalski shouted after her. "What do you think you are doing? You think you're flying this thing?"

"She called back over her shoulder, "With your permission, sir!"

Kowalski laughed. "Permission granted, soldier considering my left hand is useless. I'll copilot."

Roberta strapped herself in and ignited the turbines while her mind wrestled with what she had just heard back there at the facility. "Did she really love him? Did she love this man that frustrated her so with his indifference to everything, as if he had no passion for anything whatsoever? Why hadn't he even touched her since this mission began? Ever since he knew that she was NSA, and ever since they left Seattle, he had been cold to her!" she thought to herself. Checking her instruments for flight readiness, she decided. "He is going to be a hard one to control, but damn it! He is a great dancer! And, he promised me a warm beach somewhere! If he follows through on his promise, as he did with the dance at the Governor's mansion, I'll make it worth his while! Then let's see if this Tatyana still has his heart!"

Before Nick, Zubkov, and Anatoly got there, the rotors were already spinning, and before the slider door was shut, they were in the air. Kowalski was in the copilot's seat helping her with the instruments. Nick was in back talking to Victor, and Victor's men were racing for the airshaft beyond the facility walls to meet up with Timmons and Ulyana.

"Can I trust you, Victor?" Nick shouted over the turbines. "This *Semya* technology was going to make you a very wealthy man, which makes our partnership in this mission unlikely."

"I am already a very wealthy man, Nicholas. Yes, you can trust me! I just recently learned of my blunder."

"What are you talking about, Victor?" Nick shouted back over the screaming turbines.

"The *Semya* technology. Only yesterday I learned the truth behind it! I was going to offer to destroy it, but I wanted something first in return."

"What's that?" Nick asked.

"The Stalintsia Steel merger must go through! And I have long-term commitments for launch facilities that must be met!"

"Go on," Nick replied.

"I am a patriot, Nicholas. My father died before I was born defending his Motherland, and I swore on his grave, never to betray my country—ever!"

"But," Nick yelled to be heard. "If you knew about the danger of the *Semya*, why were you going to sell it to a madman like Bentley?"

"I didn't know about the Obvyet project! I had read all the classified reports about this wonderful new technology that was buried by the Russian government, and I believed the reports to be true as written! That all the problems surrounding the *Semya* chips revolved around a flawed, and a corrupted operating system—something I could fix! I assumed that the Soviet high command had only buried it for someone else to profit from later. I assumed further, that it would eventually be sold on the black market anyway, and so I surreptitiously sold off the holdings for Laboratory 173 to a European consortium that I controlled. I bribed the officials who witnessed the destruction of the Semya chips to look the other way while I replaced all the boards with blank boards, and the Soviet high command had so many other worries at the time that no one noticed. I then spent millions of dollars to have an entirely new operating system designed for it, and I thought I had fixed all the problems with it. When I was finally convinced I had, I sought out a buyer for it."

"What changed your mind?" Nick asked.

"Ulyana Baronova did," Zubkov replied. "I think you know her! She is your operations manager, and everything she has told me about you indicates that you are a man of principle, a man of purpose. She is also my biological daughter Nick, my only blood child! She was born out of wedlock, of course, because I was already married to Tatyana when she was born. Her mother has been my secret mistress for more than twenty years now. Ulyana knows me only as her Uncle Victor, though I provided the means for both her and her mother to have a good life all these years. I got her an education, and I got her into the KGB when she was very young. She has always kept me informed of important matters, though on a need-to-know only basis. She never discusses your business with me, has never divulged any secrets, unless she discovered something that would put me in harm's way. If she did hear of something that might do me harm, she would slip me a warning! It was never very detailed mind you, but enough to make me think twice about whatever the subject might be. She has saved my bacon on several occasions! She never told me the name of her boss or of the firm she worked for, and I never asked her!"

"This time it was different though," Victor went on. "This time, Ulyana had her mother deliver a note to me—something she had never done before! I knew immediately that it must be very important! She had left me a stack of documents, top-secret files containing a Soviet strategy to build an impregnable defense network that was flawed only because of a computer that became hostile! As I read the documents, I realized what I had inadvertently done, which wasn't what I had intended to do."

"And what did you do?" Nick said loud enough to be heard over the turbines. "Did you intend to get even richer?"

Victor scoffed at Nick's naivety. "As I told you, I am already wealthy— don't be such a fool Nicholas! My interest was in supporting the Russian space program. And the Russians made the Soyuz launch vehicles I leased! And they made them in Russia! My purchase orders brought jobs to the Motherland! Likewise, Russian engineers wrote the code for the new operating system to drive the *Semya's*. I didn't enlist the help of any foreign workers. I brought jobs to Russia, plain and simple! It takes money to make money, Nikki. So, I made my money early on, and I was using it to refuel Russian innovation—Russian technology! The Soviets had one thing right."

"What was that?" Nick asked.

"The importance of educating every young boy and girl in Russia, and then finding something for them to do! And, they accomplished that goal very effectively. Russia has the highest educated populace in the world by far. Illiteracy was nearly zero ten years ago, but now we have doctors and engineers sweeping the streets for tokens—because we have no jobs for them! We have Generals selling off battleships on the black market, and we have a mafia more powerful than our own government is! I was determined to change all that one brick at a time through free enterprise! I accomplished much, but I failed in this venture.

"After reading what Ulyana had gotten to me," Victor went on. "I realized my mistake, but I asked myself, 'Why lose my entire investment if I could barter a deal with both the Americans and the Russian Federation? And, in the process we can all accomplish what we want?' I wanted to get here first to grab the *Semya* boards, and then cut a deal directly with the two governments! But, there was another flaw in my plans! Someone else was intent on stealing this technology too! Your close friend Alexander Mayakovsky got here two days ago, and there is one board missing."

That revelation complicated matters further! But, Nick put it aside for the moment.

"You knew that Alexander was planning to run off with Tatyana, didn't you?" Nick said.

Victor laughed loudly, and Nick stared back at him skeptically, wondering why he was laughing. "That is what I thought too, Nicholas! I have known about their affair for years! I even came to the conclusion that Tatyana deserved to have her own life with anyone she wanted to! I further realized that it was in Natasha's best interest to let her mother be happy. No Nicholas, Mayakovsky had no intention of running off with Tatyana! He used her to get the access codes to Laboratory 173 so he could steal the *Semya* technology! You asked me how I could be involved with a madman like Bentley, but I am not! Alexander found him! And, it was Alexander that befriended General Krushensky too, whom he met at one of my social gatherings years ago. Alexander has been playing me for the fool for many years! But in reality, he has played us all for fools!"

Nick stared at Victor Zubkov intently. He was sure the Russian wasn't lying to him. He could not see any sign that the man was anything but utterly sincere. Victor continued. "Did you think for one minute that I didn't know that Alexander was a spy for the CIA? I kept him close to me, to feed the CIA what I wanted them to know about me, and over time, I actually came to like him. I underestimated him though, so yes I am the fool too! I too thought his only ambitions were to steal Tatyana away from me! But his real ambitions were far greater than love—his *real* ambitions were to become wealthy! So, he used you as his cover to disappear so he could beat me to the *Semya*, and then deal directly with Bentley himself! Bentley is a scheming bastard! So it wasn't difficult for Alexander to persuade him to cut me out of the deal altogether. That bastard thought he could bring me to my knees with the Stalintsia Steel deal—and break me financially, winner take all!"

"If you knew all this, why didn't you just run with the technology yourself last night?"

Victor smiled. "Because, my friend, I didn't know who Alexander had in his back pocket within the Russian Federation military. Now that I know it is Krushensky, we can deal with this situation."

"We?" Nick replied.

Victor laughed again. "Oh Nicholas, you crack me up! You are in charge of the only private international intelligence agency in the world. How many millions do you take in per year for the collection of intelligence?"

Nick didn't reply.

Victor laughed again. "I didn't think you knew the amount! You are, and always have been, a covert agent Nicholas! You never will be a good businessman! God bless you! You are a purist and a real soldier! You count lives, not dollars. Am I correct?"

Nick, once again, failed to respond to his remarks.

"I am proud to have met you, Nikki. That is what your friends call you isn't it?"

Nick nodded.

"Then, may I call you Nikki too? It would be an honor for me."

Nick grimaced at the thought of being friends with the likes of Zubkov! But, he had to admit that Zubkov didn't appear to be the ruthless thug his legend proclaimed him to be. Besides, if what he said was true about setting Tatyana and Natasha up for life financially, and letting them go, to live as they chose to live, then he was a different man altogether from what he had been told. And if he was Ulyana's father, there must be something good about him anyway! He knew that Ulyana dearly loved her uncle, who it now turns out to be him! Ulyana was as good a person as Nick had ever known and so he extended his hand and shook Victor's.

"Call me Nikki," he said. "Now, what about this we?"

Roberta was on the COM. "We're at the mine entrance. What are my orders, Nikki?"

"Put us down close to Seahawk 3, and have Kowalski get in the air to back you up, Roberta. Victor, Anatoly, and I are going in. After Kowalski is in the air, take us all the way down into that pit—to the mine entrance. Then pull back with Kowalski. I don't want anything getting out of here until we have swept the mine front to back."

"Sir," Kowalski replied. "Alexander and Krushensky have at least a dozen men in there with them, probably more. How are the three of you going to take them out?"

"We're not going to take them out, Kowalski. We are going to hold them here until Timmons arrives from behind, and then we are going to squeeze them into submission. I am more worried about the support they may have already called in. Russian assault choppers are probably on the way."

"We are low on fuel and ammo," Kowalski replied. "And between the two of us, we only have a few air-to-air missiles left. Roberta's gun is half empty, and she is nearly out of fuel to boot!"

"Do what you can to find some fuel," Nick barked back, assuming the role he hated, as he thought about how he was putting Roberta in harm's way once again—for the sake of some damned mission! "Don't take them on head-to-head! Instead lure them in and jump them! Remember, they won't be expecting you. Use your craft's stealth features to your advantage. General Krushensky and Alexander Mayakovsky don't have a clue yet that we are waiting for them."

"How do we know they are even still here?" Kowalski shouted back.

"We'll know that soon enough," Nick muttered.

"Roger that," Kowalski replied.

Roberta dropped Kowalski off at Seahawk 3, and then she immediately took to the air again, sweeping down into the largest man made hole she had ever seen before! It was a huge quarry the size of the Grand Canyon, or so it seemed, and it had roads that spiraled down to the bottom for the earthmovers to bring the rock up to the surface. As she dropped into it, what appeared to be little Tonka trucks moving like ants in a procession, one line going up and one line going down, weren't. They became behemoth monster machines several stories tall, as one got closer to them. At the bottom, they dispersed into various tunnels that went in different directions.

Nick, Victor, and Anatoly scrambled out of the chopper, and Roberta lifted off to meet up with Kowalski, who had just lifted off too. On the ground, dust was swirling everywhere, and the men had to protect their eyes and noses until Roberta had gained enough altitude for the air to settle down again. When the dust settled enough, Nick shouted to Anatoly, "Which tunnel?"

Anatoly pointed. "That one over there, but we are going to get stopped by security." He pointed to a fleet of 4WD SUV's racing down into the pit to intercept them. "They will be trouble, Mr. Nick. They have already set off alarms because we weren't cleared to land here."

"No they won't," Victor replied. "I am a major shareholder in this operation!" He was already speed-dialing a cell phone number, and when his party answered, he replied. "You know who this is?"

"Of course sir, Comrade Zubkov. What can I do for you?" the voice at the other end replied.

"I am at the Alrosa mine in Yakutsk on some personal matters," Victor barked into his cell phone. "There is a fleet of security personnel on their way to intercept me. Can you please inform them who I am?"

"But Comrade Zubkov, what are you doing there, and why was I not informed of your arrival?"

"Some National Security matters have come up quite suddenly, I am afraid. Tell your men to stand down, or we will have to kill them," Zubkov said without emotion.

"But Comrade Zubkov," he pleaded with him. "I don't have the authorization!"

"I do! So, make the damned call before we kill some good employees!"

"Yes sir," the man replied. "This will be my job on the line."

"Only if I die comrade," Victor snapped back. "They will be upon us in a few seconds. What will you do?"

"Consider it done, Comrade Zubkov."

The six black American-made armor-plated Hummers came to a screeching halt, surrounding them. Anatoly had his rifle already shouldered and was taking aim.

"Stand down, now soldier!" Nick commanded in Russian. "Roberta,

Kowalski, get in here quick!"

Seahawk one and Seahawk three made an appearance over the pit and hovered. "Do we take them out, Nikki?" Kowalski radioed back.

"Show them some firepower, Kowalski, but without killing anyone."

"Roger that," he replied, and he put his gun on one of the Hummers that appeared to be empty—the guards now all in front of it. He pulled the trigger on his GAU-17A Gatling gun and chopped the vehicle in half. Riddled with bullets, the SUV slumped like a broken horse, and then burst into flames, and exploded.

Victor raised his hands emphatically as he got up from the ground where he had thrown himself down at the sound of gunfire. He said in Russian, "Everyone stand down! We are on a mission of the utmost importance! I am Victor Zubkov, the Minister of Heavy Industry, and within minutes, we will all be under assault by traitors to the Motherland. You must trust me—we are here to defend the Motherland!"

"Comrade Zubkov," one security man spoke up, also picking himself up from the ground. "We have no orders to support your allegations." By now, there were a dozen Alrosa mine security guards surrounding them with automatic weapons pointed in their direction.

"You do know who I am, son?" Victor replied.

"Yes, sir. You are indeed the Minister of Heavy Industry."

"Then stand down, or these Americans will have to kill you. You have seen the firepower, yes?"

The young guard nodded, but he was unwilling to stand down.

"You will get the authorization soon, and we will wait here patiently until you do."

Victor slowly lit his last cigar, relishing the aroma, while he worked his injured shoulder, which was painfully stiffening up. He then swallowed another codeine pill for the pain, took a few more puffs off the fragrant Cuban, then threw it to the dirt and crushed it out. The Russian guard's radio crackled, and the guard listened intently. Finally, he nodded. "How can we help you sir?" he said to Zubkov.

Timmons and Ulyana gathered with their team in the granite chamber below Laboratory 173. "This is going to be a bitch!" Timmons muttered to Ulyana. "All of us going into that narrow tunnel in single file—in the dark, is nothing short of a nightmare for me!"

"Are you afraid of the dark?" she chided him.

"No, just claustrophobic!" Timmons replied angrily. "Tight spaces give me the willies. Mind if I go in front?"

She smiled. "You get the first bullet then, so be my guest!"

Timmons nodded, and got in line behind the guide at arm's length. Ulyana put her hand on his shoulder and said, "Okay, we can go."

Alexander Mayakovsky and General Krushensky clambered up into an earthmover while the Spetsnaz team took the running boards or clung to the sides of the huge machine now filled with ore. "I thought you had control over this, General," Mayakovsky spat out. "Your people were to take out the Americans on the Kamchatka peninsula. How the hell can you miss three Sikorsky's?"

"You have what you came for," the General muttered dryly.

"We are in a diamond mine hundreds of feet below the ground, and a blizzard has shut everything down! We should be in the air by now and halfway to Greece! What happened to your choppers? What happened to the snowmobiles? Where is plan-B?"

"The Americans got through, so what am I to tell you? Where were you for the past two days?" Krushensky fired back. "Victor Zubkov found out about Oleyenka somehow, and Oleyenka's birds were destroyed by the Americans! We were to refuel at the lab, but the American's were there first! Plan-B was the team waiting for us with three attack helicopters, and the Americans took care of them too! Now we go to plan-C and get the hell out of here. There is a military base not far from here, and we will commandeer a transport plane to Sochi. From there, you can easily slip into Greece with your precious cargo."

Alexander lit a cigarette impatiently, and took a deep drag on it. "You are an idiot, General!" he muttered, and he took his gun from the holster, put it to the general's temple. Without further hesitation he pulled the trigger, blowing his brains all over the cab. The driver of the earthmover stopped it and clambered out, running into the mines covered in blood, and brain fragments. Alexander opened the door and pushed the general's corpse out, which landed at the feet of his men. The general's men had clambered down from the earthmover, weapons at the ready. "Anyone here have a problem with this?" Alexander called out to them in Russian. "He is a disgrace to Russia, the fat sleazy whore! He let the Americans through, and they want this!" he said holding up a satchel. "This is Russian technology! It must not fall into the hands of the Americans! I am taking it back to Moscow. Who is with me?"

Alexander had chosen his words well, knowing that he was addressing soldiers whose loyalties to the old Soviet Russia were still strong, and who were frustrated by the corruption within the Russian military. Besides, Americans were always a good motivator for Russian soldiers. They were trained to hate them!

One man stepped forward. "He was a general, our general, and you killed him!"

"This general, this whore, was selling out to the Americans! How else can three-dozen of Russia's finest be defeated by a handful of Americans? He was prepared to have you all slaughtered so that he could hand over this satchel to them when we get topside. They will be waiting for us when we get there. What's your name, soldier?"

"Evgeniy Lutrova, sir."

"Here Evgeniy, take this technology, and together we will return it to where it belongs." Alexander tossed the satchel down to him. "The Americans will not make fools of us anymore! They will not come into our country and steal what is rightfully ours! Your General knew what they were coming for, and from where and when. How do three American warships get over the Kamchatka peninsula? Can anyone tell me how? My orders are from the FSB! They are to get this technology back to Moscow—pronto! How many comrades have we lost already? We are heading into an ambush, and the support the General said would be there, won't be. Why? Here is why." He tossed down an envelope.

Evgeniy picked up the manila envelope and opened it. In it were documents detailing various financial holdings, transactions in the Middle East, and photos of Krushensky's young mistress. Evgeniy examined the documents and passed them around. "What do you want us to do, and who are you?"

Alexander clambered down from the hauler and addressed him face-to-face. "Here are my credentials," he replied, handing him a document written on FSB letterhead. "And here is my badge. Evgeniy examined both and nodded.

"I don't want any more deaths here today," Alexander called out to the rest of them. "The Americans will be waiting for us above, and they will kill us all if you resist them. It is imperative that Evgeniy and myself get this satchel to Moscow. Does everyone understand? I want you to offer some resistance, enough for Evgeniy and me to slip away, but that's all! Once we are clear of here, you must stand-down—those are direct orders!"

Topside, Kowalski and Roberta flew back and forth across the pit looking for any signs of trouble while watching their instruments for bogies or incoming. Down below, Timmons gasped for breath when they finally got to the end of the tunnel and into the main mineshaft. He regrouped everyone, tasked one of the Russians to flag down a hauler, and got on his radio. "Nick, can you hear me? We are in place and moving toward the exit."

Nick radioed back. "I hear you. We have the front door covered. Get moving, and let's squeeze them."

Zubkov tapped Nick on the shoulder, and Nick turned to him. "He won't come out this way," he said.

"What are you talking about, Victor? We don't even know if he is in there!"

"He is in there alright," Victor replied. "Have you seen any sign of military aircraft? After you destroyed everything, their assets are all gone! No further forces will be coming. This will be the last stand."

"How do you know this, Victor?" Nick replied.

"Plan-A was Oleyenka and his birds. Plan-B was the Spetsnaz team off site with three attack choppers. There is no plan-C, Nikki! The general had to abandon his own helicopter because he had no fuel! General Krushensky is too stupid to think that far ahead, but Mayakovsky isn't! He has a map of the mines, and there are dozens of airshafts everywhere. He will figure out a way to slip out. We need to be in the air, not down here. Let these men do the police work. If Krushensky is still alive, he is stupid enough to think he can drive one of these haulers out of here, and get to a military base that is not far away. But, Mayakovsky will know this is stupid, as stupid as the General is simple minded! Mayakovsky already has another escape plan, his plan-C. So, my belief is that they are still in the mines."

Nick remembered the snowmobiles that had been at the ready, and agreed. "So what are we looking for, Victor? We can't have a team on every airshaft?"

"No, but Alexander came in through the mines, so he has transport nearby. My guess is it's a snowplow. He didn't come in with Oleyenka or Krushensky, and with the weather the way it has been, he would have had to plow his way in. He probably stole one of the plows in Yakutsk and plans to leave by rail—he wouldn't risk the airport."

"Victor, you're brilliant!" Nick said, clapping him on the shoulder. "Kowalski, Roberta, put the birds down now!" he commanded. "Timmons," he called out on the radio. "Walk the mines. Mayakovsky is looking for a way out, probably an airshaft somewhere. Do you copy?"

"Roger that sir, but we are three kilometers in, and we don't know where the airshafts are."

Ulyana tapped him on the shoulder. "Yes we do. I have maps."

Timmons got back on the radio. "You have a very efficient operations manager here, boss! She has the maps! Where do we start?"

"Just check out every airshaft between you and me, and keep pushing these guys forward. We are coming toward you doing the same. If you can avoid a firefight, do so."

"Roger that—avoid body bags," Timmons replied.

"Okay, Victor. Get the mine's security team over here. They know where all the airshafts are. And Victor," Nick said. "Those choppers are low on fuel."

"Done!" he said, and went off to find out where they could be refueled.

Chapter 32

"We can't defend ourselves from an ore transporter, men. We'll use it for cover to walk out," Alexander instructed them. "Get a driver up there and get this thing moving! When the bullets start flying, only take positions for defensive fire. Give Evgeniy and me some time to get away. I don't want anyone killed here. Is that understood? Throw your weapons down if need be. The Americans don't want to kill you or die themselves either—they just want this parcel."

"C'mon Evgeniy, pick out five men. We need to go this way," Alexander instructed.

"But, I can't leave my men. Where are we going?"

"Not far," Alexander said. "Grab the damned parcel. The Americans will be here soon!"

Roberta was flying over the Alrosa mine in the direction Anatoly instructed her to when she spotted the snowplow. "There it is Nikki," Roberta shouted over the COM. "A snowplow, off the road, and close to an airshaft."

"Well done," Nick replied. "Put us down."

Roberta landed nearby, and Nick and Victor scrambled out. "How do you want to do this, Victor?" Nick said to him.

"I didn't see any footprints in the snow. Did you?" Victor replied.

Nick shook his head.

"If this is the truck Alexander used to get here, it has been sitting there for a long time, long enough for the blizzard to sweep away his prints. It is my guess that he is down there then, and this is where he will come up. It's much warmer down in the mines than it is up here, especially now that it is getting dark. I say we check it out before we all freeze to death."

Nick ordered Roberta and Anatoly out, and they all approached the airshaft with weapons ready. The padlock on the door had been sheared.

"I would say that this is where he got in," Victor said.

Nick nodded. "Then let's go."

The ventilator shaft was twenty meters in diameter, and the walls were made of poured concrete until much further down, where they reverted back to solid granite. A steel-grated floor was underfoot, and in the center was a labyrinth of steel stairs, descending hundreds of feet to the bottom. The steel work was anchored to the circular walls with structural steel beams, and high overhead was a huge fan driven by an enormous electric motor. The air flowing through the grating and towards the ceiling was warm. Low voltage lighting dimly lit the stairs every few feet. There were twelve steps down to a small landing, then another twelve steps at right angles to another landing, until the rectangle was complete. The center area was completely open, and Nick noticed the steel cables hanging from high above with large steel hooks dangling idly. He assumed they were used for lowering heavy equipment into the mine. The stairs were wide enough for four people to use comfortably side by side, and he thought they must have been designed as an escape route in the event of a fire or explosion. They all stood there listening, but the only perceptible noise was the steady hum from the fan above, and the rumblings of machinery from down below. "We go down one by one," Nick instructed. "When I reach the first level, then one of you comes down. That way we can cover each other all the way down."

Victor interrupted him. "It would be best if the woman stays here, Nikki. Not only is she the best pilot, but if Alexander gets by us, she can pin him down on the stairs until we can back her up."

Roberta objected. "Victor, you should stay here, not me! How are you going to hold up on these stairs at your age and being wounded too?"

"She's got a point Victor," Nick said. "If we control the situation and capture Alexander with the *Semya*, I'll need her to verify what we've got anyway."

"As you wish." Victor sighed. "I'll stay here." The disappointment was evident in his tone. "Anyone have a cigar?"

No one did, and Victor sat down by the door, feeling left out of the action and hating it! Nick got on the radio. "We're in, Kowalski. Are you ready?"

"Affirmative, Nick. I am on the ridge above the mine, missiles and guns targeted on the mineshaft. They have halted all transport into and out of the mines, so if anything comes this way, I can take it out. No bogies on the horizon.

"What about the rest of the group?" Nick responded.

Kowalski replied, "Everyone is moving in as ordered."

Then, deep within the mine, Nick heard small-arms fire and grenades exploding. "We're moving in, Kowalski. In a few minutes the radio won't work, so keep your eyes open."

"Roger that," Kowalski radioed back. "Good hunting."

Nick took the first set of stairs, then motioned for the to others follow." As more shots and explosions echoed up from below, Nick threw caution to the wind and scrambled down the stairs three at a time. Anatoly and Roberta followed the best they could. Zubkov decided he could not stay behind if there was a firefight, and he started down the steps cautiously. An Alrosa Hummer had taken the first hit from a rocket-propelled grenade, which had flipped the machine over. The armor shielded the two Alrosa mine guards from the blast and certain death. Other Alrosa security members in two more Hummers veered off sharply in different directions, and slammed on the brakes, skidding sideways and broadside. Bullets pelted the glass, but failed to penetrate either it, or the vehicle's body armor. "They'll be hitting us with the RPGs next!" one guard yelled over the radio. "Get out now!" he commanded. "And move for better cover!"

However, the firing ceased as quickly as it began. Cautiously, the men exited the Hummers and took up defensive positions behind boulders not far away.

"This is weird," the head security officer radioed to his team. "They had us! Why did they stop firing?"

"I don't know," a voice belonging to one of the security team for Alrosa answered.

The security officer called out for the intruders to lay down their weapons, and the immediate response was another volley of small-arms fire. "Stay where you are, Americans! We do not want to kill you!" one of their attackers yelled.

"Where are you, Timmons?" Nick barked into the radio.

"We have them," Timmons came back. "But if we start shooting, we will kill the Alrosa people in the crossfire. Give me a few minutes to flank them. Then I will put one burst in the air to let them know we are here."

"Don't forget that you are in a solid granite tunnel here, Timmons! Bullets have a way of bouncing around in here! Put your bullets in the dirt," Nick cautioned him.

Timmons complied, taking Oleyenka's men by surprise. Realizing that they were outflanked, they laid their weapons down.

"We have them Nikki," Timmons radioed back.

"Is Mayakovsky there?" Nick panted, breathing hard after the breakneck rush down the stairs.

"We need a few minutes to confirm that. I'll get back to you."

Roberta and Anatoly were right behind him when he finally found the bottom step. "What happened, Nikki?" Roberta gasped, trying to catch her breath. Anatoly immediately took up a defensive position behind some rubble, waiting for orders. The airshaft had led them into an enormous tunnel that was well lit by Halogen lighting. Nothing was moving, and all machinery had been shut down. No workers were in sight. The Alrosa mineworkers had all disappeared.

"He is not here," crackled Ulyana's voice from the radio. "No one is talking. They are obviously stalling us, Nikki."

A volley of bullets flew past them and smashed into the granite walls behind them, ricocheting everywhere. Roberta felt a richochet enter her back between her shoulder blades, but the bullet had lost velocity after bouncing off the wall, and did not penetrate very far. "Damn!" she muttered at the pain, and pushed Nick to the ground with her. Immediately, she tried to find a target.

"You are hit, Roberta! How bad?"

"It was only a ricochet, and probably only a fragment at that," she replied as if it were nothing. "I'll be okay." Nick looked at her with concern, and it was then she knew she had a chance with him! The bastard really did care for her after all! The lug just couldn't express it!

Mayakovsky and his men had heard their mad scramble down the steel flight of stairs and had taken up positions to ambush them. "Nikki," he shouted out, the words echoing in the expansive chambers. "Throw down your weapons and I'll spare your lives."

Nick, who had no idea where Mayakovsky and his men were until he looked at Anatoly, who was pointing upward had nothing to say back. Alexander and his men had taken up positions high up the granite walls, in the scaffolding used for planting dynamite. At least three rifles were aimed at him and Roberta.

"I don't want to kill you or your friends, Nikki. I just want the chopper you came in with, and to get the hell out of here alive!"

"You can't fly it Alexander," Nick shouted back to him. "It takes a special code to fire the turbines! Give me the *Semya* chips, and I'll give you the code."

"I don't think so, and who is the woman, Nikki?"

"Just a technician, Alexander! She is a cryptologist to identify the authenticity of the boards you have. She is no threat to you, so leave her out of this!"

Alexander laughed. "If she meant nothing to you, you would have just tried to take me out. You are so predictable, my old friend! I wonder how you have survived for so long in this business! I am coming down, Nikki. Tell your man behind the rocks not to be a hero. I have five guns pointed at you all."

Nick looked at Anatoly and shook his head, then grabbed Roberta by the arm and made a dash for cover with her. Anatoly opened fire to cover them. Shots echoed off the walls everywhere, and bullets bounced off the granite walls in all directions, intensifying the danger.

Alexander clambered down the scaffolding despite the gunshots, and Nick had him in his sights when bullets pelted the rock he was behind. He fired anyway, and Alexander dropped to the dirt unscathed. He fired back and yelled out, "This is not the way it has to end, Nikki!"

"So, how should it end, Alexander? With you stealing the *Semya* technology and getting rich for your efforts?"

"Nikki, listen to me! This is not what you think it is. Right now you think I am a traitor, and you think that I have no intention to marry Tatyana—but you would be wrong on both counts! There is still much you do not know," he said in English.

Evgeniy couldn't understand what was being said between the two in English, and he motioned for his men to flank their enemy's positions. Anatoly saw what they were up to and opened fire, taking two of them out. But, their return fire hit him in the head, and he fell dead to the ground. Nick got his sights on another soldier and pulled the trigger, and the man dropped off the scaffolding to the ground below. Alexander stood up, sprayed a volley of rounds toward Nick, and scrambled across the tunnel for better cover.

Evgeniy and his remaining two men opened fire on Roberta and Nick, effectively pinning them down while Alexander worked his way toward them using the granite walls of the mine to shield himself.

Roberta slipped the safety off her weapon and put it to automatic. There were only three men left! Three men that she was certain of anyway! If she could take out one of them, Nick could take out the remaining two—and this thing could be all over with! One of Evgeniy's men made a mistake, and tried to clamber down the scaffolding to assist Alexander. He probably thought he was out of sight or that everyone else was pinned down. She aimed below him, and pulled the trigger, Recoil from the weapon walked the bullets upward until they found their mark and pulverized him. Ten bullets riddled his body, and he fell screaming in agony to the dirt below, where he fell silent. She couldn't see another target behind the boulder she was behind—so she sprinted toward Anatoly's position, and spotted another of Evgeniy's men. Bullets started flying everywhere again, and she dove for cover behind his dead body.

"What are you doing, Roberta?" Nick shouted at her, emptying his own clip and reloading.

"You are being flanked by Alexander," she shouted back. "Besides, what do you care, this is just a mission, remember?"

Nick grimaced at her words, and Alexander laughed from somewhere unknown.

"So, she is nothing to you, Nikki? I think not! So, I will take care not to injure her."

"He is moving up on us on this side of the tunnel," Roberta called out loud enough to be heard. "If they kill me, they won't have the code for the Seahawk to fly out of here." She said this for Alexander's benefit. "He said that he had five guns on us," she went on. "Anatoly got two, you got one, and I got one, which leaves only one more. I saw him on the scaffolding a moment ago, but now he's gone! All we have to do is hold out long enough for Timmons and his team to show up."

Alexander almost chuckled to himself. He had purposely misrepresented the number of guns at his disposal! Evgeniy's men plus Evgeniy made a total of six. Evgeniy had now taken up a position against the granite wall only a few yards away from where Nick and Roberta had taken up their positions. There was also still a shooter high up on the scaffolding with a sniper rifle.

"Nick," Alexander called out in English. "Your woman was incorrect. There is one more shooter on the scaffolding, at two o'clock. Can you see him?"

Nick squirmed around for a better position, and he peeked over the boulder he was behind. "Yeah, I see him, but I can't get to him from my position. What are you getting at, Alex?"

"As I told you. You don't know everything. There is more to this than meets the eye, and I am only doing my job."

"What job is that, Alex?" Nick shouted back.

Alexander pulled the trigger on his automatic and sprayed the scaffolding. Nick watched as the sniper tumbled to the ground, and then he saw Alexander turn his weapon on Evgeniy and shoot him too. "To protect US National Security, what else?" he replied as he stepped out into the open with his weapon pointing down.

"I'll throw down my weapon and surrender if you give me a chance to explain."

"Lose the weapon first," Nick replied.

Alexander complied, tossing his rifle to the ground in clear view of Nick and Roberta, and he raised his hands high—and put them behind his head. Nick stood up from behind the boulder, his rifle aimed directly at him. "Pat him down, Roberta."

Roberta got up from behind the rubble, stepped over Anatoly's body, and cautiously approached Alexander to frisk him.

"He's clean, Nikki."

"Where are the Semya boards, Alexander?"

"In that satchel up on the scaffolding, next to the corpse of one of General Krushensky's men." Alexander pointed, and then returned his hands to his head.

For the first time, Nick noticed the blood stains on her back. "Roberta," he shouted to her. "You are hurt! Are you okay?"

"I am alright, Nikki!" And to prove it, she cautiously crossed the cavernous tunnel to the opposite side and started clambering up the scaffolding to retrieve the satchel. When she reached it, she opened it, and examined the contents. "It looks like everything is here Nick," she called out weakly, as the bullet in her back caused her difficulty in breathing. Nevertheless, she verified the authenticity of one board, and then called out, "It's genuine."

"Let's go then," Nick yelled back to her.

Nick walked up to Alexander. "What's going on here, Alexander? You have something up your sleeve. What is it?"

Alex grinned. "You're the eternal pessimist, Nikki. Let me guess. You think I am here to steal the *Semya* technology and then sell it to Nathan Chadwick Bentley?"

Nick nodded, but he was more concerned about Roberta, now that the situation was under control. "Everyone associated with this op seems to think so, too," he replied, as he watched Roberta clamber slowly back down the scaffolding, and noticing her struggling and pausing for breath.

"Except for one man, who knows the truth," Alexander replied. "And that's Smith."

"What the hell are you talking about, Alexander? Smith is the one who sanctioned this mission in the first place."

"Yeah, of course he did, Nikki! He also was the one who wanted you to carry the attaché case and who arranged for the Letter of Congress."

Nick looked puzzled, and he said as much. "But why would he make you out to be the fall guy, Alexander?"

"To start me over with a new identity in a new life, that's why. Besides, while everyone is looking one way, he can do something else."

"What's Smith up to?" Nick demanded.

"Do you really think that Smith was going to dismantle the cloned Magic Mountain project? He thinks that this President is a madman for trusting the Russians in the first place, and for letting the Russians get proprietary rights to the technology that is being developed around this chip. Smith has the support of some very prominent people, both in the government and within the military ranks, who are backing him up on this. Hey Nikki, Presidents come and go, some good and some bad. Do you really think that national policy is dictated by the whims of presidents?"

Roberta approached them with the satchel and noticed the look of confusion on Nick's face. "What's wrong?" she asked, breathing hard.

"I'm not sure," Nick replied, going to her and putting his arm around her. "Roberta, are you okay?"

She smiled at him. "I think that bullet might have pierced my lung. I am having difficulty breathing."

"Can you make it up the stairs, Roberta?"

She nodded. "I think so Nikki."

"Let's go then, up the stairs, Alexander." He motioned toward the stairs as he supported Roberta's weight. "The amount of blood looks bad, Roberta. Are you sure you can make it"? Can you breathe?"

"I can make it," she replied. "I don't know if I can fly the chopper, but I can make it out of here, and you don't need to hold me up. I'll lead the way while you keep a gun trained on Alexander's back."

Reluctantly, Nick let go of her shoulder and she started up the steps. He took up a position behind Alexander, and they headed up the stairs.

"So what is Smith up to, Alexander, and why are you here?"

"He wants your mission to fail, Nick. If it does, the Russians boot the Americans out of Magic Mountain, and the clone facility continues to operate. The United States President is on his second term now, and the Russian Federation President has declared he won't run for another term. Once they are both are out of office, both sides start with new leadership. You were chosen Nick, because of World Trade. World Trade will take the blame for botching the whole thing up, and Smith wants World Trade shut down too—it's been far too above board in providing Intel to the United Nations! Exposing to the world that you were working for the United States on a covert mission taints the credibility of the whole organization, and all your funding gets yanked."

"You haven't told me yet your involvement in this," Nick said angrily.

"Zubkov is my involvement," Alexander went on. "Smith found out that Zubkov was close to taking the *Semya* to market, and he couldn't let anyone else have this technology. You know how he thinks, Nikki. As long as both the Russians and the Americans have the same capabilities, they balance each other out. But if another country gets it, then two countries can gang up on the other one, and the balance of power is lost. He sent me back in to get everything, effectively defeating your mission and discrediting your agency."

"But Zubkov told me that it was you who brought Bentley to the table in the first place," Nick answered.

"Bentley came to me first with a well laid out plan, and I passed that on to Smith. Smith came back with his own plan, and I just followed orders," Alex answered.

"Then why equip us and send us in? Why provide us with information about the facility and move heaven and earth to get us here if we were to fail?" Nick asked Alexander as he watched Roberta struggling to get her breath up ahead.

"Hold on a minute, Roberta," he called out to her. "I'll radio Zubkov to lower the cable. You will never make it in your condition." Nick then radioed Zubkov and ordered her to sit down on the steps while they waited.

Victor was already nearly to them, and hearing the radio, he called down to them.

"Nikki, I am almost to you now! I'll stay with Roberta and Alexander while you go topside. You can take the stairs faster than I can."

Nick replied, "Hurry up, Victor! I think she is about ready to pass out."

Victor started scrambling down the remaining flights of stairs to meet them, and Nick said to Alexander,

"Continue the story. Why would Smith go to all the trouble?"

"One, he had to make this mission look good to keep the American President from getting suspicious. Two, he never expected you to make it across the Kamchatka Peninsula, much less the Sea of Okhotsh."

"I can't believe he would kill me, Alexander?" Nick stated angrily.

"Nick," Alexander said to him tersely. "He didn't really want to kill you, but like everyone else, you are expendable! You are no longer useful to him, and at your age, what more could he get out of you than the ultimate sacrifice? He was after the woman here as well. She found his money trail and she seeded document trails all over Washington, and he wanted her dead and discredited too! You were both only collateral damage to him."

Alexander's words hit Nick hard, but he said nothing.

"You thought it was all about the money, didn't you?" Alexander laughed. "It's not about money, comrade—it's about freedom! People everywhere are willing to die to try to achieve it. Aren't they, Nikki? Most don't even know what freedom really is, and yet they will die for it. Why should I be any different, old friend? This package is freedom for me! Once I deliver it, I can disappear and be sane again, and I can stop watching over my shoulder for someone wanting to kill me."

Nick took a seat next to Roberta and put his arm around her. "So, what's your angle, Alex? Who do you work for?"

"I don't work for anyone anymore! Freedom, remember? Nothing is ever going to stop these two countries from mistrusting one another, or stop people like Smith from hoping they never will. My deal was to prevent Zubkov from getting this technology to market and to get it to Smith. In return, I get a new identity and a very fat bank account so I can be free. You are here to make the effort look genuine. Everything was staged, Nikki—everything!"

"So, I am disposable and so is Roberta?" Nick said disgustedly.

"Everyone is disposable, Nikki! Why do you think that there is one missing board? I have it—it is my insurance policy! I can use it to keep you and your woman alive too—otherwise, everyone is supposed to die, including me! Nikki, you are my friend, and we go back a long way. I could have had you killed, but I didn't. Think about it!"

"And what about Tatyana and Natasha, Alexander?"

"They are part of the deal I have with Smith, and they will be okay."

"Do you love her, Alexander?"

"Nikki," he replied. "I was in love with her from the moment I first set eyes on her! I watched her grow pregnant with your child. I watched her when Victor Zubkov courted her—and when he eventually married her! It took me many painful years of standing in the wings, before she even ever noticed me! It took many more years before she even knew my name. I promised her I would be in England with her, for our flight to America together."

From two flights above them, Zubkov yelled down,

"Look out!" They all looked up to see him aiming directly at them. Nick got up and aimed at Victor, thinking he was aiming at Alexander, confirming what he knew about the man all along, that he was just a ruthless killer!

But before Nick could pull the trigger, he saw Evgeniy down below—aiming upwards, who had been left for dead! He fired, and Alexander fell to the steel grating having caught several lethal bullets. Victor pulled his own trigger sending a volley of bullets downward, killing Evgeniy! And Nick once again shook his head at his misconception of Victor, as he lowered his own weapon.

One second he was ready to kill this Russian, and the next he was going to have to thank him for saving his life!

Alexander lay on the steel grating bleeding profusely. He was fading rapidly when he pulled Nick closer to him. "I do love her, Nikki! You have to believe me! My ticket is in my vest pocket to prove it." He shuddered from the pain as he pulled the ticket from his coat. "The last *Semya* board is in New York City, in a safe deposit box at the Chase Manhattan Bank there. The key for it was mailed to a post office box two days ago. The key to the PO box is in my pocket."

Alexander started trembling even more and coughed up more blood, and then he chuckled one last time. "I almost made it, Nikki! I almost made it out, and with the woman of my dreams! I would have been here before you!" Alexander coughed even more blood up. "I went to New York City first—with the board of *Semya* chips first! It was necessary to protect her! Tell Tatyana that I love her! Please, Nikki! Promise me you will do this for me!" But, before Nick could reply, Alexander sighed and then fell limp. Nick knew that Alexander was dead—he had seen too many others die this way. Helpless to do more, he searched his pockets and found the mailbox key and took the ticket from his dead hand.

Zubkov clambered down the remaining flights of stairs to meet them. Roberta started crying, and Nick looked up remorsefully.

"We need to talk, Victor," he said. "This is not over yet!"

Chapter *33*

Six months later: Melbourne, Australia.

The sun was just rising at the beach cottage. Already the gulls were squawking outside, circling overhead, and examining the waters below for anything edible. The telephone jangled, and Nick instinctively reached for it. "Yes," he muttered into the receiver, still half asleep. He listened intently for a few seconds, and without saying anything more, he hung the phone up.

"Everything okay, Nikki?" Roberta asked.

Nick nodded and pulled her closer, savoring the feel of her warm flesh against his. "I think we should go into town later—there are things we need," he murmured softly.

Roberta answered with something indistinguishable, and then fell back asleep. She instinctively wrapped her legs around his. Nick lay there, quietly enjoying the feel of her beside him. He scratched at the bandage on his forearm where the scars had been removed by laser not long ago. It was healing nicely—the forearm was, and he hoped his past life could be as easily erasable as it was.

Morgan hung up on the other end of the phone line, and smiled. On the table in front of him was the Chicago Tribune. The latest headlines read, "Multi-Billionaire Murdered by his Executive Purchasing Director, Love Triangle Suspected." The second story down was, "Congress Approves Stalintsia Steel Merger to Providence Steel, Stock Market Plummets."

He called up his broker on his cell phone. "Yes, I'll take a thousand shares of CodeSource," he instructed him. Leaving the lounge, he headed for Kennedy airport in a taxi, glad that it was finally all over with. World Trade had been completely dismantled months ago. Victor Zubkov had brokered his deal with the US government, gotten his merger approved, and the American and Russian governments had taken up his launch pad commitments. His new operating system was being franchised to Samuel Forester's CodeSource. The *Semya's* had all been destroyed, except for one last remaining chip, an insurance policy for Nick Peters who had to change identities for the final time. The Magic Mountain project in Russia had been de-funded and shut down! And Blakely, well Blakely had been right after all! He'd finally had that dreaded discussion with Anne Marie, and his wife finally sued him for divorce! But, he was getting over it.

The real twist to the whole thing was Smith! When the Soviet Union crumbled, and the Cold War ended, the world order had become destabilized, and it drove him too the edge between sanity and insanity! It drove him there because it left a vacuum—a vacuum that now many players were trying to step into! The clone to Magic Mountain was found on an island off the coast of Brazil. It was discovered that Smith and his cronies were working on the laser defense system that the Russians nearly had in place when the *Obvyet* went berserk, just before the Chernobyl incident. He had military funding for it, and his intention was to make America impenetrable to nuclear attack, thereby allowing the American military the ability use the first strike nuclear option! When everything was exposed, suddenly Smith's backing dried up, and everyone cut their ties to him! He was deported to Russia in disgrace, and executed shortly thereafter! This time he was cremated, end of story!

Roberta and Nick had recovered fully from their wounds. They destroyed all but the one *Semya* chip. It was securely hidden away by Nick to ensure their freedom—freedom from reprisals from either government! The big stick Nick held over both governments was the threat of turning over the last remaining *Semya* chip to Iran, a country who wouldn't hesitate to use it in the most threatening way! They were both granted their new life without interference from any governmental agency.

Nick had been haunted about Smith over those past months, obsessed with thoughts of the missions they had been on together, their friendship, and all that Smith had done for him—including the house he had given to him. But, it was his allegiance to the man that bothered him most. The thought that Smith had considered him collateral damage in completing a mission was disquieting enough, but he could rationalize it away if he worked hard enough at it. After all, any agent had to be considered expendable, and to play favorites could be dangerous, even if the agent in question was like a son, the virtual triggerman like a father! But, the fact that Smith was willing to kill Roberta to cover his tracks, an utter innocent who was nevertheless imperative to the success of the mission, made Nick realize that indeed Smith was a madman willing to leave blood anywhere to reach his goal. The whole purpose of a democracy was to protect the rights of the innocent, the common man, and the public. Somewhere along the way, Smith had lost sight of that! Somewhere along the way he had become consumed with notions of world power, albeit keeping power in balance. The means to that end were just as heinous as if Smith had wanted the power for himself!

Smith's trial was fast tracked in America. And rather than try to prove him guilty of anything here, it was determined that he was an illegal alien and he was deported back to Russia to stand trial there for his actions. He was executed in short order, and Nick never had an opportunity to stand up in court on his mentor's behalf. But, the truth of it was, the very thought of defending Smith made him deeply uneasy. Not only had the man betrayed all the principles that Nick had lived to endorse, but Nick felt as if he would be betraying his love for Roberta! Betraying her because of how Smith had nearly been the cause of her death.

Smith sent him a brief note that read,

"Old men have no fear of dying Nikki, only of the legacy that they leave behind them! You are my legacy Nicholas, so no matter what happens to me, it doesn't matter! I know you will carry the torch even though you may not know it yet. You still don't know it all Nikki, so watch your back. Governments are not controlling the world order. That is just an illusion that they want the masses to believe. The people who do control the world order—have carefully orchestrated my death because I failed! I failed in my efforts to expose them, which was my true mission regardless of what you might believe now. Should you choose to carry the torch any further to expose these people, I have left crumbs for you to follow that only you can. My suggestion is—that you don't! Marry the girl instead, and be happy!" The note was signed only "Smith."

It was a troubling note that Nick had dwelled upon for days—even months! And, he knew he was never as brilliant as Smith was, and besides, he was tired of the cloak-and-dagger life anyway. Finally, he destroyed the note, hoping never to think about it again. And when he came across the first "crumb" Smith had left behind—came across it completely by accident, he looked the other way, thinking of Roberta.

Morgan paid the cabby and grabbed his bag. His flight to Melbourne was officially to convince Nick to return to the CIA. But, on his way to the terminal, he dropped his letter of resignation into the USPO drop box there. He smiled when he did. There was no way Nick was coming back to the CIA! But, he might as well let the CIA pay for his ticket! Nick had promised him a new identity when he brought him the last *Semya* chip, and it was in his carry-on baggage now!

Later that day, when Nick and Roberta returned from shopping, there was a package left at the front door of the beach cottage from Fed Ex. Nick smiled when he opened it—it was from Victor! The note read, "I thought you might enjoy this, comrade."

Nick took the video DVD and inserted it into the player, turned on the TV, and sat down on the couch and waited until it began.

"What is it Nikki," Roberta asked him when she returned with iced tea. She smiled at seeing his expression! His face was plastered with a big grin! She sat next to him, eager to see what was pleasing her man so.

"It is a video of Natasha at her most recent dance recital for the Julliard Dance Academy in New York City," he bragged. Then he kissed her, and pulled her closer. Together they both watched with tears in their eyes as Natasha danced her heart out—to the beautiful music of Tchaikovsky's *Nutcracker Suite*.

9 781935 361190